THE LUNA MONOLITH

Hard Science Fiction

BRANDON Q. MORRIS

BRANDON Q.
MORRIS
HARD SCIENCE FICTION

The Luna Monolith

Dewar Crater, March 2, 2082

LIWEI WAS SWEATING. THE ASCENT WAS PRETTY STEEP, AT least for lunar terrain. And, crucially, here at the southern edge of the crater he had to be careful with every step he took. He'd already gotten one of his boots stuck in a narrow crack between two boulders and he'd needed Jinjin to come to his rescue. How much further did he have to go? He looked up to see the slope shimmering in the direct light of the sun. Liwei even thought he could see the reflections of a mirage, but it must have just been a lens flare in the visor of his spacesuit. It was still about two hundred meters to the rim of the crater, which followed a fairly straight line here.

He stopped, leaned forward, and took a deep breath. It was distressing how out of shape he was. In his boss's position, he would have immediately ordered himself to do special training every day. This kind of thing was to be expected when using the Sky Snake for every mission, for the sheer convenience of it. But Liwei commanded the advance team himself, and unfortunately was one of the last taikonauts left who still enjoyed the freeze-dried food available on the makeshift station. When he sat on the suction chair or took a shower, he'd try to ignore the clearly visible bulge on the front of his body. That worked fine until he had to get into the spacesuit that had been specially tailored to his physique.

Liwei straightened up again and tugged at the top of the suit, which was digging in painfully under his arms. He really needed to eat less and exercise more. Or at least be sure to make plans that didn't involve him walking in direct sunlight. A lot of it was reflected by the suit, but not all of it. That, combined with his own body heat, pushed the cooling system about as far as it could go. Liwei looked around and saw the bottom of the crater far below. From up here, his all-terrain rover, the Sky Snake, looked like a toy. He had parked it next to one of the excavators that were preparing the terrain for the installation of the hypertelescope.

The hypertelescope! Liwei was proud to be from the country responsible for this key astronomical project on the far side of the moon. The Europeans' gravitational wave observatory, with its two little arms, looked tiny in comparison. They would mold the bottom of the crater, which was forty-six kilometers in diameter, into the optimal parabolic shape and equip it with mirrors made not of glass, but rather of a special liquid.

He pictured the crater shining silver. Secondary mirrors would float over the structure on gigantic cables, though there was still a lot of work to be done before that happened. This was primarily because the crater was presenting more problems than the engineers on Earth had ever imagined.

He could feel a vibration from the arm of his spacesuit. Jinjin's face, with a black strand of hair falling across it, appeared on the display attached to the top of his wrist. She was his representative at the makeshift base, where most of the work was actually done by autonomous robots. Together, the two humans were responsible for creating the best possible working conditions for them.

"Taikonaut Yang Liwei, what's taking you so long?" asked Jinjin.

They were actually on a first-name basis, but Jinjin liked to tease him by using his full name, which he shared with the first-ever Chinese astronaut – a legend. Liwei couldn't tell if this had helped or hindered his career at the space agency.

"I'm just getting the lay of the land. Why are you bothering me, Jinjin?"

"Excavator Five is complaining now, too," she explained.

"It's working on the eastern edge of the crater, right?"

"Correct. It's experiencing the same malfunctions as Seventeen."

Number Seventeen was the reason why he was here in the first place. The machine was adapted to regolith, the relatively soft rock that covered a large portion of the lunar surface. The excavators would broadly scan their work area in order to avoid harder ground. Repairs would be costly, and it would be necessary to bring in replacement parts from Earth.

"At what depth was the obstacle located?" he asked.

"Twenty meters," said Jinjin.

For Excavator Seventeen, it had only been fifteen meters.

"Do you think they're encountering the same problem?" he asked.

Both he and Jinjin had access to all the data. But he had been trained as an engineer, whereas she was a geologist.

"It's possible, but not certain. You'll have to inspect them both up close."

Liwei sighed. Originally, his plan had been to be picked up by the Sky Serpent on the other side of the crater and return to the base where Jinjin was waiting. Now he'd have to walk back.

"I did warn you about the walk," said Jinjin.

She had. And it was precisely that warning that had prompted him to leave the rover. Of course he was capable of climbing the ridge of a crater!

"It's probably just a cryptomare," he said.

Jinjin had explained to him that cryptomaria, located beneath the lunar surface, were hard magmatic deposits created over 3.8 billion years ago by widespread volcanic activity at that time. If Liwei was right, they would need to replace the normal excavator with an even costlier specialized machine that could handle the harder basalt.

5

"Not every abnormality is necessarily a cryptomare," said Jinjin.

Of course he was aware of that. But here at the Dewar Crater, which they'd been excavating for six months now, it had always turned out to be a cryptomare.

"But if two excavators report something simultaneously, it's highly likely that..." he began.

"Don't forget that Seventeen is working on the southern edge and Five is on the eastern. The fact that they are so far apart could indicate different causes."

Liwei sighed again. There was no point disagreeing with Jinjin about geology. Or about anything, for that matter.

"Okay, let me go up these last two hundred meters. Then I'll get back to you and we'll talk about the rest."

THE RIM OF THE CRATER WAS MADE UP OF A COLORFUL collection of small boulders. It was possible to see how the meteorite had pushed, heated, and tossed up the material when it struck. The large fragments had remained farther down, whereas the smaller pieces had made it to the rim. The view was magnificent. This was the real reason he made the trip. From down below, the moon always felt small because the horizon was so close, but from five kilometers up, it looked completely different. The view was dominated by the Stratton crater to the south-southwest. It looked a bit like it could be the Dewar Crater's grandfather, because it was so much more eroded. The crater's rim had not formed a continuous line for a long time.

Liwei looked for a good place to sit down. Then he took off his backpack and pulled out the scanner, which looked like a nineteenth-century camera. He stood up the tripod, steadied it, and established a radio connection to his suit. The scanner, which ran on ultraviolet light, came to life. It systematically swept across the area between the two craters. Liwei mirrored the data on his display. Where previously only regolith had been visible, now there were small, virtual elevations of thorium, iron oxide, and titanium oxide. The higher they were, the higher the concentration they indicated.

It was quite obviously a cryptomare. He'd been right. That must be what Seventeen had detected. But the volcanic inclusion was located beyond the crater, so it shouldn't cause any further problems for the operations taking place inside it. But there was another elevation, colored dark blue, visible in the image. There must be another substance in addition to the thorium, iron oxide, and titanium oxide. This wasn't unusual, given that the scanner was specially calibrated for those three substances and was therefore unable to identify every deposit. Perhaps it was carbon or water residues. Hadn't an American mission landed between the Stratton and Dewar craters many years before?

He stood up and rotated the scanner one hundred and eighty degrees in the hopes of immediately sorting out the message from Excavator Five, though he was pretty far away. This would have the enormous advantage of allowing him to return to his original plan. The image had actually brought him both good and bad news. Good because he had been able to identify the reason for Excavator Five's error message. Bad because that meant he would have to start up the special excavator again.

"Jinjin, can you hear me?"

"Loud and clear," she answered like a shot, as if she had been waiting at the radio the whole time. She probably had. Jinjin was extremely ambitious and dedicated, just as he had been at her age.

"I was right," he said.

"A cryptomare? That's not good. We're going to fall behind schedule."

Unfortunately, he had to agree with her. They only had one special excavator that could handle harder ground, meaning that work in one location would have to be suspended.

"You could start preparing Excavator Zero. That would save us time."

"You know that's against the rules, Liwei."

"And what if, as your superior, I command you to do so?"

"It would still be a violation. You are the engineer and are responsible for it. Could you please remember to bring me the samples?"

Dang it. He struck his transparent visor in frustration. He'd almost forgotten about the samples.

"Of course I'll remember," he said.

The connection crackled and ended. Liwei sat back down on the boulder. He needed to program the Sky Serpent to collect the samples for him before coming to pick him up at the foot of the mountains. He pulled the data from the scanner back up on the helmet's internal display. The result from the first measurement looked really strange to him. The blue area formed a configuration that appeared to emerge from the depths of the moon. The only time he'd ever seen anything like it was in images of the geysers on Enceladus. But the Earth's moon wasn't filled with ice and water, just solid rock.

Mare Orientale, March 3, 2082

AN ALARM! A SIREN WAS WAILING AND A LIGHT IN HER ROOM had come on and was flashing. Antonia threw back her comforter and jumped up, then tried to run to the communicator but tripped over the blanket, which was caught between her legs. She fell in slow motion. Shit. Because of the low gravity, she didn't hit anything, but this wasn't the ideal way to start her day. And then Bree came sailing in! Her dog landed right next to her and licked her face. As a Cavalier King Charles Spaniel, about thirty centimeters at the shoulder, she didn't often get the opportunity to do this.

"Off, Bree!"

The dog immediately obeyed. Antonia pulled herself up and scratched Bree's head. It had been easy to get permission to bring her to the ESA facility. Antonia attributed this to Bree's friendly personality, which must have won over the general director during a ministerial-level meeting. Or maybe it was political, a favor to the Italian side.

The alarm. She'd momentarily forgotten about it. Bree played an important role in sometimes letting her forget about her stressful, monotonous everyday life. But now she had to deal with this racket.

She took a long step towards the communicator.

"Ernie?"

It wasn't Ernie, her colleague. It was someone from mission control in Darmstadt. It was a woman, but she didn't introduce herself. She'd probably just been woken up.

"It's getting serious," she said.

A shiver ran down Antonia's spine. Those magic words, at long last! She would have to tell Ernie.

"Thank you, whoever you are."

The connection had already been terminated. Now every minute counted. Antonia pulled open her cabin door and cool air rushed in. She shivered in her thin pajamas, but there was no time to change clothes.

"Bree, stay!" she commanded.

The dog followed the order and looked at her expectantly. She was probably hoping that Antonia would make breakfast, but that would have to wait. Instead, she hurried into the control room in long strides. Ernie was already there, also in his pajamas, leaning over the loudly humming quantum computer. It took a long time to get it up and running, since the inside had to be cooled to temperatures close to absolute zero.

"Are the lasers ready yet?" she asked.

Ernie shook his head. He was a man of few words.

The laser controller was located at the other end of the control center, which was about the size of a classroom, alongside a rectangular window with a view of the first emitter. Antonia checked the settings. They had prepared everything weeks before, and now she just needed to activate the right measurement program. She switched on the generator, which provided power specifically to the laser sources and was completely independent of the station's power supply. The detector would still work even if they ran out of power at the base.

An ordinary person might find it strange that measuring was clearly the top priority. But as a physicist, Antonia was absolutely fine with that. People could be replaced, but the event they were measuring today would never occur again. Something similar might happen elsewhere, but this fusion of two black holes smaller than stellar size was so special that she would give anything to observe it. Or almost anything – with the exception of Bree, of course.

"Running lasers," she said.

Antonia stepped in front of the window to observe the emitter. It didn't look any different from before. Outside in the vacuum of the moon's surface, the laser's light was invisible. But she knew that at that very second, two beams perpendicular to each other were shooting into the darkness at 300,000 kilometers per second. On the horizon, they encountered a deflector that was mounted high on a mast, which rerouted them by a few degrees so that they hit the next deflector. This continued until the photons on both sides, after traveling around nine hundred kilometers, reached the outer ring of the Mare Orientale. There they were reflected by one hundred and eighty degrees so they would turn around and meet back up again in the receiver, also located in the emitter's unassuming mast. The strength of the gravitational wave that had passed through their experimental arrangement would tell them how strong the interference was.

Hopefully. This wasn't the first gravitational wave to be recorded, but this was the first one since starting up the MIGI, the Moon Interferometer Gravimeter Instrument, which they had collaborated on with other astronomical research facilities. They'd heard from one of their partners about the impending event, and if everything went well, various telescopes on Earth and in space would now have the site of the event in view.

Ernie came over to stand next to her, and they both looked at the emitter. The interferometer made such precise measurements that it was noticeable if the gravitational wave – essentially, a bump in space-time – lengthened or shortened one of the detector's two laser arms by even a fraction of a millimeter. They themselves wouldn't be able to sense it, though Antonia constantly had the feeling that she was being hit by gravitational waves. That must be sheer anticipation. She had worked on the Advanced Virgo in her home country for a long time, but the facility on the moon far exceeded that interferometer's capabilities. Back on Earth, they'd only dreamed of being able to detect the fusion of small black holes. The lack of atmosphere, the far lower number of seismic events, and the lack of interference from human activity were enormous advantages, allowing for the construction of much longer arms at a lower cost. And, unlike a detector placed in outer space, the system was easy to maintain and repair.

Now something just needed to happen.

"Hm," said Ernie.

The lanky German was clearly tense. She looked at him and he blushed. Ernie lived up to so many clichés! That was why she'd been so surprised when she caught him playing the guitar the other day. He even had a pretty good singing voice.

All of a sudden, the computer beeped. They both jumped up simultaneously and nearly bumped heads. The reason for the beep was subtle vibrations, too uniform to be mistaken for a moonquake.

"You notified the Chinese, didn't you?" asked Antonia.

Ernie slapped his forehead. "Weren't you going to...?"

She shook her head. Ernie flew over to the communicator and typed something.

"Jinjin, was that you?" he asked.

Jinjin was a nice young woman. They had never met in person, since they were way too far apart. But being a part of the same four-person human delegation on the far side of the moon had definitely forged a connection between them.

"You need to stop whatever you're doing right now," Ernie said. "Please."

Antonia noticed that he was staring into the microphone, as if he could convince Jinjin that way. Then he smiled.

"What a sweetheart you are, Jinjin," said Ernie. "I owe you."

Whew. Evidently the Chinese woman had agreed. Ernie turned back to her.

"They need to clear out a magma pocket, but they'll put it on hold until we give them the green light."

"Thanks, Ernie."

Antonia breathed in deeply. It appeared that everything had turned out well yet again. It would be unbelievably embarrassing if the collaborative project failed because she hadn't been able to coordinate everything.

"I think it's amazing that we can feel the vibrations from their construction work all the way over here," said Ernie.

"The material of the moon is pretty rigid, so the waves aren't dampened all that quickly. At least that's how Jinjin explained it to me one time."

AFTER HALF AN HOUR, ANTONIA SUSPECTED THAT NOTHING else was going to happen today. Some time later, she remembered Bree. She ran into her cabin, where the dog was still sitting on the floor in the same place she'd left her. She wagged her tail happily.

"Come on, Bree," she said. "It's time for breakfast."

Bree followed her into the canteen. There were two major advantages to the small, square room that was centrally located on the base: It had a dome in the middle that looked up to the starry sky, and it was always well-heated. Antonia tended to get cold quickly, whereas Ernie liked it cooler. The temperature in the canteen was their compromise. That way, Antonia could always go there if she wanted to warm up.

Her dog barked. Antonia had been lost in thought again.

"Yes, Bree. You're right."

She opened the storage cabinet and took out a packet of food, then shook it. It sounded like cereal. Fortunately, Bree would eat almost anything. If she were the kind of dog that refused dry food, they would be in trouble. Antonia took a bowl from another cabinet, put in some food, then set it down in front of Bree, who descended on it eagerly.

Antonia sat down at the table and crossed her arms

13

behind her head, watching Bree eat. Before too much time had passed, she was startled by a beep. She got up and went into the control center to see what was going on.

"E-mail from mission control," said Ernie, making room for her in front of the computer.

Judging from his slumped posture, she could guess what it said.

"To all partners: This was probably a false alarm," she read. "The system is, visually and in infrared, still in its old, metastable state, as the WZST has just confirmed. Thank you for your cooperation. We will get back to you tomorrow."

That was a shame. It was the Wang Zhenyi space telescope that had provided the first indications of the rare constellation of comparatively small black holes. Antonia crossed her arms. But that was how astronomy worked, whether with telescopes or a gravitational wave detector. It was only possible to record what actually happened.

"Do you think anything will come of it?" asked Ernie, swiping across the screen.

A planetary system appeared. Someone looking at it would have thought it was perfectly normal before noticing that two of the orbits overlapped. They didn't just overlap – they didn't have planets, as did the other parallel orbits, but two X symbols. This X was precisely what they wanted to observe. After the WZST had discovered this system, astronomers had, based on the existing motion data for the star, determined that there must be at least six planets. However, even the best telescopes could only detect four of them. The conclusion was that two of the four must be invisible black holes – the X symbols in the diagram. These would be the first detected objects of that magnitude, but for conclusive proof they needed to record the moment that they merged.

"The funny thing is that this all happened a long time ago, before we were even born," said Antonia.

The system was 86 light years from Earth. The light she saw from it now had been emitted a year before her mother was born. And yet it was in the Earth's close cosmic neighborhood. Outer space was really enormous.

"Or it never happened at all," said Ernie. "But I wouldn't dare to make such a prediction based on the existing data."

He did have a point, given how high the uncertainty was. Yet there was at least a possibility that they would be able to observe such an event. If the system were twice as far away, their equipment probably wouldn't be able to take sufficiently accurate measurements. Proving that smaller black holes existed would be a major advance in cosmology.

"I'm not all that unhappy about the change," she said.

"Well, if you get bored, you're more than welcome to take over for the next maintenance interval."

The computer responded as if it had been listening the whole time. Antonia opened the diagnostic program and saw that one of the masts was out of alignment.

"All right, I'll handle that. When's the next time a merge event could occur?" Antonia asked.

"Tomorrow evening, standard time. But I didn't really mean that. Of course you don't have to..."

"No, you're right. It's my turn. Tomorrow morning, I'll take a look at the mast."

Dewar Crater, March 3, 2082

LIWEI SHIVERED. IT WAS COLD DOWN HERE IN THE LAB. JINJIN liked it that way, and since she was the one who worked here most of the time, she was also the one who decided on the temperature. He came up behind her and looked over her shoulder. She didn't react and remained focused on the diagrams in front of her, which probably represented spectra. Every so often she'd mumble something. Then, instead of clicking away the diagram before her, she'd move it to a special folder at the top of the screen.

He cleared his throat. It wasn't a wise move to disturb his colleague, but he had a lot on his plate today and needed to interrupt her.

"Yes?"

"Good morning," he began, since this was the first time they'd seen each other today.

Jinjin turned around in her chair and leaned back with an exasperated look.

"You too. What is it? Of course you can see..."

She pointed behind her towards the screen.

"Is everything okay with the samples I brought you yesterday?"

"Yes, of course. If there was a problem, I would have complained already."

"I'm only asking because I'm about to take Zero out. I could collect a few more samples."

Jinjin shook her head. "They just confirm what we already knew. A cryptomare. We really need Excavator Zero."

"Dang it. That'll cost us at least three days. But that's still better than unpleasant surprises."

Jinjin nodded. "Surprises are the devil's handiwork. But now that you mention it, three of the samples did catch my attention. I found excessive amounts of hydrocarbons in them."

"What does that mean?"

"I have no idea. Maybe at some point a ship landed there. This material could have come from an exhaust jet. Based on the concentration levels I'm seeing, I assume it must have been a pretty big ship. But it couldn't actually be that. I checked, and there was never a spaceship that landed in Dewar Crater."

Liwei felt his cheeks growing hot. He'd taken three additional samples in the outer area, which was not at all their concern, between the Dewar and Stratton craters. He had mislabeled them so that Jinjin wouldn't ask too many questions. It was supposed to have been a routine check. Sometimes she took the rules a little too seriously, in his opinion. But maybe that was why he didn't have the kind of career she did. She was young enough to be his daughter and was already his second-in-command. Apparently they had considered making her his superior, but they didn't want him to lose face. She probably would actually be a better boss.

"Maybe it was a private ship. You know they aren't too meticulous about registration."

There were in fact more and more private trips taken to the moon every year.

"Yes, it's a terrible habit to record things incorrectly."

Jinjin looked him straight in the eye. She must suspect something. If there was a time to come clean, this was it. Liwei shook his head. How would that look? He was the boss, and he didn't owe Jinjin an explanation. If he decided to take three samples from somewhere, she had no right to question it.

"Yes, well, it's not a crime," he said. "And if it's only a matter of a few exhaust deposits, it doesn't really matter."

"I'd still report it to mission control," said Jinjin. "Just in case someone left us a nasty surprise. You know, a bomb or something that would destroy the finished telescope."

"Who would attempt something like that?" Jinjin had really bizarre ideas sometimes.

"I have no idea. The Russians? Maybe they're jealous because they feel left out. I mean, we've been a successful world power for years, and they..."

"No, I'd sooner suspect the Americans. But not with a bomb. They would be more likely to try to spy on our measurements."

"That's utter nonsense. After all, we've agreed to make all results available to the international community, like the ESA with its MIGI."

Liwei shook his head again – not because he wanted to contradict Jinjin, but because the entire conversation was pointless, since he hadn't collected the samples in the crater.

"If you don't report it, I'm going to have to disclose the data," said Jinjin, who had probably misinterpreted his shake of the head.

"Come on, I'm your supervisor. Of course I'll do it," he said.

Jinjin had crossed a line by making that threat. He turned around abruptly and left the room without saying goodbye.

Liwei already had on the LCVG, or the cooling underwear for the spacesuit, when the image from the previous day popped back up in his mind. He hadn't told Jinjin about it. This mass flow from the interior of the moon, located past the edge of the crater ... had anybody else taken an interest in it? Was that why there were traces of hydrocarbons on the surface at that exact spot? And what if the inclusion itself was made up primarily of hydrocarbons? Perhaps it was the remains of a meteorite strike? No, it was more likely the remains of a comet, rich in both water and carbon, that could have crashed into the moon at some point. Wasn't that how the Earth had gotten some of its water? Such a discovery would cause quite a sensation in the scientific community. But it was strange that such volatile substances hadn't evaporated into space. Unlike the Earth, the moon was too light to hold on to its water.

Liwei sniffed. Thinking about all that water made him have to go to the bathroom, and he took off his cooling underwear. The moon toilet worked almost like one on Earth, except that it worked with negative pressure. Sitting on it too long could leave telltale marks on the backs of the thighs. As he took care of business, washed his hands, and put the LCVG back on, he kept thinking about the strange formation. He would have to take a closer look at the data from the spectrometer. Now was a good time since Jinjin, who was responsible for it, would certainly still be dealing with the samples a while longer.

It was quiet in the control center. Liwei no longer heard the constant noise from the life support system. He sat down in front of the computer that Jinjin usually used. Though he had to log in with his own data, as a supervisor he could also access the areas she used. As was to be expected, the measurements from the day before had been sorted perfectly by time and location. But he couldn't find the scans of the outer area that he'd made from the rim of the crater. He clicked through to the trash. Of course. Jinjin had tagged them as unnecessary and deleted them. He ground his teeth and saved the data to his own area, then loaded it into the analysis program.

At first, he got the same image he'd seen the day before: some kind of outflow making its way up from the deeper regions of the moon. But then he started simulation mode, and the software showed how the mass could have spread through the ground. All of a sudden the direction reversed:

The inclusion had probably come not from below, but from above – in other words, from outer space. The program accounted for known factors such as the density and hardness of the regolith, along with the typical speeds of smaller celestial bodies in the solar system. A given amount must have melted when it struck the lunar crust. The object had drilled its way into the moon like a bonbon descending into a very thick pudding.

He took a look at the statistics. The software indicated a sixty-three percent likelihood that this was what had actually happened. That was low, even if the probability that the mass flow had come from within was less than twenty percent. Hmm. What was he supposed to do with this? He saved the analysis in his own area that Jinjin couldn't access. She would grumble whenever he addressed matters that weren't designated as part of their actual job. And what about that threat she'd made? Liwei shook his head. He got stubborn whenever somebody tried to pressure him. He most certainly wouldn't be passing the data on to the control center. He logged out and switched off the screen. It was time to put the special machine to work.

AND ... GO! THE CLATTER OF THE CHAINS WENT STRAIGHT TO his bones. Liwei pushed both levers forward simultaneously and a loud clicking noise came from somewhere in the gears. The heavy machine sped up with a groan. Liwei accelerated a bit more to the right, steering it onto the rough terrain alongside the road used by the rovers and the ordinary excavators. A mixture of ice and dust, the surface wasn't thick enough for this hulking behemoth. Up here, four meters above the lunar surface, the horizon was also a lot farther away. Ah, it felt good to move through the gray landscape this way.

He glanced at the screen, which showed the terrain behind him. The control center disappeared into the darkness, and behind him a rover traced long, straight lines on the ground with its two headlights. It was following him in auto mode, and he'd be able to take it back to the control center after setting the giant to work.

But he had no desire whatsoever to drive back with the rover today. Even as a kid, he'd always dreamed of operating a powerful excavator. It seemed very satisfying to him – pushing the shovel into a pile of sand, lifting and moving a big load at the touch of a button, and leaving behind a trail of falling rocks and crumbling grains of dust. And that was exactly what Excavator Zero, with him at the helm, would do. Although he didn't really need to be in the cabin, he didn't need to be in the control center either. All he could do there was write dumb reports for mission control. They could wait a little longer.

The light on the control panel flashed, signaling an incoming call. Liwei accepted it.

"It's me. Jinjin."

Liwei had thought it might be her. He was still angry and had no intention of saying any more than necessary.

"Liwei here."

"Are you making good progress?"

"As planned."

He looked at the map on the screen. Actually, he was currently twenty minutes behind schedule, because he'd taken the time to analyze the data earlier.

"Good. Did you report the data?"

He took a deep breath to avoid shouting at her. That wouldn't help. And Jinjin really was in the right.

"Yes, of course."

That was easier than he thought. He didn't even feel guilty. Jinjin couldn't see what he'd done under his login, and she certainly wouldn't go so far as to check with mission control.

"Okay."

He didn't answer. But they were still connected.

"There's something else I want to say..." she began. He realized that she was struggling to find the right words. "I apologize. I took things too far earlier, and that wasn't right. I shouldn't have questioned your competence."

Was that really an apology? Liwei couldn't tell. She'd phrased things in such a way that he could save face. Sometimes he thought Jinjin acted like someone was monitoring all their communication and using it to judge them. But that wasn't possible. Maybe that was how she'd grown up? He knew nothing about her background or her family. It was strange, actually, given that they'd been working together for so long in an isolated facility on the moon. He shrugged his shoulders. It would be best to take it for what she'd said it was: an apology.

"Thank you, Jinjin. I'll put it out of my mind."

"Oh, that's a great relief to me. You're the best supervisor I've ever had."

Liwei couldn't help but smile. What she said was so over the top that there was no way it was true. But Jinjin said it as if she were acknowledging the leader of the Communist Party – that is, as if she were speaking with true conviction.

"I'm honored," he said. *Even if I don't believe it.* "But now I have to focus on driving."

THE ASCENT WAS QUITE SOMETHING. BY NOW THE SLOPE WAS eighteen degrees, but the excavator rolled uphill tirelessly. Digging through the layer of dust down to the hard rock, the chains provided a secure grip. Liwei had thought long and hard about the sequence for carrying out his plan. Should he finish everything he had to do in the crater first? There was no real hurry. The other machines could, of course, keep on working until the following day.

So he decided to indulge his curiosity, and he intended to drive Excavator Zero directly over the ridge of the crater towards Stratton Crater. Even though there was a flatter route that would take him along the developed road over a pass, the machine wouldn't take the rougher terrain any slower. The direct route was only half as long, which would save him a considerable amount of time. He would be back before Jinjin was done analyzing the soil samples.

The rover that had brought him there didn't have it quite so easy. They had long since left the road, and while its balloon tires worked well on flat terrain and especially in deep dust, they were no good on inclines. Liwei had given the navigation system full autonomy so it could make its own way. Still, the rover was lagging behind him. But there was no way he'd send it to the control center, because then Jinjin would find him out.

Whatever. Liwei looked at the map. It was still around ten kilometers as the crow flies. If the rover failed to find a suitable route, it would probably just drive in circles until he came back to get it. Since he didn't plan to take any more than two hours for the trip, that seemed like it would work out fine. After that, he'd go help with Excavator Seventeen, then Five.

THIRTY-SEVEN DEGREES. TO LIWEI IT FELT LIKE HE WAS LYING on his back, even though that would be a few more degrees. According to the manual, the machine could handle inclines of thirty-five degrees. But that was likely an understatement. Still, just to be on the safe side, Liwei had rotated the three heavy instruments forwards so as to prevent the vehicle from rolling over backwards.

Another ten meters... Seven, four, then... He tilted forward. He'd made it to the ridge of the crater! What an amazing view! Liwei took it in for almost too long, and before he knew it the tools projecting from the front dragged the whole machine forward. Into the abyss. He quickly pressed the three buttons connected to them and rotated them back, and the excavator's center of gravity stabilized again. Liwei sped up a little. The ridge of the crater was a little steeper on this side, so the machine practically drove itself. He looked at the image from the rear camera. The cloud of dust he left behind him must be visible from orbit.

THIS MUST BE THE SPOT. LIWEI PULLED THE CONTROL LEVERS into neutral, then compared his position with the data from the UV scanner. The ancient comet, or whatever it was, was almost directly under him. But he really needed to lower his expectations. He probably wouldn't find anything. The material had probably melted on impact and bonded with the moon rock. There would be nothing to see for those who didn't have spectrometers for eyes.

Liwei nodded to himself. Once he'd come to this understanding, everything was easier. First, he unfolded the excavator shovel and made his childhood dream come true. He would be able to clear about a meter of loose regolith. Underneath that, the ground was harder – there was material that had melted into magma, and he'd have to loosen that first. Excavator Zero had a spur-drill combination. He guided the rotating spur so it slammed into the ground from above until fissures formed. Using a third tool, he could break them open like an eggshell to reveal the mysterious layer underneath.

He pulled in the shovel and activated the spur. An eccentric motor slammed the spur, made of the heaviest and stablest material available, against the ground and lifted it up again. The impacts were powerful enough to shake the cabin. Liwei increased the frequency and the machine started making around ten strokes per minute. He rolled it forward slowly so as to cover a larger area.

Boom. Boom. Boom. It felt amazing. It occurred to him that they should take Excavator Zero out of the garage more often.

All of a sudden, the call light started to flash. It was Jinjin. She must have caught him.

"Liwei? You've got to stop that right now," she said.

"Yes, of course. Hold on, I'll explain..."

"It's not about you. The ESA people have established that the vibrations coming from Zero's spur can be seen in their measurements."

"I'm almost done anyway."

"Um... I don't want to tell you what to do, but we've been instructed to always cooperate with our neighbors' scientific institutions. Every minute counts."

Liwei sighed. His plan certainly seemed ill-fated.

"I understand," he said. "What if I just work with the shovel?"

"This is important. International cooperation. If we failed in this regard, it would make us look bad in front of the entire world. You wouldn't want that."

No, he wouldn't. It would be an inexcusable mistake.

"You're right," he said.

"Thank you for your understanding. I know you want to finish the work on the crater as quickly as possible. But we're going to have to call it a day."

"That's okay. I'll come back."

"So does that mean you'll be back in half an hour? I'll cook something yummy."

Liwei's mouth started watering. Jinjin had mastered Szechuan cooking, his favorite. But then he remembered where he was. It would take him at least two and a half hours to get back to the base.

"Oh, don't go to the trouble," he said. "I'm carrying around a few extra kilos I should lose first."

"As you like. I'll see you later, then."

Mare Orientale, March 4, 2082

It was good to get off the base again. Mare Orientale was a very special place. Antonia took giant strides as she headed away from the base, with Bree following her in long, low leaps. She seemed to be taking special care to make sure her transparent helmet didn't hit any rocks. Antonia was proud of her sweet girl. Every so often, whenever Antonia got too far away from her, she'd hear her barking over the helmet radio.

Bree hadn't forgotten how to move in the low gravity of the moon while wearing her specially adapted spacesuit. It seemed as if Cavalier King Charles spaniels had been made to roam around extraterrestrial celestial bodies. On their way to the moon, Antonia had feared the worst; Bree hadn't been able to get used to the constant feeling of falling, which was unavoidable on the part of the journey that didn't involve acceleration, and on the Gateway.

But her sweet girl had been quick to adapt after they landed. The fact that they rarely went out for EVAs was not because of Bree, who loved going for walks, but Antonia, who always felt too cramped in a spacesuit. At least when she thought about how small the personal spaceship she was moving through the deadly vacuum in was. She gulped and checked her progress on the arm display of her suit.

The mast she was looking for was situated partway to the first mountain range, the inner Montes Rook. Three of these rocky rings formed concentric circles around the station. Past the inner Montes Rook was the outer one, which itself was surrounded by the Montes Cordillera. Once they'd made a trip there to catch a glimpse of the Earth. Mare Orientale was so close to the edge of the far side of the moon that under certain conditions it was possible to see the Earth.

They wouldn't be traveling to any of the rings today. The trip was virtually impossible to make on foot; even the inner-most ring was more than two hundred kilometers from the base. They would have had to use the air-conditioned rover, and even then it would take two or three days. Much further away, but in the same direction, was the Chinese astronomers' base. And yet the vibrations resulting from their construction work made it all the way to Mare Orientale.

That was probably because the ground there was relatively thin. Basalt only about a kilometer thick extended across the basin like the skin of a drum. This meant that there were few differences in elevation, which had been helpful when building the detector. But when vibrations reached here, they shook the entire plain, nine hundred kilometers in diameter.

Bree barked. Antonia stopped and turned around. The dog was waiting in front of the shadow of a little hill. It was no more than fifty meters high, but because the sun was still quite low, it cast darkness behind it like an enormous cloak.

"Come on, Bree!" Antonia called. But her sweet girl didn't follow.

What was wrong? Antonia made a long jump towards Bree and landed next to her. She tried to pick her up, but she resisted. Could it be that she'd somehow become afraid of the dark? The best remedy would be to get Bree to confront it. She stroked her helmet and murmured to her soothingly, so that Bree finally allowed herself to be picked up.

But as soon as she stepped into the shadows with her, Bree started to whimper. Antonia wouldn't let herself be dissuaded, however. They couldn't avoid every shadow. It would take too much time, and their EVA suits couldn't sustain them out there forever.

"All right, Bree," she said in a low voice as she got ready to jump. "I'll carry you through, and then you'll see that there's nothing..."

Whoa. Her foot should have been touching down on the surface, but when she looked down, all she saw was blackness where gray dust should be appearing in the light from her helmet. Crap! This must be one of the magma caves characteristic of the inner area of the crater. She should have consulted the map before setting out, since every large rock there had actually already been measured by radar. But now it was too late. She couldn't break her fall when there was nothing under her feet. Antonia leaned forward a little, and that was when she saw the ground. She hit it with her boots. She bled off momentum by running a few steps, but she overlooked a knee-high boulder, hit her knee, and fell onto her stomach.

Bree howled. Antonia let go of her and she started to run around her, barking. The suit showed no signs of damage. Good thing! She turned around, sat up, and felt her knee. There was a bruise on her lower leg, but she could bend her leg without any problems. She got up and Bree promptly calmed down again.

"See, everything's okay," she said.

Bree barked once. It sounded like, *I warned you.* Or was it just her imagination? Dogs could see in the dark better than humans because they had more rod cells in their retinas, but the shadows on the moon could hardly be compared to dusk on earth.

"Did you want to draw my attention to that hole?" asked Antonia.

Bree barked again, just once. At times like this, Antonia often felt as if her dog understood her. But she was a scientist, and she knew that it was mainly her own projection and years of training.

"We've got to get out of here," Antonia said.

She picked up Bree and shone her helmet light upwards. Those last few steps had taken her down into the magma cave. The ceiling seemed stable, but she still preferred to return to where she could see the sky above her.

Antonia extended her arm up along the edge. It didn't reach the ceiling, but there was only a little space between her gloved fingers and the rock. The surface probably was no more than two and a half meters away. Maybe three, she corrected herself. Without the EVA suit, that wouldn't have been a problem. At just about sixty kilograms, she could have easily managed the height with a bit of a running start. But the suit would be a problem: first, because it weighed forty kilograms itself, and second, because it made her movements stiffer. She couldn't jump as well in it.

Antonia put Bree down again. "We need to build a little ramp," she explained, looking around and picking up a stone with an edge as long as her forearm.

It felt like it was made of foam. Antonia bent down and held the lump in front of the dog's nose. Bree sniffed it, though of course she couldn't smell anything through the helmet.

"Look, Bree! We need something like this. Go find it!"

Bree hopped like a young goat, which made Antonia laugh. Then she vanished into the darkness. Was she now suddenly no longer afraid, or had she never been afraid? *Stop*, Antonia thought, but she bit her tongue and didn't call Bree back.

Fifteen minutes later, there was an impressive staircase at the bottom of the magma cave. It was half a meter across and one and a half meters high, reaching up to her chest. Antonia had placed the stones rather loosely, but she only needed to use each step once, so that should be good enough.

She was sweating. Where was Bree?

"Bree? Come!"

Antonia heard the sound of her bark come from the speaker in her helmet, but she couldn't tell what direction she'd run or how far away she was.

"Bree! Come here!"

Another bark. Of course, Bree had no idea that it was harder for her owner to follow her barking out here. It was Antonia's own fault for not bringing a leash. But since there was no way they would meet a random pedestrian out here and Bree was always obedient, she hadn't thought it was necessary.

"Bree!"

More barking. She looked around. The magma cave ended in a tapered wall on one side. She stood with her back to it, then looked to the left, where it descended deeper into the moon. Looking at the structures in the wall, she thought she could detect the magma that had once flowed there. But of course she wasn't a geologist. She took a few steps inside. Bree came barking towards her.

Whew! What a relief. Antonia crouched down and petted Bree through her spacesuit. But the dog was not content. She turned away from her and nudged her right boot.

This probably meant, "Come."

"All right," Antonia said. "What do you want to show me?"

The dog backed away from her, barking, as if she had to make sure Antonia was following her. They took maybe ten steps into the cave. Little by little, she started to feel queasy. These magma formations had often been left untouched for billions of years and were just waiting to collapse under the impact of some force.

Antonia stood still. Surprisingly, Bree didn't complain and just pawed at the dust with her front legs. Antonia shone her light around the area. Something glittered. What could that be?

Suddenly, she heard Ernie's voice asking, "How are things going?"

Twenty years before, nobody would have been able to reach her in this cave. Since then, the Americans and the Chinese had joined forces to set up a network of satellites around the moon, ensuring radio reception at almost every location. It also provided coordinates.

"I'm... I'm just taking a short break."

"You should end it now," said Ernie. "I just got a message that the next possible merge event is in three hours. The mast should be up and working again by then."

"Got it. We'll set out immediately."

Antonia looked at the clock on her helmet display. Three hours was enough, though this discovery would have to wait. It was probably just some scrap metal anyway. At first glance, Antonia had spotted a few characters that reminded her of Chinese script.

"Come on, Bree, we've got to go."

The dog looked at her with her head cocked. Antonia bent down and petted her.

"You did a great job finding this. But come now."

She picked up Bree and followed the beam from her helmet light to the stairs. Then she took a running start and floated nimbly up the steps like a ballerina. After landing on the surface of the moon, she shone her light into the hole once more and watched the staircase collapse in slow motion.

"I'VE GOT TO GO UP THERE NOW," SAID ANTONIA, POINTING TO the top of the mast.

Bree's eyes followed her finger. The dog scratched in the dust with her hind legs as if she was about to race upwards.

Ernie's voice came in over the radio. "Toni, it's getting really tight now," he said.

Antonia hated it when he called her that. She took a deep breath. There was no point in getting upset. After all was said and done, she would enjoy getting some rest. She walked around the mast. At the base was a small structure that looked like an outhouse. Inside it was the power source, probably the most expensive component of the entire MIGI since it contained plutonium, which had become extremely expensive. There were solar cells on the roof, but they were dependent on the sun, which didn't always shine.

A ladder led up the side of the structure. Antonia bent down and patted the dog again.

"I'll be right back," she said, and Bree barked in confirmation. "Sit!" she commanded. Bree sat down obediently.

Antonia climbed onto the roof of the little hut. Another ladder led from there to the deflector high above. The diagnostic program hadn't been able to establish why it was out of alignment. A micrometeorite from outer space might be the cause, but it very well could have been a moonquake, or vibrations from the Chinese facility. Fortunately, the deflector wasn't damaged. It just wasn't positioned perfectly anymore, and she needed to correct that.

"Ernie? I'm climbing up now," she said.

From the control center, Ernie would see when she'd finished. Then he would send out a laser pulse, and if it followed the exact intended path, that would indicate she'd done a good job. Antonia had never thought she'd enjoy doing such manual tasks, but she welcomed the change after being cooped up in a bungalow in the desert for weeks on end.

She reached for the mast, but the ladder wasn't there. Antonia looked up. Of course. The ladder hung at an inaccessible height so that nobody unauthorized could climb up. Safety was an especially high priority at all ESA facilities.

"Ernie, how do I get to the ladder?" she asked.

"Oh, sorry. I'll have to unlock it from here. Done."

Antonia looked back up. The ladder was still just hanging there.

"Nothing's happening here," she said.

"It's probably stuck," said Ernie.

Damned temperature differences. If the ladder was in the sun, the material would expand; if it was in the shade, it would shrink. Some materials could handle this better than others.

"I'll take care of it," said Antonia.

"Listen, I've got a call with mission control soon. There's probably new data from the merge event. Can you hold out that long?"

"And the laser?"

"It's been activated already. If it takes the right path, the computer will report the success to you."

"Got it. Well, say hello to Earth for me."

She ended the connection. If there was new data, this task didn't seem quite so urgent anymore. But she wanted to start heading home. Antonia climbed back down from the little hut and Bree started to jump around happily. But this was no time to play. Antonia walked around the tiny building. There must be a tool cabinet in there. There! She opened it. At least that worked all right. And she saw what she was looking for clipped to the side wall: a telescoping pole.

She took it out of the cabinet. It had a hook at the end and when extended, was about two meters long. She tucked it under her arm, closed the tool cabinet, and climbed back onto the roof of the hut. From above, she saw Bree walking around the base of the ladder. It didn't look like she'd dare go up, though. She didn't like climbing stairs, let alone ladders.

"All's well," Antonia said, speaking over the private channel, and Bree gave a short bark.

Now! Antonia extended the pole to its full length, tilted her head back, and grabbed the ladder with the hook at the end of the pole. The hook encountered some resistance. Antonia tugged it gently, but nothing happened. She pulled harder. Ugh! The ladder was still stuck. Who had come up with the dumb idea of setting up an anti-theft device on the moon? It was probably cheap technology from Earth that was only adapted to the conditions there. Antonia gripped the pole with all her might.

Finally! The ladder slipped. The hook came loose and the pole fell out of her hand as she lost her balance. She had to hold on to the mast. Bree ran around excitedly and barked at the pole, which had landed on the ground next to her, stirring up a cloud of dust.

All of a sudden, a sharp pain shot through her left foot. Antonia whirled around. She'd been struck by the base of the ladder! She tried to pull her foot out from under it but couldn't. Now the suit was reporting that damage. The air pressure started to drop and red numbers flickered across the helmet display. *Stay calm.* She took the sealing spray out of the tool bag. This wasn't the first time she'd used it. Out on the moon, any sharp-edged stone could damage the EVA suit. But, thanks to the spray, that kind of thing wasn't a problem. She squatted down, shook the bottle briefly, and sprayed it over the spot where the ladder had come down on her foot.

The suit calmed back down and the air pressure stabilized. Antonia stood up again and breathed in deeply.

"Ernie?" she ventured.

No answer.

"Ernie? I've got a little problem."

That was probably the understatement of the year. She tried to pull her foot out, but as soon as she started to pull hard, the suit started to impede her. The metal rod at the end of the ladder must have gone through the material. She could push the ladder up to pull her foot out, but what if that just exposed a big hole? The sealing spray was only meant for minor tears. Bigger holes needed to be patched, but that couldn't be done in the vacuum of the moon's surface.

If someone could come with the rover... It had a pressurized cabin. The spray could at least keep the hole sufficiently sealed until she was safe inside.

"Ernie? Please say something!"

What did he have to talk to mission control about for so long? He should kindly get back to doing his job.

"Beep-beep-beep-beep..."

That was the suit. The sealing spray must not have done the trick after all. Antonia switched it off. The suit was losing oxygen. Not so much that she'd die immediately, but enough that she'd run through her supply in three hours.

"Ernie? I need you right now."

Still no answer. The device in her helmet didn't have a strong enough signal to communicate directly with Earth. She could try Jinjin, but Ernie wouldn't be any easier to reach from the Chinese base.

Bree barked, and Antonia had an idea. What would be the best way for her to tell the dog to run home as fast as she could?

"Bree, go home," she commanded.

The dog barked three times.

"Bree, you're my last chance. I'm going to die if you don't get help for me."

Antonia heard the dog clawing at the ladder. The sound stopped, and then she heard it again.

"What are you doing, Bree? You'll ruin your suit."

Right then, a little astronaut's helmet peeked over the top of the roof. Bree pulled herself up as if she'd been doing it all her life and pranced over towards her human.

"You did a great job."

Antonia petted Bree through her spacesuit. It hampered the dog's movements considerably, and it was something of a miracle that she'd been able to make it up the ladder. But this didn't help Antonia, although it did mean she wouldn't have to die alone. Personally, however, she would prefer not to die at all.

"Bree, I need you to run home for me. Home. Do you understand?"

The dog looked at her. Her eyes looked so infinitely sweet, even through the helmet screen. Maybe she shouldn't send her away after all? No, if Ernie didn't get in touch, this would be her only chance. She was starting to get angry with him. He'd probably been chattering away about personal matters for a long time now.

"Bree, go! Home!"

The dog tried to put up her ears, but the helmet prevented her.

"Home, Bree! To Ernie!"

Bree ran over to the ladder, but stopped and whimpered. Antonia could certainly sympathize. Given the dog's size, it must seem like a skyscraper. Climbing up must have been easier.

"Come here," said Antonia.

Bree ran to her. Antonia grabbed her with one arm, squeezed her eyes shut instinctively, and threw her off the roof. Poor girl. Bree yelped as Antonia released her, and then again a few seconds later, presumably as she landed on the ground.

"Bree?"

She answered with a bark.

"Back home. To Ernie. Off you go!"

Antonia looked around with the light from her helmet. Sure enough, Bree was heading towards the control center. She sure was fast! Antonia sighed. Now she was all alone. And now, of all times, the suit was complaining again. She sprayed fresh sealing spray on the hole. The bottle was already alarmingly depleted. She should have packed a fresh container before she left.

Lunar Gateway, March 4, 2082

Ron pulled off his T-shirt and threw it aside. It hit the floor with a smack. JP would scold him when he noticed the wet spot. The ESA astronaut was fussy when it came to matters of hygiene, or his idea of it at least. But that was why Ron had put the thing on in the first place! All because a few drops of sweat could fly off his godlike body. Ron started to pedal faster again. The module they trained in was specially lined on the inside so that a few splashes wouldn't immediately fry the electronics.

Whew. The machine wouldn't let him dismount until he'd generated a certain amount of energy. The clamps around his thighs were constant reminders of that. Officially, their purpose was to press his body against the contraption in zero gravity. But since they didn't reopen until he'd completed the task, they also bound him to the torture device. He even had to serve as his own torturer! If they had told him all this when he applied to NASA after his stint with the Navy... He still wouldn't have decided any other way. Ron liked to complain about everything he could, but all in all he loved his job.

"The food will be ready in ten minutes," JP called through the circular bulkhead that separated the module from the rest of the station.

"I'll be there soon."

The meals Jean-Pierre made were not to be missed. In this respect, Jean-Pierre conformed to all the stereotypes Ron had about the French. He was somehow able to turn convenience foods into something not just edible but delectable. He made use of seemingly unlimited stores of spices, which were replenished whenever the Lunar Gateway received visitors. All space-faring nations now used this intermediate station, with the exception of the Russians. For years there had been a Chinese spaceship docked at one of the modules, serving as an emergency reserve for that country's two lunar stations.

The most recent visit, however, had come from India. This had provided Jean-Pierre's cuisine with a whole new dimension of flavor. Ron's mouth was already watering. It was time for the final push. The indicator was at 96 percent.

●

AFTER TAKING A SHOWER AND DONNING FRESH CLOTHING, Ron floated into the central module. It was a living room and an office in one. Ever since JP had come on board, they also ate there. The Frenchman wouldn't let anyone into the small kitchen module until he'd tidied up. He cooked twice a day – lunch and dinner. At first, mission control had been against this, but the two astronauts didn't end up gaining any weight. They actually shed pounds. JP's cooking was obviously healthy. Ron was really glad to have him on board. Unfortunately, his French colleague would be leaving in three months to be replaced by a Japanese astronaut – a woman. Ron had never been so unhappy about the prospect of having a female visitor.

"What's on the menu today?" asked Ron.

JP never answered that question, but he also wouldn't serve the meal until Ron asked it. Now he was bringing a pot in from the kitchen. Ron couldn't help but laugh at the deliberate way JP moved, as if he were about to perform a magic trick. But in low gravity, any sudden movement could potentially cause the food to fly out of its container. That was why they used deep bowls that could be covered easily. JP brought an aromatic scent with him in from the kitchen that transported Ron to India. He could detect cardamom and nutmeg.

The terminal sounded. *Not now!* Ron just sat there, but Jean-Pierre paused and nodded his head toward the computer. Ron sighed. His colleague must be a favorite down at mission control, because he always responded whenever he got a call and carried out all orders to perfection. This seemed to be a hallmark of ESA astronauts. All the Europeans Ron had worked with had invariably followed orders more strictly than his old friends in the Navy had.

Ron sighed, stood up, and floated over to the terminal.

"Gateway, Ronald Hudson here. What's up?"

"Lucy from mission control. I have a somewhat sensitive issue."

He and Lucy only communicated over the radio, and he'd never seen her. She had a high-pitched, somewhat squeaky voice that made him picture her as some kind of Barbie. But she probably wore a cowboy hat and smoked real cigarettes. Based on her accent, he guessed that she was from the Midwest.

"You want to invite me out for a drink when I get back?"

"Astronaut Hudson, that's five dollars in the chauvinism jar."

"Okay, okay, I'm sorry. What's up?"

"I can't tell you that straight away. You've got to go to your cabin and wait to have a conversation there."

Ron had a sassy retort on the tip of his tongue, but restrained himself. Who knew how many people at mission control were listening right now?

"I'll be available in an hour," he said. "Jean-Pierre's cooked. Too bad you can't smell it through the radio. You'd get right on the next starship and join us."

"Um, bad news, Ronald. This needs to happen immediately. So, now. Dinner will have to wait."

"You're not serious, are you?"

"Yes, that's the way it is. I'm sorry."

"Crap."

Ron pressed the button that terminated the connection. Jean-Pierre never waited to eat, as he'd demonstrated on two prior occasions. Ron pinched his lips together and pointed to the bulkhead.

"I'm very sorry, mon ami, but there's something I've got to do immediately."

He pushed himself off and floated over to the bulkhead, then opened it and pulled himself through. While he was still floating through the corridor, he heard the terminal sounding again from behind. He held on to a strut, listening. Was it possible they'd changed their minds? But since nobody called out after him, it must be for JP.

HE HAD JUST REACHED HIS TINY CABIN WHEN THE communicator on the wall started vibrating. He pressed the answer button.

"This is Major Hufman," announced a deep male voice.

"It's a pleasure. Ronald Hudson. NASA astronaut. You can call me Ron."

"We don't have the time for ... fine, Ron. I'm something of a liaison between NASA and certain organizations that are responsible for the security of the United States. This is about a concern that these ... friends have communicated to us."

"You don't want me to spy on my colleague here, do you?"

"No, no need to worry about that. Mr. Jeunet comes from a nation we are on friendly terms with, after all. But he shouldn't find out about what we're discussing here."

"I see. That's the reason for the secrecy."

It seemed like this was going to be a long conversation. He took the communicator from the wall, then floated over to the bed and strapped himself into it. How he missed being able to fling the whole weight of his body down onto a mattress!

"I don't think you understand, Ron."

"If you say so..."

"It doesn't matter. It's about unusual activity on the moon. We'd like to ask you to keep an eye on it. Very inconspicuously."

"I'm sure you've got one or two spy satellites that take much better photos than we could from the Gateway, right? And wouldn't us doing our own thing here violate the terms of the Artemis treaties?"

"You know, of course, that our Chinese friends have never acceded to those. Our cooperation is bilateral and designed so that we can visit our partners' facilities at any time without being able to make any demands."

"There's still the matter of our telescope's low resolution, Major."

"Resolution isn't everything. You know that, Ron. The human intellect is still indispensable. Besides, none of our satellites down there can check it out first-hand."

"You want me to land on the moon?"

"Possibly. At the moment, there is only ... greater interest."

Ron frowned. He was missing his dinner for this? Some guy at the CIA must have a serious case of suspicion. But there didn't seem to be any concrete reason.

"So what exactly do you want me to do for you now?" he asked.

"Observe discreetly. If you notice anything..."

Blah blah blah.

"Got it, you can count on me." Ron bit down on his hand to keep himself from laughing out loud. "What did you see down there anyway?"

"It doesn't appear that our Chinese friends are sticking to their own plans. They intended to convert the Dewar crater into an antenna, but now they've also begun excavations on the southern side of it."

"Maybe the antenna needs a new power station or something? The whole infrastructure is probably outside the crater."

"We did consider that, of course. But we've seen the plans.

China's never thrown them out the window like that. There must be a reason for the excavations."

"Maybe the ground at the intended location isn't suitable, or something to that effect. There are a lot of possible explanations."

"We're aware of that. But why was there no official change of plan? Whatever. You have your mission. And one more thing – just in case you need to land on the moon, please board the lunar module alone. Your nice French colleague will certainly want to keep cooking on the Gateway."

What? He was supposed to leave Jean-Pierre behind and basically steal the lunar module?

"Major, that could..."

"You have your orders. I'm ending the connection now."

Ron leaned back. That had certainly been a strange conversation, and it seemed to him that the Major knew more than he could, or wanted to, admit. But he could very well be mistaken. When he was in the Navy, he'd met a few people who were very good at pretending to know things.

HE MET JEAN-PIERRE IN THE CORRIDOR. THE FRENCHMAN was still wearing his apron, and in the weightlessness it billowed out in front of him as he pushed off on a crossbar. Ron stopped and looked around. There didn't seem to be any cameras or microphones here. Of course, it was impossible to be sure, but since the Gateway was an ancient international project from the 2030s, they were probably safe from eavesdroppers.

"Jean-Pierre?"

The Frenchman grinned. He seemed to have some idea of Ron's intentions.

"The food is still on the table," he said. "I'll warm it up a bit."

"What did they want from you?" Ron asked.

"I'm not allowed to tell you," answered JP.

"Oh."

Hm. He'd actually wanted to join forces with the French-man, to defy the demands made by the stupid secret services. But JP seemed to be taking it seriously.

"Don't look so grumpy," said Jean-Pierre. "I'm cooking Chinese food for a week starting tomorrow, by the way. What do you think?"

Ron grinned. "I love Chinese food."

"Maybe we'll even pay a visit to our friends at the site where the hypertelescope is being built. I could really use some original recipes."

Ron raised his hand and they high-fived each other. The Frenchman was all right.

Dewar Crater, March 4, 2082

"I PROBABLY WON'T BE BACK FOR LUNCH."

Liwei was holding the bottom part of the EVA suit. He didn't have to wear it since Excavator Zero was docked directly to the control center, but it was always safer to bring along a spacesuit just in case.

"Jinjin?"

She was staring at the screen in front of her and didn't move a muscle She always looked like that when she was thinking hard about something.

"I'm heading out. Otherwise the ESA is just going to get in our way again."

"Hold on," said Jinjin.

She turned around and then looked down. Uh oh. She was embarrassed. That meant she was about to say something inappropriate to a superior.

"What is it?"

He smiled encouragingly, even though he didn't really want to hear it. Liwei couldn't help it.

"I saw the excavator's log. Just by accident. You took it out of the crater. That's why it took you so long to get back yesterday."

By accident. Of course. But could he blame her? Liwei would have looked into it if she had behaved the way he had.

"By accident. I see."

Jinjin smiled. "Well, the fact that you were okay with skipping a meal certainly got my attention. You haven't ever done that before!"

He sighed. "You caught me." The only question was, at what? Should he come clean to her? Could he even try lying to her?

"That's what I thought," said Jinjin. "I also saw your scans. The ones of the area between the Dewar and Sutton craters."

"I thought I had..."

"Yes, you probably saved them in your own area of the computer, but you didn't overwrite the deleted files in the public area."

Jinjin had recovered his files? She really was spying on him! Shouldn't that make him angry? But what good would that do? He had to make sure she didn't rat him out to mission control. If this showed up in his file, his career would be over.

"Oh. Just my luck," he said.

"Not at all. I found your data very interesting. The structure you found is really mysterious."

"But it's none of our business. You're absolutely right, Jinjin. We should stay focused on the work being done on the hypertelescope."

"Now just relax, boss. I have no intention of talking to anyone about this discovery. Not until we know more."

Liwei let out a deep breath. She didn't want to tell on him. The scientist in her must have won over the rule-follower.

"Oh, that's good." He grinned.

"But next time, tell me right away if you find something that exciting. We're in the same boat, after all."

She was probably right. They hadn't known each other very long, but it was hard to keep a secret within the confines of the control center.

"Okay, it's a deal. So tell me, what do you think of it?" he asked.

"I don't think it's a natural phenomenon."

"What makes you say that?"

"No celestial body would leave so few traces upon impact. Given its dimensions, it should have created an enormous crater. But you discovered the object between two craters that don't seem to have anything to do with it."

"What if the object hit the moon when it still had a liquid surface?"

"Then it would have spread out more, because the material would have melted. I measured the differences in concentration. This thing couldn't have a diameter of more than twenty meters. Take a look."

Jinjin turned to the screen and pulled up a graphic.

"It looks as if somebody drove a huge sword into the moon," he said.

"Good comparison." She ran her fingers over the screen as if trying to draw the imaginary sword back out.

"But where could the object have come from? You don't think it was extraterrestrials, do you?" Now it was out. The "e" word.

Jinjin burst out laughing. "Extraterrestrials? You're funny. If they existed, we'd be living in a totally different world. They'd be everywhere by now."

"But this structure..."

"I think it was some kind of experiment that went wrong. Maybe it was the Russians, maybe the Americans."

"Or it could have been China."

Jinjin raised her slender eyebrows. "We can't rule that out as a possibility either. And that is why we've got to proceed cautiously."

"What kind of experiment could it have been?" asked Liwei.

"I heard that in the 2040s, the Russian RB Group intended to set up a secret project on the moon. A giant laser.

But it was stopped because it made a number of nations feel threatened."

"The Starshot program, right. I remember that." Liwei nodded.

The project had almost led to the dissolution of the Sino-Russian Union. The lasers had been set up on various moons in the outer solar system instead. But was the structure really the right shape for that? He leaned forward and clicked around on the graphic. The mysterious material pierced the moon's surface almost vertically. Close to the surface, it had lateral protrusions that resembled the crossguard of a sword designed to protect a fighter's hand.

"Maybe it's a linear accelerator," he said. In that case, the bulky protrusions beneath the surface that looked like a cross-guard would be powerful electromagnets.

"Or maybe they were going to try to build an X-ray or gamma laser," Jinjin ventured. "High-energy photons would be more effective at accelerating a spaceship."

She was obviously talking about the legendary gamma laser, which nobody had made yet because it was physically almost impossible. Then the facility would have been filled back up with moon rock so it wouldn't be noticeable from the outside. But why wouldn't they have realized from the outset that they wouldn't succeed? Politicians. Physicists and engineers might have warned them, but been overruled.

"That would also explain the high carbon content in the upper regolith," Jinjin said. "A lot of spaceships would have landed here to provide the material for the accelerator."

"But wouldn't that have gotten out to the public?" Liwei asked.

"Not necessarily. The secret services would surely have noticed it, but maybe they'd made some kind of standstill agreement. Plus, there's so much private traffic these days that it could have been hidden as secondary cargo on tourist flights."

Liwei sighed. Who knew what the politicians had been thinking at the time? Maybe this had all happened ten years ago when everybody was distracted by the black hole that had suddenly entered the solar system. Liwei's memories of what had happened then were hazy at best.

"If this really was an attempt to set up a gamma laser, our people will be very interested in it," he said.

"Yes, they definitely will."

"We would surely be forgiven for deviating from the plan a little."

Jinjin smiled. "I'm in agreement with you about that, too. I've also worked out how we can use Excavator Zero without delaying the construction of the hypertelescope."

"Great. What's your plan?"

"Drive to Seventeen on the southern edge of the crater and remove the top layer of cryptomare there. Then the normal excavator can keep working in automatic mode. After that, cross over the ridge of the crater with Zero and continue to work on our discovery."

Our discovery. Liwei smiled, even though he had been the one to find the structure. It felt better to have Jinjin on his side.

"What if it really is an alien object?" he asked.

"Now stop that, Liwei. That's nonsense. Even if there was a second civilization somewhere, why would it go to the trouble of flying through space for many, many years in order to hide something under the regolith on our moon? You're familiar with Occam's razor. When there are several possible explanations, the simplest is the most preferable. Therefore, if a discovery is made on the Earth's moon, by all means consider humans first. Somebody buried a little secret beneath the lunar surface, and we're going to find out what it is."

Liwei nodded. Jinjin was definitely right. The simplest explanation was that there had been plans to build a gamma laser there for the Russian RB's Starshot project. As an engineer, he was curious about how the Russians had intended to do this. All he knew about developing a gamma laser was that all attempts had failed so far. The main problem was probably that heat was needed in order to produce enough gamma photons, but cold was also needed to put them into a homogeneous laser state in which they more or less oscillated in unison. The moon would be a good location for it, because it was relatively easy to create a vacuum there.

"Liwei?"

"Sorry, did you say something?"

Jinjin smiled. "I think it would be good to get going now."

He looked at his watch. She was right. It would take him an hour and a half to get to Excavator Seventeen.

"Okay. Until tonight, then."

"Good luck! I'll keep mission control off your back. But you have to promise me something."

"Yes?"

"When you've dug this thing up, let me know so we can look at it together."

THE EXCAVATOR RUMBLED DOWN THE SLOPE. THE SPECIAL model didn't only have wheels, but also feet that looked like spider legs and were very useful for climbing. There was practically no natural formation on the moon that it couldn't handle, apart from the ancient caves beneath the surface. It was simply too big for them.

Liwei switched the windshield to data mode. A silvery layer appeared between him and the world outside, presenting him with information from the scans of this region. The area where he'd already been active was reddish in color. But the structure that interested them was much farther under the surface. Hopefully Jinjin had calculated correctly. If he took more than three hours, there was a greater risk that Excavator Zero would be needed somewhere else.

Liwei came across a curve in the wall of the crater. He continued steering the excavator horizontally, braked, then pushed down his helmet visor and prepared to get out. The life support system sucked the air out of the cabin, and he only trailed thin threads of vapor behind him as he exited and climbed down the ladder. Along the way, he thought of something he hadn't told Jinjin about yet and that he wasn't going to share.

Liwei walked around the excavator. With its legs unfolded, it reminded him of the fat spiders he used to see at his grand-parents' house. They'd lived in the countryside in southern China, and sometimes his mother had left him there for weeks on end while she was away on business. The excavator had a narrow hump on its back, and underneath it was a kind of tarp. Liwei opened the flap, which was secured with two latches. The dark opening was about three meters wide. Dust started to trickle out, and he felt guilty because he obviously hadn't cleaned the tarp properly last time. He reached into the opening, grabbed the edge of the tarp, and pulled it out. More dust fell onto his suit and boots. *It's your own fault.* This time, he wouldn't forget to clean it.

Liwei held the edge of the tarp between his fingers while moving away from the excavator. This wasn't easy, because he needed to overcome the resistance of the material, but he could only use part of his weight to do so. He braced himself almost horizontally against the back wall of the excavator until the tarp extended about one and a half meters from its container. At that moment, he started to feel it in his fingers: the material was reawakened. It had a shape memory that activated after being in an extended state for two minutes. Liwei ducked down as the tarp began to slide over him on its own. Then it arched up, crossed the cabin, and grew in height until it was several meters above the excavator, just beyond the reach of its tools. The tarp curved and extended down-wards to form a kind of tent.

It was now dark around him, and he switched on his helmet light. He walked around the excavator. The tent covered the device itself as well as its working environment. The tarp was designed to protect the area from the dust that would inevitably be stirred up. This would be important at the location where the hypertelescope's mirrors would eventually be installed, since the fine regolith was any mechanical system's greatest enemy.

Out here beyond the ridge of the crater, however, the tent was actually unnecessary. It served a different purpose. Liwei looked up at the sky. He couldn't see the Lunar Gateway at the moment, but he didn't want an audience while he dug up what was possibly an unfinished accelerator. Liwei climbed back up towards the cabin. While he was still on the ladder, he knocked the dust off his suit. He opened the door, climbed in, then closed the door and let the life support system build up pressure. With his helmet open, he sat in the driver's seat and steered the excavator to the spot where he had already begun digging.

IT WAS A GOOD HOUR LATER WHEN THE SWORD'S CROSSGUARD emerged from the ground. Liwei was making use primarily of the excavator shovel. Beneath a thin, very hard layer, the ground consisted of somewhat compacted regolith. This was exactly what it would look like if Liwei himself had buried an unsuccessful project here: he would have covered the construction site using the dust amply available in the surrounding area, maybe bind the excavated material with a little water, and then spread a thin layer of molten volcanic rock over it for camouflage. Liwei could just imagine how furious the people in charge must have been, having to bury such a considerable investment under the surface of the moon. What could it be? Whatever it was, he hoped his home country wasn't behind it. If anybody found out, it would mean a loss of face. This made the presence of the tent all the more important.

Liwei moved the excavator half a meter forward so the shovel could more easily slide under the block that ran parallel to the ground, and had looked like a crossguard on the scan. It was actually a cuboid that gleamed under the spotlights mounted in the roof of the tent. Everything looked gray up here, but this thing was definitely black. The shovel slid into the regolith underneath it. Liwei moved it back a little so he could remove the material better. Just then, a crack appeared where the crossguard and the "blade" met. Dang it. Had he damaged the object? The black cuboid snapped free, and Liwei's seat suddenly rose a few centimeters. Apparently the entire weight of the cuboid was resting on the shovel, and its leverage had managed to lift the excavator, which weighed several tons.

Liwei switched the motors off and established a connection to the control center.

"Jinjin? I've got a situation here."

"What happened? Don't tell me we won't be able to keep to the schedule."

"The shovel is stuck under part of the crossguard."

Liwei shared the camera stream with his colleague.

"Why don't you just pull it out?"

"That's not possible. The cuboid is too heavy. It lifted the entire vehicle."

"I would estimate that the object is five by two by two meters, which is twenty cubic meters. Excavator Zero should be able to lift that easily."

"But it can't, Jinjin. The density of the material must be extraordinarily high."

"Maybe they're lead supplies that were going to be used later to create a shield."

Liwei switched on the drill controller. One of the spider arms rose, and its titanium tip lowered onto the cuboid. Liwei felt slight vibrations in his back. A warning light flashed – the drill tip was overheating. He turned the device back off.

"It's not lead," he said. "The drill can't even get in one millimeter deep. We can machine any material except diamond, and this thing is too heavy to be diamond."

"So it's an unknown material," said Jinjin.

"Extraterrestrials, then?"

"Nonsense. But I find this reassuring. If the material can't be found in our databases, then it's not a Chinese project that we've accidentally dug up."

He admired Jinjin's pragmatism. The whole thing looked pretty alien to him. But she was right, of course. Occam's razor and all that. Why would extraterrestrials travel many years just to sink a sword into the moon?

"I have an idea," said Jinjin.

"Yes?"

"I'll send you a normal excavator. Use it to dig out the shovel from underneath. The object is much wider than the shovel, so you should be able to pull it out."

If they took an excavator away from the work taking place in the crater, it would put them even further behind schedule. How was he supposed to explain that to his superiors?

"Mission control won't be happy about this," he said.

"It's your turn to come up with an excuse this time. Nobody knows you left the crater with the Zero, by the way. Officially, you're inspecting Excavator Seven right now."

Liwei sighed. There were enough satellites orbiting the moon to keep a constant eye on the surface. He would have to come up with a good reason for why he was here. Unless what he discovered got him off the hook because his superiors considered it valuable.

"I just hope I dig up a great surprise here."

When he said the word "surprise," a shiver ran down his spine. Liwei had been a taikonaut for so long that he hated such things. Surprises were almost always fatal. It was thanks to plans and checklists that he was still alive.

EXCAVATOR TWELVE PUSHED ITS SHOVEL INTO THE LOOSE regolith, about one meter behind the spot where the mysterious object had pushed Zero's shovel to the ground. Liwei was controlling the excavator's power with the aid of the joystick. Since his own machine was currently not moving, it wasn't a problem for him to operate the other one.

The shovel overcame the resistance of the lunar soil with surprising ease. But that really shouldn't surprise him. Everything he was seeing must have been filled in only a few years ago, meaning it wouldn't be as solid as untouched moon rock. He pulled the shovel out again and poured the spoil onto the same heap he'd started with Zero. Dust rose as the mixture fell to the ground. He'd had to open the tent halfway because of the extra machine, and this meant that some of the dust cloud made it outside. *Keep calm, Liwei.* It was still half an hour before the American Gateway's next flyover.

Now for another try. The shovel went in again. It was a strangely satisfying feeling to be able to watch it in action, and something he remembered from his childhood. If someone had told him back then that he would one day be driving an excavator on the moon... Liwei pulled back the powerful shovel. Now there ought to be about thirty centimeters of space beneath Zero's shovel. Should he try to pull that out? Suddenly the cabin rose a bit more, just as the handle of a rake comes up when you step on the tines. The strange object had answered his question by descending into the cavity, along with the shovel.

"Jinjin? Our nice little plan isn't working."

"Why?"

"The object immediately sank into the cavity before I got a chance to pull the shovel out."

"Wow. It must be really heavy."

He could hear the anxiety in Jinjin's voice. Evidently she'd run out of explanations. The object certainly wasn't made of lead. What purpose could it have served? Nobody would bring such a heavy object to the moon for no reason. It was way too expensive.

"Told you so."

"Well, what do you want me to do about it?"

"You had the idea of the second excavator, so I thought..."

"But you're the engineer."

That was true. He should come up with a solution himself instead of relying on other people for ideas. Liwei pictured the shovel's position. He would need space underneath it to be able to pull it out. The regolith wasn't stable enough to prevent the object from sinking further down, so he needed firmer material. The spoil left over from the cryptomare! They'd have to get Excavator Eleven to remove the igneous rock from the ground. Then he'd need to place it beneath the object somehow to keep it from closing up the hole he'd taken so much effort to dig.

"The cryptomare," he said.

THE REGULAR EXCAVATOR PULLED BACK INTO THE TENT. ON its powerful excavator shovel were several wedges of the material from the cryptomare outcrops that had been removed earlier. Liwei spit into his hands and wiped them on his pants. Now it was his turn.

He put his helmet back on and evacuated the cabin. He made a long jump from the outside ladder and landed on the excavator's shovel. The magma wedges were too heavy to lift on his own. He did, however, manage to knock the two largest ones off the shovel and onto the ground. He jumped down after them, then pushed the first one up to the level of the stuck shovel, though slightly to one side. Now came the hardest part. Groaning, he lifted the first wedge. The idea was to ram it into the ground with an oversized hammer so it could serve as a stable base for the heavy object as he cleared away the moon dust around the shovel.

Liwei groaned. "Now!" he said, then turned away.

Jinjin was controlling Excavator Eleven remotely. The shovel moved towards him noiselessly, then suddenly stopped in mid-air as if it had hit an invisible wall.

"What's wrong?" he asked.

"You're too close to the top end," Jinjin explained. "If I hammer the wedge into the ground, the shovel might hit you."

Liwei considered the powerful device. He'd assumed that

he could get out of its way quickly enough, but on closer inspection this did seem doubtful. He moved his hands a little further down and bent his knees. But this change in the way his weight was distributed meant that he was only just able to keep the upright wedge stable. After ten seconds, he started to have sharp pains in his arms. After twenty seconds, the wedge started to slip from his grasp.

"You've got to hold on to it for me," said Jinjin.

"I'm trying."

Liwei leaned over the wedge and pushed it back up with all his strength. But as soon as he slid his grip closer to the center of gravity, the wedge prevailed and sank down again. He just had to be fast enough.

"Jinjin? Why don't you just forget about the fact that I'm close by when you have the excavator strike with the shovel? I'll get out of its way."

"Are you sure? If it hits you, all that will be left of your head will be mush. It'll look like a walnut that's been run over by a tank."

Jinjin certainly had a vivid imagination. Or maybe not. That was probably an apt description of what would happen if he didn't manage to get out of the way before the wedge disappeared into the regolith.

"Yes, there's no other way."

"Are you saying that as my supervisor?"

"Correct. That's an order."

"Got it. Just say when."

"We'll count down from three. Then you strike on zero."

That was pretty obvious, but he didn't have anything other than precise instructions to offer in terms of safety.

"Sure," said Jinjin.

He braced himself against the wedge. The life support fan in his suit started going at full blast. The suit must have noticed that his heart rate had sped up.

"Three, two, one, zero."

Even as he pronounced the last word, he released the wedge and threw himself backwards into the dust. His head hit something hard. Everything else was erased by the pain. His eyes went black.

⬤

"Liwei? Say something! What's going on?"

"..."

There was a word on the tip of his tongue, but it vanished before he could say it.

"Liwei? Say something!"

He knew that voice. It was... damn it. His sister? The darkness was impenetrable.

"Liwei! You've got to wake up! The Gateway is about to fly over your location."

"..."

He tried. This time, his words were drowned out by alarm signals. Was there a fire somewhere? Liwei opened his eyes to see scrolling columns of data and, above him, a light that was far too bright.

"Liwei, I know you're alive. You have to wake up and close the tent or we're going to be in trouble. It's me, Jinjin."

Why hadn't she said so right away? Jinjin, that was... He tried to scratch his head, but his index finger encountered something in the way. A helmet! Liwei sat up. He was in a spacesuit. It was dark around him, though perfectly straight beams of light illuminated some kind of construction site in black and white. The moon! Of course. He was overseeing the preparatory work for the hypertelescope, and Jinjin was his sole employee.

"Jinjin? Tell me again what you want me to do."

"Close the tent, quickly!"

Tent, tent... What did she mean? He looked up. Somebody had pulled the anti-dust tarp over the equipment, but behind him it was open since there was an excavator in the way.

"Can you bring the excavator a bit closer?" he asked.

"Hold on. Sure. But this time, you're going to get out of my way."

What did she mean by that? He certainly wasn't going to let the giant machine roll over him. Liwei took a few steps backwards and climbed up onto Ex Zero's ladder. The other machine stopped right in front of him. He grabbed an edge projecting from the front, pulled himself up, and climbed over it. Now there was enough room behind the vehicle for him to pull the anti-dust tarp all the way down. All the memory material needed was a push in the right direction for it to assume its original shape.

"Perfect, Liwei. That was close. How's your wedge looking?"

Wedge? Again, he didn't understand what she meant. Liwei climbed back over the excavator. A large, wedge-shaped chunk of rock had drilled its way into the regolith between the two machines.

"Is this what you mean?" he asked, sharing his camera feed.

"Exactly. You wanted to use two wedges like that to keep the cuboid object from sinking."

Right. Suddenly the memory exploded in his mind like a ripe pimple, and the sensation afterwards was similar, too — raw and vulnerable.

AFTER THE GATEWAY STATION DISAPPEARED BEYOND THE horizon, they drove a second wedge under the other side of the mysterious object. All of Liwei's memories had returned, and it wasn't entirely pleasant. Without his memories, he'd felt free somehow.

"Now I'm going to dig the shovel free," he said.

Liwei sat back in the cabin. Since he didn't have a direct view of the working area from there, he used the excavator's camera feed, which he streamed into the visor of his helmet. That made him feel almost like an excavator himself as he cleared the dust and rubble away from beneath Excavator Zero's shovel.

"Don't you think that's enough?" Jinjin asked after a while. "You don't have to fill the shovel all the way."

"I just wanted to be sure."

"Well, in any case, it's a matter of speed. The two wedges certainly won't hold the cuboid's weight forever."

"You're right."

Liwei switched to Excavator Zero, and the lights in his crosshairs went out. He took his helmet all the way off and wiped the sweat from his forehead, then reached for the shovel controls. *Just pull the joystick backwards.* It had to work! Liwei shook out his right arm, put his hand loosely around the stick, and pulled on it abruptly.

"It worked!" he shouted.

"How far have you gotten, Liwei? Mission control is getting on my case because we're behind schedule."

Liwei chewed on his fingernails. There was a miracle taking shape right before him, and the only thing that interested those nitpickers on Earth was the schedule. Well, then, he'd just have to work overtime! It would be easy enough to make up for the time they'd lost.

"Tell them I'll stick to the plan no matter what, even if it means doing a night shift."

"Then they'll start in with work safety again. You're not allowed to be out there for more than six hours. After that, you have a break."

"I don't need a break. If you could see what I'm seeing..."

Liwei had switched off the camera stream because mission control could see what he transmitted to the control center. And if that happened, the game would be over. This was neither a linear accelerator nor a gamma laser. Humans had never created a technical device with such a wonderful form.

"Well, you do have to take a break. It's the law," said Jinjin.

"But not when there's danger."

"Are you in danger?" Jinjin's voice had gotten louder. The question sounded like an accusation.

Liwei shook his head. "No, not that I know of. But the world as we know it could be in danger."

"Huh? You're speaking in riddles. Did it turn out to be a weapon after all?"

"I don't know. It doesn't look dangerous."

"You just mentioned danger. Why don't you open the camera stream?"

That was a good question. In all honesty, he couldn't have cared less about mission control. It would be two or three days before the necessary specialists from Earth arrived, so there was plenty of time to finish the excavation. No – he wanted the picture for himself. He, Yang Liwei, was the first and only person out of almost nine billion members of his species to have the opportunity to behold this marvel. He wanted to enjoy this exclusive privilege for as long as he could.

"Liwei?"

"I'm here."

"I'm starting to worry about your mental health. You're not responding very quickly. Maybe it's an effect of getting hit on the head?"

Liwei smiled. If he were mentally unfit, Jinjin could take over. But she wouldn't take things that far. They'd always gotten along well, and he was a good boss – at least he thought he was.

"I'm quite lucid, Jinjin. Don't worry. I'll open the camera stream in a minute. I'd just like to tidy up here a little bit."

Jinjin sighed. "I'm worried that you're losing it. But you're the boss. Please contact me as soon as anything changes."

"I promise."

Liwei ended the connection, then turned the main camera above the cabin around once in a circle. The excavator was in a pit about twenty meters wide that he'd dug himself. Its slopes looked higher than they actually were because of the spoil stored beyond it. Plus, the second part of the "crossguard" had broken off when the loose regolith was excavated. It had probably never been firmly connected to the actual object, which they had always imagined to be a sword. But that had been a mistake. The structure didn't point downwards. Its base was located at the bottom of the pit, and it pointed to the sky like an admonishing finger.

It was a monolith, and it was so black that it looked like a small hole in the fabric of space-time. Liwei felt a shiver run down his spine and had to turn away.

LIWEI'S FIRST STEP OUT OF THE CABIN FELT STRANGE. HE turned around again. The screens around the controls were black, and just a few status lights were still flashing. He'd switched the machine off completely, even though he was going to be right back. What had come over him? Nothing. He shook his head.

The spotlights in the roof of the tent lit up a scene that would soon be on the front pages of all the media on Earth. But for now, it still belonged to him. His legs were shaking as he climbed down the ladder. The stele looked almost pompously unreal, as if it wanted to prove with every millimeter of its being that it had not been built by human hands – that it actually hadn't been built at all, because it had been there since the beginning of time.

But that was silly. Somebody had covered it with regolith and then added a layer of igneous rock on top. So the stele did in fact have a history that might include humans. Maybe the Americans had discovered it back in the 1960s but hadn't been able to do anything with it. Others would have to clarify all this.

Liwei was particularly interested in its composition. He approached slowly. The crunching of his footsteps on the dusty ground was transmitted to his helmet as a mechanical vibration. He was walking downwards at a forty-degree angle, which forced him to lean back so far that it was uncomfortable. But the stele towered so high above him that he could still see it. Its square base was around one and a half meters on a side. It was about twenty meters tall, and the diameter tapered to half a square meter.

Liwei couldn't detect any design on the surface or even any kind of structure. But the stele did obscure the view of what was behind it, so it did actually exist in this reality. It didn't appear to cast a shadow, however. The spotlight in the dome of the tent shone so brightly that it should have cast a shadow, but there wasn't one. Liwei himself, on the other hand, was preceded by a flat, black silhouette that had just made its first contact with the stele. It looked as if his shadow was embracing the pillar. For a moment, it absorbed it completely, only to spit out a growing fragment that extended behind the pillar.

It was a fascinating optical phenomenon that would have delighted physicists. Liwei walked around the stele at a constant distance while observing his shadow. He stopped when the spotlight at the top of the tent vanished behind the pillar. If it had had a shadow, it would have fallen right on him. But it wasn't dark around him, but bright. The spotlight doubled in size, and was visible to the left and right sides of the stele.

This phenomenon sounded familiar to him. Heavy objects in space acted as gravitational lenses and seemed to bring distant galaxies closer together. But the stele wasn't nearly heavy enough for its gravity to deflect the light that way. To be capable of doing that, it would need to have the density of a neutron star, in which case nothing could keep it from drilling far deeper into the moon.

There must be another explanation. The physicists would come up with something. Liwei looked up at the sky. At the end of the excavation process, he'd had to open the tent slightly on one side. He'd deliberately stirred up a lot of dust to make it more difficult to see, but it had settled back down again. If he wasn't mistaken, the Lunar Gateway had just reappeared above the horizon. After the sun and the Earth, it was the third brightest object in the lunar sky. Though the Americans would have a good view, the stele was so narrow and dark that they probably wouldn't notice anything special.

He moved a little closer to the stele and the hairs on his back stood up as if there were some kind of electrical field there. But there was no humming noise coming from anywhere, and his devices didn't register anything. The stele was just standing in the pit, doing absolutely nothing. It had been forgotten at some point, and it seemed to sense this. In any case, it hadn't asked to be dug up. It was all due to of his curiosity, and the object didn't seem to care about his presence.

"This is about something bigger, isn't it?" he asked. Now he was talking to a stele! What had happened to the cool, calculating engineer he'd been before? It must be the sheer awe inspired by something that would leave all humankind baffled, something whose nature he couldn't understand. The Indigenous peoples of America must have felt the same way when they first became aware of the deadly power of firearms. That didn't stop them from wielding such weapons themselves later on, and the researchers would probably find some use for this stele, too. Humans had a gift for making use of the things around them.

But for now, it was just him and the stele. It was an honor, and it was the most sublime moment of his life so far. He wanted to enjoy it accordingly. Liwei took another step towards the stele. Now he could touch it, but he wasn't quite ready yet. He stretched out his arm and held it so it would disappear behind the corner of the stele. He laughed. He could still see his hand! It was impossible, but it was undeniably clear. The stele was bending the light, which meant he could see around it.

However, the effect had its limits. If he moved his hand too far around the corner, his fingers would disappear bit by bit into the impenetrable blackness of the stele. Wow! Wow! Wow! His heart was hammering in his chest. Liwei had cut the radio connection to the control center because otherwise Jinjin would keep nagging him about the plan. As if that still mattered! His country was spending billions building the hypertelescope so as to find out more about the secrets of the universe. This stele would take them so much further. And it was standing here free of charge, excavated by a curious engineer known as Yang Liwei, whose name would certainly go down in the history of mankind and whoever it was who had built this stele.

Liwei felt a tear running down his cheek. It was a sublime feeling to be standing here. Humankind was making real contact with the universe for the first time, even if it was pretty one-sided, and he was responsible for it. Liwei shook his head; he didn't really like such grandiose thinking. It must be the stele that, by its mere presence, had changed him. Hadn't one of the early astronauts once described how seeing the Earth from orbit alters the way you think about the planet? Liwei felt something similar now that he'd encountered this object, which for him represented the universe as a whole.

Oh, man. When the main characters in a movie started off with such a clusterfuck, he preferred to skip ahead. Liwei stretched out his hand and took the last remaining step forward. His middle finger touched the stele first. This was especially noticeable because an intense sensation of cold spread rapidly across his body from it. His hand and arm froze before his eyes. He tried to tear himself away from the stele, but it was too late. Pain raced through his shoulder into his neck and chest, and his heartbeat stopped at almost the same moment that the electrical activity in his brain stopped. The last thing Liwei saw was blackness – a blackness that had never been so bright.

Mare Orientale, March 5, 2082

IT WAS PROBABLY THE COLD THAT WOKE ANTONIA UP. HER entire body was shivering. She must have slept. Good. That would mean that her body had used less oxygen. When she checked the status indicator, the numbers were blurry because her hand was shaking. Two o'clock. Was that possible? Morning or afternoon? The moon had a talent for keeping such information a secret. But it must be nighttime, because otherwise her tank would already be empty.

Dang it! The merge event. They'd missed it, and it was all her fault. She looked up and saw that the deflector was fully extended. Awesome! So they'd done it after all! She laughed so hard it sounded like she'd lost her mind. But she was happy for her colleagues all over the world. Too bad she wouldn't get a chance to see the data. The analysis would take months, and she'd be dead in a few hours, if not sooner.

At least Bree was safe. She hoped so, anyway. Her sweet girl had a good sense of direction even if she couldn't follow her nose there. Ernie would take care of her. He'd told her that he'd never had any pets in the course of his long life, but nobody could resist Bree's charms. On many occasions she'd observed him playing with her, caught up in the moment like a little kid.

Antonia gulped. She didn't want to die out here, but it

looked like that was what was going to happen. She applied the sealing spray one last time, but now it was as good as empty, and the suit was complaining about the continued loss of pressure. It could still replenish it from the oxygen tank, but she could see how much longer that would last. According to the display on the helmet screen, there were exactly thirteen minutes left. Shit. That was sooner than she'd expected. So these were going to be the last thirteen minutes of her life.

She squatted down and groaned in pain. The leg that was pinned by the ladder had fallen asleep. Along the edge of the hole a thick layer of ice had formed from the moisture in her breathing air, which was escaping from the crack in vertical plumes. Antonia watched it and saw the air rise in a straight line, undisturbed by any wind. Antonia blew out forcefully, but all she got was a film of mist on the inside of her helmet, which quickly dissipated.

The moon was a proper celestial body. Before, she'd thought of Luna as a gentle goddess, but anybody who spent more than three days up there realized just how severe a deity she was. Luna was unforgiving of mistakes, and she punished those who made them for all eternity. If Ernie didn't extricate her dead body from the bottom of the ladder, she would have to sit here until she turned to dust. Good thing she wasn't immortal. It was just a shame that she couldn't have one last glimpse of the Earth. There was a possibility that she could see it from the top of the mast, but that was just as inaccessible to her as the Earth itself.

Antonia wiped at her foot and tried to break off the ice. It didn't come loose until she used a wrench from her toolkit. When she pressed the tool against her foot, it felt like it didn't even belong to her anymore. Maybe she should have sawed it off. She even had a laser cutter that would do the trick. But she wasn't the type who could clench her teeth and amputate a part of her own body in an emergency. She was an astronomer and wanted to see the stars from as comfortable a position as possible. She had owned a telescope when she was a girl, but while it stood out in the field next to her parents' house, she had controlled it from a computer in her nice warm room.

She sighed, but she realized immediately that she wasn't all that sad. As close to dying as she was, shouldn't she be? All of a sudden, everything seemed so trivial to her. The great merge event! Who cared if two black holes were merging? The two objects certainly didn't, and it wouldn't ever affect the people on Earth in any way. They'd had to build the MIGI first to even witness it.

Eight minutes to go. Her stomach was cramping. She didn't feel grief anymore, but it had given way to fear. Asphyxiation was supposedly not a pleasant way to die. Why did the cold have to wake her up? She had always wanted to die in her sleep. Play with Bree in the evening, go to bed, fall asleep and then never wake up again – that was how she'd imagined it. The only thing she was worried about was what would happen to Bree. There hadn't been much room for other people in her life, since she'd preferred to give her attention to the stars.

Antonia rummaged around in her tool bag, which also contained a first aid kit. Didn't it include some pills that made dying easier? She took it out of the bag and actually found a few sedatives inside – but how was she supposed to take them? What if she were to just open the helmet visor? That was probably what a real astronaut would do. Better to meet a terrible end than... But that would mean giving up her very last minutes of hope, and she couldn't do it.

She stood up again. The pain in her leg was excruciating. She pulled herself up the ladder and roared. Bree answered with a bark. She was still on the private channel she used to communicate with her sweet pup. But why did she have reception? The control center was too far away, wasn't it? *Oh, Bree, you didn't turn around, did you? Please stay with Ernie.* She looked in the direction the dog had run in, and she saw a dust trail too distinct to have been stirred up by Bree's long leaps.

It was a person approaching her at an impressive speed.

"Bree!" she called out.

"Toni!" Ernie called back. It was, of course, her colleague, bounding over the uneven terrain in giant strides. "Why are you on the private channel? I thought you'd already run out of air!"

Why hadn't she noticed sooner? It must have been the fear. Antonia read the displays on the inside of her helmet and closed her eyes. Three minutes left. Ernie was at least two kilometers away. It wasn't going to work. Tears coursed down her face and she started to sob.

"What's going on?" asked Ernie. "I'm almost there, and I've got oxygen. What happened?"

"I'm about to run out of air. It was nice of you to come, but it's too late."

"Now don't be silly. I'm almost there. Tell me what the problem is. Bree wasn't able to help me with that."

Her dog, her sweetheart. Antonia wept uncontrollably. It was a mixture of relief, hope, love, and a fear of death. Something that she would hopefully never feel again, regardless of how things turned out.

"I need you now, Toni," Ernie said sternly.

Antonia sniffed. "The bottom of the ladder went through my boot. When I pull the metal out, the hole in my suit opens up and I suffocate."

"But you won't. Just stay calm. Do you have a plastic bag handy?"

What did Ernie want with a plastic bag? "To put over my head?" she asked.

"You're going to put it over your foot after you've pulled the ladder out."

"But won't the bag explode?"

Of course it wouldn't. She almost felt like slapping herself on the forehead. The pressure difference was less than one atmosphere.

"Forget I even asked that question," she said, digging around in the toolkit. The first aid kit had been packed in a baggie! Where had she put it? The baggie wasn't in the toolkit anymore. Antonia looked around. Then she saw it lying on the roof of the hut, right next to her. But it was halfway over the edge. With a groan, Antonia crouched down, let go of the pole she was holding on to, and toppled backwards. She landed hard on her back, and her head briefly bounced inside the helmet.

"Is everything OK?" asked Ernie. "I'll be there in five or six minutes."

"I'm just getting the baggie," she said.

Antonia stretched out her hand. At all costs she had to keep from knocking the bag off the roof. At least she didn't have to worry about a sudden gust of wind. She lifted her arm, which suddenly felt especially heavy, and slammed down on the bag with all her strength. Ouch. She groaned, but as she pulled her arm closer to her body, the bag moved along with it. Phew. She turned onto her side and sat up.

The bag was small, but not too small. It should be the right size for her boot to fit inside. But it was stiff from the cold. While maneuvering her foot into the bag, she had to be absolutely certain not to damage it. But first she'd deal with the ladder. Antonia pushed the bag under her trapped leg, then used both hands to grasp the metal brace that had pierced the foot of her suit. It took her a moment to prepare herself mentally. It was sure to hurt like hell. The metal seemed to have pierced her skin, too. But she couldn't really tell based just on the sensation in her foot. Fortunately.

She was ready. "One, two, three." On the count of three, she pulled as hard as she could. The bottom of the ladder moved upwards, but her foot didn't want to get out of its way. It didn't react at all, as if it didn't belong to her anymore. She couldn't hold the ladder for very long. She told her other foot to do the job and started kicking her own leg until it was far enough away from the base of the ladder. She was sweating. Finally, she could let go of the ladder. She thought she could hear the metal clanging on the roof, though that was impossible.

She had to act quickly. The suit was complaining loudly about the drop in pressure. The reserves were being used up.

She picked up the bag and tried to warm it up a little between her hands, but it didn't work since she was wearing gloves. She carefully slid the bag over her injured foot, which involved lifting the entire leg briefly with her free hand. It worked! She pressed the opening of the bag against the lower part of her leg and fixed it in place with the last of the sealing spray.

Whew. The suit was still giving warning signals, but the reserves were only being used up slowly. She'd bought herself a few minutes ... make that many years, hopefully. Ernie was on his way and would take her to safety at the control center. Hopefully! He wasn't there yet.

"WAIT, I'LL CARRY YOU," SAID ERNIE.

That was out of the question. She'd gotten herself into this situation, and she was going to... "Ouch!" It hurt like hell when she stepped on it. Hopefully the metal rod hadn't gone all the way through her foot. But then wouldn't she be bleeding? Or were those black spots she saw blood? She leaned on Ernie's shoulder.

"I'll be fine," she lied, hoping it would come true if she just believed it.

"Are you going to climb down the ladder, too?" asked Ernie.

"No problem."

"Really?"

"Yes, but thank you for asking."

She actually would have liked the help, but Ernie had already saved her life with his idea, and she didn't want to impose on him any further.

"Great, then I'll take care of the deflector," said Ernie. "Thanks so much for getting the ladder down for me."

"My pleasure." Antonia grinned. It was a miracle that she was able to joke again. It must be the shock. It was actually a miracle that she was alive at all, but here she was, already taking it for granted.

"But be careful, Ernie. I wouldn't be able to come to your rescue right now."

"Don't worry. I'll be right back."

Antonia pulled herself down to the ladder. She was grateful for the moon's low gravity, since it meant she didn't have to stand so firmly. A certain amount of weight transfer, however, was unavoidable. It was even more noticeable on the ladder, since all the weight was concentrated on the narrow rungs. She decided to skip the ordeal of the last six steps and jumped, leaning slightly forward to break her fall with her arms. She landed in the dust. It was a good thing Ernie wasn't watching, because he definitely would have made fun of her.

"That jump was so elegantly executed, Toni. You just need to work on your landing."

Dang it! She saw the cone of light coming from his helmet.

"Just take care of the deflector," she said.

"You already fixed it. Great job! The research consortium is very pleased."

"Why didn't you bring the rover to get me?" she asked as Ernie set her down in front of the lock like a piece of luggage. She'd tried to walk for a while, but their progress had been too slow, so Ernie had ended up carrying her after all.

"Ahem," said Ernie.

She shouldn't have asked that. When you're rescued, you don't ask questions. In Ernie's place, she would have been irritated too.

"It doesn't matter. The important thing is that we're here now."

"That's not what I meant. That's a totally fair question. Unfortunately, the rover isn't working. I was actually repairing it when you ... er, when Bree got here. Then for a while I tried to get it going. At a certain point I gave up and ran. I'm so sorry. I didn't want to keep you waiting that long. If I had set out running right away... But I thought maybe your suit wasn't working anymore at all."

"No worries. I'm so grateful you came to rescue me." Antonia pulled herself to her feet and dragged herself over to the control center airlock. It was open. Ernie really must have been in a hurry. As a German who always did everything properly, he always closed every door behind him. It seemed he'd even sacrificed his principles to save her.

"Once again – thank you, Ernie," she said.

"Sure thing," he replied.

"Are you coming in too?"

"I've still got to check the laser. Following every measurement, that's standard procedure."

Antonia grinned. Could she have managed to do such things so soon after going through all that? But that was just like Ernie. He'd just saved another person's life, and it was back to his daily routine. The laser, which had never shown any signs of a problem, needed to be checked. It said so on checklist ZFR81.

She pulled herself into the airlock chamber, closed the outer bulkhead, and hit the pressurization button. When it lit up orange, she pulled the helmet off her head and breathed in greedily. The air had never tasted as good as it did now. Now the light switched to green, meaning she could open the inner bulkhead. Just as she was pushing herself through it, a black and white ball shot towards her and began licking her face.

"Eww," she said, not in reference to Bree's wet tongue but rather the dried sweat on her skin. She set the dog down on the floor.

"Give me a second to change, okay?"

Bree let out a short bark, apparently in agreement. Antonia removed the heavy top part of her suit, set it down in the airlock, and closed the bulkhead. Then she opened the outer bulkhead. That way, the suit could air out a bit. Then she moved to the console and pressed the call button.

"Reporting for duty from the control center," she said.

"Great. I just reached the laser."

A yellow light on the control unit started flashing, signaling that somebody was trying to reach her. Antonia accepted the call.

"I hope I'm not disturbing you." It was the woman from mission control, whose name she still didn't know. Ernie had seemingly said nothing about his rescue mission. There probably had been no time to do so, and nobody from Earth could have helped them anyway.

No problem, I just came back from the brink of death. "Not at all. We're really looking forward to the assessment."

"I have good news."

"Everything's progressing a lot faster?"

"There's going to be a second event, and it will be very soon. Are you ready?"

All of a sudden, the fact that she had just feared for her life didn't seem important to her anymore. There was going to be another merge event! She'd slept through the first one, but now she would be able to witness the first demonstration that smaller black holes existed! Antonia was back to being the astronomer she'd been all her life.

"We're expecting it in eight minutes. Our friends at WZST found characteristic vibrations that only..."

"Thank you, we're nearly done with the preparations," she said, and terminated the connection.

They'd have to be quick. Hopefully Ernie had called the Chinese astronauts this time.

"Ernie, how's it looking?"

"I'll have it in a second."

"Okay. You need to wait up there."

"I need to what?"

"I want you to stay up on the mast of the laser. We have a second event and it's going to start soon. If you climb down while it's happening, you'll create vibrations that could interfere with the measurement."

"Got it."

After Ernie was done checking the laser, she switched the system to measurement mode so that the quantum computer in the control center would immediately start evaluating the interference patterns. In the past, this would have required a supercomputer, or they would have had to wait days for the results. Bree barked, and Antonia put her index finger to her lips. "Shhh." Bree probably just wanted some attention. She didn't know, of course, that an event the world of astronomy had been waiting so long for was happening right now. The quantum computer delivered the first data and converted it into a diagram that at high magnification currently showed a mostly smooth line. It wasn't perfectly straight because even the measurement setup on the moon had a certain amount of background noise.

There! A first blip. If the theory was correct, it wouldn't be the last. And there! Again! The curve twitched back and forth. The deflections went up and then back down. But there was one strange thing: The result was asymmetrical and vaguely reminiscent of the cross-section of a crater's ring. The physicists wouldn't be happy, since they'd predicted a symmetrical course. She and Ernie would have to double-check all the data; they would surely be treated with skepticism. But all of a sudden, the deflections started all over again. They were very pronounced, but now the process was repeating itself in mirror image. It divided the curve in the middle and the end mirrored the beginning. It matched almost perfectly! What had she just seen? The intensity of the gravitational waves matched the predicted objects, but the sequence was different from what had been projected.

Well, it would be up to the physicists to figure that out. At least her name would be on the paper that announced this great discovery. Sometimes she was happy just to be an astronomer and observe, without having to constantly think about what her findings meant for the theories behind them.

All of a sudden, Bree started barking like crazy. Antonia leaned down and reached out to pet her, but she bared her teeth and tried to bite the palm of her hand. Antonia only just managed to pull it back before she was thrown against the main computer's controls. Her spine collided with a sharp edge.

Ernie came in over the loudspeaker.

"Shit, what's going on here? Did you go to the Chinese... Aaah, I'm falling!"

Oh no! Was that a moonquake? Seismic waves of this magnitude had never been recorded here before. No, it must be something else. Maybe a lander had crashed, or a deliberate explosion? She pulled herself to her feet. Bree licked the hand she had almost bitten a moment before. The diagram on the screen showed an enormous deflection, but it really must be a mistake. Surely the tremor had misaligned the MIGI, for nobody had ever measured a gravitational wave that powerful.

Ernie. "Ernie?" she shouted into the microphone. "Ernie, what's going on? Please say something!"

"Arggglll," came in over the loudspeaker as she was standing in the airlock, about to put on her spacesuit.

"Ernie, was that you? Please come in."

"I... Yes, everything's fine. I should have held on tighter."

"Are you hurt? Do you want me to come get you?"

She still had no idea how to get the suit over her injured foot, but if Ernie's life was in danger, she'd be able to suppress the inevitable pain somehow.

"No, I'm standing in front of the lock. I just can't get in..."

Dang it. Why hadn't he said something? She was blocking the airlock. She let go of the suit, limped into the neighboring workshop, and closed the bulkhead. Soon the pumps that extracted the breathing air started up. Something rattled loudly and she heard the pumps again. As soon as the switch on the airlock lit up green, she pressed her hand on it. There he was, standing in the middle of the airlock and taking off his helmet.

Antonia jumped over to him and hugged him. She didn't mind that the dust on the outside of his spacesuit smeared her tracksuit.

"Now, Toni," said Ernie.

She let go of her colleague and grinned. She'd almost forgotten that he didn't much care for her emotional greetings.

"Good thing nothing happened to you," she said.

"We need to vacuum the airlock," said Ernie. "If all that regolith dust gets into the control center, it could cause us a lot of trouble later."

"You're absolutely right." Antonia looked around, but there wasn't a vacuum cleaner in the airlock.

"That certainly was a powerful jolt," said Ernie. "That couldn't have been the gravitational wave, could it?"

"No, that was a moonquake. The strongest one we've ever measured."

"Again? This old, cold ball of stone seems to be coming back to life."

"Maybe it's some kind of midlife crisis," said Antonia. "You should know something about that."

"Hehe." Ernie grinned. "Is that any way to talk about the person who saved your life?"

Lunar Gateway, March 5, 2082

"RON HUDSON? ARE YOU THERE?"

Ron blinked and tried to make out the display on the alarm clock. It was a little before four in the morning. If Earth was reporting at this time of night and directly into his cabin, it could only be one particular person.

"I'm listening, Major," he replied.

"It's time."

"What time?"

His brain didn't really function at this time of day. What did Major Hufman want from him?

"Your excursion. It's starting. The ferry. Do you understand me?"

"Oh yes. I remember. You wanted me to visit our Chinese friends."

Ron took a deep breath. He didn't like this at all. Though he'd served in the Navy for fifteen years and was accustomed to such assignments, he'd had his reasons for signing on with a civilian agency.

"Right," said the Major. "We've already loaded the destination coordinates onto the ferry. It'll be a quick excursion."

"I don't like it," said Ron. "And why can you issue me instructions anyway?"

"I can't," said the major. "I'm asking you to do something for your country, just as your country..."

"I get it."

Ron laid his head back down on the pillow. It was that same old thing. If he hadn't been dead drunk that one time, his second-in-command wouldn't have had to fill in for him – and never return. NASA had never been informed of this. He'd been promised that what happened in the Navy stayed in the Navy. He should have known they would come and ask for a favor at some point. Actually, he had known. He'd just blocked it out.

"You should leave in thirty minutes," Major Hufman said.

He jumped up. Half an hour? They were crazy. "What's the sudden urgency?"

"We were able to persuade a Chinese surveillance satellite to not look closely for a moment as you land with the ferry. But this satellite is only responsible for the target area for a short period of time. Normally there are two or three, and we can't influence them all at the same time."

"Understood. And on the ground? Isn't everything there monitored too?"

"We have special suits for you that will minimize your infrared radiation. If they don't know what they're looking for, they won't find it."

"Infrared? That won't make me invisible."

"No. You'll have to stay in the shade as much as possible. Shadows together with infrared shielding make you invisible."

Ron reached into his underwear drawer to get a clean pair to replace the ones he was wearing.

"And what is my assignment, exactly?" he asked.

"To observe. We need to know what the Chinese have discovered down there."

"Is it dangerous?"

"We don't know enough to provide an assessment."

"I mean, if the Chinese catch me."

"According to the Moon Treaty, they aren't allowed to have weapons..."

"Haha, Major. Who are you kidding?"

There were, of course, no functioning weapons aboard the Lunar Gateway. But he knew exactly which components he could use to assemble a powerful crossbow in record time. The lunar module also had everything he'd need for that.

"Fine. Our friends very well may react somewhat ... nervously. But don't worry, there are just two of them."

And I'm alone, you jackass. If his information was correct, all Chinese space travelers had to undergo military training first. Maybe they didn't have his experience. But he really wasn't some kind of special agent who could deal with being outnumbered.

Fine. He knew somebody who would be happy to accompany him.

"Is that all?" he asked.

"Good luck, Commander Hudson."

No one had called him that for a long time. Ron couldn't help it – he felt a shiver run down his spine.

⬤

As he approached the lock to the landing ferry, he heard a clattering sound from behind it. Ron grinned. So that was why JP hadn't opened it for him. That son of a gun must have been given a similar assignment. Ron got a bar from the workshop and used it to open the cover of the airlock. Just as he'd anticipated, a fist shot out of the dark opening.

"Merde," said JP.

Ron burst out laughing. "At least you tried. Your boss will give you a lot of credit for that."

The light came on in the open hatch and JP's head appeared. He could knock him unconscious with the pole. But he'd always been one to interpret orders creatively. Major Hufman had certainly known that from reading his file, but had he planned for it?

"Truce?" JP asked, pinning the metal rod against Ron's hand.

"Hey, if I'd wanted to hit you with it, you'd be unconscious by now."

"Okay, you win." The Frenchman raised one hand, while his other held onto the ladder leading down into the lunar module. "Should I come out?"

"Quite the opposite. You'll direct the ferry to the surface. I'm coming along. We need to leave in exactly six minutes."

JP grinned. "So that's the American plan?"

Not exactly, but Jean-Pierre didn't need to know that. Ron just nodded.

THE PILOT AND CO-PILOT SEATS WERE NARROW AND SITUATED close to each other in front of the controls, which had been designed so that they could be operated from either seat.

Ron settled in as comfortably as possible and fastened the lap and shoulder straps. They still had four minutes before the Chinese satellite would temporarily stop watching.

"Where to?" asked JP.

"I was told that the coordinates have already been entered."

"Um, I'm afraid I overwrote what was there."

Ron laughed out loud. This was going well! "Then we'll fly to where they wanted to send you. I hope you have good information."

"My destination should be about fifty kilometers west of Stratton Crater."

"Stratton? That doesn't ring any bells. Aren't the Chinese building their hypertelescope in Dewar Crater?"

"Stratton is next door. The interesting spot is right in between."

Ron's bracelet vibrated. One minute left. "All set? We need to head out."

"I'm ready."

"Then press the launch button. We can talk more on the way down."

THE FERRY DROPPED SO RAPIDLY THAT RON WAS GLAD HE hadn't eaten anything today. Had that been a part of the plan? But perhaps it also had to do with the change of destination.

"What would you have done about the Chinese watching you?" he asked.

"Nothing," replied JP. "What are they going to do? The moon belongs to everyone. Nobody can occupy part of it."

"Be that as it may, visits made without prior arrangement are frowned upon."

"But they can't fight back. There are no weapons down there."

Ron had to restrain himself from laughing at how naïve JP sounded. But surely he wouldn't mind it if he handed him a gun.

"Supposedly it's three, sometimes four days before one of their spaceships can get here," JP explained. "I think my superiors were a little afraid of how the Americans might react. A private ship might only need two days from Florida. That's why we're doing this here, so that I would definitely be the first to reach our Chinese friends. By the way, the people at the ESA were surprised that you hadn't prepared a launch at all. But it turns out that's explained by your mission."

"Right," said Ron. Should he be happy about that? Apparently his superiors were trying to get the desired information as inconspicuously as possible. It was actually a clever strategy not to alienate the other powers too much. The only thing he didn't like was that he would have to take the heat for it. But there was nothing to be done about that.

"Did they tell you what this is all about?" asked Ron.

JP hesitated. "I... screw it, either we'll both see it or neither of us will. The science squad says there must be a mass concentration. That's probably what the MIGI measurements showed."

"MIGI? It sounds so funny."

"It's a gravitational wave detector," JP explained.

"I know that. Sounds funny anyway."

"You're one to talk! You guys specialize in crazy acronyms."

"But seriously," said Ron. "You know more than I do. A mass concentration, then. Whatever that looks like."

"I was wondering the same thing. Maybe it's fragments of an asteroid or a dense inclusion of an especially heavy ore. Maybe it's what used to be the core of an iron meteorite."

"So you mean we're like modern-day prospectors?"

"Such a core directly in Earth's orbit would be worth a great deal."

"So much that people would go to war over it?"

Ron pressed himself into the back of the seat. He'd been to war and wouldn't wish it on anyone. And this time he'd end up in the eye of the storm. That mustn't happen.

"No, I don't think so," said JP. "The elements in it aren't all that valuable. Only the high concentration would make extracting lucrative. But not to the point that people couldn't reach agreement about it."

Very reassuring. Ron nodded. "Thank you for telling me all this. I'm sorry I can't reciprocate." That wasn't a lie. He was really irritated that he'd been given so little information.

"Hold on," JP said, as if that would be any help in the event of a crash.

Ron reacted anyway and pressed himself against the backrest. The ferry was floating downwards and seemed to be plunging into a deep, dark hole. JP leaned forward and switched from the optical camera to radar. Now Ron recognized the crater slope extending to the east. How high could it be? Two hundred meters? In the low gravity, that shouldn't be a problem. Its shadow would provide them with much-needed cover, once the ferry's engine cooled down.

All of a sudden it bucked several times, then switched off

completely. Ron checked the radar. Another twenty meters to the surface. They should survive. Fifteen. Ten. Five. Impact.

He was pushed against the back of his seat. Then the ferry slowly tilted to the side. To the left. He was on his left side. Ron unfastened the straps as quickly as possible and threw himself to the right, landing first on JP, then on the floor to his right. His head hit a metal strut and started thudding with pain. But it wasn't over yet. A body fell down on top of him. The ferry slowly tilted back into a vertical position and stabilized.

Lucked out. "Could you get off me?" Ron asked.

A boot hit him in the shin and JP rolled off. As soon as Ron was free, he sat up. His skull was ringing like a church bell, but it was getting better by the second. JP went around him to go to the control computer.

"What happened there?" asked Ron.

"I'm checking that now," JP answered. "It looks like we had a little bad luck with our landing site."

"What kind of bad luck?"

"A regolith dune on the wall of the crater. The moon dust was stirred up by the engine and unfortunately stuck to it."

"Stuck? Can't we remove it with a duster?"

"No, at these temperatures, the dust grains have melted. We'll need better tools than that."

Okay. They'd made it down to the surface alive. That was good news. The Europeans probably hadn't done enough research when choosing the landing site, but he couldn't complain – he hadn't even asked for coordinates.

"How about you take care of the engine and I'll take a look at what the Chinese have discovered?"

"Haha, nice try. I'm coming with you. We can clean the engine later. It has to cool down first anyway."

It had been worth a try. Major Hufman certainly would have been happier if he'd gotten JP out of the way. But as long as he could keep from resorting to violence, that was what he'd do.

JP jumped up and started to put on his spacesuit.

"Not so fast," said Ron.

"Shouldn't we be quick about it?"

"There are two things I've got to show you first."

"You Americans live up to all the stereotypes," said JP, cradling the small crossbow in his hand.

"I can assure you that the Chinese and the Russians have personal weapons too."

"And this thing here works?" JP turned the screw to wind the crossbow and pretended to aim at something.

"Much better on the moon than on Earth. Trust me, you wouldn't want to be shooting in a pressure chamber with our friends' guns. A crossbow bolt isn't as dangerous, but it's enough to perforate a spacesuit or cause painful injuries. Plus, you can improvise ammunition."

Ron grinned. JP must think he'd known about this for a long time, but he'd actually only recently found out. But it all made sense, and whoever had come up with it had earned his respect.

JP nodded. "Still, I hope I won't have to use the crossbow."

"Nobody wants that," said Ron. "All we're doing was creating a balance of power, which is the prerequisite for the prevention of violence."

The old doctrine had proven itself over the course of millennia. Whenever he thought long and hard about it, it seemed wrong to him at first. But the longer he kept at it, the more convinced he became. Facing an enemy unarmed was only an invitation for the adversary to exploit their advantage.

"Then let's go," said JP.

"One more thing." Ron held up a cape that had been folded into a rectangle. "We need to drape this over our spacesuits."

"But it's shiny! Isn't that ... counterproductive?"

"No. In the shadows, there's no light to reflect off of it.

The shiny layers let almost no heat radiation through, so when we're in the shadows, it's guaranteed that nobody can find us."

"What if we can't find any shadows?"

"Then we'll have to hurry, so we can disappear back into the shadows again."

THE FERRY HAD BURROWED SO DEEPLY INTO THE DUST THAT IT took a tremendous amount of effort to open the outer bulkhead of the lock. When they were finally able to get out, sand trickled towards them. Ron forced himself not to think about the engine, which of course made him ruminate about it all the more. If they wanted to leave the moon at some point, they would need to dig the shuttle out completely. From the side, the engine wasn't even visible.

Ron was reaching for his head to switch on the helmet light when JP stopped him.

"You're right, buddy," he grumbled, adjusting the cape over his head.

This is a dumb plan. Back up in the Gateway, it had seemed terribly clever. Down here, it was obvious that its plain and decisive drawback was that he couldn't see past his feet. And everything outside the shadows was so brightly illuminated that it wasn't possible to see any details there either.

"You have to lean forward at an angle," JP explained. "So far that on Earth you'd fall on your face."

Ron tried it. "Go on," said JP. Ron obeyed. "Keep going." He fell on his nose. JP laughed. "Sorry, I couldn't help myself. That was a little too far. Before you fall down, you have to push yourself off. Imagine you're a panther."

"Grrrrrr," said Ron.

"Good start."

"Grrrrrr." Ron leaned farther forward and jumped.

Before long, JP was next to him again. "Is it possible that you've never been to the moon?"

Ron nodded, then remembered that JP could barely see him. "That's right."

"You live in the Gateway but never come down? That must be deadly boring."

"God knows I've had enough variety in my life."

He'd evidently said that in such a way that JP didn't dare press him any further. Great. There was still a risk that they'd have conflicting interests at the end of this mission, in which case it would be a disadvantage to know each other too well.

THEY MADE GOOD PROGRESS. RON, HOWEVER, HAD underestimated how exhausting it would be to move around in a spacesuit. Maybe he should have taken a trip to the moon, at least once. Even after eight hours on a Gateway spacewalk, he had never been as exhausted as he was now after half that time. Plus, the distance seemed to increase instead of decreasing, because they had to keep detouring in order to remain in the shadows for as long as possible.

In the early afternoon, the instrument on his arm still showed a distance of about forty kilometers to their goal. They probably wouldn't make it today.

"We're moving way too slowly," said Ron.

"We can't go any faster," JP replied.

"I know. Should we turn around?"

"You mean give up?"

"No. We could try to get closer with the shuttle."

"You saw the engine. Or didn't see it, I mean. It will take us a day just to dig it out. If we keep walking, we'll catch up with our friends by tomorrow afternoon."

Ron sighed. They'd have to sleep in their spacesuits. He wouldn't be able to make it that far without an extended break. JP was younger and in better shape.

"I'm going to have to sleep for at least a few hours," said Ron.

"Same here."

Whew. He'd feared that the Frenchman would want to go on without stopping. His biggest concern, however, was his stomach, which had been giving him trouble for a while. He knew he'd have to relieve himself at some point. He wasn't dreading that so much as what would come afterwards. Ron tried not to think about it, but couldn't help it. The spacesuits were designed so it was possible to spend two or three days in them, but after twelve hours it really wasn't enjoyable anymore.

But did he have any alternative? It didn't look that way.

THEY HALTED IN A TROUGH FILLED WITH DUST WHEN MAJOR Hufman contacted him.

"Look, Major, I don't have time for small talk. Do you have anything new for me?"

"Well, it seems the Europeans have lost contact with your colleague Jean-Pierre Jeunet. Has he contacted you? Do you know anything?"

"No, I haven't heard from him. As you suggested, I haven't accepted any calls from the Gateway."

"Thanks, Ron. That's what I'd been hoping. I'll pass it on."

"Maybe he jumped out in his spacesuit," Ron suggested. JP, who was listening in, ran his hand across his throat.

"Ha ha, I don't think he's ready to give up on life yet. Meanwhile, I wanted to update you on our latest findings."

"Go for it."

Ron frowned. If this turned out to be a false alarm... But no, the Major would have told him so immediately, right? Whatever the case was, he certainly was taking his time to answer.

"Sorry, I wanted to play the pictures into your helmet for you, but I don't think the connection has enough capacity for that. Yes, Henderson?"

He could hear a woman's voice in the background.

Henderson was the technician at mission control who Ron always dealt with when something went wrong on the Gateway.

"Ah, I can send you a still image. The Chinese have covered the site with some kind of tent, but it's open on one side, which gives us a glimpse inside. The perspective isn't ideal, but you can see for yourself."

A connection request appeared in Ron's helmet screen, and he accepted it. Then he saw an image floating in front of him. There was an oval pit with an angular black object protruding from the middle. It definitely wasn't of natural origin. He shared the image with JP without saying a word, bringing his index finger towards his lips. Ron could tell when the image showed up for JP as the Frenchman's jaw literally dropped. Ron grinned. The trip down here had been worth it after all.

"What is...?"

"Don't ask me what that is. Our experts aren't in agreement about it. But we don't have all the data that our Chinese friends do. Our sources say that they've brought in the Eleventh Bureau of their intelligence service in response."

"Which means?"

"They think it's an extraterrestrial structure."

"Aliens?"

"We prefer the term extraterrestrial, but if you prefer..."

Ron laughed. Someone was screwing with him. Or else he was dreaming. He pinched his thigh hard. He definitely felt real pain there under the thick fabric of the spacesuit.

"Our experts aren't one hundred percent convinced yet," said Hufman. "But we don't have their data, either. The Chinese don't tend to exaggerate or panic."

"What else could it be?" asked Ron.

"Something left behind by another world power? The Russians have been noticeably quiet. Either they don't want to upset their Chinese friends, or they've got something to answer for."

Ron looked at the picture. The pit looked freshly dug. The

strange object must have been hidden beneath the surface. Why would the Russians have buried a black pillar on the moon?

"Does it serve an identifiable purpose? Does it do anything?"

"You're asking the wrong person, Ron. We've only got these few images from our spy satellite. It didn't detect any radiation."

"Have you asked the Chinese about it?"

"Of course, but nothing's come through the official channels. They see it as their internal affair, as their property."

If the object really was extraterrestrial in origin, that was an entirely understandable reaction. What could science learn from it? The US certainly would have tried to keep such an artifact for itself.

"What about the Europeans?" Ron asked. "Their relations with Beijing have been a lot better than ours lately."

He looked over at JP, who appeared to know even less than he did. His superiors probably didn't consider him important enough.

"The military's in charge there too," the major explained.

"Well, that's good. Can't you take the most direct route?"

"Ron, what do you think I've been badgering my superiors about? But since we've largely withdrawn from there, our influence and our relationships have also dwindled."

Ron clenched his jaw. The situation seemed pretty messed up. But how could anybody have prepared for something like this? The experts had always said it was almost impossible that the Earth would ever be visited by extraterrestrials.

"Are there any activities that indicate what the other powers' intentions are?"

"Yes, of course. Every spaceport on Earth seems to be making desperate preparations to launch human missions. SpaceX and BlueOrigin have canceled all private missions, but Russia, Europe, and even Japan and India are busy getting their rockets out onto launchpads. Almost two hundred people could be headed your way within a week.

However, we're estimating that only twenty percent of them will be able to land on the surface."

That was still forty people. They could hold hands, form a circle around the object, and all sing together. Beethoven or something. *Is it even possible to sing Beethoven?* Ron imagined what that event would be like. But, knowing people, they'd probably prefer to shoot at each other. What kind of impression would that make on the extraterrestrials? He shook his head. *Who cares what kind of impression we make if we can claim this exotic technology for ourselves?*

Then something occurred to him. "Major, you didn't say anything about the Chinese."

"Very observant. It's true – the Chinese are going about business as usual. They always have an emergency backup ship with a lunar lander, which is out on the pad with a full tank, but otherwise we haven't seen any unusual activities. They don't seem to be concerned about anybody wanting to take away their toy."

"Maybe our experts are mistaken after all, and the strange thing is just an unusually shaped block of stone. Some experiment from the bygone days of space travel that was buried."

"I wish that were the case, Ron. But the fact that the Eleventh Bureau has come into play suggests otherwise."

Oh well. He wouldn't have minded getting an all-clear. "Well, what should we do now? Me – what should I do?"

"Find out as much as you can. If you have the chance to seize the object, then take it. But tactfully, please. We don't want to start a war on Earth."

"So I'm supposed to capture this column for us, but it shouldn't look like I am?"

"That's correct, Ron. Say you're there to help our Chinese colleagues with an emergency... you get the idea. No open aggression. Most importantly, no witnesses and no cameras either."

No witnesses. Ron fumbled for his crossbow. At the same moment, JP, who had been listening in, reached down. Ron spread his arms, turned to him, and grinned. JP imitated the gesture. The Frenchman was not a witness. He'd never been here.

RON WAS LYING ON HIS BACK. THE RIGID ARMOR OF THE upper part of his spacesuit was pressing into his hip. He'd put a stone under his head. The sky looked amazing. It seemed to be made up of stars rather than the space in between them.

He couldn't sleep. His stomach and intestines were rumbling. He needed to let it all go, but he couldn't bring himself to do it. The diaper wouldn't absorb everything. He tried to think of something else, but the pressure in his bowels kept asserting itself. Following Hufman's orders had been a shitty idea. Literally. Once in the Navy, always in the Navy, that's what they said. But he'd been a civilian for years. Legally, he couldn't be held responsible.

But morally speaking? What if, with the knowledge they gained from this artifact, the Chinese rose to become the undisputed dominant world power? Perhaps that was what the future held anyway. The US wouldn't be worse off just because a communist party was ruling on the other side of the world.

"I can't sleep," said JP.

"That makes two of us."

"Do you really think this thing is an extraterrestrial artifact?"

"It seems the Chinese do."

"I'm asking you, Ronald Hudson."

Ron sighed. "I don't know. Scientists have always told us how vast the cosmos is. Why would anybody spend centuries reaching our solar system only to bury a dark pillar on the moon? Couldn't they have contacted us instead of leaving something like that behind?"

"It may have been sitting there for thousands of years," said JP. "That long ago, we wouldn't have been able to talk to them."

Ron liked his slight French accent. It made him think of red wine and boiled chicken. His stomach gurgled again, and he turned onto his side. This was the only way he could curl up. His head slid off the stone and hit the ground. Ouch. Sleeping out in the open on the moon had been a shitty idea.

"But they would have to have been traveling for a hundred thousand years before that," Ron sputtered. "Couldn't they have waited a little longer? They must be pretty long-lived, after all."

"What's wrong with you?" asked JP. "You sound ... stressed."

"It's nothing. Let's talk about the extraterrestrials."

"Hey, you're not secretly dying on me, are you? I don't want to wake up next to a corpse in the morning."

"Don't worry about it. It's nothing." Nothing but shit.

"Maybe the pillar itself is the message," said JP.

"Message?"

"From those extraterrestrials who couldn't wait."

Ron chuckled. *The extraterrestrials who couldn't wait.* That would be a funny title for a serious novel. A *New York Times* bestseller.

"What's so funny?" asked JP.

"I have no idea," said Ron. He didn't feel like explaining. He probably just had a horrible sense of humor.

"Maybe there was no point in waiting for us," said JP.

"Because we're too dumb?"

"No, they placed the object here and buried it so we wouldn't find it until we were smart enough to handle it properly, whatever that means. But maybe we wouldn't have anything to say to each other. Do you know what that's like? I'm sure you do."

Ron nodded. Once, when he was young, he'd fallen in love with a woman who he thought was absolutely beautiful. He'd done everything he could to win her over, and they did in fact end up sleeping together. But afterwards, they had nothing to say to each other. When she left his apartment, they both knew they wouldn't see each other again.

He didn't have any regrets and had even forgotten her name.

Oddly enough, he started to feel sad about it now, of all times.

"Yes, I do know what that's like," he said, swallowing the lump in his throat.

"It doesn't seem unlikely," said JP. "They must be millions of years ahead of us. What could they possibly have to learn from us? And we won't be able to do anything with their knowledge until far in the future. The only useful information we can share is simply that we exist. We aren't alone. What do you think about that? I think it's amazing."

"But we do know that. Think of the Enceladus being."

"That's totally different. It's a part of us, like the whales. For us, Enceladus is a long way away, but on a cosmic scale, it's a part of the solar ecosystem, along with Titan, Io, Mars, Venus... Everything that lives here comes from the same source. Whoever built this stele came from somewhere else, and is probably of a completely different design. The extraterrestrials will have different concepts of space and time and different senses. Maybe they even live in other dimensions."

"You've got quite an imagination," said Ron.

"Hey, here we are lying on the moon, staring into the infinite universe, and we're just a few hours' walk away from an extraterrestrial artifact. This is so intellectually exciting."

Ron couldn't have cared less about the black pillar right now. Another pain jolted through his stomach. *Damned gas.* Ron assumed the fetal position, but it didn't help with the pain. He groaned, and his voice reached just the right pitch. A liberating sound left his throat and he felt like he was deflating.

He lay on his side, exhausted. The pain was gone, leaving fatigue in its wake.

"What was that?" asked JP.

"Don't ask." Ron yawned and pulled the metallic cape over his head. "I need to rest now."

Dewar Crater, March 5, 2082

"Zhang Jinjin, why aren't you in your place in the control center?" asked an unfamiliar female voice over the loudspeaker.

Dang it. She'd tried to lock out mission control. There must be a back door she didn't know about. Should she take the call? They wouldn't listen to her, but maybe she'd be able to stall them a little. It would still be half an hour before she reached the excavation outside Dewar Crater, which was where Liwei had been when she'd lost contact with him. If mission control could hack into their communications, maybe they could also influence the rover's controls.

"Who is this?" she asked.

"My name is Wang Yaping. I'm in charge of coordinating the mission to rescue taikonaut Yang Liwei."

"I've never heard your name before. Can you provide any authorization?"

This was standard procedure, so Yaping couldn't hold it against her. Anybody could have hacked into the line, after all.

"You're Zhang Jinjin, born on February 28, 2056 in Qing-dao. You attended the military aviation school in Guangzhou, where you graduated with honors. After that, you were..."

"That's probably easy enough to look up. Who's to say you're the person you claim to be?"

"I can give you..." Yaping started.

"Don't go overboard, Jinjin," interrupted a male voice.

Jinjin was startled – it was Li Guofeng, her flying school instructor. How had they gotten him to mission control so quickly?

"I'll bet you're surprised, huh? Hopefully it was worth getting me out of bed so early. You must be having quite an adventure right now."

"I am."

What else could she say? She and Guofeng had had a kind of father-daughter relationship back then; because he'd taken her under his wing, she'd graduated at the top of her class. But she hadn't heard from him since then.

"You're trying to buy time, aren't you?" he asked.

Guofeng knew her well. If she was lying, he would be able to tell.

"And if I were?"

"Jinjin, it's really important that you let others do their job. What we do here only works when we act collectively. Each individual remains in their designated place and does the job they've been trained to do. You're an excellent taiko-naut. These nice people here explained to me that they need you at the control center, not in a rover somewhere out on the surface of the moon. There are others who will determine exactly what happened. They're specialists, just like you, but trained for this kind of emergency."

Jinjin sighed. *This kind of emergency.* As if anybody knew what had happened to Liwei. She'd managed to gain access to the ordinary excavator's cameras, though Liwei had locked Excavator Zero so that only he could access it. The other vehicle also had eyes, though, and on the screen Jinjin could see what they saw: Her supervisor, stiff and rigid, was standing stock-still with his arm outstretched in front of a slender, pitch-black structure. Jinjin zoomed in. It looked like just his middle finger was touching it.

She turned the camera so she could see his face. Liwei's mouth had stretched all the way open, and his eyes had widened. Something must have scared him before he... Right, before what? Liwei wasn't moving a muscle. It looked as if he were frozen, but the skin of his face wasn't pale. In fact, it was slightly red. If he were dead, wouldn't he have collapsed? It was tiring to keep one arm outstretched, and Liwei had been in that position for more than twelve hours. And then mission control came along and claimed, in all seriousness, that they recognized this type of emergency and could send in people more competent than she was?

"That's not how it works, Jinjin," said Guofeng. "You're throwing your life away. It would be a shame to waste your potential like that. Let the specialists do their job."

"I'm sorry. You also taught us how important it is to be there for each other. It'll be at least another day before the special unit arrives. I can't leave Liwei alone that long. I have to go to him and see if I can help him."

"We're looking at the same images you are, comrade," said Yaping. "Yang Liwei isn't showing any signs of life. His suit is technically dead. We can't detect any activity. You've got to stay away from him. Otherwise you'll be putting yourself in danger. Our emergency team has a robot with them. Just wait in the control center. I promise we'll do everything humanly possible to help Liwei."

"Right. Tomorrow. What if it's too late by then?" Jinjin asked. "I promise I'll wait patiently at the control center once the team arrives."

She herself didn't think she could help Liwei. But she at least wanted to keep him company. He was so vulnerable, standing out there in front of the giant statue. And his space-suit's reserves would be depleted soon.

"That's not good enough," said Yaping. "You need to stay away from the scene of the accident. It's dangerous. You're just making our job harder."

Why was mission control so insistent that she not even enter the area? The control system had just reported another unauthorized access. It was a good thing she'd switched to manual control long ago. Yaping was probably just trying to distract her as they silently worked against her. Jinjin clenched her jaw.

"Were you and Liwei very close?" Guofeng asked.

So now he was trying to make it personal. As her former commander, it didn't suit him at all. Guofeng had always put his work above everything else and kept the professional and the private strictly separate. She hadn't even known if he had a family until she'd graduated. Yaping was probably telling him what to say. She felt sorry for him; as a military man, he was just as caught up in the chain of command as she was.

But the question wasn't outlandish. Had they been close? Not especially. Liwei was her boss, and she thought of him only in professional terms. Yet over time, something like a relationship had developed. Relationships form between people even when they aren't thinking about it. Perhaps those were even the better ones. At any rate, it was because of that relationship that she was now sitting in the rover and violating all her orders.

But that was none of Guofeng's business.

"Tell me, which ministry does Yaping belong to?" asked Jinjin.

"Ministry of State Security," Yaping replied.

"The Tenth Bureau?" That was the division responsible for science and technology.

"No. Eleventh."

"Oh please, we all know there are only ten bureaus."

"Officially, the numbers only go up to ten. But since everyone here already knows, I can tell you – the Eleventh Bureau was set up by the 15th National People's Congress in the last century."

"And what does it oversee?"

"Preparations for making first contact with another civilization."

FIRST CONTACT. THE FORBIDDEN WORDS. GUOFENG HAD always told them, *No matter what you see out there, never mention extraterrestrials.* There was always a natural explanation. She had been laughing about it just yesterday. *If they existed, we'd be living in a totally different world. They'd be everywhere by now.* That was what she'd said. And now this Wang Yaping was talking about first contact. Even if she hadn't spelled out it exactly, this meant a first encounter with extraterrestrials. Sweat trickled into Jinjin's left eye. She tried to turn down the temperature in the rover, but the display read that it was already at sixteen degrees, which was the minimum.

Was it her fault that her superior was now standing motionless in front of the column? She hadn't wanted to believe him, so he'd had to prove it. If she'd gone to him immediately in order to investigate the discovery, perhaps he would have waited for her. But one of them would definitely have touched the stele. Who knew that a simple black pillar like that could have such an effect?

"Jinjin? We need to talk," announced Yaping. Ah. Apparently the relay satellite that had given her a moment of respite as it orbited the moon had reappeared on the horizon. Sighing, she pressed the button that confirmed the radio connection. There was no harm in talking. Yaping wouldn't convince her to go back to the control center. But perhaps she would tell her more about this mysterious phenomenon.

"Okay. What can you tell me about this structure?"

Yaping laughed. "You are good. Guofeng warned me I wouldn't be able to hold you back. But that doesn't mean our roles have changed. I'm the one who asks the questions."

"Could I just ask one tiny question first?"

Yaping didn't answer, and Jinjin took this to mean that she consented.

"How is it that you're at mission control so soon? Why did this all happen so quickly? Or are you calling from somewhere else?"

"No, I'm here."

"But I only reported trouble with Excavator Zero to

mission control. So why has the Eleventh Bureau been brought in?"

"We'll discuss your incomplete report later, Jinjin. For now, we need your cooperation."

And after that? They'd drop her like a hot potato. Yaping hadn't said as much, but the emphasis on *now* spoke volumes. Yaping was honest. Amazing ... or maybe not, because how do you establish trust other than by being honest, preferably in regard to questions with answers that weren't especially important?

"We have the night-time moonquake and our American friends to thank for alerting me," explained Yaping. "They must have seen something from the Gateway that our own satellites didn't notice."

"The column?"

"We're referring to the object as a *stele*, but no, they probably haven't spotted that yet. They were looking for the epicenter of that exceptionally strong quake and detected some strange optical reflections there, a kind of Einstein ring, then started wondering how the quake and the phenomenon might relate to each other."

"So they checked in with us?"

"Ha ha, no. Of course not. They poked around in their research network until a few of our people took notice. We just had to put two and two together. Your message, the tent, the quake, the two excavators..."

"But you didn't know about the stele?"

This was her fourth question. Either Yaping was new to her job, or she was caught up in how proud she was of her own intelligence. Or it was merely part of her strategy to get Jinjin on her side. Maybe it was a combination of all three.

"Actually, we did. After the warning was issued by the network, we were able to access the second excavator's cameras. Liwei must have neglected to block them."

Jinjin smacked her forehead. Of course, the telltale cameras. The image was still displayed on the control console. Liwei hadn't moved a single millimeter.

"I know," she said.

"We know that you know. You see, Jinjin, we mean you no harm. We could have halted the camera stream to your rover at any time. We just think you'd be safer at the control center. It's a matter of your well-being."

"I'm not turning back. That's out of the question."

"I understand. We are quite willing to accept a second-best solution if there's no other option."

"And what's that?"

"For you to inspect the black monolith under my guidance."

"Okay, I can live with that."

"But you've got to promise me one thing: You'll always stay at least ten meters away from it."

Ten damned meters? No way. There was no way she would touch the monolith, but she wanted to keep Liwei company. She was certain he was alive in his spacesuit, which itself had turned into a statue.

"Deal," she said, "I'll keep my distance from the monolith."

She didn't confirm what distance precisely. That was significant. She knew it and so did Yaping.

"Great. Then here's to a successful collaboration."

"PLEASE POINT THE RADAR TO THE NORTH," SAID YAPING.

Jinjin raised the arm with the compass on it. Since there was no magnetic field on the moon for it to use, the compass oriented itself visually to mountain formations that could only be seen in a very particular arrangement from a specific point. This took a few minutes. Once it was calibrated, the device buzzed. Her eyes followed the needle as it pointed into the darkness of infinity.

She'd taken down the tent shortly after she arrived. The other nations represented on the moon had known about this discovery for a while, and scientists from across the globe were probably trying to convince the Chinese government to release the discovery site. Yaping was shielding her from all of this. Jinjin connected the radar to the power cables issuing from the hatch of the excavator and started it up.

"We're receiving data. Thank you, Jinjin. Now the spectrometers."

This was something else the excavator was equipped with. The measuring instruments normally helped it to differentiate among various kinds of rock so that it could apply the appropriate amount of force. But she had to deploy them first, which wasn't easy in the spacesuit. She couldn't work as well with gloves on her hands. The work wasn't technically demanding, however, which allowed her mind to wander.

The Eleventh Bureau. She couldn't immediately recall how responsibilities were divided in the state security department. The Third Bureau had recently made headlines for being largely responsible for China's peaceful reunification with the island of Taiwan. At least that was how the Western media assessed the change in attitude that had taken place after the island's most recent elections, which made the process possible. Jinjin wasn't interested in politics and had no opinion about it. She was surprised, however, that the ministry was also preparing the nation for contact with extraterrestrials. It did affect national security, sure. But the general scientific consensus was that such contact was totally impossible.

Did the date of the Eleventh Bureau's founding reveal anything about the motives behind it? The 15th National People's Congress – she counted backwards – had met from 2023 to 2028, long before she was born. What had happened back then? Whatever it was, it hadn't made it into the history books.

Jinjin pressed the call button on her sleeve. "Tell me, Yaping, what happened in 2026 that led to the founding of your bureau?"

"Are you making good progress?" Yaping asked.

"2026. Please. It can't be that much of a secret, can it?"

"I... All right. Let's say you've been reading Western media from that year. You're absolutely free to do that."

"Of course."

"If you were to look in the right place, the activities of a German physics teacher would come to your attention. I've honestly forgotten his name because it's so impossible to pronounce. Let's call him Schmitt."

"Did he have contact with extraterrestrials?"

"Ha ha, no. A lot of people have said they have, but not Schmitt. What this man noticed was that there were some stars missing from the sky. He discussed it with astronomers all over the world, and that's how we heard about it."

"There are stars missing from the sky?" What was Yaping talking about?

"Yes. When they're counted in sky surveys, some are always lost. That's normal. But Schmitt believed he had discovered something behind it, something with effects that were gradually moving towards the solar system. He calculated that it should reach us in a few hundred years."

"It? What?"

"This alleged wave that's extinguishing those stars that go missing."

"How fascinating. And there are extraterrestrials involved?"

"We don't know. Schmitt believed that we needed to put a satellite in solar orbit, a kind of beacon emitting a particular signal. That would protect us."

"That sounds pretty whimsical."

"I agree with you there. But our astronomers did the math."

"And the physics teacher was right?"

"He did good work, at least. His calculations were correct. Unfortunately, he died during the events ten years ago, and his data disappeared along with him."

Poor guy. But if he was a physics teacher in 2026, he must have been ancient by 2072. Jinjin remembered the reports. In

Western Europe in particular, people's sheer desperation had led to a number of uprisings and riots.

"And his satellite?"

"We took it down after a year."

"We? Who's that? The UN?"

"No, China. Except for our researchers, nobody was interested."

"What? So he did all that work for nothing?"

"For the most part, our scientists think we should keep quiet so that more advanced civilizations won't notice us. That means we should send out as few signals as possible. We can't prevent the radio noise that comes from Earth, but in its solar orbit, Schmitt's beacon was sometimes pretty far from Earth, which made the signal conspicuous."

What a nice story. Was it true, or was it a cover-up designed to conceal the truth? The ministry was capable of anything.

"Couldn't the destruction of the sun hit us at some point?" she asked.

"According to Schmitt's predictions, a lot of water will still be flowing down the Yellow River by then. We could, of course, broadcast the signal again right before then if..."

"If we've discovered what's causing this phenomenon by then?" Jinjin suggested.

"If we still exist as a civilization by then."

"ARE YOU SURE YOU'VE CONNECTED THE DEVICES correctly?" Yaping asked.

The question came as no surprise. Jinjin herself could see the curve on the screen. Curve, yeah right. It was a straight line, and it could only be distinguished from the x-axis because the system colored it red.

"Yes, I've checked the wiring several times," Jinjin said, trying not to sound too annoyed. Yaping's doubts were entirely understandable. When an object had light shining on it, some of it ought to be reflected. Then it should be possible to draw conclusions about what the object was made of, based on the reflected radiation.

"The stele is completely dead," said Yaping. "That's impossible. I studied physics."

Jinjin bit her lower lip. She wasn't a physicist, but when she'd trained as a taikonaut, she'd learned how to operate a spectrometer. Every object – really, every one – emitted something.

"There must be an error in the measurement," said Yaping.

"Like I said, I've checked everything several times." Now Jinjin did sound irritated.

"I'm sorry. It must feel horrible, but it's not that I don't trust you. It isn't that at all! The fact of the matter is that this monolith is absorbing all radiation. But as it does, it must give off heat. Which is also radiation. But I don't see any of that."

"Okay, hold on."

Jinjin closed the helmet, opened the hatch, and climbed out. She jumped over to one of the spectrometers and aimed it at the wall of the crater.

"Ah, now I see something," Yaping said, the voice coming through in her helmet. "Volcanic rock and regolith? That can't be."

"What you're seeing are reflections from the slope of the crater. I rotated the spectrometer. See? It's working."

"That... You're right. Sorry, but... As a physicist, I still can't believe it. And if I did believe it, I'd have to advise you to get out of there as quickly as possible."

Sweat was running down Jinjin's forehead again. Yaping sounded genuinely worried.

"Why is that?" she asked. "The stele isn't moving."

"If it stores all the radiant energy it receives, it must contain an enormous amount of energy. If it were to release it, nobody should be in the area."

That sounded reasonable. But anybody who'd built something like this must have considered the consequences. So it was intended to be dangerous.

"You mean the monolith is a weapon?"

"It's a bomb, at least," said Yaping. "There isn't any technology capable of storing energy indefinitely. At some point the monolith will have to release it, and the effects would be catastrophic."

It seemed like she'd better head back to the rover. What if there was an explosion soon? But there was Liwei. She couldn't leave him behind. His body was just a meter away from the stele.

"What's the point of burying a bomb under the moon's surface?" she asked.

"First of all, we don't know how the builders of the monolith think. If the stele's been collecting energy for billions of years, it could probably completely blow up the moon today. Such a weapon could be useful. That would be a deadly attack on terrestrial life. But what's more likely, in my opinion, is that the monolith can release its energy in a targeted way. Consider the shape. It looks like it's aiming at something."

"An ... energy cannon?" asked Jinjin.

"Something like that. Didn't the Russian RB intend to build an enormous laser here in order to power spaceships? If the extraterrestrial builders come to visit or have visited us at some point, this could be their return ticket. Or it has military purposes. But if that were the case, the monolith would have to be aimed at a target."

"That's not what it looks like," said Jinjin.

"I would be cautious about coming to any conclusions before we understand the technology."

"I'd better take a closer look."

"Wait!" Yaping shouted. "Don't go near the stele!"

Jinjin terminated the radio connection. She'd made a promise to Liwei that she would keep him company.

LIWEI WAS ALIVE. JINJIN WAS ENTIRELY CERTAIN NOW. SHE looked at his face up close. His forehead was slightly furrowed. The eyes were clear, focused on his outstretched hand. A gray hair was sticking out of his left nostril. His cheeks were a slightly reddish hue in the intense light of her helmet lamp, but mostly gray otherwise. His lips were slightly pursed. She could imagine him speaking some sort of greeting. He must have known that he was touching something built by extraterrestrials. Surely, whatever he'd said was meaningful.

There was a drop of sweat suspended over his right eyebrow. It was too big, and it troubled her. It should be rolling downwards, even if the gravity here was lower. She wanted to give Liwei a quick nudge so she could see the drop fall. Better not, though. The effect of the stele might be transferred to her too.

Jinjin looked around. From a purely subjective standpoint, it looked like the monolith rising from the gray rubble had been standing there motionless for a thousand years. But objectively speaking, the images from the excavator's camera showed that it had moved upwards about ten meters during last night's quake, without touching a single hair on Liwei's head. The back of his spacesuit, however, was covered with dust.

It didn't appear, however, that the stele was completely excavated yet. But if the regolith was touching this alien material, and she was standing on that very same ground, just one meter away, shouldn't she also feel the effect of the monolith? Jinjin took a step back and then laughed at her own fear. The whole moon would have come to a standstill if the effect of the stele did in fact spread through the ground. But she still preferred not to make physical contact with Liwei.

At least not directly. Jinjin bent down and picked up a little rock, and lobbed it in Liwei's direction. She watched its trajectory. The stone ... that wasn't possible. She switched on the helmet camera and threw a second rock. This stone likewise slowed down just before reaching Liwei's spacesuit, approached as if in slow motion, and then stuck to the suit as if it were magnetic.

Jinjin stepped closer. The bead of sweat was still hovering above Liwei's eyebrow. The stones must have hit him too gently to disturb it. But what about their momentum? Momentum, mass times speed, couldn't just disappear. She'd learned that in school. The monolith, however, didn't seem to have gotten the memo. Apparently the known laws of nature didn't apply to it.

She took a deep breath and stood next to Liwei, looking towards the stele. What had made him touch it? Jinjin waited to hear a voice speaking to her, urging her to do the same thing her boss had. But there was nothing. The stele was silent, and it didn't care what Jinjin wanted. She was out of place. The monolith had its purpose, but it had nothing to do with her. The fact that Liwei had touched it was just bad luck. Those who built it probably hadn't thought humans would ever come here. If they had, they would have blocked off the area with police tape.

Jinjin reached out her arm. What would happen if she touched the monolith too? Would Liwei wake up from his dream? Would she be connected to him somehow? It didn't look like he was in pain. She pictured the look on his face – a mixture of curiosity and surprise. He had been the first. That was certainly a magical word. These days, it was impossible to be the first anywhere, even on the moon. Every mountaintop and every crater had already been explored. In Liwei's place, she would have grabbed it too.

Should she...? No, not until she knew more about what was going on here. Jinjin pulled back her arm.

"I'm sorry, Liwei," she said.

Liwei didn't answer. For a split second, she thought she'd seen him wink at her, but that was only her imagination. Jinjin turned around and started back toward the rover. Hardware got dusty so quickly here! She climbed in through the hatch, closed the cabin from the inside, let air stream in, and removed her helmet. Then she established a radio connection to mission control.

"Is that you, Jinjin? Don't ever do that again!"

Yaping sounded really worked up. She must have been watching over the second excavator's cameras to see how close she got to the stele.

"I'm sorry. I had to keep a promise I made to Liwei."

"You were gone for nearly twenty hours! We thought we'd lost you!"

Mare Orientale, March 6, 2082

"GET THE BALL!" SHOUTED ERNIE, THROWING IT ACROSS THE control center. Bree ran after it but didn't slow down in time. She crashed into the wall, bounced back briefly onto the floor, and then kept following the ball, her tail wagging, under a cabinet mounted on the wall.

"You aren't supposed to play with her in the control center," Antonia said. But her words lacked conviction because, just like Ernie, she could see how much fun her dog was having.

"How's she supposed to catch a ball outside?" asked Ernie. "This is her hunting instinct. Taking care of a dog means letting her exercise it."

"Has mission control been in contact with you today?" asked Antonia.

Ernie had taken the early shift so she could sleep in. He'd even offered to send her to the infirmary, but she had to decline. Her foot still hurt, but that didn't mean she could let Ernie do all the work.

"No, they've been quiet."

That was unusual. They normally received new orders in the morning, standard time, for observations relevant to the current situation.

"Maybe teams all over the world are busy evaluating the two merge events," said Antonia.

"Then someone would take the opportunity to request their own observation times."

He was right. It wasn't normal for mission control not to want anything from them., especially not after the moonquake they'd had the day before.

"Okay, I'll keep trying my luck with the rover," Ernie said.

"If you need help..."

"Thanks, but I have to identify the error first. The fuel cell keeps turning off."

He disappeared into the workshop and the door closed. Bree barked after him. When the door remained shut, she picked up her ball, ran over to Antonia, and looked at her with her twinkling brown eyes.

Antonia sighed as Bree wagged her tail expectantly. "I shouldn't do this." But she threw the ball all the same, and the dog dashed after it. Then she turned her attention to the computer. The silence from mission control worried her, but not because of any concerns about the moon station's antenna or the relay satellites.

IT WAS A WHILE BEFORE SOMEONE ON THE OTHER END confirmed the connection. She didn't recognize the voice.

"This is Colonel Lehmann," a woman announced in clear English. "What can I do for you?"

Had she somehow reached the switchboard? But why was a colonel answering?

"This is Antonia Marucci from the MIGI. Where is our CapCom?"

"I'm sorry, but communication with the moon has been transferred to another level of command."

"What does that mean?"

"The scientists aren't responsible for communicating with you anymore. Now it's the military. However, we're still discussing the situation and will let you know what conclusions we reach."

"Situation? What's that supposed to mean? Is that in reference to yesterday's merge event? Was the data so revolutionary that it's caused a worldwide commotion?"

The idea made her smile. Science was now more important to people than ever.

"I don't know what a merge event is. But unfortunately, global commotion can't be ruled out."

Now Antonia felt scared. "What do you mean by that? Please explain!"

"I'm sorry, but I can't provide information until a clear decision has been made."

"About what?"

"I can't tell you anything about that either. Please remain calm and go about your daily activities. We'll get back to you as soon as there's anything to say."

The connection broke off. Colonel Lehmann had simply hung up. Antonia angrily kicked the base of the computer, then screamed because she'd kicked it with her injured foot.

"What's wrong? Do you need help?" Ernie stood in the doorway, looking at her anxiously.

"No, that was just my own stupidity. Did you overhear the conversation I was having?"

"No, I would never..." Ernie turned red, and Antonia shook her head.

"I didn't mean it like that. I just mentioned it because then I could save myself the trouble of explaining it."

Bree came flying in. She landed right by Antonia's foot, barked once happily, and then licked her human's thick sock. How cute was that? Antonia felt warmth spreading through her chest and she was about to crouch down to cuddle the dog when she remembered Colonel Lehmann.

"The military's responsible for us now," Antonia said, then elaborated on the conversation she'd had with the colonel.

"Which military?" Ernie asked.

"No idea." For decades Europe had been planning to develop its own army, but nothing had come of it. "NATO, maybe?"

"They aren't responsible for Europe's internal affairs."

Ernie was right. At the moment, it didn't really matter. They needed to figure out what happened, as a matter of priority. If they were in danger, they needed to know what to expect.

"Okay," said Antonia. "Do you have any idea what might have happened? Lehmann wouldn't give me the slightest clue."

"It must have something to do with gravitational waves," said Ernie.

Typical Ernie. Of course he thought it had something to do with his area of specialization.

"What makes you think that? Maybe there was a coup or something."

"No, that doesn't make any sense. If that were the case, down on Earth they'd be worrying about things other than replacing our CapCom with a soldier. It must have to do with us somehow, with the MIGI. All of a sudden, it seems we're important."

"It probably isn't related to the merge event," said Antonia. "That colonel lady didn't even know what that was."

"That doesn't surprise me. The fact that some black holes have merged isn't really going to attract the military's attention," said Ernie, wrinkling his nose. "But if it is about the MIGI, the answer should be in the data."

"Which data?" Antonia raised her eyebrows.

"Good question. If the military has taken over, the event must have already happened, right?"

She shook her head. Was that really so? Whatever had disturbed the European governments so much that they sent the military into mission control could still be going on.

"Or it's still happening," she said.

"Do you see anything unusual here?" asked Ernie, looking down and grinning. "Well, apart from a crazy little doggy."

Antonia's face broke into a smile when she saw the wild flips Bree was doing over her foot. She was probably trying to get her attention. But this wasn't the time to play.

"Well then, take another look at the data from the merge event while I take a few new measurements."

"Sounds good," said Ernie.

"Did you fix the rover?"

Suddenly a cold shiver ran down her spine. The idea of not having a way out of here didn't sit well with her at all.

"Of course," said Ernie. "It was a breeze."

"Thank you, that's a relief," she replied, nodding.

"A relief?"

Ernie knew her all too well. He must have detected the slight tremor in her voice. Perhaps it was an after-effect of the accident. She didn't feel safe on the moon anymore. She had never felt this way before.

"Oh, it's nothing."

"Gotcha. If you want to talk, I'm here."

That was nice of him, and she knew it. There was a reason the psychologists had locked her and Ernie up together in this station, where it was easy to get claustrophobic.

"I'm okay," she said.

Ernie left the control center. He liked to work in his own little room because he could fart there in peace, or so he claimed. Flatulence was a result of the low gravity here. Antonia looked at Bree, who had fallen asleep next to her foot. From zero to a hundred and back in a minute. That was her girl. Antonia drew her leg back carefully.

"Sorry, sweetie, I've got to take care of our measuring equipment."

Antonia drew herself up with a groan. She had to stretch her leg out to keep it from hurting, but there wasn't enough room at the desk with the main computer's big display on it, so she had to lean forward uncomfortably far in order to type. She'd thought about getting the AR lenses from the bathroom so she wouldn't need to use a screen, but in the dry air here she couldn't tolerate them for more than two hours.

And it didn't look like the problem would be resolved quickly. The merge event appeared to have desynchronized the path of the laser in a peculiar way. Only a really powerful gravitational wave could do such a thing, and this was something they had never observed in reality. There was no physical explanation available for it. If that was what had happened, Ernie was right, after all – it was the measurement data from the past that had made the governments on Earth nervous.

But she wasn't ready to agree with Ernie's conclusion just yet. Maybe she needed to recalibrate the system. Usually she'd have to get permission from mission control. But what recommendations could Colonel Lehmann give her? And what could possibly happen? The MIGI simply wouldn't be able to carry out new measurements for an hour and a half. Because of the lack of synchronization, it wouldn't have been able to anyway; the measured values obtained that way would be unreliable. So they had everything to gain. Antonia started the process.

"Now that really is enough," said Antonia, taking Bree from her knees and setting her down on the floor. If the dog had had her way, she would cuddle all day. But the main computer had just signaled that the calibration was complete.

Out of the corner of her eye, she saw Bree shooting off like a cannonball, probably to go try her luck with Ernie. He always kept his door closed, but on several occasions she had caught Bree pressing the button. She wouldn't be able to jump that high on Earth, but here a little head start was all she needed.

What's this? Antonia had pulled up the new calibration data, and it looked odd to her. There were two new deflections that she didn't remember. The calibration data depended on the system itself and its surroundings. Influences from the environment couldn't be avoided, even on the moon, and only on rare occasions was it possible to completely eliminate such sources of error. But that wasn't necessary, because knowing what their precise dimensions were meant they could be subtracted from the actual measurement.

Two new deflections. What could it mean? Antonia scratched her head. She retrieved the sensor values that described the status of the laser paths. Temperatures, vacuum, laser intensities – everything looked good. The MIGI itself hadn't changed. And the solar system was still the same. So the problem must be located in the immediate vicinity. Immediate – in other words, on the moon. There was no horizon for gravitational waves.

Antonia got up to tell Ernie the news. She could have called him, but she wanted to see the look on his face when she told him about the change in calibration. She pushed off in the direction of the workshop carefully, so as not to put too much strain on her injured foot. Ernie met her at the open airlock. He grinned.

"Got it," he said.

"I..." Antonia shook her head. She couldn't believe it! "What have you got?"

"The cause. It's in the merge event data. The recorded deflections only fit a cosmological model without dark matter."

"Huh?" Antonia understood what Ernie was talking about, but why would that mean that the military would take over mission control?

"New physics, Antonia! Finally, we have proof for a

completely new physics, and the standard model has been definitively buried!"

"But that's silly, Ernie."

"No, not in the slightest. I analyzed the raw data we sent to mission control. If the other facilities haven't found anything contradictory, the results are clear."

Antonia sighed. Ernie seemed to be taking science a little too seriously. But no military people on Earth thought that way!

"So you think that's the only reason why Colonel Lehmann is now sitting in the CapCom's seat?" she asked.

"New science is always..."

"Why don't you come take a look at this?"

Antonia dragged her colleague from the hatch to the main computer and pointed to the screen.

"What's this?" asked Ernie.

"The new calibration data." Antonia pressed a button to superimpose a curve with the old data over it, and the two deviations stood out clearly.

"That's ... interesting." Ernie pulled himself closer to the screen and used his fingers to zoom in on the data. "The deviations are continuous rather than discrete," he said. "That suggests a natural source. Has an asteroid hit the moon recently?"

"We would surely have noticed that. And look at the size of the deviations. That would have to be one killer asteroid."

"True. But it really does look like a gravity well somewhere in the vicinity."

"Don't you think it looks more like two?" Antonia asked. But as soon as she said it, she realized how unnecessary her question was.

"No, one. This was data from our facility, not the surrounding area. Imagine that you live on an atoll, with the lagoon inside, the reef outside. A giant wave comes from the north. First it breaks on the reef, and then it races through the lagoon and breaks again. One source, two deviations."

"Yes, my mistake," Antonia admitted. "But what's the source?"

Now it was Ernie's turn to sigh. "I have no idea."

"Colonel Lehmann probably knows something but isn't saying anything."

"Then we'll find out for ourselves."

"How about I give Jinjin a call?" Antonia suggested.

"That's a great idea."

ANTONIA INITIATED THE RADIO LINK. THE RELAY SATELLITE IN orbit responded immediately, but nobody on the other end answered.

"Oh well," said Ernie. "I was really hoping..."

"This can't be good," said Antonia.

She had a bad feeling about this. It was the signal path that bothered her. Her call hadn't even connected with the Chinese system. Jinjin couldn't have answered even if she'd wanted to. Why was that? She verified the authorizations, but it didn't look like anything stored in the relay satellites could have locked the Chinese crew out of communications. That would also be quite unusual. The various factions had been cooperating for many years, at least in basic areas like communication. It would be far too expensive to set up multiple satellite relay networks around Luna.

"The problem must be with the Chinese base," she said. "Something's happened there."

"You think so?"

"Yes. Otherwise we would at least get an automatic response."

Antonia was freezing. She went over towards the hatch and adjusted the life support system controls, which were located right next to it. If something had happened to Jinjin and her colleague, they were all alone on the far side of the moon.

"True," said Ernie. "I hope they're both doing okay."

"We should go and see. What if they need help?"

Ernie looked up at her, his eyes wide. "Are you serious?"

Antonia nodded. "Of course!"

"But it isn't any of our business."

"What? We're under an obligation to help. Moon Treaty, remember?"

Antonia narrowed her eyes. Why was Ernie so ... reluctant? Was he scared? She'd understand if he was, but he should be honest about it.

"Don't look at me like that," Ernie said. "The Chinese construction site is damned far from here."

"That may be true, but we're still the closest. Nobody can help them as quickly as we can. And you even fixed the rover."

A cold shiver ran down her spine as she realized what that meant. They would be in that tiny rover for a long time.

"Mission control would never let us do that," said Ernie.

"When you ask a lot of questions, you get a lot of answers."

"You want to drive off without authorization?"

"I wouldn't ask," Antonia countered. "Then they can't forbid us from doing it. We'd just be doing our duty."

"I've got a bad feeling about it," said Ernie.

"The rover is safe. You inspected it yourself, right?"

"I'm not talking about our vehicle. If something left traces like the ones we measured in the calibration data, it's better to keep our distance from this phenomenon. Or am I mistaken?"

Antonia sighed. It wasn't easy to dismiss his fears. But if the Chinese researchers needed help... At least with Jinjin, something of a friendship had developed.

"The advantage of an object with such a high mass is that we can't miss it," said Antonia. "And then we can get out of its way, whatever it is."

"Here at the MIGI, we are at a safe distance."

"Yes, we are. But just think of the new physics we'll find

there. Should the Chinese be the only ones to benefit from it?"

Ernie grimaced, then slumped over in defeat. "You really know how to use my own reasoning against me."

Surface of the moon, March 6, 2082

"Good morning!"

When JP's voice woke him up, it didn't look like the sky had changed.

"Morning," Ron replied, glancing at the computer on his arm. It was five o'clock in the morning. He'd slept for six hours. He rotated his head in all directions, cracking his joints. Then he shook out his arms. His right leg had fallen asleep. He hopped from one foot to the other and felt something sticky peeling off the hairy skin on his backside. Sh... He wouldn't even let himself think the word.

"Feeling better?" JP asked.

"I guess so." His stomach growled. He was better at managing hunger than abdominal pain. During his time in the Navy, he'd felt hungry almost all the time. If things here got too exhausting, he could always drink nutrient solution from a tube in his suit, though it tasted horrible.

"Let's go, then. We've still got a grueling stretch ahead of us."

JP was right. Ron looked around, but their campsite was hidden in pure darkness. He bent down and felt the ground.

"Is this what you're looking for?" asked JP.

Ron could see the two metal sheets in the weak light emitted by the little lamps inside his helmet.

"Here," said JP, handing him one of the sheets. Ron hung it over his suit. All he needed now was a lightsaber, and he'd look like a Jedi warrior. He looked down at himself. The spacesuit puffed out the sheet. He would make a pretty fat Jedi.

THE CLOSER THEY GOT TO THEIR DESTINATION, THE FASTER they went. JP seemed to be spurred on by the prospect of solving the puzzle, just as much as he was.

But then they ran out of shade. About two hundred meters in front of them was a sort of tent. It was open at the sides, and they could see two huge machines, which clearly served to tear up the ground, parked underneath.

"The one on the right is a normal excavator, and the one on the left is a special one," said JP.

"How do you know that?"

"We were just talking about it. The Chinese loaned us an excavator so we could set up supply lines for the MIGI lasers beneath the surface of the moon."

"You? Have you been down here before?"

"No, I coordinated it through the Gateway. That was the first time I was out here. You didn't even exist then."

Perhaps he should have taken a greater interest in the Gateway's guests. Ron had always felt a bit like the custodian of the station, and had adopted the surly manner of some of his colleagues on Earth.

"Do these things pose a threat to us?" asked Ron.

"They have no intelligence of their own. But they can be controlled remotely, and if one of these things rolled over you, it would flatten you like a pancake."

"How fast are they?"

"They can get up to about twenty kilometers per hour."

Well, that was faster than Ron could run. At least on Earth. Even here, it would be a close call. It seemed best to stay away from those excavators.

"Do you see the pillar?" he asked.

"No, we're probably coming from the wrong side. It's probably hidden by the machines."

"Or the Chinese have already dismantled it and taken it away. Actually, never mind. The major would have found out and passed along the information."

Hufman had gotten in touch with him two hours ago, urging him yet again to exercise caution. There had probably been contact between governments, and the Chinese had vehemently forbidden any interference. *If you get too close to the area, we cannot guarantee the safety of your people.* An overt threat, even if the Chinese insisted they had formulated it as a warning.

"If we cross the area in front of us, we'll blow our cover," said JP.

"We'd be like cardboard cutouts at a shooting range," said Ron, shaking his head. "And they could be anywhere. Look at those shadows over there."

"There are just two of them. They can't be everywhere."

"Ha ha. One is enough. On the moon, the range and accuracy of guns..."

"You really assume they're armed?"

Ron reached for his crossbow. "You aren't that naive. If there's a risk that one of them would do it, they'd all have to try."

JP sighed. "I could just go walking over there. Visits aren't forbidden, are they?"

"Um, yes, they are. The Chinese government was very clear about that. They're claiming this area exclusively for themselves. Supposedly for security reasons. They don't want anyone to get hurt here and then be at fault for it."

"That's cleverly worded."

"But pretty transparent." Ron sat down on a large stone. He himself was on the verge of following JP's suggestion and simply visiting his colleagues over there. They were humans, not predators. If he went alone, they'd outnumber him and wouldn't have to kill him straight away. Nobody liked killing.

But if he went, JP would come along, just as he wouldn't let him go alone. That complicated the calculations. Two men were a greater threat. It would be almost impossible for two of them to keep two enemies in sight simultaneously. If they acted logically, they'd take down at least one of them. Who? When in doubt, the American. Ron glanced at his upper right arm, with the prominent American flag.

"I don't like this," he said. "It's too quiet."

"Maybe there's no one here," said JP.

"That's what they want us to believe," said Ron. "It's an old strategy. Whoever makes the first move takes the bigger risk. Maybe the area here was mined too."

Was he thinking too much like a soldier? But all Chinese astronauts had military training, even if they worked as scientists or technicians.

"Do you know the Chinese crew?" Ron asked. Maybe they'd get further on the personal level.

"Zhang Jinjin and Yang Liwei," JP replied. "A man and a woman. He's the boss. She's still quite young."

"So Zhang is the woman?"

"Jinjin. Zhang is the family name. Liwei's the boss. He's been around for a while."

"Do you know him personally?"

JP shook his head back and forth. "Not really, no. I dealt with him a few times from the Gateway. He was our point of contact."

Now Ron remembered. Liwei had spoken to him when a Chinese ferry wanted to dock at the Gateway. It hadn't happened very often, and so his memories of it were vague and of no use to them.

"Which of the two is more likely to have a positive reaction to us?" asked Ron. "The woman, since she's young and naive?"

JP shook his head. "Jinjin still has her career ahead of her. It's more likely that she'll follow orders than Liwei, who's about to retire. If I remember correctly, Chinese astronauts get a decent state pension starting from the age of fifty, and Liwei's in his late forties."

"That's enviable. But would he risk his pension?"

"Neither of them is going to risk anything on our account. But Liwei's worked there so long that he has connections to help him if he has any problems. That gives him more leeway to make his own decisions. Still, you can't expect him to betray his country."

Ron didn't want that at all, and could certainly understand Liwei's position. You just didn't turn your back on your country, period. Did JP feel that way, too? Ron looked at his face. It looked like he was thinking things over. There was every reason to. If they waited in the shade, they wouldn't get any closer to their goal.

"I think..." JP began. "What do you think of waiting here in the shade? It's standard lunar time here too, so they'll go to sleep at night, and then we can take a look at what interests us without being disturbed."

"I don't think they're doing things by the book right now. They'll be guarding the artifact around the clock."

"Yes, but they also need to sleep, at least in turns. Even we took a break yesterday."

Hm. JP was right. Everybody needed sleep. Having only one opponent to deal with would make it a lot easier. The only problem was the area in front of them. Even one person with a weapon could cover it. Ron looked around. More crater walls rose to the south of them.

"We'll use the daytime to make our way around this area," he said. "Maybe everything will look better from the other side. Even if it doesn't, at least we won't have been sitting around being bored."

"Okay," said JP. "Some exercise will do us good."

Dewar Crater, March 6, 2082

"What? I've been out here for half an hour at the most." Jinjin looked at the computer watch on the wrist of her spacesuit, which she was still wearing. She held the small display up to the camera and switched it on. It clearly showed that only thirty-three minutes had passed. "There!"

"Why don't you take a look at the rover's on-board computer? Okay?"

She swiped on the control panel screen, and a large clock appeared. The numbers looked abstract to her, but below them was the date: March 6. All of a sudden, she froze. The stele had taken a whole day of her life from her. She saw Liwei's motionless face in front of her. He'd been under the influence of the object for much longer. How old might he have become by now? But no. Her own watch proved that yesterday wasn't yet over for her. Liwei wasn't ageing faster, but slower.

"I'd like to show you something," said Yaping.

A play button appeared on the screen, and Jinjin pressed it. She saw herself, filmed from the perspective of the other excavator. Circles were displayed to show the distance from the monolith. The recording showed her moving normally at first. At a distance of about four meters, she slowed down drastically, as if somebody had activated a slow-motion feature.

"Now I'm going to skip ahead one hour," said Yaping.

There was a little blip in the footage and then Jinjin saw herself standing just behind Liwei. She was lifting her right leg extremely slowly. It had taken her one hour to take a single step – the one that brought her up to Liwei.

"This goes on until you turn back."

"It all felt completely normal to me. My watch proves it."

"Yes, we believe you. But please don't ever get that close to the monolith again."

"For now, I have no need to."

Still, it was a good idea. At least now she wouldn't worry about Liwei running out of oxygen. Time was passing much more slowly for him. And that must apply to the drop of sweat above his brow, too.

"Do you have an explanation for this phenomenon?" she asked.

"It's the same as for the Einstein ring and the strange projections beneath the tent: the stele must contain an enormous amount of mass in a very small space. The mass is distorting space-time, which leads to effects like this."

"Just like a black hole."

A shiver ran down her spine. The army had managed to keep their country calm, unlike in the West. But teetering on the abyss of death for weeks had left a deep impression on her.

"I was afraid you would say something like that. But please, you absolutely must avoid using that term. Otherwise people will immediately think of the horrible events of 2072."

Jinjin sniffled. She never could have imagined this! What a surprise.

"What's different this time?" she asked.

"Everything. First of all, the mass involved. This is definitely not a black hole. The dimensions simply aren't right. The material the stele is made of is very dense, but not that dense. And second of all, we have the situation under control. We know what to do."

Control. Jinjin liked that word. She'd always had good control over her life, or she wouldn't have made it this far.

"Speaking of which, if today is actually tomorrow – shouldn't the rescue team have arrived by now?"

Yaping gulped audibly. "There are still certain delays."

The rescue workers were late for such an important mission? How could that be?

"What's wrong? It only takes a day to get here, right?"

"True. But since midnight, the Americans have closed off the orbit. They're threatening to destroy any ship that approaches the moon."

"They're able to do that so easily?"

"We aren't equipped for a war in space. At least not right now. Nobody had any idea that the moon could become a source of contention. Our government protested at the UN Security Council, of course, but we don't want to risk losing a ship. The civilian moon ferries are simply too vulnerable."

The People's Republic of China was letting itself be blackmailed by the United States. This had never happened before.

"That's ... outrageous."

"This is actually what the Eleventh Bureau predicted. We're going on the assumption that every nation must and will try to be at the front of the line when first contact is made. Otherwise their survival will be at risk."

"That's a pessimistic way of looking at it. Why wouldn't they share their findings with all of humanity?"

"Because humanity as a whole is doomed to die. By cooperating with an alien power, individual nations can hope to continue existing for a period of time that has yet to be determined, but nothing more."

"That presupposes that our visitors' aims in coming here are belligerent ones."

"Right. That is what the Eleventh Bureau is assuming. They have to destroy us before we destroy them. There's no question about that. We are too alien to each other for us to arrive at a mutual understanding."

This doctrine sounded familiar. She'd heard it discussed in politics classes a long time ago.

"But there's a counterexample, isn't there?"

"Do you mean the Enceladus creature? It doesn't meet the criteria for first contact. It's a collective intelligence poor in resources. It's not a civilization, and it didn't reach us by its own efforts. At any rate, we're monitoring Enceladus in the event that there are any changes in this assessment."

"So there's a war over who gets to kiss up to the aliens first."

"No. The equilibrium has been thrown off balance. We've blocked off the surface of the moon and threatened the Americans that we'll destroy the lander if it lands. That would be possible without entering lunar orbit."

"And the Europeans?"

"They're staying out of it and insisting on a peaceful exploration of the moon."

"So right now, everybody's looking at each other suspiciously."

"Right. But the Eleventh Bureau assumes that our country has a slight advantage."

Jinjin nodded. Liwei's curiosity was what had given them this advantage. And he might have paid for it with his life. Hopefully they'd give him credit for it later. The very thought made her shudder. She had to save him somehow.

"This is why we're going to appear outwardly calm. Ideally, we will have solved the problem before either party is forced to make good on their threats."

We? How was the Eleventh Bureau planning to solve this problem from Earth?

"And what's my role in all of this?" asked Jinjin.

"That's a very good question," Yaping answered quickly, as if she'd been waiting for it.

"Then I'd like to request an equally good answer."

Jinjin took off the top part of her spacesuit and settled

comfortably in her seat. Yaping had seemingly worked out a comprehensive research plan. Jinjin heard paper rustling in the background. If they knew enough about the monolith, surely they'd be better able to assess the danger.

"We worked out the best possible strategy years ago and calculated it over and over again using the newest supercomputers and AIs. The result was always the same."

Yaping paused. Jinjin indulged her and asked, "Which one?"

"Do you know what would have radically altered the course of Earth's history?"

"No clue. If humans had never figured out how to harness the power of fire?"

"If the Native Americans had fought back when their colonizers arrived. Systematically. They would have had to kill every new arrival and burn their ships."

Jinjin gripped the armrests. Surely Yaping wasn't serious. It was a historical comparison, nothing more. And now she was going to explain why it didn't apply in this particular case.

But instead she asked, "You understand me, Jinjin, right?"

"Yes, I think so. You want to kill the extraterrestrials."

"It sounds a bit trite, but yes."

"It is trite."

"We don't mean any harm to the other civilization. We just never want them to set foot in the solar system. It's pure self-protection."

If the Spanish, Portuguese, and Italians, and then the British and French, had stayed at home rather than conquering the other hemisphere, the United States and Latin America would have ended up looking quite different. But was that really an apt comparison?

Jinjin gulped. "I don't know if I can agree with you."

"You don't have to. You are free to think whatever you want about it, of course. But at the same time, you are under an official obligation to follow my instructions."

"It does look that way, yes." Though, at the moment, it

would probably be difficult for Yaping to force her to obey. But she also couldn't stay on the moon forever.

"If it makes you feel any better, I'm not asking you to kill any extraterrestrials. None have been seen yet, right?"

"Hm. So what is it that you do want?"

"In the control center, there are several cores for the reactors we intended to use to power the hypertelescope. You're going to extract the fuel from them and construct a small nuclear bomb that you'll use to destroy the monolith."

It did involve the stele, then. Jinjin took a deep breath. It was a shame about this cosmic miracle, but if meant maintaining peace on Earth... At that moment, she pictured Liwei's face. The drop of sweat falling in ultra-slow motion. The brief wink. Maybe he did want to say something, but she hadn't given him enough time. He would never have enough time again.

"The stele that Liwei is standing next to," she said.

"Yes. It's unfortunate, but unavoidable. He should have followed orders. But I promise you that we will give you both a national award for science and technology."

"Jinjin, what are you doing?" came the Eleventh Bureau agent's voice in her helmet.

She had expected the question to come earlier. But apparently Yaping had to clarify a few things at mission control first. Hopefully. She'd always considered the people there as friends, and assumed the feeling was mutual. Just leaving Liwei to die – the plan must have stirred up some protest. They wouldn't just accept it, would they?

"I'm trying something."

"What does that mean? What are you trying to do?"

"I'm not going to just let Liwei die like that. Maybe I can separate him from the monolith."

"Jinjin, this is taking up precious time that we don't have!" Yaping exclaimed, raising her voice.

"Give me half an hour. If it doesn't work, I'll put the nuclear bomb together in record time."

She had no idea how to construct a bomb from the cores of the small reactors, but they would surely send her a checklist. In a taikonaut's life, there were checklists for everything, even for going to the bathroom.

"You're forgetting about the acceleration of time near the stele," Yaping said. "Every minute counts. The Americans won't just sit back and watch. The more time we give them, the more likely it is they'll find a way of getting to you that we haven't thought of."

Yaping wouldn't be speaking in such long sentences if she were surer of herself. Jinjin knew people like that – people who always had a plan and proceeded accordingly. If they were forced to improvise, they started to stumble. She also loved plans, but she could do without them if need be.

"We should give her a chance to save Liwei," said Guofeng.

Those words warmed Jinjin's heart. Her old commander was standing up for her, after all.

"He's a valuable resource," Guofeng explained. "Not only because of his training, but also because of what he's experienced in his encounter with the stele."

"If he experienced anything," said Yaping. "Anyway, it's irrelevant, since in twenty-four hours the monolith won't exist anymore."

"What if the plan doesn't work?" asked a woman in the background.

"It has to."

"If you know yourself but not the enemy, you will suffer a defeat for every victory you have," said Guofeng.

The Art of War... The old warhorse had always been fond of quoting Sun Tzu.

"Yes, that's right," said a male voice she couldn't quite place. Apparently, mission control was fully staffed. All the relevant ministries had probably sent representatives.

Yaping sighed. "Fine, but we're to stay connected,

and after three hours have gone by here, you'll have to call it quits, Jinjin."

"I understand."

Although it seemed that the Eleventh State Security Bureau had sovereignty, Yaping still wasn't completely free to make decisions. For such horizontal structures, consensus was important in order to be protected in the event of failure.

Jinjin stumbled, which brought her back to the present moment. She stood with her legs apart, surveying the scene. The monolith looked even blacker than before, but that must be an optical illusion. Liwei looked small before her, almost as if he had shrunk since she'd seen him last.

"Wait!" came a voice through the helmet. It wasn't Yaping. "I have something for you that should be of some help to you."

Jinjin remembered the woman's name. It was Lydia. Her parents had given her a Western name, a practice that had been fashionable in some circles for a while. Lydia was a programmer.

"What is it?"

"A tool for your suit that tells you how severe the time dilation is for you. I'll load it onto your on-board computer. It'll just take minute."

"How does it work?" asked Jinjin, approving the installation prompt on her helmet's display. "Using the radar?"

"No, the microphone. It measures the distortion of sound when we talk to you. If the factor gets too high, you'd better come back."

"Thank you. That's a really good idea," said Yaping. "I'll make a note of it in my report."

"Yaping is right," said Jinjin.

There was no harm in agreeing with one's opponent when it didn't matter. Sun Tzu must have said something like that once. She raised her arm and angled it to see the display better. The new program had a standard icon. She tapped on it and a one appeared.

"I've rounded the values to integers," explained Lydia.

"They're easier to read that way. The factor is actually 1.018 right now."

That was almost a two percent increase, and she was still twenty meters away. The stele was a fantastic feat of engineering. And she was supposed to destroy it?

"Isn't it possible that we'd draw the extraterrestrials' attention to us even more if we blow up the monolith?" asked Jinjin, jumping forward from a standing position.

"We had lengthy discussions about that." As Yaping spoke, her voice sounded deeper and deeper. "We believe that we must not show weakness. Our actions should send a message to everyone they affect."

Her last words were hard to understand. As Jinjin landed, the counter on the display jumped to two. Now her time was only half as fast as it was on Earth. She needed to hurry.

But she still had a few steps to go before reaching Liwei. She took the retractable pole out of her tool kit. At first, she'd thought of using it to push Liwei's hand away from the stele. But then she'd be touching her boss, at least indirectly. Not a smart approach.

Jinjin came over to where she'd been standing earlier alongside Liwei, but this time stayed a little farther from the stele. The counter was now at five. She didn't have time for it, but she quickly glanced at Liwei's face anyway. The drop of sweat had made it over his eyebrow and was now hovering in the air just in front of his cornea.

That wasn't good. Jinjin's mouth felt dry. The drop was not connected to the monolith anymore, but it still wasn't free. Maybe the atmosphere in the helmet created a connection? She couldn't give up hope. Jinjin extended the pole to its full length of three meters. She drilled the back end into the regolith so that it couldn't slip, with the front end pointing to the sky.

But not for long. She pushed the metal rod toward Liwei's arm. At the same time, she ran backwards until the counter went down to three. Unfortunately, she could only estimate how much time she had left. A sum function that showed the total number of minutes left on Earth would have been helpful. The rod fell more slowly with every passing moment. The lower end moved more slowly than the upper end, which was moving closer to the monolith, and this made it look like the solid metal was bending. But that was just because of its location. In its own reality, the pole was still straight. It was space-time itself that was twisted near the stele.

In the end, it was all a question of numbers. Even though it looked to Jinjin like the pole was slowing down, from the pole's standpoint it was falling as dictated by the moon's gravity. It had a fixed momentum that would affect Liwei's arm and hopefully free him from the stele. The question was whether this would happen in the foreseeable future or in a few years. To determine the answer, she would need to know more about the properties of space-time in the immediate vicinity of the monolith.

The pole was still falling. The counter on her arm display read three. She'd waited five minutes, which was equivalent to a quarter of an hour on Earth. That meant she had to turn back. Jinjin took a deep breath, turned around, and jumped over to the rover. The pole would keep falling even if she wasn't watching. Maybe it would hit Liwei's arm in thirty minutes, maybe three hours, maybe tonight. The important thing was that it happen before the bomb went off, so that Liwei would be free to run to safety. There was nothing more she could do.

"I'm BACK IN THE ROVER," JINJIN SAID AS THE ATMOSPHERE slowly built up inside. "Now can you tell me how to assemble the bomb?"

"That will be the next step," said Yaping. "After solving one other problem."

Jinjin giggled involuntarily. It really would be a surprise if anything went according to plan. But anything that delayed the detonation of the bomb was good.

"Unfortunately, it's a serious problem," Yaping said, her tone reproachful. "We've spotted two people approaching the site of the stele from the west."

"Meaning?"

"We don't know who it is yet. They're moving in the shadows whenever possible and seem to be wearing insulating suits, so our satellites' infrared sensors can't detect them."

The ESA's new gravimeter was located to the west, but it was nine hundred kilometers away. Nobody could walk that distance in a single day.

"I don't think it's the ESA people," said Jinjin. "Ernie would have told me."

"It's possible you're mistaken," said Yaping. "What we've discovered is so unique that no nation can afford to take friendships into consideration."

Jinjin shook her head. She had never met Ernie, but he wasn't the type to immediately go through with anything his superiors demanded. *Live and let live*, he always said. He would have at least tipped her off. No, it must be Americans approaching.

"We'll see when they get here," said Jinjin. "How should I welcome them?"

"You won't be welcoming them," said Yaping. "All the powers on Earth know the site's off-limits. You'll keep the visitors from getting too close. By force of arms, if necessary."

What ideas Yaping had! Everybody knew that the Moon Treaty prohibited weapons on the moon. Should she make herself a slingshot? Jinjin smiled. Her sister had always been better than her at building slingshots. The moon would certainly be a good place to use one thanks to its low gravity, and if a stone hit an exposed helmet visor, it could cause considerable damage.

"There are weapons at the control center," said Yaping.

"Excuse me?"

"They're completely legal. We have flare guns."

"It would be almost impossible to hit someone with one of those."

"That's correct. Otherwise they wouldn't be legal. But in the warehouse you'll find a conversion kit you can use to turn two flare guns into viable firearms."

THIS WAS UNBELIEVABLE. SHE WAS ACTUALLY ASSEMBLING A nuclear weapon to destroy the stele! The core of a small nuclear reactor lay before her on the hard lunar soil. It looked like one-quarter of a tangerine. A numeric keypad was visible on the left side of the cut surface. Jinjin was sweating. *Don't press the wrong button.* She entered the password Yaping gave her, and a green light came on. She took the second tangerine quarter and pressed it against the first. She felt the two segments click together beneath her fingers. They were so perfectly joined that no cut edges were visible anymore.

The cores had been designed deliberately to equip power plants of varying capacities. Half a tangerine provided twenty megawatts, but she still needed a third quarter and would have to take care of that next. It was stored in a different module. Jinjin stood up and displayed the 3D map of the control center in her helmet. Little had she known that the components were stored there.

Following the map, she passed through a small container village that she hadn't visited for a long time. Most of the mirrors for the hypertelescope were stored there. If she carried out her mission, there wouldn't be much work on that for a long time. When the bomb went off, there would be no shock wave in the nonexistent atmosphere, but there would be one in the ground, and a lot of material would be moved around. Unless they were lucky, they'd have to do most of the work over again.

But there wouldn't be any more "them." The bomb would explode at Liwei's feet and he'd be blasted to dust. At least it would be a quick death. And based on what she knew of biology, it would be a painless one too, since the immediate disintegration of a body didn't give the nerves enough time to transmit pain signals to the brain.

Unless, of course, time really did pass far more slowly for Liwei. Jinjin thought about the drop of sweat over his eyebrow. An explosion consuming him in slow motion would be brutal. It would be best to place the bomb right next to him, or even a little in front of him. That way everything would go much faster.

And what if they were wrong? Time hadn't dilated in a linear way as she approached the monolith. What if the effect approached infinity, as when approaching a black hole? That would explain why the monolith didn't visibly reflect. There was nothing for it to reflect, because even light particles didn't reach its surface in a finite time. That would also mean that the object couldn't store unlimited energy, meaning it wasn't a potential danger. She needed to speak to Yaping about this.

The display in her helmet blinked. Jinjin was standing in front of an ordinary-looking container. It wasn't even locked. She opened the right-hand door and saw several mirrors up front on the right. There were only two on the left. There was somebody standing behind them. At first Jinjin was startled. Then she burst out laughing. It was a small group of roughly humanoid robots. At some point, they were supposed to install the mirrors, which were way too heavy for human workers. They had two arms and six spider legs that gave them secure footing in the regolith. Their eyes were dead, and there was no trace of their limited, ant-level intelligence.

As Jinjin walked past them, she kept her distance. A shiver ran down her spine as she left the group behind her. The container was surprisingly long, and the last two components for the bomb were hidden in a crate at the back wall. Yaping had explained to her that they were covered with sand for camouflage. A lock would only attract thieves. Jinjin scraped away the sand, took two more tangerine halves from the crate, and made her way back to finish the project she'd started.

Like the first two, the third tangerine quarter consisted of nuclear fuel. The last one had the detonator. The bomb was supposed to go off soon, since the first curious visitors might start arriving tomorrow. Jinjin checked the detonator and synchronized it with her spacesuit. Then she set the timer to twelve hours, just as Yaping had instructed. She didn't even pause as she thought about what she'd tried, about the very different time Liwei seemed to move in, where everything happened in slow motion. For a moment, it weighed on her conscience. Should she contact Yaping to explain to her the possible error that had influenced the instructions? But why hadn't the scientists who were surely advising her pointed out the time dilation?

Because they secretly didn't want the stele to be blown up. They were driven by curiosity, which was why they'd gone into research. But their job involved clarifying the facts, at the very least. She was here to follow orders, as Yaping had made very clear to her. If she did that, nobody could blame her.

"Jinjin, can you hear me?"

It was Yaping. *Speak of Cao Cao and he will appear...* Her face grew hot. Was Yaping a mind-reader?

"I just set the timer," she answered. "Unfortunately, I couldn't move any faster."

"Good. You're further along than I thought. What about the weapons?"

"I haven't gotten around to that yet."

"Okay. You're doing very well. I still have to ask you to hurry. The two intruders are almost there."

"I'll do my best. How should I deal with them?"

"Well, of course it depends on them. They're currently hiding in the shadow of a hill. It looks like they don't dare come any closer. That means they don't know you're alone, and it should stay that way. But please be careful. They might expect to be met by armed forces, so they probably also have weapons. But it would be preferable if you didn't shoot them out in the open. We never know who might be watching from above, and we want to avoid a war if possible."

Great. Two armed Americans. "But I may defend myself?"

"Of course. In closed areas or beneath the tent, you have completely free rein. Guofeng told me that you were near the top of your class."

"He's exaggerating. I did the best I could."

"No, the old man isn't prone to exaggeration. That means you are an excellent markswoman. Use your skills for the good of your country. It is in your best interests."

Jinjin bit her lips. This wasn't what she wanted, but what could she do? She had no choice but to obey.

"What about the bomb? Won't it...?"

"No, Jinjin. You'll be safe behind the closest crater wall. It will only have a direct effect on the moon itself."

The explosion, of course, would also have a direct effect on Liwei. And he was completely innocent. That damned stele! Maybe destroying it was the right thing to do, after all. Even if the Eleventh Bureau's theory was incorrect and it wasn't important to eliminate every trace of the extraterrestrials, the mere existence of this technology would turn the different blocs against each other. If one party gained exclusive possession of it, there would be war. The fact that her home country was freely giving up the chance of a scientific revolution by destroying this monolith, which had appeared under its charge, in order to prevent a possible war filled her with pride. The government was acting in the best interests of humanity as a whole.

Just not in Liwei's interests. But what did a single person really matter?

"Watch out, the intruders have come out of their hiding place," Yaping warned her as the rover approached the tent concealing the stele. The nuclear weapon was strapped to the passenger seat. Whenever the rover went over a bump, it shook the seat belts as if it wanted to get out.

"Where are they going?" asked Jinjin. "Maybe they aren't even going towards the stele."

"I don't think they are. We saw them near the Stratton crater. It appears they're trying to avoid the excavation site."

"Is that wise of them?"

"Yes, it is. If they come from the east, they have a much better approach without having to leave the shadowed areas."

"What should I do?"

"They've surely seen the dust that the rover sends up and noticed you long ago. But they don't know you're alone, so we aren't expecting a direct attack. Just keep following the plan as agreed."

The plan. Well, okay. Was this what Yaping called a plan? But she replied, "All right." Then she stretched and pressed herself against the backrest. She'd rather lose the bomb somewhere in the shadows where nobody would ever find it again. But then what about those two Americans? Under no circumstances should they get their hands on the monolith. An artifact that could stop time... Who knew what science would make of it?

She thought of Liwei again. He'd opened his mouth as if he wanted to say something. But she hadn't had enough time to listen to him.

Wait. Wouldn't that be a way to render the Americans harmless? All she would have to do was convince them to approach the stele like Liwei. It probably wouldn't be that difficult. Curiosity would lure them into the trap. And nobody could really hold her to blame.

She established a radio connection to mission control.

"Yaping? I have a plan."

Surface of the moon, March 6, 2082

RON WASN'T JUST SWEATING – HE WAS HUNGRY AND STINKY, too. He was disgusted with himself. The detour was taking a lot longer than he'd anticipated. They'd gone for almost a full second day without catching a glimpse of the alien object. His oxygen would last another twelve hours or so. If it got to that point, they'd have to ask the Chinese for help. Ron envisioned the embarrassing situation. *We were just in the neighborhood and wanted to, uh...* Surely their friends would use it for propaganda. *Heroic taikonauts rescue lost American astronauts.*

"You've got to check this out," said JP.

The Frenchman was a few meters ahead of him. It seemed farther than that since their route went upwards. JP was standing at the top of the crater's ridge. That was extremely careless of him, since the upper part of his body was fully lit.

"They'll see us," said Ron.

"They'll have done that anyway," said JP. "Whenever we've taken quick shortcuts where there's sun... Every square meter here is definitely being monitored from orbit."

Ron was breathing heavily as he dragged himself towards the ridge to finally stand alongside JP.

"Look!" shouted his friend, pointing downwards at an angle.

There it was. Ron remained motionless for a moment, awestruck. It seemed that JP felt the same way. Ron immediately recognized the column he'd seen in the photo. It had a rectangular cross section and tapered upwards. It looked a lot eerier in real life than in the photo. It took Ron a moment to figure out why.

"It's the black," he said. "It's darker than anything else on the moon."

JP shielded his eyes with his hand. "You're right."

"Of course I'm right."

"Do you realize the significance of that?" JP asked.

"I... Um... The column is that dark because it doesn't reflect anything."

"Exactly. Measurements would need to be taken, of course, but the albedo's got to be close to zero. Very close."

"So it's definitely a structure that's extraterrestrial in origin?"

"We certainly don't have that kind of technology. Just imagine what you could build with it – airplanes and missiles undetectable by radar."

"That's why the Chinese want to keep it to themselves."

Ron sat down on a rock. The view was truly breathtaking.

"Do you see that cloud of dust?" asked JP.

"Yes, it's weird. Somebody must have been driving around down there pretty recently."

"There are several rover tracks leading towards Dewar Crater."

"To a base."

Maybe the Chinese had gotten reinforcements. He really needed to speak to Hufman. Surely he would know if a Chinese ship had landed.

Ron slapped his thigh. "All right, let's strike while the iron's hot. The longer we wait, the more time possible adversaries have to show up."

"What's your plan?"

"There's a way to get to the stele without leaving the shadows even once."

"What? That's impossible."

"Just take a look, JP." Ron pointed to a crack in the wall of the crater. "If we make our way through this recessed area, first that hill over there will shelter us, then the first excavator, and then the other one."

"Were the two vehicles positioned so conveniently before?" asked JP.

"No clue. We saw them from the other side. The shadows were different there."

"It strikes me as strange. As if it were arranged."

"Let's get going. We've been looking for a chance like this!"

This French guy. He very well understood that JP didn't want to cross the empty area, but they needed to make the most of this opportunity. No question. Ron stood up.

"Do as you like. But I'm going down there now."

Dewar Crater, March 6, 2082

THEY WERE COMING!

Excavator Zero's radar had just reported two moving objects. That must be them! As expected, they were sneaking up in the shadows. Jinjin followed the flashing dots on the rover's control screen. She was already wearing her spacesuit so she could step in quickly.

One of them seemed to be in a hurry, whereas the other was hesitant. Because of this, the distance between them slowly grew. Was this something they'd agreed on in advance? Or was the hesitation a sign that the second American was suspicious? She needed both of them to be as close to the monolith as possible. If the distance between them was too great, the one lagging behind would notice there was something wrong with the other one.

Now the straggler stopped completely and remained standing in the shadow of a small waste heap about a hundred meters away from the stele. What was this person up to? Were they trying to watch the other astronaut's back? Not on her watch. Jinjin took over the controls of the normal excavator, which so far had provided the shadows the Americans were using for cover on their way to the monolith. She steered the vehicle very slowly towards the stele, and its shadow moved with it. She watched the flashing radar dots intently.

The second American moved forward a little, evidently to observe what was happening. He must be working it out in his head – he had about sixty seconds before the path to the stele was no longer in shadow. Either he'd have to make a run for it now or leave his friend to fend for himself. Jinjin counted silently. When she reached thirty, she exhaled in disappointment. It appeared that the second American was chickening out. He went back into the shadow cast by the waste heap. Jinjin kept counting. Now the man in the front had also paused. She couldn't see it on the radar, but maybe the two of them were waving to each other, or speaking over the radio.

There! The point that was farther away was starting to speed up. It took a big leap and landed in the shadow of the moving excavator. He kept going, though he'd slowed down again. From his perspective, the machine was moving in the right direction. This was advantageous to Jinjin as well because now, meter by meter, the excavator was obscuring the Americans' view of the rover. At some point, she would have to get out in order to lead them into the trap for good.

Where was JP? Ron's heart was beating so fast that the suit automatically performed a health check. He turned around and didn't see any sign of the Frenchman. But the enormous machine that had been providing them with a shadow to take cover under was moving. If JP didn't start running soon, he wouldn't be able to catch up with Ron unless he dared go into the light, which Ron didn't think was very likely. He didn't even bother trying to get him to join him.

"It's okay, Jean-Pierre," he said over the radio. "I can manage on my own."

If this was going to be their last conversation, he didn't

want it to be marked by anger and incomprehension. After all, they'd gotten along well on the Gateway.

"No, hold on," JP answered. "I just don't want to walk into a potential trap. Our friends here can't see me directly, but that excavator is moving for a reason. They're just waiting for us to move with its shadow."

"And you don't want to do that? I understand. I'll look at the monolith on my own, that's fine."

"I just want to avoid behaving the way they expect me to. That's why I'm only jumping at the last second."

"Ah, so you are coming with me?"

JP didn't answer, but he could hear him breathing heavily. He was probably running. All of a sudden, there was a hand on Ron's shoulder. He gave a start and instinctively raised the crossbow.

"It's me," said JP.

He hadn't seen him approaching. The shadows here were truly unique. Ron breathed in and out deeply to calm himself down.

"I'm glad you made it," he said.

"I still don't know if it was a good idea. Honestly, I was still debating it up until the last second."

"You didn't follow a plan?"

JP sniffed. "I'm way too worked up to make plans."

Ron moved to put his hand on JP's shoulder, but hit his helmet instead.

"Sorry, it's so dark," he said.

He felt two arms wrapping around his suit and smiled. JP was surprisingly sentimental for an astronaut. But he gave in to the hug and even returned it.

"Now let's get to work," he said. "The stele is right around the corner. If we walk around the excavator's big wheel, we should be able to see it."

"And the Chinese will be able to see us, right?"

Two dots were flashing close together right in front of Excavator Zero's rear wheel. Now she had them where she wanted them. They'd probably need a little more time to venture out of the shadows. The last eighty meters offered no cover. Jinjin bent over and picked up the two firearms. They were surprisingly light for weapons. They probably weren't actually made of metal, though they had a metallic sheen, which probably helped dissipate heat in the vacuum of the moon's surface.

Jinjin took another deep breath of the cabin air, then closed her helmet. She was scared. Her hands were cold. She turned up the heating in the suit a little, but immediately started to sweat. She had never shot at another person before. Would she be able to do it if the Americans didn't follow her instructions? It was different to fire at virtual opponents in the holosimulator than at real people who could die from a single shot.

A single shot. Even if she aimed deliberately for the leg, a hole in a spacesuit would kill the person wearing it. But she wouldn't aim for the leg, since she was following her instructor's directions and targeting the largest target area – the torso. Jinjin sighed and closed her helmet. Hopefully it wouldn't come to that.

She opened the hatch, which let some air out. The moisture immediately froze into ice crystals that refracted the sunlight. It looked like somebody had sprinkled glitter. She closed the hatch behind her, packed the weapons in the tool bag, and went over to the ladder that led to the top of the excavator. Even though the Americans were just a few meters away from her, there was no risk of them hearing her. Jinjin climbed up the ladder, slid across the top of the excavator on her hands and knees, and peered down into the shadows on the other side.

She couldn't see anything, which was no surprise. Her suit didn't have radar, and the two were clearly still shielding themselves with insulating sheets. If the Americans were to look up at that precise moment, they might be able to see

Jinjin's outline against the stars. But that would be a huge coincidence. She pulled back and sat down so that her legs dangled in front of the driver's cab windshield. From here, she had a good view of the way to the stele. Using her helmet visor, she tuned to the international emergency call frequency. Anybody within range of her suit antenna, regardless of nationality, could hear what it was transmitting.

Jinjin was ready.

⬤

"GOOD LUCK," SAID JP.

Ron set off running. He didn't take the direct route, but instead zig-zagged like a hare in the hopes that he wouldn't be hit immediately if somebody fired at him. It wouldn't be a problem for a skilled marksman, but maybe their Chinese friends didn't have much experience handling their weapons. After all, they probably didn't have much combat experience, unlike him.

The disadvantage to this approach was that it meant he had a greater distance to cover. After the first few steps, he was already breathing heavily. They'd decided that he'd be the vanguard. If nothing happened to him, then JP would follow. This was, of course, no guarantee that they'd be safe. Maybe the enemy would wait until both hares revealed themselves. But if they wanted to examine the monolith from up close, they had no other option.

Ron approached the pillar. He still couldn't make out any more details on it, but he could see that there was something right in front of it. No, not something. A person. He hadn't been able to tell right away because this person was standing strangely still. No living being could refrain from moving with that much consistency. The person was wearing a Chinese-made spacesuit and had one hand outstretched. It appeared to be touching the stele.

How strange. If this was one of the two Chinese astronauts who made up the local crew, that meant they'd have just one other person to contend with. This particular individual appeared to be very preoccupied – in any case, they weren't paying the slightest bit of attention to the American darting back and forth, though they must have at least noticed him out of the corner of their eye. What if it was a robot? That outer layer was definitely a spacesuit. But theoretically, a humanoid robot could be commanded to put on an EVA suit. That would also explain how whoever or whatever this was managed to stand so still. It wouldn't pose a problem for a robot. But it didn't make any sense, unless it was meant to distract two stupid Americans.

Ron stopped and looked around. Still nobody had appeared to get in between him and the stele. So why all the fuss? Why was China blocking the area to visitors? No, something was going on here that he didn't understand yet. He waved to JP, who was probably still watching him from the shadow of the machine, and gestured to him to stay where he was. Something smelled funny, and it wasn't the diaper he hadn't been able to change out of yet.

Nothing. No movement. Ron felt like he was trapped in a slow-motion video. But when he kicked a rock, it followed a normal trajectory towards the excavator. Time was passing. His imagination had run away with him. *Take a deep breath. It's the stress that's making you crazy.* He got the feeling he was being watched from the shadows, but he couldn't let that distract him. There was nothing he could do about it anyway.

Ron wanted to get a look at the face in the helmet, so he came closer to the strange robot to view it from the side. He'd been expecting the typical robot face with camera eyes and a speaker in its chin, but the manufacturers had actually made a human-looking face. Why would they go and do that? He wasn't particularly interested in robotics, but wasn't there something of an inter-industry agreement to avoid overly human-like constructs? He shook his head. No, even the HDR series developed by a Russian company didn't fit the bill. He also wasn't aware of any similar projects the Chinese were working on that involved extremely human-like robots.

As interesting as all of this was, it shouldn't distract him from his actual mission of examining the monolith. Ron stood still, looking at the strange structure towering far above him. Up close, the sinister aura he'd noticed before was somewhat diminished. It was a simple geometric figure that didn't seem to pose any riddles. He couldn't see any inscriptions, but perhaps it had some that were microscopic. The robot, which was still eight or ten meters away, appeared to be studying it intently. Maybe that was why it wasn't moving at all. If it was just a pawn to serve as a distraction, surely something would have happened by now. After all, the element of surprise had worn off. Or maybe the Chinese didn't dare take action against JP and him? They were all colleagues, after all, and maybe a certain amount of solidarity was to be expected.

Whatever. He switched on the radio.

"JP, everything looks clean. I think you can come."

"Are you sure? Isn't there somebody standing there?"

The Frenchman's voice sounded squeaky, as if he'd inhaled helium. What was wrong with the radio? This was no time for hardware issues. JP might be speaking quickly, but he always did that when he was excited, as Ron well knew. And it got everybody worked up.

"It must be a robot. The thing isn't moving and doesn't seem dangerous."

"Gotcha. You ought to check your radio, Ron. You sound like you're in a Russian men's choir."

Fucking technology! Why did this have to happen now, of all times? But a hardware analysis would take too long. There was something wrong with the frequency conversion. Maybe one of the components was running hot. Perhaps something was misaligned. The main thing was for it not to fail completely.

"So are you coming now?" he asked.

"I'm on my way."

Ron looked in the direction he expected the Frenchman to come from. Whoa, he was fast. It was as if he'd been moved by magic. Ron turned back towards the stele and had taken two steps when somebody tapped him on the shoulder from behind. This time he was able to keep it together and reached for the crossbow. JP smiled at him.

"See? That's got to be a robot," said Ron, pointing to the spacesuit that looked like it was frozen in front of the stele.

JP leaned forward. "Man, that looks awfully real. Are you sure?"

Now the Frenchman's voice sounded completely normal. Ron's favorite kinds of problems were ones like this that resolved on their own.

"Nobody could stay in that awkward position for so long," he said.

"We should examine him. Maybe he's dead. Frozen or something."

"That's not how it looked to me. Not the slightest bit of frost or ice, and the skin looks totally fresh."

"You're right. Weird. What if the spacesuit just now ran out of energy?"

"You mean with a human inside?" asked Ron.

JP nodded. Ron squinted his eyes to get a better look. He couldn't see the face in detail, but if the person was dead, it must only have been for a few seconds. JP's theory didn't make any sense.

"If you don't believe me, and I can tell that's the case from the look on your face, then let's just take it out," JP suggested.

Ron shook his head. "We'd better keep our distance. It could be a trap."

"A weird trap. Do you think when we approach, he'll make a loud 'boo' noise to scare us off?"

"I just don't have a good feeling about it. Come on, let's get a closer look at the monolith and then we'll search the area. The Chinese have got to be somewhere, right?"

JP stretched and turned around. Then he suddenly stopped and nudged Ron. "Up there, on top of the excavator."

EVERYTHING WAS FALLING INTO PLACE. JINJIN WAS WATCHING the Americans from the top of the excavator. She'd originally been lying on her stomach so that if anybody happened to look in her direction, she would be less conspicuous. But that was uncomfortable in a spacesuit, so now she was sitting up again. The two men were now so close to the stele that they no longer stood a chance. Judging from their movements, Jinjin guessed that time was half as fast for them as it was for her. If they reached for their weapons, she would definitely be able to dodge them.

All the same, it wasn't time to celebrate yet. They still had three, four, five meters to go. Now time for them had slowed down to one-tenth of what it was for her. Jinjin leaned back on her hands and smiled as she watched the Americans. They probably thought they were so clever. Or they were simply careless.

Suddenly the man on the right turned around. He seemed to notice something. Her. He touched his companion with his elbow, and now they were both staring in her direction. The man on the left wasn't just looking – he was also bending down. His hand moved towards his spacesuit's tool kit and went inside. To Jinjin, it looked as if he were making the movement very carefully. In reality, however, he was going straight and fast for his weapon. The man was a professional. That was how her instructor used to move. Whenever he wanted to teach them something, he would switch to slow-mo in order to demonstrate the exact sequence of movements.

But the American wasn't deliberately moving in slow motion, and that was to her advantage. Jinjin snatched her pistol and jumped from the top of the excavator onto the top of the rover, which was about four meters away but considerably lower. Even from there, she had a good view of the two intruders. She grinned as she noticed the American's nervous movements. To him it must have looked like she moved like Superman. Were Americans still familiar with Superman? Her grandfather had had a soft spot for American superhero comics.

She spoke into the microphone, in English. "Hands up!"

No answer. Then she remembered that the frequencies must have also gone up for the men near the stele. If she was transmitting at five gigahertz, it would be ten gigahertz for them. She entered half the value for the emergency frequency and tried again.

"Hands up!"

The man on the right put his hand to his ear. He must have heard something, so she repeated her demand. For emphasis, she jumped off the rover, took out the second pistol, and aimed at both astronauts simultaneously. Now the American on her right reacted by slowly raising his arms.

"We come in peace," he explained in English.

Jinjin wasn't very good with languages, but she thought she could hear a distinct accent. What about his companion? He was still holding something that might be a crossbow. Clever. It was probably easier to smuggle the parts for that to the moon than parts for a firearm, and the effect was almost the same.

"The guy with you too!" she called out.

The other man raised one hand over his head, but he was still brandishing his weapon with the other.

"Tell him to drop the crossbow."

The object fell to the ground in slow motion, stirring up dust.

"Push the thing away with your foot."

She couldn't think of the English word for crossbow. The man's foot moved slowly, as if it were refusing to obey, but ultimately the weapon flew several meters through the air.

"That's right. Now take a step back."

The Americans followed orders. That had been surprisingly easy! They didn't seem to have grasped the situation yet.

"One more step."

No reaction – and no answer. The frequency. Of course. She reduced it a bit and tried again.

"One more step."

The two didn't move to comply, or else they hadn't heard her. Jinjin made another adjustment to the frequency.

"One more step."

"That's not happening." That must be the voice of the man who'd been holding the crossbow. "The moon is an extraterritorial zone. We can move freely here."

"My country has closed off this area for valid reasons. Remaining here is dangerous. We have shared this information with all parties to the Moon Treaty."

"Well, it's only dangerous here because you're pointing an illegal weapon at us."

"Oh, and the ... the thing you wanted to shoot with?" Why couldn't she think of the stupid word? "In any case, I don't know what you're talking about. The only gun I've seen here was yours."

She put the pistol away and showed her empty hands. The American used the opportunity to lunge for his crossbow, but before he'd taken a single step, she had both weapons in her hands again.

"Leave it," said the other man. In her eyes, he was definitely the more likeable of the two.

"I don't know what kind of trick this is, but we're not giving in," said the other.

"It's not a trick," said the American with the accent, who probably wasn't an American at all.

Now she thought she could make out the flag of his country of origin on his suit. He was Italian or something.

"Not a trick?"

"Haven't you noticed? Time is passing more slowly for us. It must be because of the monolith."

"So it is a trick."

"Yes, the Chinese have nothing to do with it."

WHAT KIND OF BULLSHIT WAS THIS? THEY OUTNUMBERED HER two to one, yet the Chinese woman held them in check.

Judging from the sound of her voice, she was an inexperienced girl. An intern, perhaps. Of course. The Chinese hadn't known that this column would show up here, and there had been nothing to do here apart from monitoring machines. They would hardly send their top talents here.

Ron looked around. The opponent did have two firearms, but she couldn't shoot both at the same time. Yet she did have time on her side. She probably considered him to be the bigger threat. He did have the crossbow, after all. That was good. That meant that with his plan he was mainly putting himself in danger and not JP, who had cleverly not drawn his crossbow yet. He could see the handle sticking out of JP's tool bag.

What else did he have to work with? Only one thing offered cover in the immediate vicinity: the robot in the spacesuit. If he were to snatch the crossbow from JP's bag and then do a somersault, thanks to the low gravity he should be able to move behind cover, or at least close enough to keep the enemy from firing. If he could then get himself into position, all he'd have to do was fire the crossbow discreetly. The Chinese woman would have no chance of using her time trick to stay out of harm's way.

"I'd suggest we surrender," JP said, speaking over the same channel that the Chinese woman had used.

Was this a trick? A distraction? Ron didn't answer. He wasn't going to give up until he'd played all his cards. And who was to say that the Chinese woman wanted them alive? From the perspective of the Chinese, the smartest thing would be to eliminate them as witnesses. If China wanted the stele for itself, others who had seen it would just be in the way.

Ron switched to the private channel. "I'm gonna grab your crossbow and take cover over there." He pointed to the motionless spacesuit. "Then I'll deal with her."

JP was moving his lips, but Ron didn't hear anything. Was he still talking to the Chinese woman on the other channel? He couldn't seriously want to give up, could he? Ron shook his head and turned his index finger. *Switch to the private channel,*

JP. But the Frenchman didn't react. He was probably already negotiating the details of their surrender. *Without me, my friend.*

Ron checked to make sure the crossbow was still in its place, then jumped. He grabbed it at just the right moment. He managed to do the best somersault he had in years. He landed softly on his knees close to his target, but when he lifted the crossbow to aim at the Chinese woman, he didn't see her. He turned around, then caught sight of her: she was standing next to a flat rover, and JP, who had been by his side just a moment ago, was moving towards her with his hands up.

That traitor!

JUST AS JINJIN HAD FEARED, HER PLAN WAS ONLY HALF working. The American with the crossbow made a spectacular leap over to Liwei. It was fascinating to watch his somersault become slower and slower, as if he were working towards a big climax, a grand finale. But all he did was land on both feet and raise his weapon. As a precaution, she changed her position so that his friend was covering her.

But the friend was the real problem now, because she didn't know how far she could trust him. He seemed to want to surrender, and had been the first of the two to think of it. But it could, of course, also be a surprise tactic. He would lull her into a false sense of security and then assume control.

Not on her watch. The best thing would be to lock him in the rover. She could secure it from the outside so that only she could open it. He was only a few steps away now. Jinjin switched to the normal emergency frequency.

"Keep your hands up," she said.

"I don't have a weapon anymore," said the man.

"But you had one?"

He turned around briefly and pointed towards the stele. "My friend Ron is aiming it at us right now."

"That's fine, I'll move so that you cover me with your

body. But don't do anything stupid. There's a one hundred percent chance I'll hit you from this distance."

"I have no intention of doing anything stupid. This was a crazy idea anyhow."

"What was?"

"Coming here."

The man seemed trustworthy, but she couldn't let her guard down.

"I'd rather not be here myself," she said. "And you are?"

"Jean-Pierre Jeunet. Most people call me JP."

"Italian?"

"No, French. Doesn't the name..."

"Yes, of course. I wanted to check if maybe you'd just made up that name."

Her cheeks flushed. Fortunately, he couldn't see what was happening behind the pane of her helmet.

"And what's your name?" asked JP.

"Zhang Jinjin."

"Nice to meet you, Jinjin."

He took a step forward and held out his hand to her. She shook her head and moved away.

"Even if you're from the ESA, that doesn't make us friends," she said. "This is a restricted area."

"I'm sorry. Curiosity... That doesn't merit a death sentence, does it?"

Not from her. But if JP knew what her superiors were planning to do with the monolith... She had to lock him in the rover, because otherwise he'd try to save his American friend.

"No death sentence. But it's extremely dangerous here. Your friend has only himself to blame."

JP looked over his shoulder at the stele, and surely he could see how slowly the American was moving. Almost completely frozen, like Liwei. When JP turned back to her, his face was pale.

"The spacesuit that's not moving..."

"That's my colleague, Liwei. He got too close to the stele."

"Can't we get the two of them out of there? There's got to be a way. I'll help you!"

She actually believed him. And if this were a normal incident, she would gladly accept his help. But nothing about the monolith was normal, and she had almost reached the point of believing that the Eleventh Bureau's plan was the right one. Not because of the extraterrestrials themselves, but because of the misfortune that the artifact had brought upon them all.

"There's nothing we can do about the extreme time dilation in the vicinity of the monolith," she said. "We've lost them."

"We'll throw a rope and pull them back."

"Yes, of course we could do that," she said, and JP's face lit up. "But it will take the rope an almost infinite amount of time to reach them."

"Merde. There must be some way out of it, right?"

She shook her head. "The good news is that, compared to us, they are virtually immortal. And also, they won't get bored because time passes so slowly for them."

"So we just have to remove the stele and time would go back to normal?"

"Theoretically. But how would you do that without putting them and yourself in danger?"

"Let me speak to scientists on Earth. We'll all come up with a solution together."

Jinjin shook her head vigorously. "No, everything's already been decided. The People's Republic of China is going to solve the problem. I'll keep you safe in the rover until then." She gestured towards the vehicle with her pistol. "It has everything you need: oxygen, heat, water, and food. But no communication. And I shifted its controls to my console up there."

JP looked at the excavator with interest. "Wouldn't you like to show me that machine? I've only ever heard of excavators. It must feel great to drive one."

Jinjin laughed. "That might have worked with Liwei. Unfortunately he went all the way over to the stele."

"Without permission?" asked JP.

"That's none of your business. Come on, into the rover with you."

JINJIN CHECKED THE HATCH TO EXCAVATOR ZERO'S CABIN again. It was tightly closed. If JP got out of the rover, the best he could do would be escaping on foot, and that would be fine by her. Then she'd have one less problem to deal with. She'd also left him his suit with that possibility in mind. Since it had a radio installed in it, he could still use that. The range was limited, however, especially from inside the locked rover.

Back in the excavator, she freshened up as best she could. She also discussed next steps with Yaping, who told her on video that the ESA was looking for JP. Evidently he'd sneaked off of the Gateway. Yaping was very pleased with her, because everything was proceeding as the Eleventh Bureau had planned. Nobody would be held responsible if the American died in the process, since the area was officially closed. Given that there would no longer be any reason for a war after the monolith was destroyed, the experts from the Second Bureau, which was responsible for foreign affairs, predicted that the Americans would react cautiously. It wouldn't be worth it to them to make relations worse because of such an incident.

Jinjin jumped from the ladder to the ground. The bomb was still in the back of the rover, and she needed to get it, check it, and then carry it over to the stele. That was the plan. It was simple and was sure to cost Liwei and the American their lives. But would it destroy the stele as well? The scientists were pretty sure it would. No known material could withstand the resulting forces.

"What are you doing?" JP asked over the emergency frequency. He must have seen her through the windshield.

"Tidying up," she said. It wasn't a lie.

Jinjin walked around the rover, opened the cargo area, and lifted the bomb down. It was damned heavy, even on the moon. From here, it was about a hundred and twenty meters to the monolith. She could manage that. The detonator was programmed. It had already counted down most of the way. She lifted the bomb, carried it with her legs apart a few meters in front of her stomach, then set it back down. She wasn't moving very quickly.

"What's that you're dragging around there?" asked JP.

"None of your business."

That was a lie. She bit her lip. The bomb wouldn't just kill Liwei, but the Frenchman's friend too. There was no other way out of this, and she wasn't to blame. She was just doing what couldn't be avoided. But that didn't keep her from feeling guilty.

"Would you like me to help you?" JP asked. "It'll be easier with two people."

Why couldn't he be rude, at the very least? "No, thank you. You can help me by shutting up."

Jinjin carried the bomb another three meters. Whew. Most of all, it was awkward to move.

"See? It would be a lot better if we both did it."

"I could concentrate a lot better without constant commentary."

Another three meters. She was already sweating bullets. She needed to keep an eye on the time. The closer she got to the stele, the slower she would be. But by the time the bomb went off, she needed to be in a safe position behind the rim of the crater. She didn't have very much time.

Whew. She'd made it another three meters.

"What are those symbols on it?" asked JP.

"I don't know what you're talking about."

"It looks kind of like a skull. Oh, those are radiation symbols. What does it mean?"

"This is a powerful laser. I'm using it to check if the stele is reflecting anything."

"A laser? Those are ionizing radiation warnings. Now I recognize them. Jinjin, what are you doing?"

"I suppose light isn't radiation, smarty-pants?"

JP kept quiet. He was probably racking his brains trying to figure out what she was up to. Or he already suspected it, and fear was keeping him silent.

"Don't worry," said Jinjin. "Nothing's going to happen to you."

"Me? What a relief. And what about Ron and your friend Liwei?"

"Liwei was my superior, not my friend."

There was a lump in Jinjin's throat as she said that. So this was what betrayal felt like. Liwei was her boss, but of course they were also friends. When people lived together in close quarters for that long, they either came to hate each other or like each other. She liked Liwei, and she was sure he felt the same way.

"So not my friend in the strictest sense," she corrected herself.

"I'm missing a subordinate clause explaining that nothing will happen to him."

JP was listening carefully. Would it be so bad if he learned the truth? There was nothing he could do about it anyway. And by the time she drove the rover past the edge of the crater and the vibrations made their way through the surface of the moon towards them, he would know.

"Liwei and Ron can't be saved," she said. "You saw Liwei, didn't you? Did it look to you like he's still human?"

"Ron thought he was a humanoid robot in a spacesuit. I had my doubts."

"They've vanished from life as we know it, JP. You have to come to terms with that. There's no way to get them back."

"But they are alive, Jinjin. From their perspective, they're alive. Time is passing normally for them."

"We don't know that. It's possible they've assumed a crystalline state. There is such a thing. Time crystals."

She'd read about that once in a novel authored by a physicist who always wrote in a very realistic way.

"I don't think it has anything to do with their state," JP said. "Time crystals are quantum systems that change their state variables in a temporal-periodic way, just as ordinary crystals have a spatial-periodic order..."

"It doesn't matter what you think," she said, interrupting the Frenchman. "I have clear instructions."

SHE NEEDED THE EXCAVATOR TO CARRY OUT THE LAST STEP. Not because the bomb was so heavy, but because she didn't want to waste any time. Right in front of the monolith, a few meters distance made a big difference. She set the bomb down on a small mound of dirt, then climbed the ladder and entered the cabin.

The seat shook as the machine's powerful engine started running. She kept her spacesuit on to save time, since she still had to get a bit closer to the stele. Jinjin was just about to set out when she remembered the tool that Lydia programmed for her. The program used the microphone, and she needed to talk to someone so it could inform her what the time dilation level was.

She didn't want to speak with Yaping, the one who'd gotten her into this situation in the first place. It was hard to believe that she really was about to kill two people. Willingly. There was nobody here forcing her hand, and yet she was going to do it. Not because Yaping wanted her to, but because it was necessary. Otherwise, many more lives would be lost in the international battle for the artifact. The American would probably think quite differently, but she imagined that Liwei would agree with her.

"Hey, JP," she said.

"What's going on? Did you change your mind?" he asked.

His accent really was cute. It was a good thing he hadn't run after his friend. An honest answer would have been, *I just need your voice so I can measure the time dilation.* But surely that would make him grumpy.

"You've got to understand," she said. "There's a much bigger issue at stake here."

"You want to keep extraterrestrial technology from helping humanity to enter a new, golden age."

Jinjin pushed the right joystick forward and the excavator started to advance jerkily. She looked down at the arm of her suit and read 1.07 displayed on the small screen. Time had already slowed down here. But it hadn't been like that before. Had the stele's effect intensified?

"There will be a world war over the monolith," said Jinjin. "If you're being honest with yourself, you know that, too. Humanity isn't mature enough to share the technology."

"You're looking at it too pessimistically. Do you remember that close call we had with the black hole? There's a good example of how well we..."

"Okay, but there were riots and uprisings all over the world. That's not a good example."

"People were fighting for their survival. That's under-standable enough."

That was precisely the problem. They'd fight for their survival now too, against whatever world power had secured the stele's technology for themselves. Using the console, Jinjin selected the shovel as the main tool and gripped the left joystick to guide it. She pushed the stick forward and watched through the windshield as the shovel lowered to the ground. The excavator approached the mound of dirt with the bomb on top.

"Let me out of here, Jinjin. Please."

The screen on her arm flashed with a new measurement. The value was now 1.11.

"So you can move the bomb away? You know I can't let you do that."

"You could just say that I escaped. Then you won't have to live with the guilt of having killed two people."

The shovel drilled through the top of the mound of

regolith as if it were a pile of flour. The steel reached the bottom of the bomb, which tilted to the side.

"Careful!" JP shouted.

Jinjin remained calm. The bomb would be safe until the detonator went off. At that point, the three chambers would combine and deliver a supercritical mass of plutonium that would cause an uncontrollable chain reaction. She pushed the right stick forward a little more until the mound was completely inside the scoop shovel. As she used the left joystick to lift the shovel, she no longer had a direct view of the bomb.

She used the right stick to guide the excavator through a quarter-turn. Now she could steer it directly towards the stele. Her hands were sweating. She tried to wipe them, but her suit got in the way. She turned down the temperature setting, and felt a cool breeze on her back. It felt as if Father Death were standing behind her and breathing down her neck, and the fine hairs on the back of it stood up.

"There's got to be another way," said JP.

The screen on her arm showed a new value: 1.3. She hadn't made much progress yet. But the figure would climb even faster from now on.

"Have you thought of one?" she asked, just to give the software something to work with.

1.4.

"Not me. But the scientific community throughout the world can certainly find a solution."

"Do you really think we're capable of sharing the knowledge? If China were to pull back, which is definitely not going to happen, would the United States share the findings?"

"I... I don't know, to be honest. But it's not completely out of the question."

1.6. Now she saw an orange-colored field glowing on the screen. It indicated that Lydia's program was automatically adjusting the frequency of incoming and outgoing voice messages. Otherwise, JP's voice would sound a lot higher.

"What do you think the chances of everybody coming to an agreement are?" Jinjin asked.

"Hm. Thirty percent?"

"That means there's a seventy percent chance of war. You see, that's why I have to do this. It's my responsibility, and nobody's going to stop me."

2.1. Now it was going really fast. Or no – rather, slowly. All her little hairs were standing up, and the atmosphere seemed electric. But that must be her imagination. Humans had no sensory organs to detect glitches in space-time.

The radio channel came on, but Jinjin didn't hear anything. Lydia's program had to dilate the voice stream first so that it would be audible to Jinjin.

"We could at least try," said JP, his voice tinny. "If nobody comes to any kind of agreement, you can always set the bomb off then."

"In a few days, it will be too late. Spaceships all over the globe are being prepared for launch so they can bring crews here. You two were just the advance party. I was able to handle you two, but I can't do that with everyone else, all by myself. A war will set the world back a hundred years, and you can forget about your golden age."

The excavator rolled over a rock, which fragmented under its weight. She could feel the vibrations through her seat, but that didn't distract her from her intense focus. The display read 3.2. Every minute, she lost more than three times as much normal time. No, wait. The other way around. While one minute went by for her, JP became three minutes older.

"How can I convince you?" JP asked.

4.5. It looked as if the display had been waiting for him to ask his question. Things were reaching a critical point. Liwei and the American were still remarkably far away.

"You can't convince me. But you're free to keep trying."

She needed to keep talking to him so she could determine her position in the gravity well emanating from the monolith.

"A million dollars. Ten million. I bet it'll be worth that to Uncle Sam when you hand the site over to the Americans."

Jinjin laughed. As if money would do her any good if a world war broke out.

"You're not even American, Jean-Pierre. How can you promise me dollars like that?"

"I promise. I swear on everything I hold sacred. You will get the money. One hundred million."

She could use it to build a huge bunker. But what about her family? Jinjin shrugged her shoulders. There was no way that she'd betray her country for money.

"Promise me world peace, in a way that makes me believe it."

JP sniffed, and with that the display jumped to 10.2. Jinjin looked through the windshield at Liwei. She was still too far away. She silently calculated how much time she had left. If she took too long, more and more adversaries would arrive. She should start making her way back when she'd reached fifty at the latest. She'd have to get to JP and then finally to safety.

"I... I... I..." Jinjin tapped her arm. Had the software stopped working properly? Was it no longer able to adjust speech? But the orange dot kept shining steadily.

"I can't lie to you," JP finally blurted out. The display jumped to 16.9. "I really have tried. But that wouldn't be fair. There is a risk. We just have to fight it. We're here, you and me. That gives us a chance to find out what the monolith is for."

"They won't let that happen. You're being naive."

"They?"

"My government. America. Russia. India. South Africa. All of them."

She looked at the right-hand joystick. Should she drive faster? She could stand next to Liwei, and then whatever happened to him would happen to her, too. That would only be fair.

"Give the world a chance. It's better than you think it is."

JP was a hopeless romantic. It was easy enough for him to talk. He'd probably never had to make tough choices. She looked through the windshield at the shovel and gave a start. The excavator looked strangely distorted – as if it was made of a stretchy material and someone was pulling on it from the front. The dimensions weren't right anymore, probably because of the high gravity.

She checked the status displays and saw that methane consumption was unusually high. The excavator had already tapped into its spare batteries, and it looked like it had to exert more force with every meter to keep moving forward. Why hadn't she noticed that yesterday when she'd gone up to Liwei? Because her body experienced a far smaller dilation in the radial axis pointing away from the stele than the huge machine did. Time was going by a lot more slowly for the shovel up front than where she was in the back.

If the entire vehicle was moving at the exact same speed, as seen externally, the front parts would have to move a lot faster in their own time than the rear ones. The motor was located in the middle, so it had to provide additional energy to balance the front and back parts of the excavator. She displayed data for the tires and saw that the ones in the front were hotter and fuller than the ones in the back, and the control system was automatically trying to balance things out.

She had to tell someone. "You won't believe what's happening here right now."

"Is the bomb breaking down into its individual parts?" asked JP.

"No. But the excavator is being stressed by the distorted space-time. I've only seen this kind of thing in science fiction movies."

"You'd better get out of there. Put it into reverse."

"There's no way I'm doing that. I'll carry the bomb by hand if I have to."

Though that would solve one problem, it would create another: Quite simply, it would take too long. Right now, the clock was running a lot slower for the bomb than it was for her. That gave her a cushion. But as soon as she had it in her hands, every click of the counter would be a second for her, too. The effect of the explosion would spread at the speed of light. She wouldn't be able to run away, so she would need to turn back before the counter ran out.

"That's crazy," said JP. "Just leave it behind. You're risking your life. For what? Have you thought about that?"

21:6. Was he even listening to her? She'd already given him a detailed explanation of her motives, and she didn't have time to walk him through them again. Surely he didn't really want her to do what he'd told her to? Because if she didn't get to the rover in time, JP would die too. The bomb would destroy everything within a five-hundred-meter radius.

"Forget it. I'm going to keep moving forward. Just a few more meters and I'll make it."

But the excavator wasn't making it easy for her. The engine seemed to be at the end of its rope. The coils were overheating. If she kept accelerating, it would cause permanent damage, and she might have to return on foot. But then would she make it in time?

The drill! Maybe she could use that to push the bomb if the excavator stopped moving forward. She set it as the main tool and could now use the left stick to operate it. It was located at the end of a long, jointed arm which she moved behind the excavator and then pushed downwards until the drill struck the ground. Instead of drilling, she extended the arm. It worked! The excavator moved towards the target, squeaking. Just one section length at a time.

"Hey, Jinjin! It's us. Antonia and Ernie."

What? She let go of the joystick and sat back. Sweat was running down her face. She knew the two ESA astronauts well, at least virtually. They had never met in person.

"What are you doing on the emergency channel?" she asked.

"We've been watching and listening to you for a while." It was Antonia. She reminded Jinjin a little of her cousin, who was about the same age as she was and who she'd played with a lot as a girl. "We didn't want to intrude, but at this point we can't take it anymore."

"Toni couldn't take it anymore," said Ernie. "But I have my worries, too."

"Worries, okay. Doesn't everyone have them?" What could she say to them? They were nice people, and the fact that they hadn't shown up here with weapons spoke to their character. They were scientists through and through. Hadn't the MIGI recently made some kind of breakthrough? Now she suddenly remembered what she had to tell them.

"You've got to get to safety. Quickly. This area is about to turn into a nuclear inferno."

"We already gathered that from your conversation," said Ernie.

"So you're already in a safe place?"

"No, we've only just reached the rover," said Antonia. "But we thought of something."

"Please don't tell me to bring the bomb back and defuse it. It's too late for that."

Actually, that wasn't true. It was still possible to defuse the bomb before it exploded. What she really meant was that she wouldn't be able to make it this far a second time. Either she set the bomb down next to Liwei now, or she never would.

"You'll have to draw your own conclusions," said Antonia. "But we believe we've found a way to get Yang Liwei and Ronald Hudson out of their predicament."

"How?"

"We'd like to discuss it with you in person."

"Forget it."

She wasn't going to fall for that trick. No way. They must be really desperate. Unless they were telling the truth? Had they really found a solution? They certainly knew more about physics than she did. Jinjin tried to scratch her head, but the helmet got in the way. No, she needed to keep at it. She had only a few meters to go, and then her mission would be complete and she'd be done. Antonia and Ernie still had enough time to get to safety. But what interest did they have in keeping her from destroying the stele?

The Europeans seemed to be holding back, or they would

have showed up long ago. They probably hadn't even been ordered to come here. Did that mean it was really about Liwei and Ron? It would be like them, especially Antonia, who'd managed to convince her superiors to let her bring her dog to the moon. Sometimes, over video chat, Jinjin could see the two of them playing with each other, for hours on end.

"Do you have Bree with you?" she asked.

The answer was a high-pitched bark that she'd never heard from Bree before. The software didn't seem to know how to adapt the sound.

"Is she okay?" asked Jinjin.

"Yes, it's a little cramped in here, but she's cheerful as always."

Jinjin smiled as she imagined the dog in her spacesuit.

"Hey, here's an idea," said Antonia. "Why don't you come back and play with Bree for a bit while we tell you about our plan to get your colleague and the American out of there. If we aren't successful, you can still always blow the place up."

That sounded tempting. She didn't really want to be responsible for the deaths of two innocent people. She knew for a fact that she couldn't drive the excavator any farther. But that didn't matter, since she could let the automatic steering system take over.

Jinjin let out a deep breath and reached for the right joystick. "All right, then. I'll turn around."

Surface of the moon, March 6, 2082

THEY DIDN'T HEAR FROM MISSION CONTROL UNTIL AFTER they'd been on the road for three hours.

"We couldn't reach you via the control center," Colonel Lehmann announced. "What are you doing?"

Should've seen that coming. Antonia looked at Ernie, but he showed no sign of slowing down. If they kept going at this speed and there was nothing to stop them, they'd make it in a day.

"We're going to check on our Chinese colleagues," replied Ernie.

Oh. Antonia hadn't expected him to come right out and say it. He could have stalled Lehmann a bit longer. Something about inspecting the MIGI channels or whatever.

"Don't try to tell us we can't do it," she added. "We're legally obligated to help in emergency situations."

"China didn't report any emergency situation, and is also rejecting any help we offer," said Lehmann.

"We still want to see for ourselves. It's about two people, not politics."

Ernie gave her an appreciative look. Antonia was proud of herself and her arguments.

"I must officially express my disapproval," said Lehmann.

"If you catch my drift. But there is actually a certain interest here in information about this ... emergency situation."

"We understand you completely," said Ernie. "We'll continue on against your express orders, and if we find out anything interesting, we'll be in touch."

Antonia slapped him on the thigh. They made a good team. Maybe, after they were done with their careers up here, they could go into politics.

"Thank you, I'm glad we understand each other. I expect a report at least every three hours."

Instead of replying, Ernie simply terminated the connection. Antonia opened her eyes. Wasn't that really rude?

"I know the colonel. She's all about efficiency. If she had her way, we would eliminate small talk completely. After all, no information is exchanged."

"What? It's a way of finding out how other people are doing, what they think about you, and so on."

"Information in the form of facts."

"Those are also facts."

"Yes, but they aren't of any use to Lehmann."

"What is relevant, then?"

"The fact that you're alive. But you've already communicated that by saying something."

Antonia shook her head. She couldn't deal with people like that. Fortunately, Ernie was different.

"Good girl!"

Bree looked at her proudly and wagged her tail. Antonia used a bag as a glove and picked up the dog's droppings. The familiar smell wafted through the rover, and she had to hand it to Ernie for not complaining. Bree wasn't the only passenger who produced such odors on a regular basis. The rover had a mobile chemical toilet, which she was now using to dispose of Bree's business. Unfortunately, they couldn't just open the window, and breathing the same air over and over again didn't help, even if Ernie had turned up the airflow.

Antonia yawned.

"Go ahead and lie down," said Ernie.

"You still up for driving?"

"Yes. If I get sleepy, I'll wake you up."

"Thank you."

There was a loading area behind the two seats, and she arranged the crates on it to create a kind of sleeping platform just wide enough to fit her and her dog. She spread out two blankets, then climbed on top.

"Come on, Bree!"

The dog came bounding over, her tail wagging, and tilted her head to get a better look at Antonia. She was lying on her side and stretched out her hand. Bree came closer so she could pet her. Bree would have been the perfect pillow, but she'd never consented to do that. When Antonia stopped petting her, Bree made a meowing noise like a cat, hopped onto the crates, and made herself comfortable on top of her hip.

"YOUR TURN," ERNIE SAID, LEANING OVER ANTONIA. HIS shadow startled her, and she flinched. Bree fell off her hip and barked.

"It's just me," said Ernie.

The rover wasn't moving. Because of the constant shift of light and shadow, it was unwise to give over full control to the automatic driving system, at least not at the speed they were going. Antonia looked at her watch. She'd been asleep for almost five hours.

"How much further do we have to go?"

"A few hundred kilometers."

She sat up, stretched, then walked ahead with her head down. The rover wasn't tall enough for her to walk around completely upright.

"There's something I've got to do," said Ernie.

Antonia didn't need any additional details. She sat down on the left-hand side, where Ernie had been sitting. It was possible to steer the rover from either seat, but out of habit they both preferred the one on the left. When she heard noises coming from the back, Antonia switched on the radio. All that came out of the loudspeaker was static, but at least it drowned out the other sounds. Bree scurried around between her legs as if she were chasing mice.

"Did you report to Lehmann?" she asked.

"Yes, just an hour ago."

Antonia looked at her watch again. She'd have to contact mission control in two hours. Until then, she could rest easy.

"Then sleep well, Ernie."

"Thank you."

It wasn't long before she heard Ernie snoring. He had the ability to fall asleep whenever he got the chance. Antonia had turned off the radio, but now she switched it back on again and scrolled slowly through the frequencies. Every so often she thought she could hear distant music through the static. It must be an analog radio from Earth. If such a thing still existed! But maybe she was imagining it. Humans search for patterns in chaos. It's what we're trained to do from birth.

Antonia yawned. She needed to find something that would keep her awake. The best thing she could do was to speed up. The rover still had reserves. The focus required automatically made her more alert. She had to pay attention to the radar, the optical camera, and the infrared camera simultaneously. Some obstacles didn't show up on all the screens at the same time. The software would warn them if they were approaching too quickly, but finding an alternative route when pressed for time wasn't easy.

But it was fun. The rover flew over the surface, its large wheels allowing it to touch down gently over and over. If she drove proactively, minimal steering movements were enough. She hardly ever needed to step on the brakes, since there were always areas of loose regolith where the rover could slow down on its own.

Antonia pulled up the map. Between the vehicle and the Chinese control center there was just a crater ridge, which they were now driving up at a good clip. When the rover bounced over a boulder, the radio switched on. She heard an unfamiliar voice.

"We come in peace," a man said in English.

What was that? Antonia looked for the frequency. It was close to the emergency call frequency, so the radio system must have played the bit of conversation automatically. Antonia adjusted the neighboring wavelengths, but the radio remained silent. She stood up and ventured a quick look behind her. Ernie seemed to be asleep. He'd earned it.

The same thing happened when the rover reached the crest of the crater.

"Have you got one?" a woman asked.

That was Jinjin. Antonia had spoken to her often enough to be certain. She didn't hear anything more this time either. The rover drove down the slope towards the Chinese control center. It was an impressive sight. What had once been a natural crater had been transformed into an almost perfect soup bowl. Some areas clearly remained unfinished, but Antonia could easily imagine what the hypertelescope would look like. Once the valley before her was filled with mirrors, from the edge of the crater it would look like a huge, black lake with a frozen surface.

Ernie had to see this. She stopped the rover, intending to wake him up, but in the end she couldn't do it. Her colleague was smiling so blissfully in his dreams. What could Ernie be dreaming about that made him look so happy? Even though they'd been working together so long, she didn't know enough about him to say.

Antonia started the rover back up again. She'd assumed that the two radio signals had come from the control center, but it maintained strict radio silence when Antonia tried with all frequencies to reach someone there.

"Jinjin, what's going on? Please answer."

Antonia repeated the question every five hundred meters. The seventh time, a signal from the ground interrupted her. Colonel Lehmann.

"Is that you, Ernie? I've been waiting for your report for hours."

"Sorry. It's me, Antonia. Ernie's sleeping. We're just outside the Chinese control center. But it doesn't look like there's anybody here."

"Very good. I've got a request for you."

"Go ahead."

"Try to pull all the data from the station's computer. That would help us a lot. And by all the data, we mean everything to do with the artifact."

SHE WAS ALREADY IN HER SPACESUIT BY THE TIME ERNIE WOKE up. She'd also gotten Bree suited up without any problems, which was somewhat unusual. The dog was probably ready for some exercise.

"What are you up to?" asked Ernie.

"Lehmann wants me to inspect the Chinese computer."

"And she thinks they'll let you do that?"

"Well, there isn't anybody here. I just have to get in."

"Do you need me for that?"

Antonia thought for a moment. The Chinese station looked surprisingly small, and the control center certainly wouldn't be hard to find.

"No, you'd better keep an eye on the rover."

She opened the airlock hatch and Bree leapt joyfully ahead. The dog was the first to touch the ground. She kept running ten steps in front and then coming back. Antonia shone her helmet light onto the station. There were only a few portholes on this side. They walked around the flat building, which appeared to be made of brick. There were a number of containers on the other side, and the doors to two of them were open. Antonia was about to take a closer look when all of a sudden, Bree started to bark loudly.

She had evidently found the entrance to the control center and was proud of her discovery. Antonia could check out the containers later. Antonia reached Bree's side in one big leap. The outer bulkhead of the airlock was open, indicating to her that somebody must have left the control center in a hurry.

Antonia called Bree to her and entered the airlock with the dog by her side. The bulkhead was apparently controlled by an automatic system, and closed behind them. For a moment, Antonia worried that they were trapped, but then a light flickered on and a life support system flooded the room with breathable air. She opened her helmet. The air was cool and smelled wonderful. All those hours in the rover had set the bar pretty low. Bree nudged her foot. She probably wanted to have her helmet opened too, but Antonia thought it was too dangerous since the dog couldn't close it herself.

A green light turned on. She opened the inner bulkhead to enter an immaculately tidy workshop.

"Jinjin? It's me."

Her voice sounded thin. The station must be operating in economy mode with low air pressure, meaning that its occupants had left a while ago. Antonia hadn't been expecting an answer, and she didn't get one.

Two corridors led in opposite directions from the workshop. She took the one on the left and sure enough, she found a large office dominated by several control consoles and a big screen. This must be the control center. Antonia ran her finger over the surface of a desk. Not a speck of dust. The occupants were very tidy.

The computer was a classic standard model made by a Chinese manufacturer. That meant she wouldn't have to deal with playful AIs, which was a relief. Somewhere, probably underground, there must be a second computer – or at least the space for one – because this one alone certainly wouldn't be enough to analyze the future data obtained by the hypertelescope.

The screen responded when she tapped on it. She'd lucked out. It even looked like there was another user logged in. However, the interface only worked with Chinese characters. Antonia could recognize some sort of library, but she had no idea what it contained. She took a memory stick from the pocket of her spacesuit, plugged it into the standard port, and simply moved the entire library onto the stick. Hopefully there would be room for it, though Colonel Lehmann would hardly be in a position to complain if she overlooked something. After all, this was extremely illegal. But Antonia didn't feel guilty in regard to Jinjin. She was doing this to help her and Liwei, after all.

The computer beeped, and a text window appeared on the screen. Antonia recognized a triangular warning sign. The memory stick was probably full. She pulled it out and put it back in her pocket.

"Antonia? Are you still inside? We've received some interesting measurements. If you could check them..."

Colonel Lehmann. Antonia sighed. "What is it that I should do?"

"Search the rooms. There could be sources of ionizing radiation there. A satellite picked up something."

"Which rooms?"

"No idea. All of them?"

Antonia shook her head. She certainly wasn't going to dig through Jinjin's laundry. Suddenly she heard a bark.

"Bree, come!"

The dog came bounding into the control center, her tail between her legs. She nuzzled Antonia's shoes and clearly wanted to be picked up. Antonia granted Bree her wish, then lifted her up so she was looking in her face.

"Where have you been? What scared you?"

Then she heard it herself. Something in the complex rattled. It was somewhere way in the back, but definitely not outside.

"Let's get out of here," said Antonia. She tucked Bree under her arm, closed her helmet, and ran in the direction of the airlock. The clattering sound came towards her. As she reached the workshop, a door on the other side of the room opened. The airlock was closer to her. Antonia broke into a sprint. Something was coming towards her. It had four – no, six – legs. She threw herself into the airlock and tried to press the lock button on the way, but missed it. Darn. She landed in the corner.

"The button! Bree, the button! Close it!"

She heaved the dog towards the button to the right of the door. Bree could open doors, so surely she'd be able to close them too? Hopefully nothing would happen to her. Hopefully that hadn't been a terrible mistake. As Antonia scrambled to her feet, Bree instinctively extended her paws forward and hit the button. She bounced off like a rubber ball and flew backwards. Antonia leaped towards her and caught her as the bulkhead hissed shut.

They'd made it. No. The bulkhead was still open a crack. A black metal limb had pushed inside. Bree barked aggressively. Antonia tried to push the metal leg back out, but the owner resisted. Fine. The other way around, then. She pulled on it. This surprised the owner, who must be some kind of robot. She bent the leg in the other direction with all her might. It seemed that the joint it was connected to was not designed for this, and the leg came off with a crunch. She held onto it and before the robot could react, the bulkhead shut completely.

Now on the other side of the airlock, Antonia pressed the emergency button. This opened the outer bulkhead immediately without waiting for oxygen to be pumped out. Her moist breath froze into a white cloud and gave her cover. She was worried that someone might be waiting for her. As she ran towards the rover, she could see out of the corner of her eye that somebody was following her. Something. At first it moved on six legs, but when it saw that she'd almost reached the rover, it folded up four of them and sprinted on the remaining two.

"Who's that you're bringing with you?" asked Ernie.

She was focused solely on the hatch and didn't answer. A small boulder was in her way. She used it as a springboard and sailed across the last few meters, sheltering Bree in her arms. Her head hit the inner wall. The hatch closed and the rover sped off.

"Gotcha!" Ernie called out.

⬤

"WHAT WAS THAT?" ERNIE ASKED. "LIWEI NEVER SAID anything about working with humanoid robots."

"Humanoid. If you say so."

Antonia wiped the sweat from her brow. The two robots had triggered her arachnophobia. Bree seemed to have suffered a shock, too. The dog huddled against Antonia's belly, panting, and growled when she tried to put her down. Ernie drove.

"Ah, that's right, one time I asked him how they were going to set up the mirrors and he mentioned robots."

"But why are they active now?" asked Antonia.

"Maybe they're part of the security system. The computer noticed that there were unauthorized people in the building and woke up the robots."

"I don't know. The first one came at me from another room. But the computer must have known that I was standing in front of it the whole time."

"No clue," said Ernie.

"Colonel Lehmann here." So mission control had decided to get in touch now, of all times. "Do you have anything for us?"

"You could have warned us that the Chinese control center is guarded by robots," said Antonia.

"I know nothing about that. Now, do you have anything for us?"

Antonia clenched her jaw. Lehmann didn't seem to think it necessary to apologize for putting her life in danger.

"I'm uploading the contents of a memory stick," she said, "but I don't know if there's anything useful on it. The user interface was entirely in Chinese."

"Thank you anyway. We'll analyze it and let you know. Please don't interfere in the events taking place by the artifact until we've given you our okay. It'd be best for you to park in a dark crater until then."

Antonia exhaled sharply.

"Hey, at least she's saying 'please' and 'thank you' now. That's progress," Ernie whispered.

"I heard that, Ernie," said Lehmann.

"We can't just stop the rover," she said. "We're being followed."

Antonia looked at the rear radar but didn't identify any suspicious signals. That didn't mean anything, though. If they were security robots, they would have been taught to move undetectably.

"I understand the problem," said Lehmann. "Still, I must ask you not to enter into what could potentially be a global conflict until we've thoroughly prepared you beforehand. We really can't afford it. This artifact has the potential to change everything."

At the moment, Antonia couldn't care less about the artifact. Humanity was acting no differently than it had in the Stone Age. The only difference was that people now used guns instead of clubs.

"We'll do our best," said Ernie.

"I need more than that."

Nobody said anything. Colonel Lehmann didn't seem to have anything more to say either, so Antonia ended the call.

THE SOUND OF BARKING WOKE ANTONIA FROM HER RESTLESS sleep. Bree! She was immediately wide awake. Bree was standing on the lower half of her spacesuit and barking at the controls. What had gotten into her?

"Off!" shouted Antonia.

The dog obeyed and turned to her. Antonia scratched her neck and Bree wagged her tail excitedly.

"What happened?" asked Antonia.

"Get in the rover!"

"What?" Antonia frowned. What had she missed?

"All of a sudden, somebody said 'Get in the rover' over the radio. I think it was Jinjin."

"Did you answer?"

"Yes, of course. But there was no reaction."

Antonia scratched her head. Ernie was stubbornly looking straight ahead, so she couldn't try to tell what he was thinking based on his facial expression.

"I think we're picking up scraps of a conversation," Ernie said, as if he'd read her thoughts.

"But overshooting is rare on the moon," said Antonia. On Earth, this occurred when radio waves were reflected by certain atmospheric layers, which meant they could reach targets that would normally be beyond the horizon. However, this was impossible on the moon, which had no atmosphere.

"Maybe it's the artifact," said Ernie.

"You mean it works as an amplifier?"

"As a gravitational lens."

That was one explanation. The artifact would have to distort space-time in such a way that it acted like a lens for electromagnetic radiation. The effect was very important in astronomy, but of course it didn't only apply to light, but to any type of radiation.

"That would also explain why we never get an answer," said Antonia. With a gravitational lens, a lot depended on the geometry, but this changed quickly when the rover was moving. As she petted Bree, she tried to imagine an object that would have an effect like that. It would have to resemble a small neutron star, probably so small that it wouldn't be visible to the human eye.

"What are you doing?" came a male voice out of the loudspeaker. Antonia flinched. He was speaking English. She couldn't remember ever having heard the voice before.

"Tidying up." That was Jinjin.

All of a sudden, Antonia was jerked forward. The seatbelt kept her from hitting the controls, but Bree slipped off her knees. The dog whimpered until the rover came to a stop.

"What's gotten into you?" asked Antonia.

"I'm sorry. The geometry!"

Ah, Ernie was trying to answer Jinjin. But it was probably too late. It had taken them too long to come to a standstill in the loose lunar sand.

"Jinjin, please come in. It's Ernie."

Ernie was leaning forward and speaking directly into the microphone on the control console, as if that would improve the reception.

"Jinjin, please come in."

No answer.

"Jinjin, we only want to know if there's anything we can do to help. You can trust us."

The loudspeaker remained silent. "She can't hear us," said Antonia. "The geometry is too erratic. She's probably changing her location, too. That's usually necessary when tidying up."

"Tidying up?"

"That's what she said."

"Right, sorry."

Ernie was acting a bit strangely. Could it be that he had a secret crush on his Chinese colleague? As far as she knew, he'd never met her.

"Let's keep driving," she said.

⬤

"... WAS THAT SUPPOSED TO MEAN?" SAID AN UNFAMILIAR VOICE into the roar of the generator, which was running at one hundred and twenty percent of normal output. Ernie was probably trying to get the most out of the machine.

"That could be Jeunet," he explained.

"Jeunet?" The name rang a bell, but she still couldn't place it.

"The French ESA astronaut on the Gateway."

"But the signal was coming from the surface, right?" she asked.

"... radiation symbols..." the same voice interrupted them.

"... powerful laser," a woman answered.

That was clearly Jinjin. Antonia held on to Bree in case Ernie reacted the same way as before. But this time he kept driving. Antonia waited a bit, but it seemed that the geometry had deteriorated again.

"Do you have any idea what their conversation was about?" she asked.

"Jeunet saw radiation symbols and Jinjin explained that it had something to do with a powerful laser," said Ernie.

That seemed right. But any astronaut could distinguish warning symbols for ionizing radiation from ones for optical radiation. Jinjin had been making excuses. Where could the Frenchman have seen radiation symbols?

"The explanation..." she continued.

"... was bogus, of course," said Ernie.

"I wonder what Jinjin is dragging around up there."

"She talked about 'tidying up'. Maybe she meant it literally. An old radionuclide generator is sure to have tons of radiation warnings on it."

"You mean that in the presence of an alien artifact, Jinjin decided to tidy up? That would be an extreme procrastination technique."

"True. Extreme, but not impossible. At least as long as we don't have any other explanation."

The radio crackled. Antonia waited anxiously for further snippets of the conversation between Jinjin and the ESA astronaut, but it was Colonel Lehmann.

"We need to warn you," she said. "After analyzing the

data on the memory stick, we've found that the object appears to be dangerous."

"Dangerous?" she and Ernie asked in unison.

"It's extremely heavy and extremely compact. That much we can say. The physicists are very excited because, according to the data, it could consist of matter with a density similar to that of a neutron star."

"That sounds very exciting," said Antonia. "But what's dangerous about that?"

Colonel Lehmann sighed. "I'm not a physicist. I was instructed to warn you about it. Why do you have to question everything? We just want to keep something from happening to you."

"It has to do with the effect," said Ernie. "The effect of a large mass on space-time..."

"Yes, I do know that," said Antonia. "You shouldn't get too close."

"Exactly. And that's what you should absolutely refrain from doing," said Lehmann.

"How did they figure this out?" asked Antonia.

"I don't have the details. From the measurement data that Yang Liwei collected."

Liwei was Jinjin's boss. How come they hadn't heard from him yet? Was that just a coincidence?

"We have some news for you too," said Ernie.

"Ah. What is it?"

"We heard snippets of a conversation that includes the ESA astronaut Jeunet. Unfortunately, I can't remember his first name. It seems that he's on the surface, somewhere in the vicinity of the artifact."

"What? Has error been excluded?"

"Yes, he was speaking to Jinjin and referring to something they had both seen. So if Jinjin isn't on the Gateway, he must be where she is."

"That makes sense. Thank you, I'll pass that on. What was the content of the conversation?"

"We don't know for sure, because we only heard fragments of it," said Ernie.

Why wasn't Ernie telling the colonel what they knew? Was he trying to protect Jinjin? That was ridiculous. They needed to draw on every source of information in order to assess the situation.

"It had to do with radiation symbols," said Antonia. "Do the Chinese have anything on the moon that would carry those warnings?"

"What?" asked Lehmann.

"Radiation warnings. Those propeller symbols."

"It's an impeller," said Ernie. "The three sections symbolize alpha, beta, and gamma radiation emanating from the atom in the middle."

The old smarty-pants. As if that mattered in this situation! Antonia was simultaneously annoyed and amused. Ernie just couldn't help himself. But Colonel Lehmann was suspiciously quiet.

"Colonel?" asked Antonia.

No answer. She checked the connection, but it was still active. Bree, who seemed to have picked up on the tension in the air, was scurrying back and forth across her knees. Maybe being pedantic was how Ernie dealt with stress.

"Sorry to keep you waiting," said Lehmann. "I had to make some consultations first. What I'm about to tell you is classified information, and neither of you have the proper clearance for it. In light of the circumstances, clearance was granted unbureaucratically."

Unbureaucratic? Antonia couldn't hold back a smile. If that was what people at mission control meant by 'unbureaucratic,' she never wanted to be part of the bureaucracy.

"And?" asked Ernie.

"The People's Republic was planning to use several compact nuclear power plants to supply the hyper-telescope with electricity. A solar plant wasn't an option due to the location and the constant energy requirements. This is all well known. What's top secret, however, is the fact that the fuel chambers of the individual power plants can be combined to create a nuclear weapon."

Unbelievable! "A nuclear bomb on the moon?" asked Antonia.

"Yes, that of course violates the terms of the Moon Treaty. But we can't prevent someone from somehow misappropriating an object that was legally stored there."

"Somehow? We're talking about a goddamned bomb."

"A nuclear power plant is a kind of bomb, only it is detonated slowly."

Okay, Lehmann. What a weak argument. Technically, there were a few differences. The small, modern power stations used on the moon were specifically designed not to enable any self-reinforcing chain reaction. The Chinese engineers must have refrained from including this safety feature. Antonia, meanwhile, refrained from explaining these facts to Lehmann. It wouldn't change anything anyway.

"Is there any information about what Zhang Jinjin might be planning to do with this bomb?" Ernie asked.

"Please, we don't even know if there is a bomb. We just wanted to give you some useful knowledge to help you better assess the situation."

"Thank you," said Ernie.

●

ERNIE STOPPED THE ROVER ON A SLOPE. IT WAS STEEP — nearly 30 degrees — and the only reason the vehicle didn't slide down it was because the wheels had, in spite of their size, dug deep into the gravel. The slope had one major advantage: it wasn't in the shade. This meant they would definitely notice if somebody were to approach from behind.

"Can we?" asked Antonia.

She was in her spacesuit, standing a few meters up past the rover. Bree was at heel, even though Antonia hadn't commanded her. The dog seemed to sense that this was not the time to step out of line. Ernie was still messing around with the rover's bulkhead. Then he leapt to the ground and sank to his knees. He turned around.

"Okay, let's go," said Antonia.

But Ernie didn't move towards her. He bent down, picked up something she couldn't identify, and made a throwing motion. Something flew through the vacuum. All of a sudden, she heard a beeping sound in her helmet.

"It works," said Ernie. "The rover will warn us if something comes from behind. I programmed the cameras to do that."

"That's great." Antonia immediately thought of the spider robot, and a shiver ran down her spine. She started trudging up the mountain.

AT LAST – THE CREST. ERNIE HAD PROMISED THERE WOULD BE a great view from there. She climbed up between two dark, igneous pillars that looked like pinnacles and took in the landscape.

It was unreal, raw, and beautiful. She had become an astronaut for views like this. She was looking out over a basin that was relatively smooth all along the bottom. Smaller craters could be seen to the left and right, resembling two enormous, oval bathtubs. But instead of water, they were filled with darkness. Antonia tilted her head slightly; the mirror of blackness wasn't completely horizontal, but rather depended on the position of the sun.

The basin ended in another crater wall with clearly visible tracks leading down it. They must have been made by Chinese mining equipment, and led to the control center. It wasn't until that moment that Antonia realized what a long detour they had taken.

But it had been a smart decision. From here, they had a good view of the site, which stood out clearly as a foreign object. Some kind of tent was covering it on one side, but it was still quite visible from where they were. Two excavators stood near it. Antonia set her helmet visor to zoom mode so she could see what was happening down there in greater detail. The excavators were moving closer. There was also a rover made by a Chinese company.

And then there was the monolith. Ernie nudged her in the side. She could tell from the look on his face just how captivated he was. He had every reason to be. Even at first glance, the stele looked to be not of this world. The material was of such a deep black that Antonia couldn't look at it for long for fear that it would swallow her up.

"There's a much bigger issue at stake here."

Antonia was startled to hear Jinjin's voice in her helmet, even though she had redirected the radio link to it herself.

"You want to keep extraterrestrial technology from helping humanity to enter a new, golden age."

The Frenchman. What was his name? Jeunet. What was that supposed to mean? Ernie nudged her in the side again. But he didn't have to, because she could see for herself that the excavator was moving, and Jinjin seemed to be steering it. The vehicle was moving towards a small hill with an object on top of it. From this distance, it was impossible to tell what it was, but it seemed to worry Jeunet. Now they could follow the conversation clearly. Apparently Jinjin had managed to load the object into the excavator's loading shovel.

But where was Jeunet? He didn't ask her one single time to let him go. They couldn't see anybody down below. So he was either in the rover or the other excavator.

"We should try to set him free," said Antonia.

"Colonel Lehmann gave us clear instructions that we aren't to interfere until she gives us the go-ahead."

"Ernie, are you serious? There's imminent danger here. Clearly, our colleague is trapped. He said so himself. Your Jinjin is depriving him of his freedom. Who knows what she's doing?"

"She's not my Jinjin. But she is a colleague."

"I'm not here to judge her," said Antonia. "But obviously she's acting in the interests of her country and following orders she's been given. And those orders are causing harm to our colleague Jeunet."

"Jean-Pierre."

Right. Now she remembered. He referred to himself as "Astro-JP" on social media. Back then, it had seemed strange and dated to her. Nowadays, everybody was an "astro" something or other.

"So you can get rid of the bomb?" asked Jinjin. "You know I can't let you do that."

"Ernie, did you hear that? This really is about a bomb. Our colleague must have tried to prevent it from being used."

"You're right. This is a tough situation. Let's report to Lehmann and then..."

"Ernie, we don't have time!"

If he insisted on asking first, she'd do it alone. Jeunet was probably trapped inside the rover. She was sure she could break into a rover that was locked from the outside, even if it was a Chinese model. They were built for use on the moon, where the theft rate so far had been zero. She listened to their conversation. She didn't understand everything, but it sounded to her like Jinjin had orders to get rid of the stele. But what about Liwei? Why wasn't he stepping in? Had he defied the order, and then been ... removed by Jinjin?

"What do you think the chances are of everyone coming to an agreement?" asked Jinjin.

Now her voice was remarkably high. Was it excitement?

"You hear that too?" asked Antonia.

"The frequency shift? It must have something to do with the artifact. A very large mass and the resulting distortion of space-time..."

Ernie seemed happy that she'd stopped talking about her plan to set Jeunet free. But she hadn't abandoned it. She just needed to be aware of all the factors.

"It should be possible to compensate for that with an opposite shift in our radio system, right?" she asked.

"It'll take a little time... All of that can be programmed, but it will take a few minutes."

"Do you have to be inside the rover to do that?"

"No, I can do it from here."

"Great. Please go ahead with that. We can't lose the connection to Jinjin."

"Okay. I just need to go down the slope a bit."

Excellent. She'd need a bit of a head start, and now Ernie was distracted.

"Yeah, of course. I'll keep watch here," she lied, watching him walk away. "And could you take Bree with you? I don't want her romping around here."

Bree was perfectly obedient, but if she were to follow Antonia now, she'd just be putting herself in danger.

"Sure," said Ernie.

"Go to Ernie," said Antonia. Bree barked, then followed the command. She was a good girl, and Antonia was proud of her. She climbed over a gray boulder and started descending towards the valley in huge bounds.

The excavator was rolling forward. The closer it got to the monolith, the more high-pitched Jinjin's voice became. That meant the Chinese woman was definitely on board, but the Frenchman wasn't. Hopefully Ernie could adjust the radio quickly. Now Jeunet was offering Jinjin ten million US dollars, but she couldn't hear the answer. It was also taking Jinjin longer and longer to respond to anything the Frenchman said. Obviously, time was passing differently for her.

Now the Frenchman was offering her a hundred million dollars, but even that didn't convince Jinjin. Antonia would have been surprised if the Frenchman had been able to buy her off.

"Give the world a chance. It's better than you think it is."

Jeunet must be a real optimist. Or he was just afraid of dying. If that really was a nuclear bomb that Jinjin was carrying towards the stele... Even though Antonia was sweating, she felt cold all of a sudden. It should be safe behind the crater slope, and she was glad she'd left Bree there.

Finally, the rover came closer. Its windshield was facing the stele, so the Frenchman trapped inside couldn't see her.

"Is the bomb breaking down into its individual parts?" he suddenly asked over the radio.

What? What did he mean by that? She needed to know what Jinjin was saying in response, but all that came from the radio channel were scratchy sounds.

"Ernie, how's that adjustment?" she asked.

"A minute. Just give me a minute. But why are you panting like that?"

It was still about a hundred meters to the rover, so she might as well tell him.

"I'm getting our colleague out."

"What? You promised you would..."

"I couldn't just stand around while you were working. You know me."

Ernie sighed. "Yeah, I do know you. Shit."

"What's wrong? Is the radio broken?" Jinjin hadn't said anything for a conspicuously long time.

"No, it's Bree. She's not here."

Oh no. Not that. "You promised..."

"Well, what about you? She must have figured out that you were running. She does listen to us, you know."

He was probably right. Antonia was constantly amazed by how good the dog was at picking up on what she was doing. She turned around and saw something headed her way, leaving big plumes of dust in its wake. Before she knew it, Bree was crashing into her chest. Antonia held her tightly, but the momentum still toppled both of them over.

"Oh, you silly thing. Why do you have to go putting yourself in danger like this?"

Bree didn't answer.

"She definitely gets it from you, Toni," Ernie commented.

Darn it. Ernie was probably right for once. Antonia scrambled to her feet. The rover was just a few meters away, and she went over and knocked on the bulkhead.

At that moment, she heard Jeunet's voice coming through in her helmet. "You'd better get out of there. Just put it in reverse," he said.

The bulkhead wouldn't give, and Antonia examined the lock. It was primitive, and a hex wrench should do. The only reason the Frenchman couldn't get out was because there was no keyhole on the inside. She reached into her toolkit and found one that should work. No, it was a little too big. Still, she managed to work it into the slot so that it fit, then rotated it one hundred and eighty degrees, which was as far as it would go. Then she tugged on the handle to the bulkhead, and it gave way. She climbed in and waited for Bree to come in after her. After she pulled the outer bulkhead closed, she activated the pump, which started blowing air into the airlock.

But this was no time to relax. When the light on the switch turned green, she pulled open the inner bulkhead. She climbed through and saw a shadow moving towards her. At the same moment, a rock the length of her arm shot past her, hit the shadow, and then something long and hard crashed against the wall above her with a metallic clang.

"Stop! I'm not the enemy!" she shouted.

Someone yanked her around. A face came closer to her helmet and jerked back.

"*Merde*. I'm sorry, I thought you were an attacker. Who are you?" He pointed to the logo on her chest. "You're from the ESA!"

"I'm Antonia Marucci, actually one of your colleagues from the ESA. What's Jinjin doing? We've got to stop her."

"So that's why she wants to destroy the artifact?" Antonia asked.

Humans had been searching for messages from other civilizations for so long, and as soon as one showed up on their doorstep, they went ahead and blew up the whole front yard. But maybe Jinjin and her superiors were right, and humans weren't ready for it? The fact that the struggle over evaluating the data had brought them to the brink of war, as JP had reported, seemed to suggest that.

"And that's not all," said the Frenchman, who'd asked her to call him JP. "Yang Liwei, her boss, and our colleague from NASA, Ronald Hudson, are in a vulnerable position right up next to the monolith."

"Are they injured?"

"Probably not," said JP. "I think they're frozen in time. But in any case, they can't get themselves to safety, and neither can anyone else, for that matter. So the explosion will kill them if we don't prevent it."

"That's out of the question," came Jinjin's voice.

"We've got to help them somehow. There's always a way," said Antonia.

JP put his finger to his lips and pressed a button on the radio. Antonia understood: JP had put Jinjin on hold over the emergency channel while he talked to her on a private channel.

"Now we can talk," said JP. "I muted myself on the emergency channel. We've got time, since for them time is passing very slowly now. That's our only advantage."

"How can we hear them at all?" asked Antonia.

"She's compensated for that somehow with her radio equipment. Plus, we're transmitting on very low frequencies."

Ah, so Jinjin was already making use of the kind of technological fix that Ernie was working on. She could give him the all-clear that the problem was resolved, but she would prefer to speak to Jinjin from their own rover. Ernie would probably finish up soon anyway.

"We can't just let her kill two people," said Antonia.

"I've tried everything. She simply won't be convinced."

He put his finger to his lips again. "It's time for me to answer her."

JP pressed a button and said: "That's crazy. Just leave it behind. You're risking your life. For what? Have you thought about that?"

But that wasn't how it worked. Jinjin was justifying her actions in terms of the bigger picture. This was something she had to do so that humanity would survive. That was always a better argument than appealing to her own stubbornness. She didn't think of herself as important. But that only applied on a personal, individual level, and not to her loved ones.

"What if there was a way to save Liwei and your friend Ron?" Antonia asked.

"How is that possible?" asked JP.

"That's not the question. Wouldn't she want to save Liwei? She can always blow up the stele afterwards."

JP nodded. "Yes, she might try that."

"But there isn't a way," said Ernie.

"Oh, let me introduce you. Ernie Schwarz, my supervisor. The eternal optimist."

"Thank you. I've adjusted the radio system. Now we can speak to Jinjin, though with a delay."

"Great. Where are you?"

"I'm driving the rover down the slope. I'll be with you in a few minutes."

"Great. I've got a plan," said Antonia.

"Will you tell it to us?" asked JP.

"We'll tell her that we know how to save Liwei and Ron."

"But there's no way," Ernie countered. "There – is – not – one. Physics is uncompromising. Unless we switch off the gravity well."

"Let's switch it off, then," said JP.

"Haha, that's a good one. Gravity is linked inextricably to mass. Even if Jinjin blows the artifact up, its mass will remain."

"And what if we remove it?" asked JP.

"That's not possible. We're talking about... I have no idea, to be honest."

Antonia thought this over. Damn it. Unfortunately, Ernie was right. Given its effect, the artifact must be as massive as a star. But if that were the case, then the moon wouldn't be orbiting the Earth anymore, but the other way around. The entire solar system would have been disturbed. The mass therefore must be significantly less. But how heavy was it? It seemed that nobody really knew.

"We'll still say that we know a way," said Antonia.

"She won't believe you," said JP. "Jinjin seems very suspicious."

"Maybe of you. You came down here with the American, right? Europe is neutral in this matter. We've known each other for a long time, and she knows that we deal with physics at the MIGI. She'll trust us."

"Toni's right. It's worth trying," said Ernie.

Oho! What was this? Her boss was backing her up?

"And then what? Let's assume she turns around," said JP.

"Then we have to neutralize the bomb," said Ernie.

"Can you do that?"

"I'm a physicist. I can do anything."

Ha. Typical Ernie. Fortunately he didn't act like that when it was just the two of them. That would be unbearable.

"Great, then you'll be in charge of defusing it," said Antonia. "I'll try to convince Jinjin that we can save the two men who are up by the artifact."

"Forget it," Jinjin said over the general radio channel, as if responding to Antonia's thoughts. "I'm about to do it. Just a few more meters and I'll have taken care of it."

Good. They had to strike while the iron was hot. "Where do I have to press to transmit over your channel?" asked Antonia.

"I'll do it." JP turned a dial to the right and pressed a button, then gave her a thumbs-up.

"Hey, Jinjin!" she exclaimed, trying to sound casual. "It's us, Antonia and Ernie."

Now she'd have to think fast.

"What are you doing on the emergency channel?" asked Jinjin.

"We've been watching and listening to you for a while."

Dewar Crater, March 6, 2082

JINJIN HAD HER HAND ON THE RIGHT JOYSTICK, BUT COULDN'T bring herself to pull it back. Could the two Europeans be trusted? Didn't they want to get hold of the stele just like the Americans did?

But holding off on destroying the monolith didn't mean that she'd be giving it up. Didn't Antonia and Ernie at least deserve to have her listen to their plan? The two of them made up the scientific team for a powerful instrument used to measure gravitational waves. If anybody could find a solution to the problem, it was them.

What would Guofeng say about it? He'd always demanded obedience and discipline from her, but also independent thinking. *Good soldiers offer their own ideas, but follow a superior's orders once a decision has been made.* That hadn't necessarily been standard practice in her unit. Some of her fellow soldiers had been quite content not to have to think for themselves.

Up here, she was both her own superior and subordinate. And she owed it to Liwei to get him out of there. A solution that spared her colleague and the American was preferable to one that didn't. Her two different sides quickly reached an agreement.

Jinjin pulled the right joystick, and the excavator started moving slowly backwards.

AFTER WHAT FELT LIKE HALF AN HOUR, METHANE consumption returned to normal. Jinjin was anxious. Had she made the right decision? Was the deal she'd made with herself fair, or had she given up too much and gained too little? She put her hand on the joystick. It was a gesture that she alone could see, but it gave her a feeling of power.

"I need a little something more," she said.

"More? What do you mean?" asked JP.

"More information. What does this plan look like? I have some understanding of physics."

"Ernie?" asked JP.

"No, it was Toni's idea," said Ernie. "She's the one who can explain it best."

"Alrighty then," said Antonia. "The fact that Liwei and Ron don't appear to be moving is because time is passing so slowly for them. And that, in turn, is due to the fact that the stele has such a large mass."

"Please don't tell me you want to somehow shield this mass."

"No, Jinjin. That would be an insult to your intelligence. We want to get the two of them out of the immediate area of the stele. You yourself have already noticed that the distance is critical."

"But how? I've already considered knocking Liwei over with a long stick."

"That won't work. Whatever you use has to approach his location. The closer it gets, the more time it will need. It's the same effect as with a spaceship seeming to take an infinite amount of time to fall into a black hole."

That made sense. She'd already observed that effect with the excavator, time passing at different speeds for the shovel and the rear of the vehicle.

"Does your solution have something to do with spaghetti-fication?" asked Jinjin.

It was good to talk to Antonia. She had such a calm, analytical way about her, but also seemed to sympathize with her situation.

"No, the forces aren't strong enough for that. With spaghettification, the body is really stretched out. That wouldn't do Liwei any good."

"Okay. The difference isn't entirely clear to me, but that doesn't matter. How are you going to get them out of there?"

"Impulses, and here's the point, can be transmitted in ways other than by a mechanical impact."

"How's that?"

"With the help of a strong magnetic field."

"But humans aren't magnetic." She couldn't shake off the feeling that Antonia was jerking her chain, and she didn't like it one bit.

"Yes and no. Not on the whole," Antonia agreed. "But our atoms consist in part of magnetic dipoles. And the electrons, since they're spinning, also play a part in this."

"So you want to turn Liwei into an iron magnet?" An image of her colleagues being transformed into robots flashed through her mind.

"No, that's not possible. Biological material, which consists largely of water, cannot become ferromagnetic. The small magnets in the body aren't aligned in the same direction the way they are in an iron needle, but against each other. This is referred to as diamagnetic."

"So we can't pull Liwei in with a powerful magnet."

"No. But we can push him. Diamagnetic bodies are pushed out of a strong magnetic field."

"And that's going to work?"

"There are videos of floating frogs, which demonstrate magnetic levitation, on the internet. You can find them yourself. All we need is a strong magnetic field. Forty Tesla, though more would be preferable. It just so happens that we have superconducting coils stored at the MIGI. We use them to produce laser light for the interferometer. You'd have to provide us with electricity, however. One megawatt would be good."

Was this some kind of joke? Jinjin really wanted to believe that Liwei could be saved. But flying frogs? She tapped on the screen on her arm to start a search. There were actually plenty of places to find them. She pressed the play button and saw a frog floating above some kind of liquid. It was wriggling its legs, so it must be alive.

"And it won't harm Liwei?" she asked.

"Less than contact with an uncontrolled chain reaction would," said Ernie. "That much I can guarantee. Medical examinations that involve magnetic resonance imaging use strong fields that don't harm patients."

Jinjin played the video again. The quality was so poor that it certainly wasn't fake. Were Antonia and Ernie telling the truth? She wished she could ask Liwei about it. And she couldn't turn to mission control for advice. Yaping would just order her to get on with blowing up the monolith.

"How long will it take you to get the parts here?"

"Three days. The MIGI isn't just around the corner, unfortunately," said Antonia.

That was too long. In three days, all the spaceships that were being prepared on Earth right now would have arrived, and she'd lose all control of the situation.

"Okay. Well, thanks for the suggestion, but I can't risk it," said Jinjin.

It hurt to say it, because it sounded like this method could work. Magnetic fields propagated at the speed of light, even in a gravitational well. And one of the mini power plants could be operated with the fuel from the bomb in order to supply the electricity.

"Hold on. We've got the Gateway lander nearby," said Ernie. "It suffered some damage when it landed, but the three of us should be able to fix it quickly. Traveling point-to-point, it won't take us more than half an hour to get to the MIGI."

"Does it have sufficient carrying capacity?" asked Jinjin.

"A single coil weighs around four hundred kilograms," said Antonia. "To be on the safe side, we'll need two of them."

"We can make two trips."

"Then we can do the experiment tomorrow," said Antonia. "Is that good enough for you?"

Jinjin sighed. She still couldn't quite believe her luck. Could the two ESA scientists really have come up with a way to save Liwei that hadn't occurred to their own experts? Well, maybe they hadn't known about the coils in the MIGI, and it would have taken way too long to transport the material from Earth.

"Okay. I trust you. Please don't disappoint me."

1.7. THAT HAD BEEN FAST. IT ALMOST SEEMED TO HER THAT the artifact intentionally pushed objects out of its field of attraction. Perhaps it was some sort of safety measure. *Keep your distance, I'm dangerous.* How else could you teach a primitive civilization like humankind to stay away? That would also explain why the stele had been hidden beneath the moon's surface. If Liwei hadn't been so curious, humanity wouldn't be on the verge of a war now. A form of technology offering advantages as great as the stele was surely too much of a temptation for the various militaries around the world.

But maybe it would all turn out well. Jinjin thought that the cooperation with her three colleagues from the ESA was a good omen. It really could work. They didn't have to argue. If the four of them could manage it, cooperation should be possible on a larger scale, too.

All of a sudden, she noticed something moving in her peripheral vision. Somebody was climbing onto the excavator's shovel. Had this all just been a trick? Her muscles tensed. She hated being deceived, because it proved to her that she was naive. Why couldn't people just do what they said they would?

Fine. Jinjin clenched her jaw and pushed the joystick forward again. The person climbing around on the shovel fell over. It had six legs! What the... It wasn't Ernie or Antonia – it must be one of the robots she'd seen in the container. Now a second one appeared. Jinjin halted the excavator. What were the machines doing? Now the two of them were side by side, bending over and lifting something. The bomb! They intended to steal the nuclear bomb from her. Two arms extended up from the ground, where she guessed there must be a third robot.

Jinjin breathed in deeply. It must be her imagination. But she could see it on the control console: the load on the shovel was moving downwards. The two robots jumped to the surface of the moon. Yaping. Mission control must be behind this. They didn't trust her, and had programmed the robots to finish the job.

"Jinjin, there's something going on with your excavator," Ernie said.

"It's not my fault," she answered. "They're robots. Mission control must have programmed them. You've got to believe me. I had nothing to do with it."

"Don't worry. Antonia tangled with these things when we dropped by your control center."

"They were already active when you were there?"

"Yes. Toni told me they must have searched the control center."

Her heart clenched. Mission control had obviously been suspicious of her the whole time. When Ernie and Antonia had visited the control center, she'd still been driving the excavator toward the monolith. There was no doubt that she intended to carry out the mission. Okay, with some hesitation, but she'd been convinced that it was absolutely necessary. Yet Yaping had called in the robots.

"Thank you. I... It appears my bosses don't trust me."

"I'm sorry," said Ernie. "What's going on there?"

"The robots just stole the bomb from me. Apparently they're determined to set it off."

"Do you need help? Toni and JP took your rover out to the lander so they can repair it. But I could come to you."

Jinjin would enjoy the company, but it didn't make sense for Ernie to put himself in danger by coming to join her. Plus, it would take too long.

"I'll take care of it on my own."

"What are you going to do about the robots?"

"I'm sitting in an excavator, which is the best weapon there is."

"Good luck!"

JINJIN SWITCHED ON THE RADAR AND LEANED BACK. ON THE screen she saw three blinking dots, two of them close together. Those were probably the ones carrying the bomb. They weren't moving very quickly. That was good. A third dot was bustling back and forth in front of the excavator. Unlike the others, it was fast. It probably served as a scout. It was keeping its distance from the large machine; when Jinjin changed course, the dot would immediately move out of the way.

She would take care of that one last of all. The bomb was the bigger risk, and the closer the two robots dragged it to the stele, the longer it would take to recover it. The excavator wasn't a racecar. But it moved about one-third faster than the two robots, who were slowed considerably by their heavy load. That meant it would take around ten minutes to reach them. Enough time to confront Yaping.

"YAPING HERE. PLEASE COME IN."

She could hear her voice perfectly, and Jinjin was determined that her message would come through just as clearly.

"What's going on?" she demanded. "Three robots raided me and stole the bomb."

"That wasn't a raid," said Yaping, "just an alternative scenario. The three machine units are helping you to fulfill your mission."

"How come you didn't tell me about it?"

"After our simulations calculated that, based on the most recent data, the chances of you completing the mission had dropped from eighty-eight to forty percent, we didn't want to waste any time. You've got to understand that. A likelihood of less than seventy-five percent could not be considered acceptable, not by any stretch of the imagination."

So it was because of a simulation that they'd decided to hand over the assignment to the robots. What Yaping didn't know was that the simulation was actually one hundred percent right. Did she really have any reason to complain?

Still she asked, "You don't trust me?"

"Jinjin, this has nothing to do with not trusting you. It's just a matter of numbers. A sixty percent risk is too high. We had to find alternatives. Incidentally, the calculations also showed a drop in your success rate when the change of plan was communicated to you. We're simply optimizing the odds. Your new assignment is to follow the robots and help them reach the stele as needed."

Jinjin sighed. Looking at things from mission control's point of view, she might have followed the same line of reasoning. She was one resource, and the robots were another. Using both together made perfect sense.

All of a sudden, she noticed that the excavator had reached the two robots with the bomb. She used the left joystick to lift the shovel and one of the robots turned around. Even though they were moving in shadow, it had probably noticed the change in the incidence of light. A human wouldn't have noticed anything, but the machine registered even the smallest change.

Now it was all about timing. Jinjin started to speed up the excavator, which didn't bother the two robots. They didn't seem to view it as a threat, or else they generally didn't register dangerous situations. Two more meters to go. One meter. She pressed the stick. The powerful shovel moved downwards while she halted the excavator with the right stick. There seemed to be no significant resistance. Jinjin saw from the altimeter that the shovel had reached the lunar surface. She brought it back up again, just in case more action was needed.

Everything happened in complete silence. Once the shovel was three meters above the ground, two robots, as well as the bomb, had apparently disappeared from the radar. Jinjin pivoted the front camera so that it illuminated the ground. There they were. The robots had been squashed into metal packets no more than eighty centimeters high. The bomb, meanwhile, appeared to be undamaged. The surface glinted. Both the bomb and what remained of the robots had been shoved into the loose regolith soil.

That was clearly a resounding success. Should she leave the bomb there? No, that was far too dangerous. She inserted the shovel into the ground at an angle and dug up the bomb. The remains of one robot were scooped up along with it, while the other one was left to its arid grave.

Jinjin leaned back. She didn't really have time to rest, but she had to celebrate her success, at least a little. The final score was one to zero, and she was the one. The human spirit had triumphed, even if it all seemed a little too easy. It certainly wouldn't be when she had to justify her actions to the Eleventh Bureau. But the facts would speak for her—or she hoped so. Would they forgive her for disobeying? Guofeng, her role model, had once had to make such a decision himself, and still became a great instructor.

All of a sudden, there was a crash. A shadow fell over the windshield, obstructing her view. First she made out one arm, then two. The third robot! What was it doing? Its arms pounded alternately on the glass, which was specially designed to withstand the impact of micrometeorites. But could it hold up to repeated blows from a tireless robot arm? The glass was already turning white in the area where it was striking. That was due to the special inclusions that were supposed to repair small cracks immediately. Jinjin touched the pane from the inside. It was warm and dented slightly inwards.

Jinjin shook her head and knocked on the glass. "Stop it! You'll kill me!"

She felt cold. That must be the robot's intention. She had never thought of robots as posing a threat to her life. They were hard-working helpers that couldn't hurt people, at least unless someone programmed them to. A human working for mission control. Presumably it wouldn't be difficult, since these six-legged cargo robots weren't very intelligent. For example, it probably couldn't infer that she would die if the air escaped through the damaged window.

But she wasn't going to give up that easily. Jinjin slipped into her spacesuit. She hadn't taken off the bottom part, so she only needed to put the top part back on. She tightened all the fasteners and put on the helmet. The status display showed that she had nine hours of oxygen. That was more than enough. She took the gun out of her tool bag.

Come on, you robot.

It took exactly eighteen minutes for air to start escaping through the window that the robot had damaged. The manufacturer would be proud. But now everything was happening fast. Jinjin's heart was thudding in her chest as the robot stuck its leg-like limbs into the hole in the glass and used them to tear the windshield apart. When the opening was big enough, it pushed its stumpy body through headfirst. *Go away.* Jinjin dodged behind the driver's seat just before the robot grabbed onto the backrest and pulled itself into the cabin.

She slid all the way down to the floor so she was lying on her back. She was too agitated to notice any discomfort. The robot intended to kill her, and her gun was the only thing that could stop it. *Keep calm, Jinjin.* She imagined she was a soldier in a combat situation. She didn't feel like herself, all her emotions slipping away. All that mattered were the facts. Was shooting really a good idea? The cabin was already damaged, but there was a considerable risk that bullets would ricochet.

The robot, like the walls of the excavator, was made of metal.

A Taser would have been more practical. But who would have thought that their own robots might become enemies? Jinjin dug her boots into the ground and pulled herself up. Then she lunged to the side and whirled around. The robot was lying with its upper body on the seat, as if it were resting. But its little head turned in circles, obviously trying to locate its opponent. Now everything depended on how well the robot had been programmed. If she was lucky, it wouldn't recognize her in the spacesuit.

She slowly moved toward the bulkhead. If she could trap the robot in the cabin, all she'd have to do was overload the excavator's fuel cell and the machine would explode. But that plan wasn't particularly feasible; it would take at least an hour for the cell to reach the limits of its capacity. Earlier, when she'd been making her way towards the monolith, she'd been glad that the excavator's engineers had made everything so big. She hoped this would mean the explosion would be all the more powerful.

It was the only plan she had. And it was already starting to fail because the robot was able to recognize her even in the shapeless suit. The robot's programmers had done impeccable work. Jinjin raised the gun. The robot, however, didn't react. It was making its way towards her very slowly, as if it were already sure of her body. Where should she aim the gun? There were just a few sensors in its head. Most of the electronics were located in the egg-shaped belly, where they could stay heated.

But the greatest risk of ricocheting came from the robot's body. Its smooth, metallic surface reflected the light from the cabin. How would it kill her? Suffocation was one of the most unpleasant ways to die. If she had the choice, she would prefer to shoot herself.

The robot extended a kind of glowing eye from its head. The effect was a bit gruesome, like an eyeball projecting from its socket on a stick. Presumably it had been ordered to verify her identity before killing her. Jinjin took a swing at the eye, but her adversary immediately moved it aside.

A split second later, she was within reach of the robot's two arms, which sparkled on the underside. That must be glass shards from the windshield, embedded in the metal. She was no match for this robot. What could she do?

With left hand, Jinjin felt for the bulkhead behind her and managed to open the door a crack. All of a sudden, the robot's left arm shot forward. It darted towards the door and slammed it shut. Jinjin screamed as she realized that her index finger was inside the crack, and was being crushed. She couldn't pull it out. The damn robot had pinned her in place. She couldn't risk taking a shot from this distance. The bullet would almost certainly ricochet and hit her suit. She cocked the safety with her thumb and threw the gun at the robot's head.

It didn't react. The gun sailed through the cabin, bounced off its head, made its way towards the ceiling and then fell to the floor. Now she didn't have a weapon or hope, and couldn't even shoot herself. Jinjin's heart was racing and sweat was running down her face. Her body slumped over, her muscles unable to handle the strain anymore. She urinated in her diaper. So it was true that people peed their pants before dying a violent death. She was both angry and sad, but she was still thinking clearly.

Jinjin had always imagined that she would die in space. Vacuum was deadly. No matter how advanced the technology, nothing made by humans could be perfect. Eventually, her luck would run out and her name would be inscribed on a large stele at the entrance to China's largest spaceport.

She was going to die, but not like this.

Not by the hand of some robot, which was now pressing its claws against the point where the helmet and spacesuit were connected. What was it doing? She shoved at it with her right hand, but she might as well have tried to move the Himalayas. The damn thing had anchored itself to the floor of the cabin with its six legs.

Not the fastener. She heard the familiar clicking noise of the connection between the helmet and suit being released. There were five slide switches that needed to be pressed. The first click might have been an accident, triggered by its trying to strangle her. But when she heard it a second time, its intentions became quite clear. Click. Click. The robot was working its way forward efficiently. Click. She closed her eyes against the pain that she would inevitably feel upon contacting the vacuum. The robot was about to take off her helmet. How humiliating! This must have been Yaping's idea. She would have to get back at her.

In another life.

Clunk. That was a new sound. Jinjin opened her eyes and saw that the robot had lowered its spherical head. Sticking out of it was a light-colored rod with four narrow, angular fins arranged symmetrically around the tip. It might be an arrow from a crossbow. But where had it come from? The robot had stopped moving. She quickly grabbed at her helmet, which might fly off her head at the slightest disturbance, and pressed it firmly onto the neck of the spacesuit. The robot still had her hand pinned by the bulkhead. It was still as strong as ever. It probably wasn't dead, and instead was thinking about how it could eliminate the new threat without releasing Jinjin.

A beam of light shone into the cabin, through the hole the robot had made in the window. There was somebody out there! One of the ESA astronauts must have come to rescue her. She made shooing gestures with her hand. *Don't come in! It's not worth it. The damned robot will kill us both.* Jinjin swallowed the lump that had formed in her throat. She couldn't keep herself from feeling hopeful. Another arrow buried itself in the robot's body, piercing the metal like butter. This was no homemade crossbow. The arrow in the robot's head appeared to be made of a very hard but non-metallic material.

Whoosh. Apart from her heavy breathing and the pounding of her heart, it was quiet as a grave. But she did imagine she heard the whoosh of the arrow sinking into the robot's body right next to the second one. The source of the light was coming closer. Her rescuer appeared to be climbing through the hole in the windshield. All of a sudden, the robot started moving again. It twisted beneath the arm it was using to hold Jinjin and lashed out at its new opponent with its front three legs. Jinjin made the most of the opportunity to kick at the arrows in the robot's stomach. One bent to the side while the other went in even deeper.

The robot winced. More importantly, it missed its target. Then it was struck in the head by two more arrows, one right after the other, and a third went through its hand and into the wall next to Jinjin's body. What a weapon! It was clearly better suited to fighting in a vacuum than her useless pistol. Now the robot was uncomfortably close to her. It was still holding her left hand in its own, while the arrow pinned its other hand to the wall. Its head was maybe an elbow's length away from her helmet, which she still hadn't securely reattached to her suit.

Jinjin tried to click the clasp shut with her right hand, but she couldn't manage it. She was too flustered. If only she had a second hand! As if granting her wish, the robot let go of the bulkhead with its left hand. Her other arm was free! She immediately reached for the base of her neck and cried out as she tried to use her index finger. It was as if the front part had ceased to exist. She pushed away the pain and used her thumb and middle finger to fiddle with the buckle.

Click. Finally! The helmet was secured in one place, at least. That was enough to ensure that it wouldn't potentially fly off her head any time it was jostled. In the meantime, she hadn't noticed what the robot was using that left hand to do. It had turned almost all the way around and had come frighteningly close to its human attacker. What could she do? Her rescuer was fumbling with the crossbow, presumably to reload it. Jinjin caught a glimpse of his face and saw that it was Ernie, whom she recognized from all the video conversations they'd had with each other.

"Ernie!" she called, fussing with her second helmet fastener. But he didn't seem to hear her.

The arrow was still pinning the robot's right hand to the wall, but it started to swing out with the left one. If Ernie didn't get out of its reach right away, he'd be hit. And her helmet was hanging on by a single buckle. The robot struck. Its left arm would send Ernie straight across the cabin. Fuck the helmet. Jinjin pushed off the wall and kicked the robot's arm. The additional impetus sent it rotating around the arm pinned to the wall and crashing into the back wall of the cabin. Ernie, meanwhile, readied his crossbow. It was the perfect moment. The front of the robot was now facing Ernie. The arrow whizzed through the vacuum so quickly that Jinjin didn't see it until it hit. It pierced right through the narrow connection between the head and the belly.

Jinjin thought she heard the machine rattling. It grabbed at its neck like a human would, though of course it was trying to free itself from its position against the wall. As it did so, Ernie shot at the robot's free hand and got it on the second try. An arrow pierced through the hand into the upper part of the robot's body. The six legs flailed wildly, but their owner couldn't free itself.

"Ernie, thank you so much!" Jinjin gave him a big hug, but he pushed her away, pointed to her mouth, and turned his index finger in a circle. Oh, right! She was still transmitting on the frequency adjusted for the time dilation, which wasn't necessary when they were in the same place. Jinjin switched to the normal emergency frequency.

"... deactivate the thing somehow?"

Ernie was pointing at the robot, which the arrow was still holding fast to the wall. It was trying to free itself by using its legs and would eventually succeed if it didn't run out of power first. A shiver ran down her spine; in this position, the robot reminded her very much of a spider.

But maybe it was also the relief that she felt washing over her and running down her spine, mingling with the sweat as it cooled.

"Deactivate it? No, not that I know of. These things are activated by remote control."

"Then we should make sure that doesn't ever happen again," said Ernie.

He climbed around the cabin, tore a metal shelf from the wall, and took it apart.

"Here!"

He took a bar about one and a half meters long and pressed it into her left hand. She flinched, and the piece of metal fell to the ground.

"Sorry," she said, "my left index finger is mush."

She bent down and picked up the rod. Ernie didn't have to tell her what he had in mind. She moved over to the robot's right side, just out of reach of its legs. Ernie took the other side and, as if on command, they started to pummel the machine.

IT FELT GOOD. JINJIN PUT ALL HER ANGER INTO THE BLOWS SHE aimed at the machine. As long as she was hitting the robot, she didn't feel pain or exhaustion. The robot was unable to defend itself, but that didn't detract from the pleasure of beating on it – on the contrary. After all, she had also been unable to defend herself while it tried to tear her helmet off her head. She kept seeing Yaping's face in place of the robot's. It was crazy, but it didn't scare her. She would show Yaping.

Something touched her shoulder. She flinched and started to hit that too, but Ernie pushed her arm aside.

"Let it go, Jinjin. It's nothing but junk now."

He pointed to what was left of the robot. Two of the six legs had been torn off and were lying on the floor. The body was dented and looked like a shriveled orange. The head had blown apart. Cables stuck out of the cracks in the metal like straw from a scarecrow. The body was hanging from its left arm, since the right one had been torn out of the shoulder joint. Nobody would ever start this machine back up again. There was still some life left in it, though. The two toes on one of the clawed feet were rattling against each other silently.

Jinjin hugged Ernie. Warm drops of water ran down her cheeks. When she stuck out her tongue, she tasted salt. Was she crying? She breathed in and sniffed. Ernie reached for her neck, and she pulled back. Nobody was allowed to touch her there.

"Wait, just let me fasten the buckles on your helmet. Three of them are still open."

Jinjin clenched her jaw and let him do it, though she kept thinking about a predator that could rip her throat out at any time.

"Done," said Ernie.

She let go of him and tensed up.

"Thank you for coming," she said.

"I couldn't let that damn robot kill you." Ernie kicked the robot's foot with the moving toes. They stopped wiggling as if the machine was now done for good.

"It's not the robot's fault," said Jinjin. "It was just following orders."

Orders given by mission control on Earth to increase the likelihood that the plan would be carried out. *It's nothing personal, Yaping. I had to kill your robot to optimize Liwei's chances of survival.* She was still angry at Yaping even if she was just a mouthpiece, a bearer of bad news. Decisions were made at a different level.

"You can just as easily be an asshole if you follow orders," said Ernie.

Jinjin nodded. She'd almost become such an asshole and sacrificed Liwei for the sake of her mission. But there was always an alternative, as Antonia and Ernie had shown her.

"Where did you get the crossbow? I was naive enough to believe that you Europeans were the only ones who actually didn't bring weapons to the moon."

"Ron brought these from the Gateway."

Ron. That must be the American who was next to Liwei, waiting to be rescued.

"Honestly, I don't know if we have any weapons at the MIGI," said Ernie. "We didn't ask before we came to you."

"Did they send you?"

Ernie shook his head. "Quite the opposite, actually. We were ordered not to interfere under any circumstances. But obviously that's not what we did."

"That's going to cause trouble, isn't it?"

Ernie shrugged his shoulders. "I don't think so. We got really close to the stele, and our bosses can say that while we may have exceeded our authority without permission, we were legally obliged to help. Europe's off the hook."

Politics. It really was the same everywhere.

"I'm fine if you blame the destruction of the robot on me, by the way," said Ernie. "I saw the machine attack you and had no choice but to help."

"Nobody would have judged you if you'd decided not to put yourself in danger. So thank you for that. You saved my life."

"I would have judged myself." Ernie pressed his lips together. "We were the ones who convinced you not to try to solve the problem by setting off a nuclear bomb, after all."

She smiled at him. "I'm very grateful to you for that too."

Ernie's face hardened. Had she said something wrong? She didn't know him very well. Maybe he was one of those people who didn't like to be thanked.

"I ... I have a confession to make."

"What do you mean?"

What kind of confession could it be? Could Ernie have helped her fight off the robot earlier but hadn't dared? That must be it. He could have gotten to her faster with his rover. That was the only confession she was ready to hear.

"I..."

"Never mind, Ernie. It's okay. You helped me. That's the main thing."

"Yes, but..."

"There are no buts. At least not one that means anything to me."

"But you should know, Jinjin. The solution we described to you..."

Jinjin tried to cover her ears, but the helmet got in the way. Should she cut the radio connection? No, Ernie was right. She needed to know.

"So, that was an ad hoc solution. It came straight out of the blue. Nobody had done the math yet. Antonia remembered the video of a floating frog that a professor showed in a physics lecture about graphene, which Andre Geim later investigated..."

"Does that mean we can't save Liwei?" she interrupted. Where was the rod she'd used to beat the robot to smithereens? It was there at her feet. Jinjin bent down and picked it up.

"I don't know. The frogs really do float. But we don't know if we can transfer a big enough impulse to a human. Nobody's yet gotten a human to levitate that way."

"But you pitched it to me as a solution? I betrayed my country because of it!" Jinjin took a swing with the pole. She'd sacrificed her life for some spontaneous idea? She'd been under the impression that the two of them had already planned the experiment and done all the calculations for it. They'd even told her what the energy requirements were, which just happened to match what she could provide with one of the micro power stations. Or was that also not a coincidence?

"The data you gave me... Was that made up, too?" She had to restrain herself from hitting Ernie with the rod. Just a moment ago, he'd been her hero. Now it turned out that he was responsible for her getting into this situation in the first place.

"No, they were educated guesses," said Ernie. "Not just made up."

"Based on simulations? Or at least experience?"

"Estimates based on Geim's experiments. We only had a few minutes to come up with something believable!"

This was too much. Jinjin's anger got the best of her, and

she struck out with the rod. Ernie didn't resist, which made her drop her arm. She wasn't a soulless robot and couldn't harm a defenseless human.

Something believable. The words kept running through her mind. Normally, she wasn't easily fooled. If the plan sounded believable, maybe they could actually do it. She'd seen the frog, and for the purposes of the experiment, the differences between frogs and humans really weren't all that significant. Maybe she ought to give Antonia and Ernie a chance.

"Okay, okay, okay." Jinjin dropped the rod. She watched the weapon fall to the ground in slow motion, bounce briefly, and then come to rest. They were on the moon. The magnetic field only needed to generate one-fifth of the force they would have needed on Earth. If necessary, they could connect several small power plants together. But that would take too long. The others would arrive in three days, and the experiments would be over.

"We're going to try that now," she said. "No more lies from now on. We're in the same boat."

At least for the next three days. After that, Jinjin would have to account for her actions. It would be easier with Liwei by her side than without him.

"Deal," said Ernie. "I'm really sorry we lied to you. We didn't see any other way out of the situation."

Jinjin nodded. Maybe in three days she'd be happy about it. If not, the bomb would have killed them all.

Surface of the moon, March 7, 2082

"I've got good news," Antonia said into the microphone. JP observed that she was already working the lander's console like a pro. "Could you pass me on to Ernie, please?"

"Were you able to fix everything?" asked Jinjin. "Ernie doesn't want to be disturbed. He connected the rover's and the two excavators' on-board computers in order to simulate the conditions for a magnetic field within a distorted space-time."

"Yes, we did. And we're just about to go ahead with the first launch. Cross your fingers for us."

"Good luck."

"Thank you."

Antonia ended the connection, leaned back, and fastened her seatbelt. "Good to go."

JP had a sinking feeling in his stomach. They'd been able to patch up the landing gear, but they hadn't been able to get rid of all the baked-on deposits on the engine. That might make steering more difficult. And he had so little experience with the ferry. Ron should be the one sitting here.

He pressed the button to start the engine, and he could feel the vibrations in his back. He slowly turned up the power, and suddenly there was a force lifting him up. The lander was rocking back and forth, which he countered with the vernier thrusters.

"The main thrust was a bit off-center," he said.

"But not so much that it can't be offset with the vernier thrusters. Under no circumstances do we want a rolling motion."

Antonia spoke as if she were a pilot herself. "How do you know that?" he asked. "It sounds like you learned that somewhere."

"I did learn it somewhere," said Antonia. "Just like you. Thanks to NASA cooperation on the Gateway, the ferry is what we'd use to leave in an emergency. Everybody who wants to work at the MIGI has to be able to fly it."

"Oh." Then he could have let Antonia sit in the driver's seat. Ever since he'd seen how even Ron Hudson, despite all his experience, had almost caused a crash, his respect for the skill involved in navigating a lunar module had given way to a slight fear. "Then why aren't you sitting where I am?" he asked.

"Because you went ahead and sat there, as a matter of course? Do you want me to take over for you?"

The unpleasant feeling in the pit of his stomach grew stronger. The higher up they went, the harder he had to counter-steer. The ferry moved jerkily due to constant use of the vernier thrusters. He would have loved to hand the wheel over to Antonia, but now wasn't the right moment.

"Next time," he said, swallowing down the taste of bile that had risen in his throat.

"We're high enough," said Antonia. "Here's the route."

The screen in front of him was now providing him with instructions on how to steer the ferry. JP couldn't remember Ron using such an aid, but he really appreciated it. He couldn't fight his nausea and think about transposing abstract positional information to concrete course corrections at the same time.

"You're doing great," said Antonia.

He'd imagined the division of labor in the cockpit some-what differently, but the main thing was for them to reach the destination safely so they could pick up the solenoid. JP bit his lips. He attentively followed the changing instructions on the screen until he suddenly felt a kick in his rear.

Antonia clapped her hands together. "Hey, that was really great."

JP released his seatbelt buckle and jumped out of the lounger, then rummaged around in the clean-up station for a bag and threw up in it. Antonia patted him on the shoulder.

"Really, great job," she said.

HALF AN HOUR LATER, JP WAS SITTING ON THE FLOOR OF THE airlock with the outer door open, his legs hanging down. Antonia was still busy securing the solenoid. There wasn't room for two people in the cargo bay. Cargo bay, ha ha. JP sniffed. It was just an empty space between the landing gear and the cabin. It hadn't been easy to hoist the solenoid in, especially since it would have weighed almost half a ton on Earth.

"Will you be done soon?" he asked her over the radio.

"Yes, you can start going through the checklist for the launch."

JP sighed. Antonia wouldn't even grant him a short break. He stood up and looked at the landscape. The MIGI hadn't impressed him very much. He'd imagined a sea of shining mirrors, but Antonia had just laughed when he'd pointed out a few. He would have recognized that it was a solar power plant himself.

He moved inside. It felt good to be able to peel off the spacesuit. This time, he sat down in the co-pilot's seat. The checklist was printed out and hanging beside the controls. He went through it step by step and for the first time realized how satisfying an activity it could be. To complete his sense of well-being, all he needed now was for a hairdresser to run a comb through his hair, or to take a warm shower.

THIS TIME, THE FERRY DIDN'T TEETER BACK AND FORTH. JP looked at Antonia's hands. She wasn't even touching the stick that controlled the vernier thrusters.

"How do you do that?" he asked.

"I'm not doing anything. The solenoid is helping me out. Four hundred kilograms of extra weight right near the center of gravity is a natural stabilizer."

But when it was time to land, Antonia did have to steer. They needed to set the solenoid down as close as possible to the excavator, since they were going to set up the experiment on its shovel. That way, they could easily move it over to the test subjects. Of course, it was important that the ferry not cause any damage, to itself or the excavator.

"Fifty meters," said JP.

Antonia actually could have read how high up they were herself, but she'd asked him to announce their altitude since she was navigating with her eyes closed. She seemed to completely merge with the spaceship, sensing as it swung slightly in unwanted directions and compensating for it by lightly nudging the stick.

"Forty meters."

Getting there. Now the engine was starting to stir up sand. Hopefully Jinjin, who was probably putting the small power plant together, had accounted for this. Regolith dust could be very inconvenient.

"Thirty meters."

An alarm sounded, and Antonia opened her eyes. The ferry was shaking. JP checked the status displays and observed that the steering engines were running low on fuel.

"Apparently they used too much on our way out," said JP.

"Why didn't you notice that when you were going through the checklist?"

He felt his cheeks growing hot. He'd checked how full all of the tanks were. Or so he'd thought. He reached for the checklist, where every item he'd finished was marked as complete. There was no checkmark next to the vernier thrusters.

"Oh no! I'm so sorry! Now we're going to crash."

"No we won't. Don't worry. Only roll is empty. Pitch is still working." This meant the pilot could still raise and lower the nose and the tail, but not the starboard and port. Antonia closed her eyes again, but now she was also gripping the control stick for the main engine.

"Twenty meters."

The ferry started to sway too much. She tilted it forward briefly, gave it a boost with the main engine, and returned it to a vertical position. Now it was swaying less.

"Ten meters."

Though it was certainly better, it was still swaying. If they landed at an angle, the landing gear they'd fixed would break. That would cost them time and maybe even the cargo. And it was his fault! He could have redirected fuel from the main tank. Now, while in flight, that was no longer a possibility.

"Watch out, there's gonna be a bang," Antonia warned.

Now the ferry was swinging back and forth like a pendulum. JP had some idea of what Antonia was up to. She waited until the pendulum was perpendicular to the ground and switched off the engine.

"Now!" she shouted.

JP clung to the lounger as the ferry rushed towards the ground. The counter moved faster and faster. Five, four, three, two, one. Touchdown. The metal screeched so loudly that it was painful to hear, but the landing gear held up.

"Okay, let's open up our present," said Antonia.

As JP JUMPED TO THE GROUND FROM THE AIRLOCK, BREE came running towards him. The dog quickly realized her mistake, circled him twice, and then barked at the ladder until Antonia finally got out. She was limping slightly. Antonia took Bree in her arms and started talking to her. Quick to obey her human, the dog stopped barking.

JP ran over to the excavator's shovel. Something that looked like a rotary clothes dryer had been set up on the left-hand side. But instead of laundry, thin sheets of metal hung in the middle. They were shiny and silver. The whole arrangement had been stuck like a shrub in a pot, which bore the typical symbols for ionizing radiation. Jinjin was aligning the metal sheets to make sure they were distributed as evenly as possible. She was using only her right hand.

"Making good progress, Jinjin?" he asked.

"Yes, we've been waiting for the solenoid. Were there problems? It took you a long time."

He could understand that Jinjin was under a lot of pressure, so he tried to give a friendly answer.

"The thing is incredibly heavy," he said. "Also, this isn't what I thought the reactor would look like."

"What you're looking at here are just the radiators. The reactor is cooled with a special liquid metal solution. It releases the stored heat here in these areas."

"Is the location a problem?" he asked.

"It is. The radiative transfer isn't homogeneous in every direction because the excavator is in the back. Really, these power stations are supposed to be lined up in single file. But I don't want to have to lay down long cables first. And if everything works, we can shut the reactor down after a few minutes."

"It's really as simple as that?"

"Yes, the Russian RB developed these small power plants specifically for use in space. They're really great for setting up a new station before other sources of energy can come into play."

"A nuclear power plant for dummies?"

"I wouldn't describe myself as a dummy. Let's just say it's easy to maintain and safe."

How reassuring.

"Come on, let's get the solenoid," said Ernie.

"SHOULDN'T WE WAIT FOR THE WOMEN?" JP ASKED. HE AND Ernie were standing in front of the ferry's landing gear.

Antonia was still petting Bree and was making no move to help them. At the MIGI base, they'd had a mechanical loading aid, but here they were on their own.

"Antonia hurt her foot and Jinjin hurt her hand. Come on, we'll take care of it."

JP sighed. He wished he'd stuck to cooking on the Gateway. This was what he got for being too curious.

"On the count of three. One, two, three."

JP felt like the whole spaceship was sliding into his arms, but it was just the huge solenoid. Under lunar conditions, it weighed eighty kilograms. He managed to slow its fall, but he couldn't hold it alone. Ernie walked around the base – he'd pushed from the other side – and pointed to the solenoid, then to the shovel.

"We have to move it about fifteen meters out, and then one and a half meters up."

"Can't we just move the shovel down a meter and a half?" JP asked. "I have no idea how we're going to lift the solenoid."

"No, we can't do that. The power plant has to stay level."

WHEN THEY DROPPED THE SOLENOID IN FRONT OF THE SHOVEL, JP had reached the end of his rope. Forty kilograms per person didn't sound like much. But moving something that weighed that much while wearing a spacesuit that restricted your mobility – that was a different story. And then there was the sweat running into your eyes and ears. He had no idea how they were going to get the thing onto the shovel. It just didn't seem possible.

"We could activate another robot," Ernie suggested.

"Are you crazy?" asked Jinjin.

"I was just joking. I'm glad they didn't send any more of those after us. What's stopping them, anyway?"

Jinjin shrugged her shoulders. "There were probably only three that were ready to deploy. They actually weren't supposed to be activated for a few more months, when the crater was ready for the mirrors to be set up."

"I hope you're right," said Ernie, "and they're not lurking in the shadows until we feel like we're safe."

JP turned around. Up there close to the poles, there were a lot of shadows. Too many shadows.

"But maybe your idea isn't so bad," said Jinjin. "The robots have a modular design. We can separate the hips from the torso and the rest of the body. Then we can use them separately. Most of the intelligence is in the torso. We'll just use the legs and control them remotely."

"Think about what that thing wanted to do to you," Ernie said.

"I'll never forget it. But wouldn't it be fair for it to help us with our work now?"

JINJIN NEEDED ABOUT AN HOUR, WITH ERNIE'S HELP. ANTONIA went for a walk with Bree. JP, meanwhile, was glad to rest and enjoy some peace and quiet. He sat down on the excavator's left wheel housing, where he could lean against the cabin and observe the black monolith. The longer he looked at it, the more sinister it seemed to him. It really didn't seem to be of this world. How could Jinjin's colleague have taken it into his head to get so close to it?

All of a sudden, somebody tapped him on the shoulder. It was Jinjin. She was sitting on a four-legged stool. No, not a stool. JP flinched as he recognized the legs. They had belonged to the robot. When completely extended, they were long enough for Jinjin to reach him on the wheel housing.

Now she tapped something onto the screen on her wrist and the legs bent at the knees.

"It works," she said, "and don't worry – this is pure remote control. There's no way that the legs have their own intelligence."

"But they're just legs," said JP. "Don't we need arms, too?"

"Nope."

Jinjin tapped another command and the legs spread out like a four-legged camera stand until Jinjin's feet touched the ground. She dismounted and the structure lowered still further.

"That's thirty centimeters. Surely you can lift the solenoid that high?"

"One – two – three," Ernie commanded.

On "three," JP pulled on his side of the solenoid with all his might. It lifted up and tipped over, landing on the platform with the four robot legs attached to it.

"Now make it nice and stable," said Jinjin.

Antonia, Ernie, and JP tried all together not to let the solenoid slip back down as the four spider legs moved back together. They were powerful. Even carrying such a heavy load, the platform rose. As soon as it reached chest height, Jinjin halted it. Then she moved the robot close to the raised shovel. She adjusted the height again. Now all they had to do was push the solenoid onto the shovel. Ernie counted to three again, and the three of them pushed the object into the correct position.

"Success!" shouted Jinjin. "Antonia, can you help me with the wiring?"

"Shouldn't we test it on a human first?" Antonia asked.

Jinjin shook her head. "We don't know what effect the field has on a healthy person. Liwei and Ron are a different story. We might be able to save them. At most, it will harm you."

She was right. JP had seen the measurements, and they were clear. The solenoid could generate a field with a maximum of thirty-four Tesla. That wasn't quite the forty they'd wanted, but they didn't need Liwei to fly, just move a few meters away from the monolith. It was difficult to calculate how strong a force would be acting on his body. It might be too much. Was it a wind, a storm, or a hurricane? It wasn't the poison, but the dose.

"We should get started," said JP. "You all have to consider the time dilation. The whole experiment will definitely still be going on tomorrow."

"Not 'you all.' Me," said Jinjin.

"You want to drive to the stele on your own?" asked Ernie.

"Yes. Better to put as few people as necessary in danger."

"You could use the automatic system to drive the excavator," Antonia suggested.

"And what if Liwei or Ron are in urgent need of help? Somebody should be there with them."

JP nodded. Again, Jinjin was right. One person in the excavator was enough, and the rest of them would secure the perimeter. They couldn't be sure that other robots mightn't also be ready for operation.

"Thank you for coming up with such a great idea," said Jinjin.

Something made up on the fly had become a real invention. Now JP also believed it could work. Jinjin hugged Ernie first, then Antonia, and then him. Finally, she petted Bree for the first time. JP had always thought Jinjin wanted nothing to do with dogs.

"We're really sorry we weren't honest with you right from the beginning," said Antonia.

"I might not have accepted an honest answer," said Jinjin. "That would have been a shame. I've got a good feeling about this and I'm glad that when I was so outraged at first, I didn't take Ernie down."

"You wanted to kill Ernie?" asked Antonia. JP could see her eyes widen, even through the front of her helmet.

"Yes, I was about to. But he didn't defend himself, and that's what saved him."

Excavator Zero, March 7, 2082

JINJIN WAS ABOUT TO START THE ENGINE WHEN A FOUR-LEGGED spacesuit flew into her arms. She gave a start and fell backwards. It was Bree. The dog barked and tried to lick her, but of course she couldn't because of the helmet.

"Bree, off!" Antonia called out over the radio channel.

Jinjin patted the dog's suit. It fit snugly against Bree's back, and Jinjin imagined she could feel the animal's warm, soft fur through her glove and the fabric of the suit. She picked Bree up so they were looking right into each other's eyes.

"What are you doing here?"

Bree answered with a short bark, and Jinjin put her down on her lap. The dog had jumped into the excavator cabin through the hole in the windshield. They'd started to repair the damage before they realized that this would severely obstruct the view of the outside. So Jinjin had bitten the bullet and was making the trip in her spacesuit. The cabin had its own oxygen and energy supply, so she could take the suit off for a while in the airlock. They'd put some food and water there, along with a bucket for her to relieve herself in.

This was no romantic getaway. When she saw the stele, a shiver ran down her spine. It was easy to see through the crack in the windshield.

"She probably wants to say bye to you," said Antonia.

"Is that what you want?" Jinjin asked, planting a kiss on the dog's nose as best she could with two helmet panes in the way.

Bree didn't answer.

"Come on, Bree. Heel!" called Antonia.

The dog stood up and wagged her tail. She didn't seem sure whether she should leave Jinjin yet.

"Yes, it's okay. I've got to do this alone," said Jinjin.

Bree barked briefly, then took three steps before jumping through the hole back into the darkness.

THE MONOLITH WAS GETTING INTO HER HEAD. THE LAST TIME Jinjin had come this close, she hadn't felt it. It was as if she was surrounded by loud voices shouting at her, but she couldn't hear them because there was a transparent but impenetrable barrier between her and them. She didn't know what they were shouting, just that she had a terrible headache. Maybe they were warnings, or else the effects of the distortion of space-time on her brain. Before this, no human had ever moved in such a gravitational potential, and how it acted on the biochemistry of the head was unknown.

The machine faltered. Last time, this had been the moment she'd used the drill to push the excavator closer to the stele. This time, she had to do without it. Such violent shocks might cause the precious arrangement on the excavator's shovel to shift.

"How are you doing?" Antonia asked over the radio.

Because of the time dilation, communication was very slow. What she answered now wouldn't reach the others for some time. So she said nothing, preferring to use the time to carry out her mission. She navigated the excavator so that it was pointing the shovel directly at Liwei. Before she'd headed out, they'd set up an aiming device in the hole in the windshield. When Jinjin leaned back in her seat, she needed to see the cross over her target. That would mean the person was right in the center of the magnetic field.

Still a bit to the right. The generator was running at top speed, and the metal groaned as it was exposed to different lines of gravitational potential. Gravity wasn't pulling as strongly on the left wheel as it was on the right. The excavator was built for extreme loads. These forces would probably have torn a rover apart by now. They didn't, however, seem to be dangerous to individual people. Was that a coincidence, or was it intentional? Maybe those who built the stele had wanted to attract individuals possessed of a certain curiosity. To then leave them standing around nearby? No, there didn't seem to be a strategy behind it. Or she just wasn't smart enough to figure out what it was.

"Zhang Jinjin, please come in."

It had been a long time since anybody addressed her so formally. She didn't recognize the voice. It didn't use the general emergency frequency like Antonia and the others did, but the same one as mission control. The radio controller software she'd modified had automatically adapted the voice playback.

"Zhang Jinjin, please come in."

Whoever it was obviously didn't know where she was and that she therefore couldn't answer immediately. In any case, she didn't have time to talk to mission control right now. Every second here was precious. She started to calibrate the magnetic field. For this purpose, Antonia had set up a rod about one meter long pointing from the solenoid towards the target, and attached a measuring device at the end. If anything shifted during the trip, the device should be able to detect it.

"Zhang Jinjin, please come in."

Whoever it was certainly was persistent. A wheel turned slowly, taking one minute to make a single revolution. The display read: *Calibration complete*. Then she saw a diagram showing the approximate dimensions of the magnetic field projected by the solenoid. There was a clear dip on the side closer to the monolith, meaning that only part of the field strength was reaching the target. Antonia and Ernie had worried something like that would happen. Of course, the magnetic field was also subject to the effects of distorted space-time.

Jinjin tapped on the edge of the diagram and corrected it with her fingers until everything was more or less symmetrical again. A list of values appeared below the graphic, some of which needed to be entered into the solenoid's control program. She'd have to go outside to adjust some of the others. The solenoid had to be moved slightly in the x, y, and z directions.

She sighed. She had really hoped she would be spared this step. It was so depressing out there that it felt like she wasn't even on the moon, which she'd never found threatening. But here, just thinking about stepping out through the window filled her with a primal fear.

"Zhang Jinjin, please come in. This is Hao Haidong. I'm in charge of the Eleventh Bureau. Wang Yaping is no longer responsible for you. I need to speak to you urgently."

Jinjin hesitated. It seemed that Yaping had been dismissed. Was that good or bad news? It was hard to tell from here. And what did it mean for her? If Haidong was contacting her personally, it must be really important. Either the Eleventh Bureau's assessment of the situation had changed, or they'd found another way to destroy the stele and were being kind enough to warn her in advance.

But she wasn't going to find out. She couldn't afford to wait for an answer.

"Zhang Jinjin here. I'm experiencing communication problems. What is it that you wanted to tell me?"

That would have to do. That way, she didn't give away where she was right now, though her location could probably be triangulated by the relay satellites in orbit. She'd have to live with that. Jinjin stood up and climbed over the control panel to the window.

IF SOMEWHERE IN THE UNIVERSE THERE WAS A DARK FOREST where hidden creatures waited for her to reveal herself so that they could attack her, then this was it. Jinjin felt as if she was surrounded by whispering voices giving her unintelligible advice, laughing at her, or calling out insults at her. The suit was also putting up more resistance to her movements than it usually did. It was almost like having to make her way through a crowd of people, even though the space around her was empty.

She activated the helmet microphone and measured the zero level. The background was no louder than usual. There was a bit more air from the life-support system since her heart was beating so fast, but apart from that, the suit wasn't using significantly more energy. So it was all happening in her head. That was as much frightening as it was reassuring.

Focus. She was standing on the shovel and had to make sure she didn't trip over the cables that had been laid out there. The little power station seemed to be glowing, the black housing standing out against the equally dark surroundings. Another illusion. The outside temperature was less than minus one hundred degrees. Jinjin checked her arm display for the numbers that showed how often she had to turn the corresponding screw on the solenoid in (for minus values) or out (for plus values) in order to achieve the desired effect. Antonia had tried to set it up so these adjustments were as simple as possible. There were nine screws she needed to adjust.

She took care of the first three without any problems, but with the fourth, she counted wrong. Fortunately, Antonia had marked the zero position in the thread, so it was easy enough to start over again. As she was turning the sixth one, Yaping suddenly appeared next to her and struck her on the fingers. She dropped the screwdriver. It fell to the bottom of the shovel, but she didn't bend down fast enough and it bounced off the shovel and disappeared into the sand.

Darn. Jinjin leapt after it. She shone her helmet's light across the area, but couldn't spot the tool. Instead, the loose regolith turned into black, bubbling mud before her eyes. She squinted and the gray dust returned. Still no screwdriver. This wasn't working. She got down on her knees and felt around on the ground. The tool must have worked its way beneath the surface.

At the very moment that her left hand felt the screwdriver through the sand, she remembered that Ernie had packed her a spare tool. She was so happy that she forgot about her injury, grabbed it too tightly, and dropped the tool in pain. It didn't disappear this time. And it didn't startle her to see Yaping sitting on the edge of the shovel, casually dangling her legs. She wasn't wearing a spacesuit, which made it easier for Jinjin to tell that it was all in her mind.

But was it really just her head messing with her? Now, all of a sudden, Yaping appeared in a spacesuit. When Jinjin realized that it was abnormally clean, it was immediately covered in a thick layer of dust. Maybe she was experiencing a temporary form of schizophrenia. Did such a thing even exist? She had no idea, but whoever was feeding her these illusions must be able to access her consciousness directly, meaning it was most likely herself.

Jinjin was usually able to calm herself down with such thoughts, but it wasn't working this time. The suit was already reporting that her health was at risk. She quickly adjusted the remaining screws and climbed back into the cabin, where she leaned back in her seat and closed her eyes for a moment. As soon as the rhythm of her breathing normalized a little, she cautiously opened them.

The whispering beings hadn't followed her. Even though the windshield had a gaping hole in it, she seemed to be safe in here.

"We have changed our assessment of the situation," said the Eleventh Bureau chief. He was still speaking to her directly. It seemed that the matter was of utmost importance. "Your top priority now is to rescue the taikonaut Yang Liwei.

I repeat, it is necessary to rescue Yang Liwei. He could be an invaluable witness. The artifact won't be cleared for detonation until he has been saved."

Liwei was a witness – but to what? Apparently, the Eleventh Bureau believed he'd discovered something that could be important for all of humanity. Otherwise they wouldn't have made such a radical change to their priorities. Jinjin restarted the calibration. This time, the field had the symmetrical shape that she wanted, with a potential maximum in the front region. The cross-section was shaped like a club, and the intention was indeed to use it to knock Liwei away from the stele.

There was just one problem. Jinjin's hand flew to her heart. That wasn't possible! She looked at the hole in the window where the target aid was hanging. And even though she turned on all the headlights and the excavator's radar, she couldn't see Liwei.

Surface of the moon, March 7, 2082

THIS WAS TAKING WAY TOO LONG. ANTONIA TAPPED ON THE armrests of the pilot's seat. It was just before midnight. Bree was sleeping on her knees, but she herself was unable to rest. Not because of the dog's quiet snoring, but because she'd stopped hearing from Jinjin. Did it have something to do with the discussion she'd had with mission control? The connection was encrypted, and all they knew was that the conversation was on the frequency that was always used to contact Chinese mission control.

What could they have said to Jinjin? Could they be blackmailing her? But that didn't explain why she'd remained silent, and why she'd stopped doing anything. She'd calibrated the field twice. After that, the excavator had stood still. If someone was trying to force Jinjin to use the bomb, she would have tried to tamper with the power plant long ago.

"Antonia here," she tried, using the emergency channel. "I'm worried about you. What's happened? Can we help you?"

Bree woke up briefly, repositioned herself, then resumed snoring. Apart from her canine companion, she was alone. JP and Ernie were out tinkering with the Gateway's lunar module. If the rescue operation worked, they might need it to take several people into orbit. There was a distinct possibility that Liwei and Ron would need urgent medical attention.

Antonia clasped her hands and twiddled her thumbs. Patience had never been her strong suit. But not even a physicist could do anything about physics in strong gravity, despite what many people believed. *Can't you do anything about it?* Such people were accustomed to having a doctor's diagnosis followed up by a treatment. That didn't work in physics. The only thing worse was wishful thinking, which was also widespread in the world of medicine.

"I... I have..." It was hard to understand Jinjin. Was she crying? "I didn't... Liwei!" she cried out, as if she were having a nightmare. "Liwei... Liwei..." Her voice became softer, almost inaudible. Antonia turned up the volume. "Liwei isn't there anymore. Isn't there anymore. He's ... gone."

What? Jinjin must be imagining things! Antonia started the rover, which didn't have a direct view of the monolith from where she was. Bree stretched sleepily, hopped off her lap, and made her way over to a bowl filled with moon sand that Antonia had set out for her as a makeshift potty. Antonia steered the rover around the second excavator, but since she was sitting so low, there were still small boulders blocking her view. She turned around and drove to where the slope of the next crater ring started, then used her helmet to zoom in on the stele.

The artifact, presiding silently over the lunar surface, looked the same. The excavator with Jinjin inside was in front of it, its front pointing towards a person. Antonia set the magnification to the highest level. One person, yes. Not two. She couldn't tell if it was Liwei or Ron, but there was definitely just one person standing there.

She radioed Ernie, who'd switched to a private frequency to work with JP on the lander.

"Please get back on the general channel," she said. "Liwei's gone."

Then she switched to the emergency channel herself. "Jinjin, what happened? I don't see Liwei anymore either."

"I ... I don't know what happened." She already sounded a lot better. "When I was calibrating the field, I dropped the screwdriver. Then I went back to the cabin and saw that Liwei had disappeared. Ron is still there."

"Are you sure?" asked Ernie.

Since Jinjin's answer wouldn't come through right away because of the time dilation, Antonia jumped in. "I checked it out. I can only see one person by the stele."

"Then we should get him out as quickly as possible," said JP. "It doesn't matter who it is. We don't want him to disappear too."

Excavator Zero, March 7, 2082

BUT IT DID MATTER WHO IT WAS. SHE'D GONE THROUGH ALL this trouble for Liwei's sake. Not for the American who had come butting in without asking. Fate had betrayed her! The black monolith had betrayed her! Jinjin would have loved to turn the power station back into a bomb. If Liwei was dead now, what was the point? She could set the bomb off without getting to safety first. The Eleventh Bureau wouldn't be happy, but she didn't care. All that would remain of her would be a few ashes.

"Antonia here. We need you now, Jinjin. Ron needs you. He's counting on you to help."

Ron. The American. She had to slide a little sideways in her seat to see him. He was probably running out of time, just as Liwei had. Jinjin could see her colleague's face in front of her. It was still, but the drop of sweat had moved. It wasn't frozen like ice, but rather solidified like glass. An amorphous form of life that moved at a different pace than hers did.

Maybe that was exactly what happened when somebody touched the monolith: They were beamed away somehow. She had no idea how the extraterrestrials would do that, but figured it had taken so long to notice because of the time dilation. That meant the American was also long gone. She just couldn't see it because the information hadn't gotten through to her yet – like a star that from Earth looks like it's about to become a supernova, but in reality has long since exploded.

If that was what had happened, Liwei might still be alive. And Ron offered an opportunity for her to test that theory. If he was already long gone, the magnetic field shouldn't affect him. After all, it couldn't displace a body that no longer existed. At least not in this reality.

Jinjin took a deep breath. She owed it to Liwei.

"Okay, Antonia. I'll give it a try. But don't get too excited. I have some idea of what might have happened here. And if it's right, Ron was lost long ago. You'll be able to tell if the magnetic field doesn't do anything to him."

It was funny – at first she'd really hoped that Antonia's wild idea would work. But now she was hoping it would fail, since that would give her new hope. Jinjin didn't wait for Antonia's reply. She turned the excavator very slowly so as not to misalign the solenoid. She didn't have it in her to do another calibration. When she'd brought the bulky figure into alignment with the crosshairs, she took a deep breath, released the magnetic field, and closed her eyes.

Surface of the moon, March 7, 2082

HE WAS FLYING! ANTONIA PLAYED THE RECORDING AGAIN. IT looked fake because Ron's body moved in slow motion at first, then much faster. The magnetic field had worked as expected. Hopefully Ron would cope well with being a little shaken up. It was difficult to watch in real time how slowly the excavator Jinjin was operating had moved at first. She could feel the walls of gravitational potential against which it was now sliding down faster and faster.

When Jinjin's figure, which looked tiny when she wasn't using the zoom feature, finally climbed through the windshield, Antonia could no longer stay in her seat. Bree seemed to sense her excitement and gamboled around the cabin. Jinjin climbed over the front of the excavator and down the shovel. Now she knelt down. Ron was only a little bump on the surface of the moon, but now his upper body straightened, making him human. Had Jinjin helped him, or had he moved on his own?

"He's alive," Jinjin said over the radio. "Hold on, Ron, not so fast!"

The American jumped up, reached for his belt bag, and pulled out a tool. Darn it. That wasn't a tool. It was a gun. He pointed it at Jinjin.

"Don't, Ron. That's Jinjin! She saved you," shouted JP.

But Ron didn't respond and instead walked slowly backwards, away from Jinjin and towards the stele she'd just saved him from.

"Other channel!" Ernie shouted.

Great. Ron couldn't have known they were communicating over the emergency frequency. The connection crackled as JP and Ernie switched to the Americans' frequency from the rover.

"They're talking to him, Jinjin," said Antonia. "Stay calm."

Hopefully she'd be able to keep her cool. She certainly wasn't happy about the way Ron was thanking her for rescuing him. But if he got any closer to the stele now, she'd need to rescue him a second time.

Finally, the American halted. He lowered the gun, put it in his tool bag, and collapsed. Jinjin waited a moment and then rushed towards him. She pulled his limp body up by the arms and dragged it to the excavator.

WHAT A MORON. JINJIN WAS IRRITATED AS SHE HEAVED THE American up the ladder towards the airlock. She could have rescued him sooner if he'd let her. She'd already seen in his pale face that he wasn't feeling well at all. He'd probably suffered internal injuries from the violent shock.

She opened the bulkhead and pushed his body into the airlock. His legs were too long, and she had to push them forward onto his body in order to close the airlock. Finally, she was able to get it closed. She locked both the inner and outer doors just in case Ron tried to escape again. Before the green light came on, she checked his belt bag. The gun was real and loaded. It wasn't even secured. She felt cold. She'd been on the verge of leaping at him to disarm him and bring him to the excavator. Evidently he would have fired at her in cold blood.

"What's wrong with you people?" she asked. "Do you always shoot at people who come to your rescue?"

"No," said JP. "Not even Ron. He was just confused. From his point of view, nothing was happening all that time, and then all of a sudden he was lying on the ground next to you. It must have looked to him like you were the one who'd given him a beating."

A beating? Maybe JP was right. She made sure the green light was on and removed Ron's helmet. One side of his face was covered in bruises, which continued along his upper body. It looked like somebody had slapped him hard across the face with an enormous hand. His blood pressure appeared to be stable. She couldn't determine if he had any internal injuries. He definitely needed a thorough examination. She took a painkiller and a sedative from her emergency supply and injected him with them.

Jinjin didn't bother taking off the lower part of his space-suit. If they wanted to meet up with their colleagues, they'd both need to be suited up. She closed the top part of his spacesuit back up and put his helmet on. She could tell from his calm breathing that the drug was already working. Good. She could drive the excavator back home in peace.

BAM, BAM, BAM. IT APPEARED THAT RON HAD WOKEN UP. SHE checked the airlock camera. The American was standing in the tiny room without a helmet, banging on the inner door.

"Can you please tell your friend that isn't a good idea?"

"Okay," said JP.

Ron stopped.

"Please tell him that we're all on the emergency frequency," said Antonia.

"Oh, man, can someone explain to me what's happened here?" asked Ron. "And, more importantly, get me out of this stinking hole?"

Jinjin grinned. She'd completely forgotten that the airlock

had also been serving as her bathroom. But it was his own fault for taking off his helmet. Then JP started telling her a story, the likes of which she'd never heard before.

The Frenchman had a nice voice, and she had to be careful not to fall asleep as he told his story. But then he mentioned Liwei for the first time, and it was a dagger to Jinjin's heart. For all the joy that Ron's rescue brought, one thing was clear: the experiment had failed, and her theory had been disproved. The black monolith didn't beam anybody away.

Or... Wait a minute! There was one critical difference between Liwei and Ron.

According to Ronald Hudson, he'd never touched the pillar.

Sometime, somewhere

THE WORLD WAS MADE OF JELLY. EVERY TIME LIWEI MOVED, he had to overcome resistance. The jelly was completely transparent, but it seemed to have a structure. For example, when he drew in his arm and then extended it to the side, the structure seemed to massage his muscles through the space-suit. It was a pleasant feeling. Liwei closed his eyes and focused his attention on it. The pressure was like that of a massager tool, but with elliptical rollers the size of a soccer ball.

He imagined that he was floating in a liquid filled with such rollers. On Earth, there was a drink – bubble tea – that was somewhat similar. But the only thing Liwei smelled was his own sweat, probably because he was still getting his air from his spacesuit.

Where was he? Before this, he'd been standing next to the strange black monolith, where nothing seemed to have changed. Maybe it made more sense to ask: What was he? It seemed that a big change had taken place. Liwei smiled. He'd never liked to think about death. He'd always felt that the day he was going to die was just as far off as it had always been. That was probably why he now found it so difficult to admit to himself that he'd died.

But he'd always believed that when people died, their

consciousness also disappeared. Maybe he'd been mistaken. That actually made him rather uncomfortable. Life after death was a topic for the various religions of the world. Liwei had always prided himself on employing the scientific method.

Fine. Who said it was impossible? He observed himself. In order to be able to come up with a theory about his condition, first he had to learn as much as possible about it.

Item one: his physical reactions. They worked. When he imagined chocolate cake, his mouth watered. If he pictured a naked woman, his penis got hard. If he moved his arms back and forth as fast as he could, sweat started running down his forehead.

Item two: the outside world. He scraped his feet in the moon dust, stirring it up. He took a step forward and his helmet knocked against the monolith. One step to the side... Hold on. That hadn't worked. He couldn't step to the side. This wasn't the reality he was familiar with. Or was it? When you reached the North Pole, a step in any direction headed south. It was impossible to go east or west. And of course it wasn't possible to go north, either – otherwise you wouldn't be at the North Pole.

There were two possibilities. He might be at one of this world's poles, and everything started here, at least locally. There could of course be other poles, but they were far away. For now, it didn't matter what kind of pole it was. It depended on the geometry he was moving in. What we see is not what actually is. A road that looks completely straight actually follows the curvature of the Earth.

Or – and that was precisely it, the Or was still missing. Or he was dreaming? What a stupid scenario. If he assumed that he was dreaming, he might as well believe that the religions were right and that he'd ended up in heaven or hell. Paradise was in fact nothing more than a perpetual dream, and its opposite was a nightmare. It wouldn't be unpleasant for him, but it would be dull.

Thesis: He was alive at one of the world's poles. In order

for that to become a theory, it had to be possible to disprove it. An idea that couldn't be refuted could not be used as a scientific theory. He had to find a way to show either that he was dead or that he could still move forward. Or backwards.

Liwei looked at the clock display on the small computer he wore on his wrist. Even though the battery was still almost full, it had stopped. But it couldn't stop. His suit's system clock kept it moving ahead, one microsecond after the other. So no time had passed since he touched the stele. For a moment, which under these circumstances could have been a lifetime, he was startled. Was this all just a dream? He walked forward far enough for his helmet to come up against the stele. There he turned around. His gaze fell on a person in a spacesuit with Chinese national emblems on it. Liwei gulped. It was him.

Around the campfire

Dear readers,

I had a lot of fun traveling to the moon with you this time. Even when I was a boy, I was fascinated by the "extraterrestrial" celestial body that's closest to us. I thought it was amazing that there were people walking around on the stark disk I saw looming so large in the night sky. However, since I grew up in East Germany, I wasn't so much influenced by the images of the Apollo landing as the "Lunokhod" lunar mobile, similar to the NASA rovers on Mars today, that the then-Soviet Union drove around up there.

Later, I lost sight of the moon. As fascinating as its landscapes may be, it's pretty dead up there. Unlike the large moons of the outer solar system, for example, we won't be finding life on Luna, and even finding traces of past life, as is hoped for on Mars, is pretty much out of the question on the moon. What would it be like if Enceladus orbited the Earth? Cosmologically, this is quite impossible, not because Enceladus is too big for the Earth (Saturn's moon is a lot smaller than Luna), but because in the early days of the solar system, no icy moon could have been born so far from the ice edge.

Meanwhile, NASA – along with many others – are making serious efforts to return to the moon. The technology is essentially still the same, only slightly modernized. What have changed are the standards (today, nobody would fly into space with the safety margins considered acceptable in the past) and the organization. It is much less a race motivated by a desire for prestige and much more of an international cooperative, meaning that equipment from many countries is being used on the moon. I'm very excited about what the future has in store, even if I won't be there myself. I don't think there will be any tourists flying to the moon in my lifetime (I'm fifty-seven). I'm certain that I'll make it into orbit (William Shatner, "Captain Kirk" of the Enterprise, was ninety years old when he took a trip into space), but not any further than that.

That said, there is something of a competitive element this time, since China has also announced that it has a lunar program. The US would certainly lose its status as the number-one space power if China were to surpass it in this regard.

How likely is it that we'll dig up a monolith on the moon? I do address this topic a bit in the novel. The truthful answer is: very unlikely. But that applies to pretty much every fictional storyline. Being murdered on the German island of Sylt or falling in love with a prince are also very unlikely. The main problem with the universe is how unimaginably big it is and the overwhelming number of worlds it contains. Why would anybody leave something behind on the Earth's moon, of all places? A typical human response would be, "because of us." The question is, of course, whether we really are so special in the interstellar competition that it would be worth traveling thousands of years to pay us a visit.

And who was Cao Cao? Jinjin quotes a proverb, the Chinese version of "speak of the devil," containing this name. Cao Cao was a general, a strategist, a politician, and a poet who lived from 155-220 CE. It is said that he was a tyrant, who ruled without mercy but also acted with military wisdom. He later turned to poetry and wrote about the art of war. He is an especially sinister figure in Chinese opera, which explains the blatant threat in the proverb.

In my work, I always try to portray both the locations and the people involved as realistically as possible. There is, however, no "Eleventh Bureau." China's Ministry of State Security is divided into ten bureaus, and each one has a different set of responsibilities. While writing the novel, I made the assumption that the state believes in the "Dark Forest" theory, which is very popular in China and which Cixin Liu expounds on in his "Three-Body Problem" trilogy. That is quite likely. As I experienced last fall with the Chinese translation of my novel *The Disturbance*, being a science fiction author in China means being asked about this theory in practically every conversation you have.

It is a relatively bleak theory, since it states that any civilization that wants to survive needs to destroy any other civilization it encounters. This is based on the idea that real communication is impossible – and thus, so is an agreement that people don't want to destroy each other. Humanity, then, is moving through a dark forest full of predators. And what is it important to avoid doing there? Screaming and attracting the predators, which is just what we're doing with the messages that we send into space.

And what's my opinion on this? I believe that any civilization developed enough to visit us would have no need to destroy us. It would also have developed a way of communicating with us. If it hadn't, why would it make the long voyage? Nobody would be willing to do that unless there was a mutually satisfying conversation at the end of it.

Just like this one that we're having around a campfire on a warm summer night. Branches are crackling in the fire and the moon's just risen above the horizon. It looks so big that maybe we could even see the Dewar crater if it weren't on the far side.

I look forward to continuing the conversation at the end of my next book!

If you liked the book, may I propose to write a short review here? hard-sf.com/links/4542900

Kind regards,

Brandon Q. Morris

PS: What happens next at the black monolith? Where the hell is Liwei? Will there be an international conflict? What will Ron Hudson do when the others try to save him? In *The Luna Monolith 2*, we once again set out for an exciting space journey. I promise that the ending is quite a surprise. Pre-order now: hard-sf.com/links/4542979

PPS: Would you like an overview of the locations mentioned in the book? I used this great map from NASA. You can even print it out! https://www.lpi.usra.edu/resources/mapcatalog/LMP/lmp2/300dpi.jpg

PPPS: As always, you'll get a color PDF of the moon biography if you sign up for it at hard-sf.com/subscribe.

PPPPS: The "event" referred to in this book is described in detail in my novel *The Hole*. A young astronomer discovers a black hole heading for the Earth, but nobody believes her. You can find the novel here: hard-sf.com/links/527017

facebook.com/BrandonQMorris

amazon.com/author/brandonqmorris

bookbub.com/authors/brandon-q-morris

goodreads.com/brandonqmorris

youtube.com/HardSF

instagram.com/brandonqmorris

The guided tour to the moon

THE MOON HAS ACCOMPANIED THE EARTH ALMOST SINCE THE beginning, 50 million years after the formation of the Earth. This celestial body that our ancestors marveled at by night, and in some cases prayed to, was probably caused by a grazing shot. A protoplanet roughly twice the size of Mars is assumed to have impacted the young Earth, moving at a speed of a few kilometers per second. This caused large pieces of the Earth's mass to be flung into its orbit, which eventually formed the moon. The culprit then integrated its mass (including iron core) into the Earth.

This whole process would have taken a year at the most to complete – the blink of an eye in astronomical terms. At that time the moon hovered at a very low orbit (30,000 to 50,000 kilometers) above the Earth, and only later did it move to its current orbit path, in several stages.

A double planet

The result was a system that is otherwise unknown in the Solar System, which more closely resembles a binary planet. No other moon is as large as ours in comparison to its planet; in the entire Solar System, the moon takes fifth place in terms of size, and even the planet Mercury is not much larger.

However, the mass ratio is 81:1. The center of gravity between the Earth and the moon is therefore located very close to the center of the Earth, about 1600 kilometers below the Earth's surface. This makes it look from the outside as though the moon is simply circling the Earth.

The moon's orbit is elliptical; sometimes it's 356,410 kilometers from the Earth, sometimes 406,679 kilometers. This is not insignificant for space missions to the moon. But this distance does not influence our perception of the moon in the sky. Though it sometimes looks much larger when it's just above the horizon, this is an optical illusion.

The moon's structure

The internal structure of the moon was determined by the way it formed. After breaking away, its surface was completely melted due to the energy released by this process. This allowed lighter substances to rise to the surface, where they formed a thin crust, while the substances with more mass were drawn toward its interior. When the moon was young, its crust was continuously bombarded with large asteroids, which caused it to fissure and allow new magma to flow out. In addition, the moon was heated by the strong tidal forces exerted on it by the Earth.

The bombardment ended over three billion years ago. Due to its changed orbit, the gravitational heating also ceased to be a factor. So only the residual heat in the core remains, at 800-1400 degrees Celsius. Nor is volcanism any longer apparent on the surface. The moon's core is relatively small, which means it doesn't have a strong magnetic field like that of the Earth.

The effect of the Earth's pull on the moon is nevertheless still evident – on one hand through moonquakes, which register up to 5 on the Richter Scale and reduce the tension caused by gravity.

On the other hand, the shape of the moon has altered slightly. Like the Earth, it's thicker at the equator than at the poles. There is also slightly more mass concentrated on the side facing the earth than the far side.

How the moon influences the Earth

Of course, the moon also influences the Earth – and in a completely non-esoteric way. Anyone who lives or vacations near the sea knows about tides that exist due to the pull of the moon. The tides are created because the ocean forms a bulge at the point directly in line with the moon. A second bulge forms on the other side of the Earth, because the centrifugal force of the Earth-moon system is particularly strong there.

This ebb and flow probably greatly simplified the transition of life from sea to land. This phenomenon would still exist without the moon, because the Sun also contributes to the tides due to its enormous mass, but only about half as much as the moon. In fact, only 30 centimeters of the tides are caused by the moon – the rest is created by the ebb and flow of related currents that are able to swell to stronger tides. The tides are highest when the Sun and the moon are in line, that is, at the full and new moon.

The moon also stabilizes the position of the Earth's rotational axis, which currently deviates by only plus or minus 1.3° from its mean of 23.3°. If there was no moon, the Earth would be considerably less stable in the long run, as shown by computer simulations. Within two million years, the tilt of the axis could change to anything from 0 to 60°.

Snow at the equator, 80 degree heat at the poles, seasonal temperature fluctuations from minus 25 to plus 45 degrees Celsius in the temperate latitudes – life would certainly look different without the moon.

Taking a walk on the moon

Unfortunately, when you land on the moon, you can't take off your helmet. Due to its low weight, the moon was only able to retain a very modest atmosphere, consisting of helium, neon, hydrogen and argon. This was largely transported by the solar winds. The noble gas, argon, comes from the interior of the moon, as a byproduct of decaying radioactive potassium isotopes. The pressure on the moon's surface is quadrillions of times lower than that of the Earth.

Because the moon only possesses around a sixth of the Earth's gravity, you can theoretically move across its surface in huge leaps. Unfortunately, it looks a bit different in practice. This is because of the way the 'jump' phenomenon works. Your maximum jump height depends on the depth of your crouch, your body's strength, its mass and the pull of the celestial body.

If you were able to jump 50 centimeters on Earth, and could beam yourself onto the moon in a tracksuit, then you'd need a room at least five meters high in order not to hit your head on the ceiling.

However, if your movement is restricted by a spacesuit (which you also need because of the temperatures ranging between minus 160 degrees and plus 130 degrees Celsius), which also adds more weight (at least another 50 kilograms – but don't worry, they only feel like eight kilograms), then you can count yourself lucky if you even manage to match your Earth jump height.

Water on the moon

The early bombardment of the moon is still easily discernible in its craters, which reach sizes of up to 2240 kilometers across, such as the 13 kilometer-deep South Pole-Aitken basin. On the far side of the moon their number is even higher than on the near side. The crater walls often look steep on images from space probes. But this is due to the shadows that enhance this effect.

They actually only have gradients of a few degrees. So, driving into them would not pose problems for our moon mobile. Not observable from Earth are the grooves: these could be lava flows that have erupted over time. Even longer are the lunar furrows (up to 400 kilometers), created by tensions in the lunar crust caused by the cooling of the celestial body.

Water has never flowed along the channels on the moon. Erosion on the moon is caused exclusively by the relentless solar winds. However, the moon is not completely dry, as shown by NASA's LCROSS experiment in 2010. This involved crashing two missiles into areas near the poles that are not illuminated by the sun. Water ice crystals were detected in the resulting loosened material, probably deposited on the moon by meteorites – similar to Mercury. The possibility of extracting oxygen from the regolith means that at least the most important substances are available for the construction of a permanent moon base.

Anyone wanting to survive on the moon long-term (for example in a base there) would need water. Although it's long been known that there is water to be found in the depths of the lunar rock, it's obviously easier to acquire it directly from the surface. A research team led by Shuai Li of the University of Hawaii and Brown University, using data from the NASA's Moon Mineralogy Mapper (M3) instrument, revealed that there is water in the craters at the South and North Poles just waiting to be extracted.

The M3 was launched in 2008 aboard the Indian Chandrayaan-1 probe. Most of the ice is located at the poles, specifically in craters that are never reached by the light of the Sun. The temperatures there never exceed 110 Kelvin (minus 63 degrees Celsius). However, the researchers found surprisingly little ice overall. They suspect this is due to the fact that only very occasional water-rich bodies have landed there. Existing ice deposits could have been destroyed during a pole migration.

No dark side

There isn't actually a dark side of the moon. But it does always turn the same side to the Earth. We can speak of a bound rotation: the moon turns exactly once on its own axis each time it circles the Earth. However, the side that has long been hidden from human view is not darker, but is in fact somewhat lighter than the side that faces us. The Sun shines on it just as often, but it possesses a significantly thicker crust. This meant that it was rare for dark 'seas' to form here when the moon was young. Many asteroids were unable to disrupt the surface. This is why the far side appears lighter from a distance.

But not only that – on the moon you can even find areas in permanent light. The edges of the Peary Crater near the north pole are perpetually lit by the Sun.

Exploration of the moon

The moon is so far the only foreign celestial body that humans have set foot on. The race to the moon, won by the US the end, is legendary.

Apollo on the moon

In July 1960 no American had yet entered the Earth's orbit. Nevertheless, NASA and the space industry met in Washington to work on further plans for space travel. At first, they were only considering circumnavigating the moon. Abe Silverstein of NASA suggested the name of the god Apollo for this.

When, on April 12, 1961, Yuri Gagarin was launched into space and the Soviet Union won the first space race, the moon quickly became a top priority. On May 25, President John F. Kennedy gave his famous speech to Congress, calling for a human to be sent to the moon and returned that decade: "I believe that this nation should commit itself to achieving the goal, before this decade is out, of landing a man on the moon and returning him safely to the earth. No single space project in this period will be more impressive to mankind or more important for the long-range exploration of space; and none will be so difficult or expensive to accomplish."

It was not certain at the beginning what a spacecraft would look like. At first we thought of a single spacecraft for outward and return flights and landing, because the technology for docking maneuvers in space was not yet available. The following concepts were available to choose from:

• Direct flight with a rocket from the surface of the Earth to the surface of the moon and back

• Assembly of the ship in orbit, then direct flight

• Flight with rendezvous maneuver in orbit

• Direct flight with refueling on the moon's surface – an automated supply ship having landed the fuel there prior

It turned out that none of these concepts were able to be realized. The Saturn V rocket was too weak for the direct flight, and assembly in space would have required many launches (up to 15). In the end, spacecraft and lander were separated. That allowed each to be better optimized for its purpose.

Initially, NASA made provisions for seven missions leading up to the first landing, assigned the letters A to G, later adding H to J.

A: Unmanned test of Saturn V and Apollo spacecraft (Apollo 4 + Apollo 6)

B: Unmanned test of the Lunar Module (Apollo 5)

C: Manned test of the Apollo spacecraft (Apollo 7)

C': First moon circumnavigation at the end of 1968, unscheduled

D: Test of command module and lander in a low Earth orbit (Apollo 9)

E: Test of command module and lander in a remote Earth orbit (canceled in favor of C')

F: Test of command module and lander in moon orbit (Apollo 10)

G: First moon landing (Apollo 11)

H: Moon landing with additional experiments (Apollo 12 and 14)

I: Manned flight into moon orbit for research without landing (canceled)

J: Moon landing with rover (Apollo 15, 16 and 17)

The program ended with Apollo 17, although NASA would probably have liked to have continued it. The USA spent a total of 23.9 billion dollars, which is equivalent to about 200 billion dollars today.

The series of Apollo tests began with a catastrophe. During a test on the ground, a fire broke out in the capsule later called 'Apollo 1'. The astronauts Virgil Grissom, Edward H. White and Roger B. Chaffee died as a result.

The program reached its goal on July 20, 1969, with Apollo 11 landing on the moon and returning safely. On July 21, at 03:56:20 MEZ, Neil Armstrong stepped into Mare Tranquillitatis as the first human on the moon, with the famous sentence: "That's one small step for man, one giant leap for mankind."

So far a total of twelve Americans have walked on the moon. Eugene Cernan – commander of Apollo 17 – is the last person to have been on the moon to date.

How the Soviet Union missed out on the moon

After the launch of Sputnik 1 in October of 1957, and Vostok 1 carrying the first man in space, Yuri Gagarin, in April of 1961, the Soviet Union had twice won the race of the super-powers. Two days after Gagarin's return, President Kennedy had initiated the race to the moon, a fact known to very few at that point. On May 25, Kennedy announced the program officially.

The Soviet leadership reacted to this hesitantly – perhaps shying away from the costs. The challenges were huge. The launcher load capacity had to be increased from under ten tonnes to around one hundred tonnes. The previous space capsules were far too small for a multi-day journey to the moon. The docking technology was still in its teething stage, and there was no landing module. And the scientists would actually have preferred to get to Mars, as it was significantly more attractive as an object of exploration than the moon. As early as the 1950s, Soviet engineers had been planning a comprehensive expedition to our neighboring planets. Among them was the design bureau OKB-1, today known as RSC Energia. N1 designer Korolev later explained that the first designs for the heavy-lift rocket came about as part of a possible Mars expedition.

The plans were phenomenal: with 20 to 25 N1 launchers in orbit, they wanted to build a 1600 tonne Mars spacecraft (MPK) that would reach the red planet after 270 days of flight time, depositing a lander there. A year later, the ship was to fly back to Earth. However, the concept was soon classified as unrealistic and was downsized. The 'TMK', designed in 1959, was to weigh only 75 tonnes and fly to Mars manned by three cosmonauts. A modified concept included an additional circumnavigation of Venus. In 1966, shortly before all resources were concentrated on the race to the moon, Korolev's bureau designed yet another comprehensive landing mission that was to launch in 1980.

In 1962, OKB-1 then began to evaluate various moon flight projects. Based on the Mars concepts and the 75-tonne-capacity N1 rocket, the preferred scenario at first was to bring a lunar spacecraft into orbit with three N1 launchers and two tankers that were to supply the lunar spacecraft with the necessary fuel. But a lunar station (L4) was also discussed, intended to serve as a launching point for further space exploration – in other words, an early precursor to NASA's Lunar Gateway. These complex schemes were then reduced to the L3 project, which consisted of the N1 rocket, the 'LOK' spacecraft equipped with two boosters and the 'LK' lander. There were to be two cosmonauts on board, one of whom would have performed an EVA (extravehicular activity) while in the moon's orbit and transferred into the LK, using that to land for 6-24 hours.

At the same time, Vladimir Chelomey OKB-52 space agency was working on concepts for orbiting the moon based on the Proton rocket and a two-seater Soyuz capsule. On August 1, 1964, this allocation was confirmed by decree of the Council of Ministers. "We must not leave the moon to the Americans," Nikita Khrushchev is supposed to have said. "We will provide everything that is needed."

However, Khrushchev was already history by the time the L3 project was officially adopted in February of 1965 – with its first flight to the moon planned for November, 1967. The division of the moon program between various design bureaus, which had long developed into independent companies, delayed development. A total of 500 organizations from 26 Ministries participated, all of which had to be coordinated. Chief designer Korolev died in 1966. It soon became obvious that the lack of powerful propulsion units was a disadvantage in the development of heavy-lift rockets. The N1 was originally designed for 75 tonnes. But a lunar spacecraft had to be able to handle 95 tonnes. Although the first stage of the American Saturn V only required five of the huge F-1 propulsion units, the first stage of the N1 required 30 propulsion units, which were difficult to coordinate.

Korolev's successor Vasily Mishin evidently lacked the political influence and skill to move the project forward quickly. In February 1967 a new government decision was issued that prioritized the program and, significantly, now included the military, who completed the groundwork for the launch facilities. However, when the launch ramp was finished, it could only be tested with a dummy. The first fully-equipped rocket wasn't ready until 1968. It was to be launched for the first time on February 21, 1969 – but it was a false start. The second attempt, three weeks before the US moon landing, ended with an explosion that destroyed part of the launching system. Launches three and four in 1971 and 1972 were also failures, at which point, in 1974, work on the N1 and the moon landing program was terminated.

The part of the program concerned with moon circumnavigations was no less plagued by problems. Unmanned L1-series (later 'Zond') spacecraft launched by Proton rockets kept dropping out at various stages of their journey. Some attempts at a rendezvous between two Soyuz capsules in space were successful. In September of 1968, five unmanned (but with two turtles on board) Zonds reached the moon, approached the far side at a distance of 1960 kilometers from the surface, flew back to Earth and finally landed, not in Kazakhstan as planned, but in the Indian Ocean. The two animals survived, but were dissected 39 days later. Zond 6 repeated this performance in November of 1968, but was beset by so many problems that a manned flight was deemed too risky (this time the turtles died upon landing). If Zond 6 had been successful, they would still have attempted to beat the Americans at their (announced) manned circumnavigation of the moon in December. By then it was too late, with Armstrong and Aldrin landing on the satellite in July, 1969.

And yet the efforts of the Soviet Union were not completely unsuccessful – a fact that is sometimes overshadowed by the failures of the landing schedules. Luna 2 was the first man-made object on the moon, in September of 1959. A month later, Luna 3 sent the first photos of the far side of the moon. On January 31, 1966 the Luna 9 probe managed the first soft landing on the moon, in Oceanus Procellarum. The probe measured radiation levels on the surface and sent images to Earth. The probes were all launched by launchers derived from R7 intercontinental missiles. Even today's Soyuz rocket comes from this line.

The lunar orbiting program, which relied on the Proton rocket, demonstrated successes with unmanned probes from 1970 onwards. Luna 16 (September 1970) was able to bring the first moon rock back to Earth. Luna 17 deposited the Lunokhod 1 rover – the first vehicle to explore another celestial body. From November 17, 1970 to October 4, 1971 it covered over ten kilometers, created 20,000 images and analyzed 500 ground samples. Even more successful was Lunokhod 2, which landed on January 15, 1973 aboard Luna 21 on the southern edge of the Le Monnier Crater in the transition zone between the Mare Serenitatis and the Taurus

Mountains. It was controlled remotely and covered 39 kilometers on the moon in five months – a record that was only broken in 2014 by the Opportunity rover on Mars. Lunokhod 2 – 1.35m high, 2.2m long and 1.6m wide – drove across the landscape on eight wheels at 2-3km/h, explored the terrain and shot over 80,000 suitable TV images. Anyone who grew up in former East Germany would be more likely to recall these images from childhood memories than the words of the first American on the moon. An interesting fact: Lunokhod 2 now belongs to an American. Sotheby's auction house auctioned it together with Luna 21 in December of 1993 as the first object not located on Earth, for 68,000 dollars. The buyer was Richard Garriott, son of the US astronaut Owen Garriott, who reputedly paid 30 million dollars to be a private astronaut on the ISS.

After the failures of the past, Russia now really wants to be part of the next planned conquest of the moon. This was declared at the start of 2019 by the head of the rocket building company Energia, Vladimir Solntsev. But the nation does not want to enter into a race. For example, Andrey Ionin from the Russian Academy of Cosmonautics denounced President Trump's plans to put an astronaut on the moon by 2024, and described the plan as being "motivated by domestic policy". The Russian plans are also less ambitious. A four-sided, reusable spacecraft currently in development, called 'Federatsiya' (which also replaces the Soyuz series) is due to launch on the new, super-heavy 'Yenisei' rocket from 2028 and set down cosmonauts on the moon for the first time in about 2031.

Where moon journeys meet jade hares

Not only Russian and US satellites have reached the moon – it's already had visitors from five other countries.

On April 10, 1993, the first satellite not built in the Soviet Union/Russia or the USA arrived on the moon: 200 kilograms of Japanese electronics that future visitors are likely to find on the edge of a crater at 34° 18′ south and 55° 36′ east. The JAXA space agency launched the 200 kilogram 'Hiten' probe in preparation for later scientific missions. It only contained a sensor for measuring the concentration of dust between the Earth and moon. It released its sister probe 'Hagoromo' in orbit, but contact with this was soon lost.

Hiten was the precursor to a new race to the moon, which at the turn of the new millennium no longer involved just the two old superpowers, but also aspiring nations such as Japan, China and India. The next visitor to the moon was the Lunar Prospector from the USA in 1999, but by this time Europe was also lining up. SMART-1 reached lunar orbit in 2004 with the help of an ion thruster, and touched down on Earth's companion on schedule in 2006. The main goal of SMART-1 was to test a new type of propulsion, but the probe also analyzed the composition of the moon's surface. Even the impact in the Lacus Excellentiae formation was used for this purpose: the probe was made to hit in a way that the material thrown up by it could be studied via telescope on Earth.

The age of poetic probe names began in 2009. 'Kaguya', a Japanese moon princess, 'Chang'e', a Chinese moon goddess and 'Chandrayaan-1' (Hindi for 'moon journey') all reached the moon. Chandrayaan-1 is still in orbit today, but dropped a 29-kilogram Moon Impact Probe (MIP) that hit the surface on November 14, 2008, the birthday of former Indian Prime Minister Jawaharlal Nehru, after having sent pictures and data during its descent. The Japanese Kaguya probe delivered the first HDTV images from the moon, discovered evidence of moon caves and measured the surface three-dimensionally. For example, it was the first time the depth of the Pythagoras Crater was measured precisely at 4800 meters.

Chang'e was the beginning of a whole series of successful Chinese lunar missions. Chang'e-2 visited the moon and the near-Earth Toutatis Asteroid. Chang'e-3 dropped the 'Yutu' (jade hare) rover on December 14, 2013. It only managed 114 meters and then refused to travel further, but has remained in contact with the ground station for years. Chang'e-4 landed the Yutu-2 rover on the far side of the moon for the first time on January 3, 2019. In addition to cameras, radar and spectrometers it also has a neutron and radiation dose detector from Germany on board.

In April, 2019 Israel also became a 'moon nation' with its Beresheet probe. The partially privately funded project, which among other things was to plant an Israeli flag on the moon, only managed a hard landing. But a successor, the Beresheet-2, is planned.

And in the future the moon will continue to have visitors. Chandrayaan-2 will come from India, China is already planning Chang'e-5, which is intended to bring back ground samples. South Korea wants to go to the moon for the first time with 'KARL' (Korea Pathfinder Lunar Orbiter). And Germany is another: the PTScientists development team based in Berlin intends to deposit two rovers using the 'Alina' lander, near the Apollo-17 landing site. Sponsors include Audi and Vodafone, and the rovers are currently called 'Audi lunar quattros'.

Seas, mountains, rivers

Best you pack a moon mobile for our little tour. Make sure you have reasonable tires, as the surface of the moon is almost completely covered in a meter-thick layer of dust and sand composed of ash-gray regolith. This is a material that has been pulverized by numerous meteorite impacts, caked together again and then loaded with other elements by the solar winds.

We'll begin at a 'sea', a Mare (plural Maria), as the dark lowlands are called, and which early astronomers mistook for oceans. Here the bottom consists of dark basalt, solidified lava that sprang from holes in the moon's crust caused by asteroid impacts over three billion years ago.

The seas are bordered by highlands, as you'd expect, recognizable by the name 'Terra'. These are up to 4.5 billion years old and formed the original lunar crust. They are traversed by valleys (typically only a few hundred meters deep) and mountain ranges that rise up to ten kilometers in height.

The lunar seas – their beauty, and how they were named

Mare Crisium

The wide plain presents its best side in the lunar morning sun.

Despite the name, these remarkable landscape features ('maria' from the Latin, stressed on the first syllable) are obviously not open bodies of water. They are large basins, mostly impact craters, which were filled with cooling lava billions of years ago. In early times long before the invention of the telescope it was thought that these dark marks, visible to the naked eye from Earth, were seas. But for about four hundred years we have conclusively known that they are solid ground. There are no waves breaking on a coast and no breeze to be felt.

The Mare Crisium ('Sea of Crises') is the largest self-contained 'sea' on the near side of the moon. It is roughly oval, 570 by 450 kilometers, with its longer axis extending east to west. Seen from the Earth, it lies on the eastern edge of the satellite. It appears to be higher than it is wide, because its proportions are distorted by the oblique angle. Thanks to its peripheral position and distinctive shape, it's a good indicator of libration even without a telescope.

Libration is the slight oscillation of the moon, a 'wagging' motion during the course of the month. This means that from Earth we see 59 percent of the surface; only 41 percent is perpetually hidden. Due to libration, the details of the landscape also shift, which is particularly noticeable at the edges. Looking at the Mare Crisium an experienced observer can tell which stage of libration our satellite is in.

When this oscillation brings the eastern edge more into view, the Mare Crisium is particularly easy to recognize.

When the celestial body turns to the west, the sea shifts to the edge and appears significantly narrower. When there is a waxing moon in the evening sky, the libration favors the Mare Crisium; as the cycle progresses, the Sea of Crises is pushed closer and closer to the edge of our satellite.

The oval, clean-edged Mare Crisium throws a clear shadow along the night-day boundary of the thin, right-side crescent moon, like a dent. A day later, when it lies in the rays of the lunar morning light, the sea offers a spectacular view – especially through a telescope. Then it looks like an enormous, flooded crater (which it is). To the west, rugged mountain ranges rise, gleaming in the light.

When lit obliquely, a concentrated pattern of furrows is visible. These ridges are located about fifty kilometers from the edge of the Mare and form a partially broken inner ring. The most massive furrow, the 300-kilometer-long Dorsum Oppel, extends in an arc up from the filled-in Yerkes Crater (36 kilometers wide) along the north-western periphery of the Mare. In the northern section, the Dorsum is crossed by several ridgelines coming from the edge of the Mare.

To the north-east there are smaller furrows such as the Dorsa Tetyaev group (150 kilometers long) or the Dorsa Harker (200 kilometers). When the Sun climbs higher, its rays play across the marbled surface of the Mare Crisium in varying colors: for example, in the light from the bright impact crater, Proclus (28 kilometers across, to the west). At noon other such craters appear, including Picard, Peirce and Greaves.

A few days after the full moon, the Mare Crisium begins to throw shadows on its western edge and its eastern extremities disappear into the dark of the night-day boundary. The mountains to the west gleam in the sunlight. On the eastern edge there is a noticeable gap, through which lava flows once blazed their way. Among other things, they formed the Mare Anguis ('Serpent Sea'), one of the smallest lunar Maria. This appears as an irregular, 200-kilometer long mark.

From the south-eastern edge a mountainous promontory

juts into the Mare Crisium – the Promontorium Agarum. There is much more to see in this sea and its surrounding areas during the two weeks per month in which it is lit – a great object of study.

Tip

The Mare Crisium is particularly impressive when you observe it through a telescope or similar. In the morning sun it appears as a mighty, flooded crater. An additional moon filter increases the contrast and suppresses disruptive light reflections.

Mare Humboldtianum

During favorable libration, this sea is a fascinating object to study.

Let's turn to the extreme edge of the moon and take a look at the Mare Humboldtianum – a sea only just visible from the Earth. It lies in the north-eastern part of the satellite, a dark spot about 270 kilometers in diameter. This sea is on the near side but its eastern spurs reach 90 degrees of longitude.

As the moon needs exactly the same amount of time to turn on its axis as it does to circle the Earth, the same side is always facing us. This should lead us to conclude that the Mare Humboldtianum would always be visible when it is lit by the Sun. That this is not the case is due to the phenomenon known as libration, described under Mare Crisium.

Libration has various causes, but the main effect is triggered by the moon's elliptical course in combination with its monthly axial spin. Libration sometimes causes landscape features on the far side to come into view, and sometimes areas on the near side disappear temporarily from the focus of the telescope – this includes the Mare Humboldtianum.

When libration is unfavorable (when the south-western section of the moon is easily visible), the Mare Humboldtianum shifts towards and over the north-eastern edge until you can no longer see it. Favorable libration, on the other hand, brings the north-eastern spurs into view (if the lighting is good). The sea can then be easily made out through binoculars.

This is the case in March, for example; a good opportunity also to see the smaller, lesser-known seas on our satellite more precisely. But let's stick with the Mare Humboldtianum. It's a dark patch of solidified lava, with a diameter of 273 kilometers, in the center of a large, old impact crater itself measuring 650 kilometers, the eastern spurs of which stretch a long way around the far side of the moon. The impact took place around 3.8 billion years ago.

Later impacts furrowed the Mare Humboldtianum. Smaller ones threw up rock that displays different colors depending on the light. On the north-eastern flank of the sea the 200-kilometer Bel'kovich Crater has created a breach. The name Mare Humboldtianum was coined in 1837 by the German astronomer Johann Mädler, in honor of his compatriot Alexander von Humboldt. This explorer's indomitable spirit, which led him at the end of the 18th and beginning of the 19th century to the discovery of previously uncharted parts of the Earth, was likely an inspiration for Mädler, whose moon globe was in turn praised by Humboldt. Another lunar crater was later named after Mädler (and one on Mars). From above, the Mare Humboldtianum resembles a wide sickle. It was first photographed in October, 1959 by the Soviet Luna 3 probe.

Favorable libration and a waxing moon tip the north-eastern region into view for three to 13 days. That's when the Mare Humboldtianum is especially easy to see.

If you want to observe the Mare Humboldtianum in the evening, the time of maximum libration is the best. The dark spot on the north-eastern edge (top right) is easy to detect with binoculars. A telescope shows even more detail, even when the Sun is high and the lunar landscape relief is not casting long shadows.

Tip

Get this sea in your sights when the libration pulls the north-east edge of the satellite towards us during a waxing moon. An additional moon filter increases the contrast and suppresses disruptive light reflections.

Mare Undarum

Right on the eastern edge of the moon lie a few seas that are only completely visible during favorable libration.

We previously took a look at the Mare Crisium (the 'Sea of Crises'), a large, oval plain on the moon's north-eastern edge – a lunar sea (Latin: Mare) of sufficient size to be able to make it out as a dull patch with the naked eye. The Mare Crisium can be imagined as a large impact crater whose interior was flooded with lava that flowed sometime after the bombardment of the crust.

The libration – the slight oscillation of the satellite on its axis over the course of a month – leads the Mare Crisium to repeatedly tilt into clear view. Either way, the Sea of Crises lies completely on the side of the moon facing us; you can observe it any time the sun is in the right position. But there are groups of smaller seas to the east of the Mare Crisium. None of these formations describe a crisp, oval outline. They are more irregular patches in a variety of shapes.

Roughly one hundred kilometers south-east of the Sea of Crises lies the Mare Undarum (Sea of Waves). It consists of a number of lava-filled craters. Similar to the Mare Crisium, the Mare Undarum is also always on the side of the moon facing the Earth. So, it remains visible regardless of the libration phase. The outline of the Mare Undarum is irregular. It measures about a hundred kilometers from north to south and double that from east to west. The only effect the libration has is that the appearance of the seas – seen from Earth – is more or less squashed. Further to the east of the Mare Crisium lie two other seas of considerable size. They lie directly on the 90th eastern degree of longitude, which forms the border between the visible and the hidden sides of the moon. These are the Mare Marginis (Sea of the Edge) and the Mare Smythii (Sea of Smyth).

The Mare Marginis is located to the east of the Mare Crisium. It has an irregular outline, is 360 kilometers wide and lies in the libration zone. During strong oscillation this Sea disappears almost completely from view. Normally, however, you can make it out from a waxing half-moon up to a full moon. The Mare Smythii (named after a British astronaut) also lies in this region. It measures around 200 kilometers in diameter. Its silhouette is almost circular, but quite faintly defined.

During favorable libration the Sea of Smyth presents itself to an Earth-bound observer to its full extent, but the oblique angle makes it seem narrower than it is. Like the Sea of the Edge, it consists of several lava-filled craters and sometimes disappears beyond the edge.

Mare Imbrium

The much visited eye of the man in the moon.

One of the first science fiction films appeared in 1902: 'A Trip to the Moon' by cinema pioneer Georges Méliès, based on two Jules Verne novels on related topics. One scene shows the distressed face of the 'Man in the Moon', who has an oversized projectile in his right eye (left for the viewer); according to Jules Verne, the capsule was fired from a giant cannon. When we look up today, the eye is luckily unscathed – the Mare Imbrium, or Sea of Rains.

Like all large lunar seas, the Mare Imbrium is also an impact basin – a crater formed in the early days of the solar system when a celestial body hit the moon's surface. Scientists surmise that a 250 kilometer proto planet impacted here 3.9 billion years ago. The collision left behind a 1,200 kilometer wide pit that today is known as the Mare Imbrium.

Even through binoculars the Sea of Rains looks impressive. Manned and unmanned spacecraft have landed on it and it has become apparent that the Mare Imbrium is indeed a fascinating place. The vast plain of frozen lava is strewn with countless craters. To the east rise the Apennine Mountains, to the north is the Plato Crater, with its dark floor, and in the north-west its edge bulges out to form Sinus Iridum, the Bay of Rainbows. When the Sun's rays hit at a sharp angle, you can see that the seemingly smooth surface is as wrinkled as unpressed linen.

Over the years, several large missions have selected Mare Imbrium as a landing site, due to the highly interesting and diversified geology that's evident there. The Russian Luna 17 probe landed there in 1970. On board was the Lunokhod lunar vehicle, the first rover to explore a celestial body. A year later, Apollo 15 landed near the Hadley Rille, a 1.6 kilometer long, winding moon valley. Dave Scott and James Irwin wound through here with the Lunar Roving Vehicle (LRV). It was to be another forty years before another vehicle left its tracks in the dust of the Mare Imbrium: the Yutu (jade hare) rover, set down by the Chinese Chang'e 3 probe. This rover functioned for 31 months and transmitted numerous spectacular images.

The Sea of Rains lies in darkness until the terminator (the night-day boundary) wanders across the peaks of the Apennine Mountains to the east of the plain. A few days later, the Mare Imbrium is already half illuminated, and a few days after that it lies in full sunlight.

This is the best time to observe the most prominent craters in the eastern half – Archimedes and its smaller northern neighbors Autolycus and Aristillus – and the many ridges and furrows. The Sea of Rains presents itself in its best light for ten days, until the terminator roams back over the surface and the region disappears again into the darkness of the lunar night.

Tip

Observe the Mare Imbrium when the terminator has just reached it; then you can see all the small craters and details.

Mare Orientale

An impressive structure that we only rarely get to see.

Most of the landscapes and places of interest that we have visited on our tour here can be quite clearly made out – deep craters, long, jagged mountain ranges, large plains and so on. The place that we are now concerned with is a bit more challenging. To be precise, it can only be observed from the Earth for a few days.

The Mare Orientale, with its surrounding mountains, forms one of the largest and most imposing structures on the moon. If it lay on the side facing the Earth, it would dominate the face of our satellite and would have found its expression in diverse religions and cultures. But the original crater was blasted out so far to the west that today's plain is mostly hidden from view. Only if the libration – the oscillation of the moon on its own axis – is particularly strong, can we sometimes peek around its western edge. Then a truly breathtaking landscape is revealed.

Only the amazed, wide eyes of the Apollo astronauts and the clicking cameras of the rovers have glimpsed the Mare Orientale in its full splendor. One of the youngest impact structures spread out before them, blasted out almost four billion years ago by an asteroid measuring over sixty kilometers.

The catastrophic hit left a 327 kilometer crater behind, which later filled with lava; then it cooled to form a vast plain. If you include the concentric rings of the surrounding mountain ranges you have a structure measuring over 900 kilometers in diameter. If you imagine that the Mare Orientale lay on the near side of the moon, our satellite would have a kind of giant cyclops eye staring down at us. Now imagine that during a lunar eclipse, when the scene is drenched in blood-red light. It's interesting to ponder how priests from various religions would have interpreted such a spectacle.

However, the opportunities to glimpse the sea are few and far between, and the visibility window is narrow. If you ever get the chance to see the Mare Orientale, you should use it. If the moon's libration turns it in such a way that its western side turns far enough towards us, the 'Eastern Sea' reveals itself with all its encircling mountain ranges. But you need good binoculars, or even better, a telescope. Even then, it's not much more than a region of stark contrasts of light and shadow. But the discovery is still exciting every time.

Where exactly should you look? The easiest way to find the Mare Orientale is to imagine the lunar disc as a dial. The Eastern Sea will appear tilted. When the libration is strongest, point your binoculars or telescope at the 8 o'clock position; here is the dark Grimaldi Crater. To the left below it, at the very edge, you will see something like a number of dark lines that resemble scratches on the surface – that's the Mare Orientale with its numerous mountains.

Of course, the stronger the magnification settings, the more details and landscape features reveal themselves – but even with maximum zoom the circular outlines are not noticeable. And yet that's not so important. What counts is that you've come face to face with something that is normally hidden from view. You can enjoy the fact that you are looking at a structure that most humans have never seen.

Tip

Get hold of a contrast-increasing moon filter if you can. That way the details will appear more clearly.

Mare Tranquillitatis

This is the sea in which humans first set foot on the moon.

The 'Sea of Tranquility' is one of the most famous regions of the moon, for two reasons: it's easy to locate, and the historical Apollo 11 landing took place there. The sea – actually a dark basalt plain – was formed about four billion years ago. At that time there was still volcanism on the moon, before our satellite cooled and retired, so to speak.

The Mare Tranquillitatis has a total diameter of almost 870 kilometers. To illustrate, that's roughly the distance from Indianapolis to Washington DC as the crow flies. When the region lies in sunlight it's not difficult to detect the Sea of Tranquility; you just need good binoculars.

It's best to view the region at times when it's brightly lit. At those times the pale gray surroundings are distinguishable from the dark basalt floor. To find it, you can orient yourself on nearby formations, for example, the Mare Serenitatis (Sea of Serenity), which looks like a snowman. The Mare Nectaris (Sea of Nectar) also borders the Sea of Tranquility, but it's significantly smaller. The Mare Tranquillitatis is quite dark. This makes it difficult to distinguish individual formations, but the shadows especially around the edges display the most differentiated colors.

It's assumed that the region originated in the so-called pre-Nectarian period, that is, a period from 4.5 to 3.9 billion years ago. If we fast-forward to the present, we see a strip of land that has been scarred by countless small impacts. There are ridges, notches and volcanic channels from geologically active times. But when walking around, the feeling is supposed to be like moving around on a layer of powder – the moon is covered with fine dust.

The region became world famous on May 20, 1969, when Neil Armstrong and Buzz Aldrin landed there in the Eagle lunar module from Apollo 11 and climbed out. It was the first time in history that a human had set foot on a foreign celestial body. The landing site was given the name of Tranquility Base. The two of them walked around for six hours, collected ground samples and took photos. They planted the US flag and when they left, they left their ladder behind. This carried a stainless steel plaque that reads "We came in peace for all mankind" and the signature of President Nixon, among others.

It's fun to track down these places and other landing sites of the Apollo missions. All you need is a halfway decent pair of binoculars that can zoom in to the craters on the surface. To find the precise touchdown point of Apollo 11, it's best to search the nearby Theophilus Crater. Once you've located that, draw an imaginary line up towards Mare Tranquillitatis, to where the small but distinct Moltke Crater is located. Directly north-west of there is the landing site. If the telescope and the viewer's eyes allow it, you can also spy three more, very small craters: Aldrin, Armstrong and Collins. The third was named after Michael Collins, the pilot of the Apollo 11 Command Module.

Even before the legendary moon landing, the Sea of Tranquility had had a visit from Earth: on February 20, 1965 the Ranger 8 NASA probe performed a (planned) crash landing, having taken 7,137 photos of the lunar surface during its nosedive.

Two years later, the Surveyor 5 probe managed a soft landing, although it braked too late and ended up thirty kilometers away from the planned landing site. The Mare Tranquillitatis is one of the most well-researched regions of the moon, and inspires the imagination of people all over the globe, which shows up in numerous books and song lyrics.

Tip

The Apollo 11 landing site is easiest to find in direct sunlight; then the small craters around it are also visible.

You may already know that you can receive a colorful PDF version of this biography with lots of images if you request it here: hard-sf.com/subscribe.

Excerpt: The Luna Monolith 2

Dewar Crater, March 8, 2082

"LET ME SEE YOUR FINGER," SAID ANTONIA, WHO WAS standing at the dining table in the kitchen with a cup of tea in front of her. She was smaller than Jinjin remembered her. That was what happened when you only ever saw each other on video chat.

Jinjin raised her left hand, pulled off the protective cap and loosened the bandage around her index finger.

Antonia carefully grasped it by the base and frowned. "It doesn't look good, but surely you know that?"

Jinjin nodded. The finger was blue-black up to the second joint. She didn't feel any pain, but that was because of the injection she'd given herself earlier.

"It needs to be seen to professionally," said Antonia. "Preferably on Earth."

"I'm not leaving the moon without Liwei."

Antonia sighed. "I kind of thought so. I never got the feeling that you were so closely ... connected? Sorry if that's too private for you."

The ESA astronaut was right. The age difference alone was enough to establish a fixed hierarchy. But Liwei had always been very tolerant and encouraged her to make her own decisions.

He's out there somewhere, even if no one can see him anymore.

"I'm only now realizing how much I miss him. Liwei was just always there, like a piece of furniture or a kettle that you need every day."

Antonia smiled and lifted her cup, which had a lid with a spout. "Here's a cup of tea!"

"I hope you don't take that wrong," said Jinjin. "It isn't meant in a derogatory way."

Antonia shook her head. "Not at all. I understand what you mean. But we have to do something about your finger. Sepsis could kill you in a few days. Can we arrange for a shuttle to take you to a clinic on Earth?"

"I don't want that."

"Not without Liwei—I see." She pursed her lips. "Can I take a picture? I'd like to show it to someone."

"Of course."

Antonia took a tablet out of the pocket of her tracksuit, which was a bit too big for her. Jinjin had lent her clothing from Liwei's stock, since her own clothes didn't fit the European woman at all. There was a click as Antonia took a picture of the injured finger.

"Thank you. I have a friend at the military hospital in Turin, an orthopedic surgeon. He'll take a look at it."

"And if it's as bad as it looks?"

"Then we'll have to..." Antonia extended her index and middle fingers and brought them together.

Jinjin swallowed. If there was no other way, it had to be done. She wouldn't leave the moon without Liwei.

●

THERE WAS A KNOCK ON HER BEDROOM DOOR. JINJIN OPENED her eyes. Hopefully it wasn't Antonia. Somehow she suspected that she would have to do without her index finger in future. She looked at the bandage. The finger had started throbbing a while ago. That definitely wasn't a good sign.

Another knock.

"Come in!"

The door opened. She recognized JP first, then Ron. Both were wearing the bottoms of their spacesuits. Ron's face looked like he'd been badly beaten up, but only on the right side. He'd taped a strip of foam to his face, running from the top of his head to his chin.

"Your effect on women is stunning," JP commented. "I told you so."

Jinjin lowered her head. She hadn't even noticed that she was staring at the American. That wasn't proper.

"It's all right," said Ron. "The foam will keep me from contacting the inside of the helmet. Touching it still feels pretty painful at the moment."

"I'm sorry about that," said Jinjin.

"Don't be. You must be worse off. I've heard that..." Ron imitated a pair of scissors with his index and middle fingers, just like Antonia did earlier.

Jinjin had to swallow. Had the orthopedic surgeon already answered? Antonia probably didn't want to disturb her.

"We wanted to say goodbye," said JP.

"What?" The spacesuits, of course. But that wasn't necessary. They could accommodate and feed a hundred astronauts here. "You're welcome to stay a little longer. I thought we might cook together. Ron raved about your culinary skills."

"Oh, I would love to. But your Chinese superiors see things differently," said JP. "They insist that we leave this base. It's for our own protection."

"After seeing what your robots are like, I actually believe them," Ron added.

Jinjin sighed. What happened to traditional hospitality? Li Guofeng, her instructor, still upheld traditional values. He would never send anyone home without feeding them.

"But we can give you a lift," said JP. "Your bosses can't

forbid us to do that. I'm almost certain you could get a connection from the Gateway to Earth orbit pretty quickly. Then specialists can take care of your finger. I mean, no offense to Antonia's skills, but she only had one crash course in medicine."

"No, I'm staying here. I'm not leaving this place..."

"...without Liwei," Ron finished her sentence. "We've already heard that from Antonia. But I don't think you can help him with that hand of yours."

Jinjin shrugged her shoulders. No one could know what would help her colleague. But if she were in his place, she wouldn't like to be alone when she unexpectedly returned. Not to mention that he might need help. What if his oxygen was almost gone, for example?

She stood up. It was time she took care of her finger. Then she'd grab the rover and drive back to the monolith. Maybe Liwei was already back, waiting.

"All right," she said. "Have a good trip. Have you refueled?"

"Yes, Antonia gave us access to the base's reserves," said Ron.

The ESA astronaut was certainly smart. She obviously knew her way around here better than they did. Hopefully she and Ernie wouldn't be kicked out soon. Had she even told mission control about her two ESA colleagues? Maybe she'd accidentally forgotten them.

Ron opened his arms and they hugged. JP said goodbye with kisses on the cheeks, confusing Jinjin. She laughed and immediately felt annoyed that she sounded like a little girl.

A girl with nine fingers. That would make a good romance title.

"Good luck with the operation," said Ron.

"You're cordially invited to the Gateway," said JP. "We'll have a cook-off. Best food wins."

"I'd love that." Jinjin smiled politely, but didn't truly believe it would ever happen. The stele was still in place. She hadn't completed her mission. The first curious people would be here tomorrow at the latest. Mission control would definitely not allow her to leave.

"Zhù lǚ tú yú kuài," she wished them both.

"Xiè xiè," Ron thanked her.

An American who spoke her language?

"Nǐ shuō hàn yǔ ma?" she asked back.

Ron raised his hands defensively and laughed. "I don't understand a word of what you're saying. *Xiè xiè* was taught to me by a friend of Chinese descent."

"I wished you a happy journey."

Ron bowed. "Then I answered correctly."

"Come on, we have to go," JP said, and opened the door.

JINJIN LISTENED TO THE FOOTSTEPS ECHOING THROUGH THE long corridor. She still had a little time. Antonia would have to say goodbye to the two travelers. Jinjin sat down on her bed, undecided, took off the bandage and looked at her finger. A few hours ago, she had used a felt-tip pen to outline the area where the digit was turning dark. In the meantime, the skin on the other side of the line had also changed, even though she had been injecting herself with antibiotics every four hours. The glove of her spacesuit, in which she had been injured by the robot, was probably not particularly germ-free.

It wasn't helping. She moved the index and middle fingers of both hands like a pair of scissors. The middle finger on the left remained rigid. She only had control over the lowest joint.

The watch on her right arm vibrated, and an ESA logo appeared. Strange. Until a few days ago, Antonia was just a distant astronaut to her, and she hadn't even saved a photo of her. Now the woman would have to cut her finger off.

She accepted the call with a wave of her hand.

"The two guys have just boarded their shuttle," said Antonia.

"That's a shame, really."

"Yes, it's too bad. But that's not why I'm getting in touch with you."

"I know. I'm on my way."

A shiver ran down her spine. Jinjin forced herself to stand up and walk to the door. There, she leaned backwards and slowly slid down.

"I'm sorry, but you'll have to come get me."

"So, sit here," said Antonia and pointed to a stool.

Ernie guided her by grasping her shoulders. He gently pushed her down. In front of the stool on the table was a machine with a knife with a metallic sheen clamped in it. The tip was stuck in a rotating hinge.

Antonia lifted it up and slowly guided it down. There was an unpleasant noise as it passed a metal edge. The knife looked familiar to her. It came from the kitchen at the base.

"Ernie built the machine," said Antonia.

"It's about making the process as quick as possible," explained Ernie. "Of course everything has been disinfected."

There were bandages on the table, which would probably be used to bind the wound.

Jinjin didn't want to know exactly. The two ESA astronauts seemed to have asked around.

"I asked my friend in Turin," said Antonia. "He thinks it's best..."

Jinjin shook her head. "No details."

Antonia smiled a motherly smile. For the first time, Jinjin saw the wrinkles on her face. She must be over fifty, twice her age.

"Give me your finger, then."

Jinjin unwrapped it from the bandage, revealing the discoloration which seemed to have advanced a little further. It was like death was trying to eat away at it, millimeter by millimeter.

"Here are the images, by the way," said Ernie, placing a

tablet on the table. Jinjin scrolled through the photos with her right hand. The first two joints were just a pulpy mass. The knuckles were also unnaturally squashed together, and it looked like something was trying to crawl out at the ends. Jinjin shook herself. That damn robot! The force with which it must have pushed the door shut... Top quality Chinese construction, she had to give it that. But it was still a shame about her finger. Even the best surgeon couldn't fix it.

Ernie put his hand on her shoulder. "There are very good prostheses these days that look almost indistinguishable from real fingers."

"Thank you, Ernie." If only the process was that far along. First, she had to get through this damn operation. Did an orthopedic surgeon really use this surgical technique? Didn't they use saws to cut bones...? She had to shake herself. The large knife looked very sharp and heavy. One or two seconds, it wouldn't torture her more than that.

"I'll put your finger in place now," said Antonia.

The astronaut gripped Jinjin's wrist with her left hand and took hold of the base of her finger with her right. She inserted her finger into the machine. The metal felt cold. There was a scraping sound as Ernie unrolled some surgical tape.

"Is that necessary?" asked Jinjin.

Antonia nodded. "It would be bad if you pulled your finger away at the last second. Then we'd have to start over. We don't want that, do we?"

Jinjin nodded. They definitely didn't want that. With a hissing sound, Ernie sprayed her finger with disinfectant spray. It was even colder than the metal, so cold that Jinjin began to lose all feeling there, which was probably intentional. Ernie fastened her arm in place with the tape and sterilized it again.

Antonia bent over her so that she could no longer see her finger and the cutting edge. That was also probably intentional. Jinjin took a deep breath, since she was on the verge of hyperventilating.

"All right," said Antonia. Jinjin was waiting for a countdown when she heard a loud hiss. Ernie moved jerkily and threw a cloth over the scene. She felt a kind of ring close around the base of her finger. It got tighter and tighter.

What was happening to her index finger? Jinjin heard a short splash, then a squeak, as if a screw-top jar were being sealed.

Only then did the pain hit her. She shivered. Something stabbed her in the thigh. Heat spread from the puncture, traveled over her hips into her stomach and back until it reached her head via her neck. Jinjin giggled. A hand stroked the skin on the top of her left hand. She felt every single hair standing up and was suddenly in the moment. She giggled as she imagined her finger floating in a jar along with some cooked pork sausages. You shouldn't waste anything that was still good.

"How are you?" asked Antonia.

"Better than I've ever been."

"I've injected you with a little mood booster," explained Ernie.

Jinjin giggled. "We have that on board?"

"Of course we do. For emergencies like this."

"How's the finger?"

"The bleeding has already stopped," said Antonia. "That's phenomenal."

"If Hao Haidong finds out…" said Jinjin.

"Didn't you tell mission control about the operation?" asked Antonia.

"They didn't even ask how I was." All of a sudden, Jinjin was infinitely sad. Tears streamed down her cheeks. A whole waterfall.

"I think they're still worried about the monolith," said Ernie.

"Exactly, and I didn't complete the mission," Jinjin sobbed. Ernie stood up. At that moment, she saw a glass on the table. It was transparent and had a screw cap. Her finger was floating in it. She had to laugh, so she giggled and cried at the same time. It worked better than she could have imagined.

"You should try this," she said.

"What?" asked Antonia, wiping her face with a handkerchief.

"Laughing and crying at the same time."

Antonia smiled gently, but it was obvious that she wasn't taking Jinjin seriously.

"Yes, really, it's great!"

"Mission control, Hao Haidong here."

Jinjin sobered up all at once. "When you talk about Cao Cao, Cao Cao comes," she said.

"Does that mean something like 'speaking of the devil'?" asked Antonia, and Jinjin nodded.

"Mission control, Hao Haidong here. Please come in." Haidong seemed to be in a hurry.

"Accept call," said Jinjin. "This is Zhang Jinjin. What can I do for you?"

"First of all, thank you for getting rid of the Americans."

"An American and a Frenchman," she corrected him. "It wasn't my doing. Whatever happened to good old hospitality?"

It must be the influence of the drug Ernie had injected her with. She didn't care that Haidong was in charge of the Eleventh Bureau.

"Jinjin, I won't hold anything against you right now," said Haidong. "The loss of Yang Liwei has certainly hit you hard. And it's largely thanks to your groundwork that we were able to solve the problem."

Only now did she notice that Haidong had switched to Mandarin. Apparently, he didn't want Ernie and Antonia to be able to listen in.

"Is Liwei back again?" Jinjin shook her head. What a stupid question. The Eleventh Bureau didn't care about their colleague.

"It's good that the Americans have arrived back at their Gateway. According to our calculations, they will be completely safe there. That's the only reason we couldn't give them the traditional hospitality that we gave your ESA colleagues who are still with you."

When would Ron and JP be safe, and from what? Jinjin had her suspicions, but she didn't want to let the thought enter her head.

"I'll have to ask you to go down to the basement and close the bulkheads while you're at it, though. Just in case. It's possible that the explosion could throw up large pieces of debris that could land on top of you."

So, an explosion—but how was that possible? The fuel from the bomb fed the mini power station that Jinjin had used to power the coil. That was how she had saved Ron's life.

"Did you bring a new bomb to the stele?" It was possible that there was more fuel stored in the containers, although that didn't make sense. Planning for the construction site of the hypertelescope had always been precise enough that no material was wasted.

"No, everything was still lying around near the stele. We activated two more robots and gave them the task of restoring the bomb. Fortunately, that worked. We can't risk the whole world dissolving into war because of this alien construct."

The Eleventh Bureau and its pessimistic Dark Forest theory. How could a simple book have such an impact? A human had made it up. There was no scientific basis to support the hypothesis.

"Anyway, I should thank you very much for your preliminary work. Warm greetings from Li Guofeng too. He is convinced that you know what you have to do."

Jinjin sighed.

"Is the pain getting worse again?" Antonia asked.

"No. It's because of..." She pointed to the loudspeaker from which Haidong's voice was speaking.

"What's he saying?" asked Ernie.

Jinjin waved it off. She felt ashamed of Haidong. But she would have to tell the two of them, at the latest when they had to hide in the cellar.

But what had Haidong said about her old teacher? She knew what she had to do. Haidong might not have understood it that way, but to her ears it almost sounded like a call to rebellion. The man who removed the mountain was the man who started carrying away the small stones. Guofeng had a whole collection of Confucian wisdom at the ready. Sometimes it had sounded as if he had invented them himself.

"Please try to calm the ESA people down," said Haidong. "The last thing we need is an enemy. The Americans will probably be very resentful. Tell them that the MIGI is not at risk."

Now she was also supposed to play politics. The Eleventh Bureau seemed to think she could do anything. But that wasn't true. It was her job to blow up the monolith. When that didn't work, plan B and then plan C were to be set in motion. Who knew what would happen if Ernie and Antonia didn't just give in?

"Is the MIGI really not in danger?"

"Not according to our calculations of the explosive force. But if your guests set off now, there is a certain risk that they will be hit. They'd better go into the cellar with you. Otherwise it would cost us a lot of goodwill."

Of course, it was not about their lives, but about politics.

"When will the blast be detonated?" she asked.

"In fifteen minutes. Hao Haidong out."

"What's the matter? Is there a problem with your finger?" asked Ernie.

Jinjin laughed briefly. The head of the Eleventh Bureau hadn't even asked about her condition. She simply had to be functional.

"They're blowing up the stele," she said.

Ernie jumped up. "What, are you kidding? After everything we've...?"

Bree barked. She must have been startled.

"Hush, Bree," said Antonia. "Don't get upset, Ernie." Antonia followed him. "It was to be expected. They've got the upper hand."

"It's my fault," said Jinjin. "They turned the power plant back into a bomb. I brought it very close to their goal."

"You couldn't have known," said Antonia.

"We should have guessed," said Ernie. "Ron, JP, you, me, and maybe Jinjin too. If only one of us had thought of it... All we had to do was back up the excavator and remove the nuclear fuel."

"Should have, could have, that doesn't get us anywhere." Antonia rubbed her temples. "What if we try to control the excavator remotely?"

"It was damaged in the fighting near the end," Jinjin said. "There's nothing we can do."

"There must be something," said Ernie.

"Yes, we have to take shelter in the basement because it could rain debris."

"And our interferometer?" asked Antonia, acting very much like the researcher she was.

"They promised that there would be no direct hits."

"But we'll have to recalibrate it," said Ernie.

"I have an idea." Antonia jumped up again and typed something into the computer. "Look at this!"

The screen showed a trajectory from the Lunar Gateway to the surface of the moon.

"What's that?" asked Ernie.

"The Gateway's lander. It could hit the place where the bomb is deposited within ten minutes, from orbit."

"And what good will that do us? It'll just set off the explosion."

Antonia narrowed her eyes. "Jeez, Ernie. I had hope for a moment."

This time it was Jinjin's turn to put a hand on her shoulder. She didn't feel hopeful at all. If they destroyed the stele, how would Liwei come back?

"We should go to the basement and wait for the explosion."

Unknown place, unknown time

Liwei woke up in the dark. He didn't feel frightened. He could feel the humming of the monolith under his glove. If the stele was near him, Jinjin couldn't be too far away. She would get him out of here. He took a deep breath. How long had he been gone? He checked the resources of his suit. He had sufficient supplies of everything. He could breathe and drink and was supplied with warmth.

Although ... that didn't seem to be necessary. The energy consumption of the heating system had dropped to zero. Instead, the cooling system was kicking in, which wasn't unusual. In a vacuum, energy dissipation was so difficult that the suit and the body in it quickly produced more heat together than could be released naturally. A refreshing breeze was now blowing in his face.

Liwei switched to the external sensors. What was that? The electrical discharge from the explosion must have destroyed all the measuring devices. The sensors were sending impossible signals. They said it was 37 degrees Celsius outside. The air pressure was 1.4 times the pressure on Earth's surface. The air contained 27 percent oxygen and 65 percent moisture. Water! There was no atmosphere on the moon and certainly no water vapor. The solar wind carried the light molecules out into space.

He let go of the stele and the world around him began to move—very slowly at first. He couldn't see anything, but the air pressure fluctuated very slowly. It must be wind! He turned. Under his feet was soft ground instead of hard regolith. Liwei bent his knees and felt around him. Were those stalks he could feel? Grass, perhaps? He sat down. This was unbelievable. This couldn't be the moon, and it couldn't be the earth either. Liwei leaned against the monolith and the world around him stopped again, sinking into silence.

But his thoughts continued to move. They revolved around the readings from the outside sensors. The air might be breathable. Unfortunately, his suit was not equipped with devices that could test for pollutants. Should he take off his helmet? The air could contain hydrogen cyanide or carbon monoxide, and nothing would warn him of that until it was too late. If this wasn't Earth, and he assumed it wasn't, he must be careful. The obvious was not always the obvious.

Liwei straightened up and detached himself from the monolith again. He might not have enough external sensors, but he did have his eyes and his hearing. Like the naturalists of a millennium ago, he could use them to examine the world and come to the right conclusions. Others had used the same means to measure the circumference of the Earth or prove its spherical shape. All he had to do was use their experience. Until he knew more, he would keep his suit on.

First the light. Whenever he touched the stele, the world stopped for him—but only for him. The world itself continued to move. But the lighting didn't change. He had no measure of the time that had passed. On earth, every part of the night had a specific darkness. Of course, it would be possible for the day-night rhythm to extend over weeks or months. But the uniformity of the lighting suggested something else: There was no day here at all. This planet had no sun to illuminate it.

But it was still warm. There was liquid water. Something was growing at his feet. The celestial body either produced energy itself in its interior, or it was supplied with energy of a different wavelength. Suppose he found himself in the orbit of a gas giant whose gravitational pull touched the interior of the object on which the stele was located. Then it would be on a moon like Europa or Titan in the solar system. Except that there was no moon with such a warm surface in the solar system.

He really could have used Jinjin's mind right now. The geologist would certainly be able to work out whether such a moon could exist. To produce that much heat, the moon would have to orbit close to its planet. But then it would run the risk of being torn apart by the planet's gravitational forces. However, higher life seemed to have developed here. So the moon's orbit must have been stable for a long time. Which was not very likely with an orbit so close to the planet.

He tried another idea. What if this celestial body orbited another one that didn't radiate in the optical range? A brown dwarf could be a possibility, but also some stellar remnant, such as a neutron star or even a black hole. If the planet was also rotating, the temperatures should show a cycle. Liwei compared the data. In fact, it was now slightly cooler than before, only 32 degrees.

Liwei went through the exoplanets he knew. There weren't many. He could only think of Poltergeist, because of its exotic name, which orbited the pulsar Lich, a neutron star. He stood up and moved a few meters away from the mono-lith. The temperature dropped a little, to 29 degrees. He looked up at the sky. It was strange. There were stars, but they were concentrated in a band that swung up at an angle of sixty degrees across the sky. It couldn't be the Milky Way. There wasn't a single star below the band.

The central star must be quite heavy. It was probably a black hole. The thermal radiation didn't come from a narrowly defined area, but from a larger one. That must be where the accretion disk was located, in which material entering the hole heated up so that it emitted infrared light.

Wait a minute. Why hadn't he thought of that right away? He switched the visor to night vision mode. This was rarely needed on the moon, because everything around was so cold that it appeared black. But here, a whole world suddenly emerged from the darkness.

Liwei stopped and froze. Figures scurried past his field of vision. They moved as quickly as massless shadows, but that must be because they were so far away from the stele. Where they were, time behaved normally, at least by their standards. He felt an impulse to go to them, but that would be unreasonable. This was not his world. If he wanted to find a way home, he had to stick to the stele.

He cut the movements first and then played them back in slow motion. The creatures he saw were fascinating. They were slightly smaller than he was, and walked on three legs. They had two arms at their shoulders and an additional arm extending from their neck. Their faces looked almost human, if it weren't for the extra eye on their forehead. He couldn't make out any gender differences; they all had long, dark hair on their heads. Their bodies appeared to be clothed in textiles.

They paid no attention to the monolith. They simply walked past it and went about their daily business, even when he waved to them. The object had probably been here for a very long time. It was embedded in a park-like landscape with hedges and trees. He couldn't make out any paths, but he thought he could detect an organizing hand. Perhaps it belonged to the sheep-like creatures that accompanied some of the residents. Were they some kind of pet?

Here, in this section, it seemed as if the sheep and the three-legged creatures were talking to each other. A planet with two different, rational species? That would be phenomenal.

Even if it didn't directly help him. Liwei turned to the stele. It had brought him here, so it must be able to transport him back. He touched it, felt it, but nothing happened. He thought of the Earth, but the object didn't read his thoughts. He spoke to it but got no answer. He shouted at it.

A dark sound resounded. But it was not coming from the stele, but from a place behind it. A three-legged person was waving madly and quickly. Liwei moved closer to them and the movement slowed down.

"Who are you?" Liwei asked loudly. The outside loud-speaker on his suit was switched on.

"Uhpuhtukoru."

The answer sounded something like that. Of course, the creature didn't understand his language. But it did express itself acoustically. That couldn't be counted on. After all, it could have morphed with flashes of light, communicated by dancing or drawn something in the grass.

Liwei moved even closer. He turned to the monolith. He must not lose sight of it under any circumstances.

"I am Liwei," he said.

"Ohpotokaro."

That was the same word as before, but a few octaves higher. That was probably what the creature's voice sounded like when it wasn't distorted by the stele's gravitational field.

Liwei pointed to himself. "Yang Liwei."

The creature imitated the gesture with its back hand. "Nux Nura."

"You can call me Liwei." He pointed at himself again. "Liwei."

The creature smiled. It opened its third eye for the first time. It was impressive and radiated pure intelligence. "Nura."

It seemed they had understood each other. Liwei smiled. Yang was his family name. Nux could be the stranger's family name. If there even was such a thing as families here. He must be careful not to anthropomorphize.

"Stele," he said, pointing to the artifact.

"Stele," Nura repeated. It could imitate his articulation perfectly.

"Stele Nura?" he tried. What is the monolith called in your language? he wanted to say.

"Stele taxtax."

"Taxtax," he repeated.

The creature laughed and said "Taxtax," the last syllable rising upwards.

He tried the same.

"Uprofti."

Liwei shook his head. Not so fast.

"I want to go home. Taxtax. Go home."

"Gaah ham."

"Go home."

"Go home."

That was perfectly pronounced. "Uprofti," said Liwei. The creature laughed again. Its third eye opened and closed.

"Home," Liwei repeated.

"Home."

The fact that Nura could pronounce the words didn't necessarily mean that they had been understood.

And now? If he had a proper computer, he could set up a language model. The small computer in the suit was not enough. He had to find another way.

"Home," he said, pointing to the monolith. "Taxtax." He took a few steps towards the stele. Suddenly Nura's back arm moved, and a hand wrapped around his wrist. It was soft and warm and pulled him back.

"Home," said the creature, pointing in a completely different direction with its right hand. Presumably it wanted to take him to its own home. Or to the military of this planet, who would likely imprison him. To researchers who would dissect him. To cooks who would fry him. He must be careful not to anthropomorphize these creatures. Liwei stopped and pushed Nura's hand away from his.

"I'm sorry, but I can't follow you so easily."

"Follow. Home."

Was it a coincidence that Nura had used the right words? Or had the creature chosen the words because of their position in the sentence? If that was the case, communication might not be that difficult.

Nevertheless. Liwei looked around for the stele. What if it disappeared if he moved away from it? Whoever programmed it could assume that he had now reached his destination. Liwei crossed his arms. "Taxtax. Home."

"Follow."

"Taxtax."

The creature closed its upper eye and moved away from him on its three legs. Damn. Who knew if the other inhabitants were as cooperative and smart? He ran after the creature. After three steps, it noticed him and grabbed his wrist again with its back hand.

"Follow."

Liwei tore himself away from the sight of some sheep standing behind a low table on the side of the road, selling items he couldn't discern the nature of. The sheep called out to passers-by, whether they were other sheep or three-legged creatures, or creatures that waddled like tall ducks, resembled horses on three legs, or looked like giant butterflies. Some reacted in the same language, and a few even bought something. No money seemed to change hands. Rather, the creatures crossed one of their limbs with one of the seller's. It must be a state-of-the-art payment system; perhaps they had implanted chips. But the fact that so many species had apparently achieved intelligence was truly astounding.

"Follow." Nura tugged on his arm. She was getting impatient. "Hix Olmutz," she said. Maybe that was the sheep's name.

A short time later, the road ended at a hedge. The surface of the road, which was reminiscent of asphalt, seemed to run directly underneath it. Liwei was wondering whether they would have to cut their way through. Nura lowered her head, rested her two main arms on it and said something that sounded like "abracadabra."

The hedge formed a passageway just big enough for the two of them. When they had stepped through, it closed again.

"Abracadabra," Liwei tried. Nothing happened.

"Aparkaparka, Nux Volom," said Nura.

The hedge opened and closed again. "Kupu, Nux Nura," he heard from an area where he would have suspected its roots to be.

Nura pulled him onwards. The hedge used the same form of address as Nura. Did that mean she belonged to the same family? Or a certain class? From the same region? This planet would be a paradise for ethnologists.

Nevertheless, Liwei had no desire to stay here. The eternal darkness alone! None of the creatures here used technical aids. They had adapted to the darkness and could therefore probably see in infrared light. That wouldn't be very helpful on the moon, but on Earth it certainly would be.

Nura led him to a building that resembled a tower. On the upper floors, creatures were flying in and out. Stairs led up to about the tenth floor, winding creatively along the outer wall. You certainly had to know where you wanted to go, because each staircase led to exactly one floor and the structures sometimes wound around each other. The construction reminded him of the children's game in which you had to find a way out of a labyrinth.

Would Nura take him to the city leaders or to the government? She single-mindedly chose a specific staircase. The ascent was strenuous because he was still wearing his spacesuit. But there was so much life here that Liwei was truly worried about his immune system—and that of humanity, should he bring micro-organisms home from here. He had to pause from time to time on the way. He used those moments to view the city from above. It consisted mainly of parks in which flat houses were scattered. This tower was one of the few tall buildings. There were also much slimmer towers from which cable cars were suspended. These presumably went to other parts of the country. The horizon was also clearly visible in infrared. It was no further away than on Earth, so this planet was probably similar in size.

Nura pulled him into a large space. Liwei had expected some kind of meeting room where the powerful would decide his fate. These beings must be interested in the fact that someone from a completely different world had arrived here.

But there was no one waiting for them here. There were boxes on the walls. Behind transparent walls, exhibits awaited viewers. There were tiny sheep in a transparent egg, tools that could be used with three hands, uniforms for quadrupeds, lots of written documents, models of buildings and objects that might be either food or cult objects—he couldn't tell.

In the middle of the room was a sphere about four meters high. Nura showed him that it was movable. She turned it so that Liwei could see the round tower. In the immediate vicinity, he saw a miniature version of the monolith. Nura turned the ball again, pointing to a cable car line with her back hand. She stopped at a cable car tower. The ride continued along a different route. Near its destination, he recognized another model of the stele.

Liwei nodded. He should take the cable car to the other stele. That was all. There was no questioning about where he came from and where he was going, no registration, and he wasn't going to be examined.

"Taxtax," he said.

"Taxtax," Nura confirmed.

"Kupu, Nux Nura," he tried.

Nura turned her head once in a circle almost 360 degrees and let out a screeching sound. Two sheep turned around to look at them. Nura led him back outside.

THE WAY DOWN WAS MUCH EASIER. LIWEI ASSUMED THAT Nura would now leave him alone, but that was not the case. She pointed roughly in the direction where he thought the cable car tower was. They set off, side by side.

They passed the sheep stall again. Nura spoke with the vendor, crossed limbs with him and returned to Liwei with a leaf. It showed a biped. Liwei's heart beat faster. Nura pointed to the drawn legs, then to his limbs. She repeated this with the arms and face. What did that mean? Had other humans visited here before, passing through from monolith one to monolith two?

But the human in the picture was naked. You could even

see a hint of his genitals. Had that person taken off his space-suit, or had he lived here? If you looked at it pragmatically, that might not be a bad idea. He could learn the language, integrate. He wouldn't even stand out among all the different beings.

Although... The damn darkness would probably get to him. No, he had to keep going, if only for the sake of the others, who surely needed him.

"Kupu, Nux Nura," he said.

Nura put her back hand on his shoulder. After another ten minutes of walking, they reached the cable car.

WHEW. THERE WERE ABOUT A THOUSAND STEPS TO THE TOP of the tower. Nura bravely walked them with him. She must have suspected that he wouldn't voluntarily plunge into the depths. Because what he thought was a cable was a simple rope onto which you had to hook yourself with the help of a primitive seat, and then let gravity carry you over great distances. On earth, they were called ziplines and were mostly intended for tourists. But there they were used during daylight, and you were on the move for a few minutes, not hours.

Nura took his hand. With the other, she wrote three signs on the palm of her hand. "Taxtax," she explained. He remembered the second cable car. He was probably supposed to show those signs at the destination of the first one so that someone could direct him to the second route.

Three inhabitants of this world were ahead of him in line. Liwei watched as a sheep skillfully chained itself to the rope and then jumped into the depths without hesitation. It was followed by a huge dog, or was that a wolf? He turned around and grumbled, apparently because the cactus-like creature waiting behind him had jabbed him in the back with its needles. Nura pulled Liwei back a little so that he wouldn't hurt himself too.

The cactus creature had a harder time. It moved on its roots, but needed them to attach itself to the rope. It first had to stand on its head, which it managed surprisingly elegantly. Then the flexible roots grabbed the seat and off it went.

Now it was Liwei's turn. He had watched carefully to see how it worked, but was still startled when the seat wrapped itself around the bottom of his spacesuit like a living creature. Nura put her back hand on his shoulder and gave him a squeeze. Liwei tried to relax. The tower still seemed a thousand meters high to him.

"Kupu, Nux Nura!"

"Kupu, Nux Liwei."

He reached for the device used to hook himself onto the rope. It supported his movement. It snapped into place with a loud click. Liwei thought about when and how he should best jump off, but the ride was already starting.

"Taxa!" he shouted without receiving an answer as he plunged into the depths at breakneck speed.

AFTER A FEW MINUTES, THE ACCELERATION STOPPED. THE rope seemed to be taut enough that the incline just about compensated for the friction. He estimated that he was traveling at one hundred kilometers per hour. The panorama was impressive. He flew over huge forests that formed geometric patterns like parks. If he leaned in a certain direction, the seat reacted and compensated for the weight.

Liwei checked his resource levels. The oxygen supply had dropped significantly. He could breathe safely here, but microorganisms were still a danger. He couldn't justify that. He satisfied his hunger with some liquid from the dispenser. This world was really fascinating. He would probably never find out where he actually was.

Why was he here at all? Had someone sent him here to save him? If so, maybe he should accept the invitation. The inhabitants of this world didn't seem to have a problem with him. It made no difference to them whether he came from another city or another world. Or was it pure coincidence which stelae were connected to each other? If so, he should stay, because who knew where the next stele would take him.

THE SEAT THAT SECURED HIM VIBRATED. LIWEI OPENED HIS eyes as he approached the ground. He must have fallen asleep. He looked around quickly. At least three other cable car towers could be seen nearby. Then the ground was beneath him. Liwei tried to run in order to catch himself. The seat automatically disengaged, but didn't drop him. It seemed to know that the journey would continue.

Two other creatures had arrived with him. They were two wolves. They embraced and spoke to each other in the foreign language.

"Taxa" he tried and held out his palm to them.

The wolves turned around. They each had an impressive set of teeth, with which they could probably tear his hand off. But they lowered their heads.

"Hix Sofon," said one of them.

"Dox Grunu," introduced the other.

"Nux Liwei."

The two stood up on their hind legs and hugged him. He hadn't expected that.

"Apraki niko furkukat, Nux Liwei?" asked Hix Sofon.

Liwei shook his head. "Taxa." He held out his palm to them again. Only now did they seem to notice the signs.

"Taxa!" shouted Dox Gronu. "Taxa furkukat solmek mikimax."

Liwei nodded. One on each side of him, the two led him to another cable car tower and pointed upwards.

"Taxa!" repeated Dox Gronu and took his hand. "Mukukat fukol." His companion gave him a tool that looked like a knife. Liwei tried to pull his hand away, but Dox Gronu held it tightly. He used the tool to add a few of his own to Nura's signs.

"Taxa!"

"Kupu, Dox Gronu. Kupu, Hix Sofon."

The two spoke in confusion in their own language. Liwei looked at the stairs. The tower seemed to be even higher than the one he came from.

THE SECOND FLIGHT WAS SIGNIFICANTLY SHORTER AND FASTER than the first. This time the seat detached from him once Liwei stood on his own two feet again. The landscape had changed considerably. The ambient temperature had dropped to below ten degrees. Instead of mighty trees, there were only bushes and meadows. A mighty mountain rose on the horizon, with a reddish glow at the top. Liwei briefly switched off the infrared visor. It must be a volcano spewing lava. In the optical range, it looked like a solitary light in the darkness.

Several paths led from the cable car station into the distance. Where was the monolith? Liwei looked around, but he seemed to be alone. There was, however, a hedge that ran around the entire area of the station. He thought of the plant that blocked the way to the town. Nura had been able to communicate with it without any problems.

Liwei tried it. He knelt in front of the hedge and introduced himself. "Nux Liwei."

"Arpokalifatax. Hix Porak."

It worked! He held out his hand to the hedge and said the magic word: "Taxa."

Fine branches with strangely shaped leaves grew out of the bush and wrapped themselves around his hand. He held it still.

"Taxa," said the hedge. "Eom kumulat Porak."

Ahh. That didn't really help him.

"Taxa," he repeated.

"Eom kumulat Porak," was the answer again.

Liwei stood up and looked for another creature. But now, of all times, there were no sheep, three-legged creatures, wolves or even cacti running around. He headed for the first road that led to the distant mountain. The hedge followed him and pushed itself in his way. He tried the next road, but it was also blocked. However, he was allowed to take the third, which ran almost directly under the cable car.

"Kupu, Hix Porak," he said thankfully.

THE STELE HERE LOOKED VERY DIFFERENT FROM THE ONE ON the moon. Firstly, it wasn't black in the infrared, but orange. Secondly, it was embedded in dense vegetation, and thirdly, it looked almost tiny after the huge cable car towers.

At first, Liwei pondered how to make his way through the dense vegetation. Then he thought about his experiences with the hedge and tried using the few words of the local language that he knew.

It worked. After he had introduced himself, the vegetation opened up a narrow strip just wide enough for him. Liwei took a deep breath. The world changed with every step he took towards the stele. Sounds swelled and became muffled. The temperature rose. The world sank into darkness because the monolith shone so brightly. Nothing grew along the last meter, not even grass. Liwei stepped onto the soft ground. His step left a deep imprint.

Liwei hesitated. If he touched the stele, he probably wouldn't ever find his way back to this place. Was it really a good idea to set off on a journey into the unknown? Who could guarantee him that the next stele had not been erected in a lava lake, or at the bottom of an ocean? Nothing. But he couldn't stay here for the rest of his life. So he might as well make the decision now.

"Taxa," he said, touching the warm metal of the alien artifact.

Dewar Crater, March 9, 2082

It was well past midnight before mission control gave the all-clear. The vibration was detectable when the nuclear fission bomb detonated. Because of the low gravity, it took a while for all the debris to fall back to the surface.

Jinjin went into the control center and used the computer to access the cameras Liwei had installed. But their images were black. Damn. They must have been damaged by heat or nuclear radiation. Jinjin tried to radio Ron and JP at the Lunar Gateway, but no one answered. The station was probably still over the horizon. She didn't want to use a Chinese relay satellite and have the Eleventh Bureau find out.

The official news channels were full of reports about an explosion on the moon. There were no photos. Most of the news was based on seismic data recorded by various stations. There was wild speculation—right up to a volcanic eruption as the cause, which would be very unlikely on the geologically dead moon. Who actually knew about the bomb? The higher ups, of course, the Europeans and the Americans.

The computer responded. JP had sent her a personal message, presumably via some kind of relay, or it wouldn't have arrived yet. "What's going on down there? I hope you're all right! My invitation to the kitchen battle still stands."

Jinjin was confused. It sounded like he was flirting with her. Yet humanity had just lost one of the best opportunities it had ever had.

She tried mission control. Wang Yaping answered. Hadn't she been relocated? Or had Hao Haidong suddenly fallen out of favor? That would mean he was being accused of failure—that the explosion didn't do its job.

"Where is Haidong?" she asked.

"You'll have to make do with me. Comrade Hao is currently briefing the Politburo."

"And what is he telling them?"

"That's subject to secrecy, of course."

Of course. "But the monolith, it's gone?"

"Some say so, others say differently."

What did that mean? Were there still no photos?

"You'll have to explain that to me," she said.

"It's quite simple—the scientists disagree. There's a cloud of dust hovering over the crater that we can barely see through. And the measurements in non-optical areas are inconclusive."

"How about if I go there with the rover? Or is that dangerous?"

"The dust there is probably radioactive."

"That won't bother me."

"Well, if you volunteer and let me know your observations promptly, I won't stop you."

You can't do that anyway. If you hadn't given me permission, I'd still be going.

"But leave the Europeans at the base. They'll all arrive soon enough to snatch the monolith away from us."

"If you say so." Of course, she wouldn't forbid Antonia and Ernie from accompanying her. On the contrary—she was happy to be able to count on their expert help. If either of them fancied a ride into a high radiation zone, that is.

JINJIN CHOSE A ROUTE AROUND THE DEWAR CRATER. THIS allowed them to cross the mountainous ring at the lowest point and make faster progress. Liwei had chosen the adventurous route across the crater, where climbing the far rim with the rover was almost impossible and took a lot of time.

The disadvantage of the easy route was that the crater ring blocked the view of the destination almost all the way. When they were about halfway along the route, JP called from the Gateway.

"What're you doing down there?" he asked.

"We're on our way to the stele," replied Jinjin.

"Are you sure?"

Jinjin sighed. He didn't trust her. She could understand

that. The dark cloud over the target area seemed to prove that she wasn't being honest.

"JP? Ernie here." The German pulled the base of the microphone towards him.

"Oh, you too?"

"Hey, what's that supposed to mean? It's not Jinjin's fault. She was tricked just like we were. They reassembled the fuel from the power plant into a bomb and detonated it. We couldn't stop it."

"Really?"

"Yes, really. That's why they wanted to get you out of there. It would have been unfortunate if someone had died during the operation."

Jinjin nudged him. Someone might already have died!

"A foreigner, I mean," Ernie corrected himself.

"You didn't suspect anything? Jinjin didn't either?"

Jinjin grabbed the microphone again. "If I had known, I would have stood next to Liwei. Then they wouldn't have dared. Maybe."

"I don't know," Ernie said, massaging his head.

Jinjin knew what he meant. But mission control would have never risked the cosmic artifact falling into the hands of a third party because no taikonaut could keep an eye on it. She had an important function here. Someone had to make sure that the Chinese territory on the moon was not violated.

"Okay, I believe you," said JP. "I'm not so sure about Ron."

"What can you see from above?" asked Ernie.

"Nothing. There's a big cloud covering the whole area. I almost think it's intentional."

"It's not," said Jinjin.

"I knew you'd defend whoever did this," Ron interjected, presumably having been listening the whole time. "Those bastards! That was an incredible treasure!"

"Ron, it's all right now," said Antonia. "Jinjin is a geologist. It's about electrical fields, isn't it?"

Jinjin smiled at Antonia. It was really nice of the physicist to defend her.

"There are two factors," she explained. "Firstly, this isn't just dust that you can swipe away with a broom. The layer is up to fifteen meters thick! The explosion must have stirred it all up. But then the stuff is also completely dry and some of the particles are tiny. When the sun shines on them, the light knocks negatively charged electrons out of the material and the tiny grains become positively charged. What happens when two particles with the same charge meet? They repel each other. Add that to the already low gravity, and it'll keep the dust aloft forever."

"Okay," said Ron. "Sorry for blowing my top. So, it's normal that we're struggling with a cloud?"

"Unfortunately," said Jinjin. "There are no air currents to disperse and distribute it like on Earth. It'll cause us problems for a while yet."

"But you should still be able to help us," Antonia added. "Do you have an L-band radar on the Gateway?"

"No idea," said Ron. "Do we have one of those, JP?"

"I'm afraid I don't know that either. I'll find out."

"Thank you, Jean-Pierre," said Antonia. "With its wavelength of fifteen to thirty centimeters, it should be able to penetrate the dust cloud relatively well."

"And why hasn't anyone else tried that?"

"In the L-band, the range isn't that great, and the current satellites in orbit around the moon aren't designed for remote sensing."

"All right," said JP. "We'll get back to you during the next orbit."

ERNIE HAD TAKEN THE WHEEL. ALL HE HAD TO DO WAS follow the automatic route-finding system, and the Chinese voice announcements didn't interfere. Jinjin sat behind him and stroked Antonia's dog. She would have liked to sleep, but her index finger was throbbing again.

"Does Bree go everywhere with you?" she asked.

Antonia nodded. "We're a package deal."

"Isn't that dangerous sometimes?"

"Oh, Bree is fine. She even saved my life one time."

Jinjin stroked the dog's head and nuzzled her neck.

"So, you're a lifesaver, huh? That's great." She laughed because she had automatically changed her voice as if she were talking to a child.

"You're not a kid, are you?" Bree looked at her with her brown eyes, and Jinjin imagined for a moment that the dog had understood her.

"Lunar Gateway here," JP announced. Bree greeted the voice with a bark. JP barked back and Bree answered. "Cut it out, you two!" shouted Antonia. JP laughed. The Frenchman was a mystery to Jinjin. How could he laugh when the world was ending? But Li Guofeng was also bit like that. Whatever happened, he made time for a good cup of tea.

"Do you have anything for us?" asked Antonia.

"I've found an L-band radar," said JP. "We lucked out—the Gateway's observation module was actually developed for a space station in Earth orbit."

They really hadn't had much luck so far, so it was about time. "And what do you see there?" she asked.

"We're just starting our flyover. I'll share the data with you."

Antonia moved quickly to the computer and switched on the screen. A three-dimensional coordinate system was built up. A picture emerged slice by slice. It seemed very coarse-grained to Jinjin.

"Is the radar broken?" she asked.

"No, it's because of the relatively long wavelength," explained Antonia. "We don't want it to be disturbed by the dust particles."

Good, that was reassuring. The slices approached a red

cross in the middle of the image. Jinjin wanted to tap her fingers on the tabletop; a sharp pain reminded her that wasn't a good idea. The slices now reached the X. It looked as if someone was using a knife to smear new layers of butter on a slice of bread. But now the picture changed. Something was sticking out of the ground. It must be the stele!

"There! It's still there...!" shouted Jinjin.

At the same moment, the monolith disappeared again. Antonia absent-mindedly touched her knee. "I saw it too."

"And did you see him too?"

Antonia shook her head without asking who she meant. Jinjin blinked, and suddenly the stele was there again. This time she tried hard not to blink, so as not to give it any reason to disappear, but it didn't help. It was gone, only to return shortly afterwards.

"Are we recording this?" asked Jinjin.

"Of course we are."

"Us too," said Ron.

Jinjin took a deep breath. The two of them had helped her find the stele. She couldn't blame them if they passed on the data. But at least she could try.

"I have a request," she began.

"I'm listening," said Ron, obviously knowing immediately that he was meant.

"If my superiors find out that the monolith still exists, they'll try again. And then maybe they'll do it for good."

"Don't worry, these pictures are top secret," said Ron.

"That's not enough. Some journalist gets a tip, and since you don't have censorship, the information is out. That can't happen."

"She's right," JP said. "What leaves this station is not one hundred percent secret. The same goes for the ESA."

"Hm." Ron took a deep breath. "All right, then. We'll keep this to ourselves for twenty-four hours. After all, we're not familiar with long-range reconnaissance and nobody told us we were going to use the L-band radar. But what do you want to do with this time, Jinjin?"

"Liwei. I have to find him."

THE CLOUD COULDN'T BE SEEN FROM THE GROUND AT FIRST. The first warning sign came in the form of an annoying beeping sound from the radiation detectors. They registered what they identified as a solar storm.

"That's my construction site," said Antonia. She examined the measuring device and nodded, then switched off the warning tone. "That's what I thought. The dust is radioactive. We shouldn't stay here forever. I take it the rover isn't specially insulated?"

"No," said Jinjin. "Normally that's not a problem."

"Hold on, I'll set us a little reminder." Antonia pressed various buttons until they heard a clicking sound reminiscent of a Geiger counter.

"The faster it clicks, the higher the radiation level in the area," explained Antonia.

Click-click-click. Click-click-click-click. It felt strange. The frequency increased with every minute.

AFTER TEN MINUTES, THE NOISE HAD TURNED INTO A background hissing. Antonia got up and adjusted the device so that it emitted individual clicks again.

"Don't worry," she said, "these are readings from outside. There's a lot of alpha and beta radiation with a relatively short range."

That didn't reassure Jinjin. She would have to get out at the end of the journey, she had no choice. Her plan was set.

Antonia returned to her seat. "Oh, look, there!" she called out, pointing to the forward porthole.

At first, Jinjin didn't realize what the physicist meant, but then she did. The sun had changed color. It was now glowing red, which must be because the short-wave parts of its spectrum were being swallowed up by the dust.

"The dust swallows short-wave..." Antonia continued.

"I know," said Ernie and Jinjin in unison.

"Okay, okay, I'll be quiet."

Jinjin looked at the red sun with fascination. For the first time in a long time, she could watch a real sunset where the nearest star to the Earth didn't just disappear behind the horizon. When was the last time she had the opportunity to do that? It must have been in her home town, out in the rice fields, which had surely given way to high-rise buildings by now.

Antonia took out a tablet and typed. "I hate to disappoint you," she said. "The sun won't set before we get there."

"Yeah, yeah, just take away all our hope, why don't you?" Ernie said and laughed.

"It's not about being romantic," said Antonia. "Without sunlight, the cloud would settle faster. It's the sunlight that knocks out the electrons. I don't like the density of the cloud."

"Do you see problems?" asked Jinjin.

Antonia nodded. "The rover isn't made for such a dusty environment, is it? Ultimately, we'll end up like the Apollo astronauts in the past, who also had to deal with dust. Even if it wasn't radioactive, the grains aren't round like on Earth. They are sharp-edged and contain tiny glass particles."

Antonia was right. The seals of the airlock and the suits could get overloaded. It would be best if she got out alone at her destination. She would automatically bring less dust back with her than if the three of them went outside. And who knew if she would return at all?

"I can measure the dust density now," said Ernie, waking Jinjin from a light slumber. He pressed a button on the steering wheel and the rover's headlights switched on.

"Now I'll measure the exposure, and then this little

program here," he pressed a few buttons, "will hopefully give us a value."

Jinjin stood up to look at the screen. It said "23."

"That's the current optical attenuation," Ernie explained. "And do you see the slight hue that the light from the headlights has taken on at the edges? Those are basically rainbows."

"Rainbows on the moon!" exclaimed Jinjin. "If someone had told me a week ago that I would see rainbows here, I would have called them crazy."

"I saw a documentary the other day that showed the first rainbow on Mars," said Antonia.

"Oh, are they that far along with terraforming?" asked Jinjin. It had only been about forty years ago that the first colony ship landed there. She knew the story from a book called *Mars Genesis*.

"It wasn't real rain, of course, but at least it was over real Martian soil under a glass dome."

Not bad. Jinjin looked out of the porthole. If she focused on the spotlight beam, she could make out the colorful streaks around the edges.

THE OPTICAL ATTENUATION HAD REACHED 50 WHEN JINJIN began feeling restless. Something was wrong. The landscape they were driving through seemed untouched. Maybe that was it. There should be traces of their previous journeys here. How many times had Liwei driven along here with the rover or an excavator? The dust must have covered everything like snow.

"What does the 50 actually mean?" she asked.

"It's an arbitrary scale," Ernie explained. "I don't have anything to calibrate the value with."

"Is the scale at least linear?"

"Yes, I think so."

Good. Then it was a little more than twice as dark as it

was when 23 was on the screen. The sun was now just a blur. It was about to disappear completely, like a sunset on a hazy horizon.

"How much further is it?" she asked.

Ernie pointed to the map. It wasn't even two kilometers. Shouldn't they be feeling the influence of the stele's gravity by now? Not if it was actually gone. Jinjin thought about the radar image that JP had taken from the Lunar Gateway. Strange, really strange. One second it had been there, the next it wasn't.

"We should measure the frequency shift to be on the safe side," she said. "That's what I learned about how time stretched the last time I was near the stele."

"But we have no point of comparison," said Ernie. "Unless we use a relay satellite in orbit."

Jinjin shook her head. No relay, or mission control would pick up too much. The Lunar Gateway was still over the horizon. The excavator, which had been just in front of the monolith, wasn't responding. It must have been completely destroyed.

Liwei couldn't have survived that. All of this was completely pointless.

"It's best if I walk the rest of the way," said Jinjin. "I'll only put you in danger."

"Out of the question," said Antonia. "I also want to see what the explosion has done to the stele."

"And someone has to look after Bree while you're both out there," said Ernie.

The dog barked.

THE ROVER SLOWED DOWN. THEY HAD ALMOST REACHED THE center of hell. Visibility was about twenty meters. The stele was ten times more distant than that.

"Do you really want to go out there?" asked Ernie, handing the helmet to Jinjin.

"It's not a question of wanting to," replied Jinjin. "I have to."

Ernie had adjusted the radio so that it would stay in contact with the rover the whole time. This allowed him to calculate the time difference and adjust the transmission of their voices so that they could understand each other.

"Antonia to Rover, come in."

Bree barked when she heard the voice. Antonia was waiting in the airlock, where she had completed an abbreviated pre-breathing program. Sweat was running down Jinjin's forehead. Bree ran excitedly back and forth between the two women. She kept stopping in front of Ernie, as if to make sure he was staying with her. Bree really was pretty clever. Jinjin took off her helmet and tested the radio.

"This is Jinjin, how are you?"

"Read you loud and clear."

"Jinjin here again," she said an octave lower.

Ernie laughed and pressed a few buttons. "Read you loud and clear," said a squeaky voice like something out of an animated movie.

Jinjin pointed her thumb upwards. It was a good thing they chose the rover with the airlock. Otherwise, they would have dust inside the vehicle later. She climbed into the narrow airlock. Antonia was lying on the floor, wiping it away with her hands.

"This is the devil's own stuff," she said, showing her a mound of sand in the palm of her glove.

"Crap. That was my mistake," said Jinjin. "The airlock must have been evacuated during the trip."

"No, it wasn't. I checked it out. There was only a slight vacuum, but there's a vacuum out there. That stuff shouldn't have gotten in."

At least it hadn't been her. That was reassuring.

"Maybe it's alive," said Antonia and laughed.

Jinjin bit her lower lip. It was a joke. The dust was not alive. But after what she had seen here in the last few days, nothing seemed impossible to her.

"You can come out," said Antonia. "It's safe."

Jinjin felt a brief tug on the leash that connected them. Antonia was nowhere to be seen. She had disappeared behind a white wall. Jinjin had never experienced such a dense fog on Earth. It looked particularly strange because there were no shades of gray, only the bright white of the reflecting dust particles and the absolute black when she turned off the spotlight.

She moved her hand in the fog and it changed its structure. The particles slowly followed her, forming dense shapes. It was as if she was stirring milk that flocculated in the process. She held her hand still and the dust settled on it, mostly on the top, but also on the bottom. She grew a kind of second glove made of dust.

The line jerked again. "Don't stand still for too long," said Antonia, "or you'll turn into a snowman made of dust."

"I can hardly see a thing."

"Follow the safety line. You can see your destination and the way there on the radar image on the arm computer."

That was good. Jinjin wiped a layer of dust off the display. Yes, there was the monolith. An X showed its location. A flashing dot pointed to Antonia's position. She pulled herself forward on the leash. She left the spotlight on. Without it, it was completely black around her, which she liked even less.

Their progress was slow. Polar explorers on Earth must have felt something like this. They didn't have to contend with cracks in the ice here, but with sharp metal fragments that were so well hidden by the layer of dust that you could easily trip over them. These must be the remains of the excavator. The explosion had apparently torn it apart. The only question was how. With no atmosphere, there would have been no pressure wave. Perhaps the machine had been bombarded with boulders? That could be it.

"Watch out, a metal hook," warned Antonia.

Jinjin stood still. Her colleague's voice sounded surprisingly deep.

"Was that on purpose?" asked Jinjin.

"What, that I warned you about the hook?"

"Your voice suddenly dropped," said Ernie from the rover. "I heard it too."

"I was speaking normally."

That was strange. Jinjin checked their distance from the stele. Another hundred meters. Under other circumstances, there would already be a measurable distortion.

"It could be the stele," she said. "Remember the radar image from orbit?"

"Physically, that's, well, impossible," said Antonia. "An object that heavy can't just appear here and disappear again."

"The radar image says otherwise," said Ernie.

"You're right. Impossible is the wrong word," admitted Antonia. "*Inexplicable* is better."

Jinjin continued walking. Suddenly she lurched forward. Shit, she had forgotten the hook Antonia had warned her about. But she managed to roll to the side. When she stood up, her vision was black. She wiped the dust from the display and took a selfie with the camera in her arm computer. She looked like a doll in the photo, but a creepy doll out of a horror movie.

"Are you all right?" Antonia asked, jerking the leash.

Jinjin laughed out loud. Her voice sounded far too deep again. The monolith was playing tricks on them. Jinjin worked her way forward on the leash. When she reached Antonia, she grabbed onto her.

⬤

"A regular rhythm has shown up," said Ernie. Since they were walking side by side, their voices were now equally distorted. "The rhythm matches the one I extracted from the radar image."

"Maybe someone is applauding us for marching so bravely to the stele," said Antonia.

According to the display on her arm, the alien artifact was still a good twenty meters away. They should be able to see it soon.

"The rhythm doesn't match," said Ernie. "I ran it through the analyzer, but it doesn't resemble anything we know. It's too early to say for sure, but it could be an irrational rhythm, something like pi or Euler's number e."

"That's impossible... err, inexplicable," said Antonia.

"Have you checked whether there's a message in it?" asked Jinjin.

Maybe Liwei had found a way to communicate with them. All they had to do was decode his messages.

"We don't have enough material for that," explained Ernie.

"If the value really is irrational, it can't be a message," added Antonia.

"Why?"

"Because every irrational number contains every possible message," said Ernie. "You just have to wait long enough, and you'll find the entire Bible in pi, or even the Communist Manifesto in Mandarin. That's a property of the infinity of those numbers."

Jinjin felt like a schoolgirl. Math had never been her strong point.

But then she had an idea. "Ha, it could be a message. The number itself could be the message. Maybe it plays an important role somewhere."

"Something like 42 in Douglas Adams," said Antonia.

The answer to the ultimate question about life, the universe and everything. Jinjin could do something with that. She smiled.

"Then we just need to find the question," she said.

"There's just one tiny little problem," said Ernie. "We

haven't caught the rhythm from the beginning. So, it could be 42, but it could also be 9942 or 0.34442."

"I suggest we stop speculating," said Antonia. "Let's stick to the facts."

"The stele is distorting voices much less than before," said Ernie.

"That means it must be significantly lighter," said Antonia. "Do we know anything else?"

No one said anything. But that was important information. Jinjin would be able to approach the monolith more easily, since she wouldn't lose as much time as Liwei or Ron. She would definitely take advantage of that.

SUDDENLY, A SHINY SNOWMAN EMERGED FROM THE FOG. JINJIN didn't manage to complete her long stride, typical for the surface of the moon, before bumping into Antonia from behind.

"Ouch," she said and fell forward.

Jinjin helped her up. "I'm sorry, you appeared so suddenly."

"That's all right, I should have said something. But I suddenly thought I felt the stele."

"Felt it? What do you mean?"

"There was this pulling sensation that went through my body. It was as if someone was holding me by the oxygen tank while someone else was pulling me forward."

"That sounds painful."

"It wasn't that bad. It's gone now, though."

Jinjin paused to check herself. But there was no unknown force, just the familiar, almost gentle pull of the moon.

"You look funny," she said, turning Antonia to face her and knocking thick clumps of dust off her suit. But they didn't fall down, they disappeared behind Antonia. To where the X lit up on the display.

"Now it's back again," said Antonia. "This time, someone is pulling on my chest and stomach."

Jinjin felt it too. Someone was trying to steal her air supply. She turned around, but there was no one there. Then she was free again.

"Ernie, come in, please," said Antonia.

"I'm listening."

"Did you just have a crash?"

"I can confirm that. Now again."

The power is back. Jinjin looked to the side, where something had moved.

"We're not alone." A shiver ran down her spine.

"I'm not scanning any life signs near you," Ernie said.

"Can you access my helmet cam?"

"If you give me permission, Jinjin."

A query appeared on the display, which she confirmed.

"Thanks. Let me scroll back. Ah, there's something. Looks like dust clumped together."

Jinjin took a deep breath. That was a good explanation. Of course, the changing gravity would also affect the dust. Where the difference was particularly large, there would be clusters. The phenomenon was similar in geology.

"Should we keep going?" asked Antonia.

"According to my scan, you're still about twenty meters away from the stele," said Ernie. "But watch out, the bomb must have gone off near there. The cloud is centered over your position, anyway."

Jinjin checked the reports from the radiation detector. The area was cleaner than expected. They were now walking on a surface that appeared to be made of tempered glass. There must have been enormous heat here. The radioactive particles were probably thrown outwards by the explosion. The detector gave them another hour or so without fear of damage to their health. The suits, designed for space EVAs, were probably also able to withstand a good deal.

"I'd best go on alone now," said Jinjin. "It's enough for one of us to put ourselves in danger."

"Are you sure?" asked Antonia.

Jinjin wasn't sure at all, but she tried not to let it show. "Yes, it's better this way. You can help me better from here, too." She uncoiled a little more of the safety line, which measured about thirty meters in total. "Ernie, you're welcome to keep looking through my camera."

ANTONIA DISAPPEARED INTO THE WHITE WALL. JINJIN TURNED forward. When the display showed the monolith just ten meters away, she stretched out her arm. Until gravity struck again and almost pulled her arm out of the socket. Jinjin groaned.

"What's wrong?" Antonia and Ernie asked at the same moment. Antonia spoke in a squeaky voice, Ernie sounded normal. Apparently only Ernie's voice was being converted to her frequency.

"I'm all right. I had forgotten about gravity."

With each additional step, walking became more strenuous. This was not how she imagined it. The rhythm of the gravitational waves accelerated.

"Do you notice that it's fluctuating faster, Ernie?" asked Jinjin.

"No, I don't see that. It probably feels that way to you because of the time dilation."

Antonia squeaked something she couldn't understand. Three steps further on, the physicist fell completely silent. She would probably be able to hear her in ultrasound. If Bree were in her place, she would still understand Antonia.

Another three steps further on, Jinjin got down on all fours like Bree. If gravity struck again unexpectedly, it would be too strenuous for her. But she mustn't crawl head-first, or the force would try to split her back in two. Instead, she approached the target crawling sideways. This way she gave the gravity differential as little space as possible.

Pause. She had to be careful not to tear the knees of her

spacesuit. The ground under her was hard and smooth, but every now and then metal bits stuck out as if they were frozen into the shiny mass. Moving on. If her display was accurate, she was almost there. The path now led upwards. She was crawling out of the depression created by the bomb. The radiation detector showed ever lower values. A nuclear fission bomb had exploded here just yesterday!

"Jinjin, can you hear me?"

Whew. "Yes, loud and clear."

"You now have a clear time dilation on your watch."

"Has the rhythm stopped?"

"No, it's now so high that there's a stretch in the average."

"How much?"

It took a few seconds for Ernie's answers to arrive each time, which told her he was right.

"About one in ten."

"Okay, that's fine." It had actually been a lot more dramatic on her first visit here.

"I'd like to get Antonia out of there. If she stays where she is, she'll get too much radioactivity in the long run."

Jinjin nodded. She pulled on the line, on which a strange, standing wave formed, moving into the white mist as if in slow motion.

"Of course. It's no good if she gets sick because of me."

"Thank you for understanding. You know how she is. Without your consent, she would never have gotten out of there. She's releasing the safety line now."

Jinjin swallowed. Ernie had just finished speaking when the line fell to the ground. Now she was all alone.

But no. Liwei was here somewhere. She turned around on all fours. The stele must be up ahead. To the side of her, dust flaked together into clumps that moved towards the artifact. They joined up with other lumps and formed a linear structure that looked almost like a standing human. The human waved its arms. Jinjin shook her head. Her imagination was running away with her.

She crawled on. Was it possible that the forces that pushed

her to the ground were fading? She stood up again. It worked. She had probably reached the maximum, which meant that no more differences could be felt. Jinjin pushed the dust away in front of her. It was like swimming in the natural lake in her grandmother's village. With her feet in the mud, she had pushed away the duckweed with her hands to reveal clear water. Just like then, a clear area appeared around her. The dust was dense enough to fall to the ground when it clumped together. Electrical repulsion was no longer sufficient as a counterforce, and the fog cleared. She herself was the nucleus accelerating the condensation. The clear space around her grew and moved with her steps.

The stele appeared in front of her. She imagined Liwei touching it. Her colleague was not there, no matter how much she wanted him to be. What would happen if she reached out? Would the artifact freeze her in time like Liwei, even though he no longer seemed to be there?

Jinjin stretched out her arm. This time, no force tried to tear it off. She took a step forward.

"Hey, what are you doing?" asked Ernie. "Are you...?"

He had reacted too late. Jinjin's fingers reached the material of the monolith.

And she grasped nothing.

The stele had disappeared. Jinjin shook her head. All this time it had been waiting for her, right in front of her eyes, and now...

There it was again! Jinjin reacted immediately. Her hand shot forward and caught the stele ... almost.

It was gone. She couldn't blame that on herself. She took a step closer, and when the stele returned, she first feinted to the right and then pushed forward with her left hand. Next to it.

Once more. This time she used her right foot, but the artifact seemed to be able to read her thoughts. Left, right, left, she danced around the shiny black structure like a boxer, but failed to land a hit. Surely this couldn't be happening!

She turned around, pretended to leave and tried a

surprise attack—nothing. She closed her eyes. If she couldn't see the stele, maybe she could catch it. Jinjin swung wildly without connecting. Why was it being so mean to her? She just wanted to find Liwei! Her swinging became desperate. Tears streamed down her face, but the stele showed no mercy. What would Li Guofeng have said? *You must strike without intention.* She tried, but even her instructor's wisdom couldn't help.

Jinjin gave up. She was drenched in sweat and grateful that Ernie didn't interfere.

"Fascinating," he said, now that she was backing away from the stele.

"I think it's pretty mean. How can such a huge structure disappear so quickly?"

"I don't think it was ever there," said Antonia.

Ah, good, she seemed to be back in the rover. Jinjin was glad nothing had happened to her.

"Never there?" she replied.

"I think we're dealing with some kind of echo," Antonia explained. "Or no, let's call it a shadow instead."

"I don't understand," said Jinjin.

"Me neither," said Ernie.

"Imagine you're an ant living in a two-dimensional world. The third dimension doesn't exist for you. Your world is illuminated by the sun, which you think is normal because you explain it to yourself as a physical property of your world. By the way, this is exactly what physicists think about gravity! Due to some change, perhaps because your world has rotated, a shadow arises, a delimited area on which suddenly no more light falls. You cannot identify the cause, as it is in the third dimension. You only notice the result, which doesn't fit in with your physics. I think that's exactly what we're observing here."

"Ugh, that sounds complicated, but understandable," said Ernie.

Something occurred to Jinjin. "Does that mean the monolith no longer exists?" she asked.

"Yes, you could say that. Not in our world, anyway."

"Great. Then you should explain it exactly like that to my superiors. Maybe then they'll shut up."

A little peace and quiet, that would be great. But she still had to find a way to get Liwei back.

"Are you actually interested in what I found so fascinating?" asked Ernie.

"Of course," said Antonia.

"I compared the rhythm with which you hit the stele to the rhythm of its appearance, which we've been observing all this time."

"And?" asked Jinjin. What did she have to do with this rhythm?

"The rhythms are identical. The stele knew the intervals at which you would strike it."

"That's..." Jinjin was at a loss for words. She was completely free to determine the rhythm of her movements. Of course, the stele had a certain influence. But Jinjin had even tried to touch the artifact with her eyes closed. And she couldn't even remember the rhythm that Ernie measured. So how was it possible for it to match her?

"Is that statistically relevant?" asked Antonia. "I mean, over what period of time did you register this?"

"The whole time. From Jinjin's first attempt to touch the stele until she moved away again."

"Did you also take the time dilation into account?"

"Of course. I normalized the two time scales, i.e. brought them to the same scale."

"Then I have no idea what the problem could be," said Antonia.

"Maybe it has something to do with your shadow," suggested Jinjin. "If this shadow is a cloud and it's dropping hail, the ants will automatically move in time with the hailstones without being aware of the cause or frequency."

"Come back to the rover first," Ernie said. "Remember, you're still walking around in radiation hell out there."

COME TO THE ROVER? IT WASN'T THAT EASY. EARLIER, JINJIN had walked most of the way with Antonia in the lead. Whenever there was an obstacle to cross, she warned her. Now Jinjin could only orient herself by the small display on her arm. The starting point of her walk could be seen on it, but it didn't seem to be getting any closer. How long had she been walking? In her memory, it had only been a few minutes.

"Ernie, is the time dilation very pronounced right now?" she asked.

"No, not at all. Antonia is waiting for you in the airlock. You don't have far to go."

Jinjin couldn't believe it. Shouldn't the veil of dust be gradually dissipating? Visibility had been better earlier.

"I feel like the cloud is closing in around me," she said.

"That's imp... unlikely," said Antonia.

"Hang on, I'll check it out," Ernie replied. "Hm. It really looks like the cloud is centered at your position. I'll compare that with the last pictures from the Gateway. Like this. Now I'll superimpose your path on it... Hm."

"What is it?"

"It may be a coincidence, but the cloud actually seems to be following you. It's always closest to where you are."

Jinjin took a deep breath. It certainly had nothing to do with her personally. It was a damn dust cloud! Maybe her suit was leaking an electromagnetic field that happened to serve as a condensation nucleus for the cloud.

"I'm sure there's a rational explanation," said Antonia. "Maybe you're acting as a kind of lightning rod for the charges. That's why they concentrate around you."

"So why didn't the cloud follow you?"

"A fair question, Jinjin. Maybe it's because of the EVA suits. Yours is Chinese-made, ours is from the ESA. Do you have any blueprints I could take a look at?"

There were maintenance plans for the suits at the base. However, there was a version of each one for when one was on the move. Jinjin searched for it on her digital assistant. There was the document. It described everything that could be repaired on the suit while traveling. Ah, right at the end: grounding.

Jinjin read out: "Your EVA Suit Red Peace is equipped with automatic grounding. It safely discharges any charges into the ground as long as you are standing on it. Please note that there is no grounding when floating in space. If the grounding strips in the sole of the shoe are torn, you can replace them with metal strip no. 36 from the emergency repair bag."

Suddenly she stumbled. She sailed to the ground in a wide arc. It wasn't a hard fall. She had enough strength in her arms to catch herself. Her leg caught just above the ground. Her hand hit the ground. Luckily it was her right one, not the left one with the missing finger. A rattling sound reached her ears. It was silent for a moment. Jinjin took a deep breath. Everything had gone well once again.

At that moment, the alarm system wailed.

"Jinjin? What happened?" asked Ernie.

"I fell. Like an idiot."

"That's not why the alarm is wailing."

"My suit must have a tear."

"Okay, take it easy. You've already got the maintenance document on your screen."

That was true. She'd just looked under "G" for "grounding."

There must also be an item with "A" for "air supply". She pulled her arm up to look at the display. It was dark, probably damaged by the impact. But she was also down on her luck today.

"The assistant is broken," she said, "I'm sorry. I'm just too dumb for this job."

"You're not dumb at all," said Antonia.

"Wait, I've got your suit telemetry on the screen. The tear doesn't seem that big, and your tank is almost full. You'll definitely survive another ten minutes."

Ten minutes—but without the screen to show her the way. How could she make it?

"How far away am I?" Jinjin stood up. A white cloud emerged from the tear, blending with the dust.

"Eight minutes, according to the computer. You even have two extra minutes."

Jinjin oriented herself. She had come from here and flown lengthwise onto her nose. So she had to go that way. She started moving.

"Antonia is coming towards you," said Ernie. "She can see you. You should meet in four minutes."

"Got it." Jinjin ran for her life. Where was Antonia's headlight beam?

"Uh, Jinjin? Could it be that you're running in the wrong direction?"

Crap. "I don't know. You tell me!"

"Turn around 180 degrees. No, you'd better stand still. Antonia will find you."

"How far away am I? An honest answer, please."

"Ten minutes."

Crap. There was only enough oxygen for six. She had to start running, shorten the distance for Antonia. Which way?

At that moment, a cloud detached itself from the dust, joined with other wisps of cloud and formed a figure that looked like a person. It pointed backwards. Jinjin turned around and ran in the direction indicated. If it was just her imagination, it didn't matter at this point.

It worked either way. After two minutes, the figure appeared again and corrected her direction. After six minutes, she fell into Antonia's arms, who took a spare tube from her breathing air tank and connected it to her suit. Together they ran back to the rover.

THE BULKHEAD CLOSED BEHIND HER. FIRST, THE ROOM WAS vacuumed. No radioactive grains of sand must get inside. Then came a short shower. Finally, the airlock filled with air so that Jinjin could pull the helmet off her head and take a deep breath.

"Thank you, Antonia," she said.

Thank you, Liwei, she thought, but didn't dare tell anyone what she had seen. It was enough for her to know, because it gave her hope.

PRE-ORDER NOW: HARD-SF.COM/LINKS/4542979

Printed in Dunstable, United Kingdom